1
De

"Laura Kenyon m.   ...ppily ever after desperately delicious!"
~ Stephanie Evanovich, *New York Times* bestselling author of *Big Girl Panties* and *The Sweet Spot*

"At times laugh-out-loud funny, and at times very touching, *Desperately Ever After* is the debut of a real talent."
~ Elizabeth Blackwell, author of *While Beauty Slept* and *The Letter*

"This story draws out the emotional side of our fairy tale princesses, while keeping the humor intact. ... It's no longer a case of just reading their stories and hoping to meet our prince charming and getting swept away. Kenyon shows that the fairy tale promise is not all that it's cracked up to be. She keeps it real and enduring for the modern woman."
~ Janice G. Ross, author of *Damaged Girl* and *Island Hopping*

"An explosive cocktail that will have you laughing out loud and wanting more and more!"
~ Lost in Chick Lit

"If you are looking for a fun and gossipy story to satisfy the holes left when *Sex and the City* and *Desperate Housewives* had their series finales (or even if you're going through *Once Upon a Time* withdrawal come season finale time) look no further than *Desperately Ever After*."
~ Chick Lit Central

"Empowering and hilarious, I think everyone should read this."
~ Tea Party Princess

Skipping Midnight

Book Three: Desperately Ever After series

LAURA KENYON

For Caroline,
with me every step of the way

"It will happen to all of us eventually. The moment will come when we ask ourselves: Where did the time go? How did the children I once cradled grow up so very quickly? How did the life I dreamt of turn into a career I never expected? And how did that woman I saw each day in the mirror become someone I don't even recognize?"

— Mary Alice Young, *Desperate Housewives*

Who's Who in Marestam

BELLE Wickenham — When she was eighteen, Belle became imprisoned by a beast who turned out to be the cursed king of Braddax, Donner Wickenham. After setting him free with her love, she became queen, a title she still retains despite their recent separation. She is now co-owner of the Phoenix B&B with her friend Rapunzel, and pregnant with the Braddax heir.

CINDERELLA Charmé — Orphaned as a child, Cinderella was raised by her abusive stepmother but set free when Aaron Charmé fell in love with her during his marital ball. She is now a venerated philanthropist, international hero, queen of Carpale, and mother of four.

DAWN Tirion — Born an eighteenth-century Selladórean princess, Dawn was cursed to die on her seventeenth birthday from the prick of a spindle. In order to stop this, a second fairy cast a new curse that put the entire kingdom to sleep for three hundred years. History says that the Great Sleep ended when Hunter Tirion woke Dawn up with a kiss. She is now a perpetual insomniac, queen of Regian, and mother to twins, **Morning** and **Day**.

Penelopea "PENNY" LeBlanche — Originally from the oppressed realm of Vashia, Penny came to Marestam seeking a better life. One stormy night, she became famous for feeling three magical peas under twenty mattresses, supposedly proving she was "a real princess." Prince Logan swiftly proposed and married her. She now lives at Riverfell Palace with Logan and her in-laws.

RAPUNZEL Delmonico — When she was a baby, Rapunzel's parents traded her to a witch named **Grethel** in exchange for rampion weed. She spent almost twenty years isolated in a tower, until her attempt to flee with a stranger (recently revealed to be Ethan Wilkins) resulted in her banishment to Carpale. She is now a cultural icon, outspoken feminist, media personality, and co-owner of the Phoenix.

SNOW White — Snow nearly died as a teenager when her mother fed her a poisoned apple because, or so the story goes, she was threatened by her own daughter's beauty. She and husband Griffin (also credited with reviving her via kiss) rule Tantalise. They are known, for better or worse, for their peace-loving, environmentally-conscious, live-and-let-live style of governance.

☙❧

Aaron Charmé — Cinderella's husband and king of Carpale.

Angus Kane — Prime minister of Marestam.

Beast — Belle's beloved rescue dog.

Carter LeBlanche — Penny's brother-in-law and the reluctant crown prince of Riverfell.

Davin Lima — Selladórean native and Dawn's childhood sweetheart. Presumed dead following the Great Sleep, only to reappear years later as billionaire Liam Devereaux.

Donner Wickenham — King of Braddax. Married to Belle but separated after having an affair with her sister **Julianne**.

Dr. Diggory Frolick — Belle's doctor and one of the dwarves who once lived with Snow.

Elmina Goodman — Reclusive pureblood fairy who saved Dawn's life in eighteenth century Selladóre by changing **Jacara's** death curse into a sleeping curse.

Ethan Wilkins — Rapunzel's beau and low-level Stularian royal. Ethan went blind while trying to free Rapunzel from **Grethel's** tower years ago, but has since regained his sight.

Gray — Belle's mysterious love interest and quasi employee at the Phoenix. He believes he was born without the ability to fear.

Grethel — Mysterious fairy who purchased Rapunzel as an infant, raised her in isolation for almost twenty years, and banished her to Carpale when she finally attempted to escape.

Griffin — King of Tantalise and Snow's husband.

Hazel Wickenham — Donner's mother, former queen of Braddax, and a pureblood fairy (the latter unknown until recently).

Hunter Tirion — King of Regian, CEO of Tirion Enterprises, and Dawn's husband.

Kiarra Kane — Angus Kane's niece and Prince Carter's sweetheart.

Letitia LeBlanche — Widowed diva queen of Riverfell and Penny's mother-in-law. She is engaged to Ethan's father, **William Wilkins**.

Liam Devereaux — Billionaire head of Perdemi-Divan distilleries. Davin Lima's modern-day alias.

Logan LeBlanche — Penny's husband, Carter's brother, and Letitia's youngest son.

Matilda Holt — Reporter for the *Marestam Mirror*.

Perrin Hildebrand — Gossip columnist for the *Marestam Mirror*.

Ruby Welles — The most famous pureblood fairy in the world, Ruby skyrocketed to fame after orchestrating Cinderella's success at Aaron's marital ball. She is often referred to as the godmother of happy endings.

Rye Wickenham — Belle and Donner's son, secretly born during an emergency procedure following his father's violent rampage at the Phoenix.

The Marestam Mirror

Diamond Ropes and Velvet Cake
By Perrin Hildebrand, King of Gossip

BREATHE, dear readers. Breathe.

Take a slow stroll through Capitol Park. Watch the sun sink into the West River. Sniff the roses at Riverfell's Botanical Gardens. Pet a puppy if you can find one, or rock your baby to sleep. Just *please* get your heart rate down before venturing beyond this paragraph. Enough people are in the hospital already. *The Mirror* won't be held liable for more.

Tickers stable? Pacemakers in control? Read on at your own risk.

A FIVE-ALARM inferno broke out last night at the newly unveiled Phoenix B&B, resulting in at least two casualties and the arrest of Braddax's troubled King Donner Wickenham—who, we now know, is the son of a one hundred percent pureblood fairy! (That's right, it turns out that the Braddax royals have been hiding much more than humility from the people of Marestam—they've been evading the magical registry for years! More on that later.)

Early reports about the melee were sketchy. But after a fourteen-hour espresso IV (the insomniac gets the worm, as they say), I've regrettably confirmed a flurry of both distressing and downright stupefying news—the most pressing being that pregnant Phoenix co-owner and technically-still-Queen Belle Wickenham was among the wounded. No details yet on the nature of her injuries, but inside sources assure me that both mama and twenty-three-week baby-to-be are "out of danger" and will be released after a few more days of "precautionary observation."

UNFORTUNATELY, the same cannot be said for Kiarra Kane, starlet niece of Prime Minister Angus Kane and the Crown Prince of Riverfell's main squeeze. Ms. Kane reportedly lost consciousness after suffering blunt force trauma to the head, and has yet to awaken. Educated forecasts about her prognosis are in short supply, but her royal beau's reaction doesn't paint a very rosy picture. In the words of Riverfell's royal mouthpiece: "In light of yesterday's tragedy, Crown Prince Carter has concluded that he cannot simultaneously focus on his beloved and learn how to run a kingdom. As such, he cannot in good conscience accept the Riverfell throne next Saturday, as expected. Instead, the crown will pass to his extremely capable younger brother, Logan, and his wife, Penelopea."

Perhaps this is an epic gesture of romantic sacrifice. Perhaps it's Carter's excuse to finally escape the responsibility he's been trying to dodge for years. Either way, if you feel the wind picking up today, that's the entire population of Riverfell breathing a sigh of relief—or Penelopea cussing out the universe. So much for that four-bedroom craftsman she was looking at.

NEEDLESS to say, it hasn't been a banner year for Donner, who was still at Marestam Central Prison at the time of publication. The beleaguered regent has come under intense scrutiny in recent months, following a very public affair with his sister-in-law and the revelation that Belle is finally carrying the heir to the Braddax throne (but is also most likely seeking a divorce). A formal indictment is expected within the next twenty-four hours, with possible charges ranging from misdemeanor offenses like unlawful use of magic and avoiding the magical registry, to felonies like destruction of property, arson, assault, and even attempted murder. (Or, if Ms. Kane's consciousness decides to leave Marestam for good, just plain murder.)

Both of his "alleged" victims are being kept under excruciatingly tight lock and key (no joke—I've tried everything!), and none of their loved ones returned calls for comment. So for now, we'll have to assess his guilt using quasi-reliable eyewitness accounts like this one from Bartholomew Mares, a corporate accountant who was staying at the Phoenix on the night in question.

"I'm not one of those anti-magic fanatics," says the numbers cruncher, who is now enjoying a complimentary suite at the Waldorf Plaza—one of many organizations that stepped in to help in the wake of this tragedy. "But my wife and I will never forget the look on that man's face when we raced downstairs to see what all the commotion was about. I swear on the cornerstone of Carpale Castle: Donner Wickenham's eyes were glowing red and he moved like something I've never seen except in horror movies. I'm not saying he had fur or claws or fangs—though I can't entirely dismiss the latter what with all the thrashing about—but I've never seen a little magic do *that* to anyone before."

Nor have I, which begs a very dangerous question: Are we to believe Donner's magical abilities are really *that* strong? Or is there something else at play here? Is it possible … just possible … that when he lost Belle's love, he also lost the antidote for the curse she broke five years ago? Could the King of Braddax be transforming back into a beast all over again?

Only time—and your faithful King of Gossip—will tell.

IN ADDITION to installing Angus Kane as temporary steward of the Braddax throne and issuing an international arrest warrant for Hazel Wickenham's deceit (unenforceable so long as she never gets nabbed on Marestam soil), Parliament has responded to Friday's tragedy by reconvening its Magical Security Committee (MSC) for the first time in half a decade.

The move has sparked both cheers and jeers throughout the kingdoms, with demonstrators from all sides converging on Capitol Park over the weekend—and ruining a beautiful candlelight vigil in the process.

When asked about the MSC's marching orders, Kane gave his usual ambiguous answer, ripe with glittering generalities and inconsequential truths. "When I laid my hand on our sacred Constitution and pledged my life to the people of Marestam twelve years ago, my number one priority was keeping them safe. A great many things have changed since that time—my hair color and daily ratio of fan-to-hate mail, for example—but my pledge most certainly has not. What happened with the Wickenhams shows a flaw in our system that must be identified and rectified before any more innocents are sacrificed, before any more blood is shed. This should in no way be interpreted as a move to divide those with magical heritage from those without. If anything, it is a way to unify all law-abiding citizens, regardless of class or title, and protect them against those who might do us harm."

And there you have it, folks: unintelligible clarity from the upper echelons.

Chapter One

BELLE

Belle vowed not to cry until her room was completely empty and her baby was safe in the hospital nursery a few floors below.

Dr. Frolick had been insisting for hours that this was the best place for him, at least for the first night while she got her bearings. The phrase was laughable. Got her bearings? Not two days ago, her handy, week-by-week pregnancy calendar said her baby was roughly the size of a spaghetti squash. It said his lips and eyebrows were becoming more distinct, and while the eyes were no longer fused shut, they'd yet to acquire any pigment. It said her baby wouldn't be fully formed for another fifteen weeks, and she shouldn't expect to hold him until the trees stood bare along Fifth Avenue, draped in fuzzy white lights.

Back then, Belle had secretly been rooting for a girl—partly because she thought Donner might give a girl more space, and partly because Belle's bloodline had thus far been a blight on the female race. But boy or girl, she just wanted to raise a happy, grounded, decent and well-rounded kid—one who could count on her mother in every way Belle hadn't been able to count on her own. She looked forward to playing and cuddling and reading bedtime stories until neither of them could hold their eyes open any longer. The little angel was going to give her life meaning where it had been almost entirely stripped away.

She'd already bought a bookshelf and had plans to stuff it with so many stories, the sides would bow weeks before the little one even arrived. Her phone overflowed with links to layette sets, which she sorted through every chance she got. Her baby shower registry was fourteen pages long the last time she checked—not that she'd actually shown it to anyone ... or purchased the books ... or assembled the bookshelf. Time had been scarce.

Belle had been too busy trying to break the magically sealed prenuptial contract that treated her child like an heirloom tchotchke. She'd been preoccupied by Ruby's theory that all broken curses would return if she didn't suck it up and go back to her vain, unfaithful, domineering husband. She'd been struggling to get the Phoenix off the ground so that *if* she managed to retain custody of her baby, she'd actually be able to support him. And as if that wasn't enough, her ramped up hormones had caused her to fall in love with a shadowy, captivating drifter at the worst moment imaginable.

But now, overlooking a sea of candles from the thirty-fifth floor of Marestam General Hospital, her superglued life was shattered all over again. Her "fresh start" was a charred mound of sticks in the Braddax Hills. Her independent source of income was going to need some painfully expensive remodeling. Her brand-new wardrobe, her journals, and the nursery she'd carved out in her haven of a bedroom were all gone. Even the second-chance romance she'd never expected was dangling in some precarious, gray area (no pun intended) between regret and redemption.

All of the sudden, none of the things she'd spent so much time fretting over mattered. Now—holding her newborn baby in her arms and obsessively tracing his swollen cheeks, his dark, curly hair, and his crinkly lips that puffed out like the crust of an apple pie — the only thing that mattered was that she was a mother.

A secret mother.

A secret mother to a premature, magical newborn who looked like a ten-week-old infant and whose life could be in danger if Marestam's Prime Minister found out he was alive.

"Angus Kane is smart and cunning and has access to every magical charm that's been confiscated under *his* laws," Ruby had said during her frantic, red-nosed rant twelve hours earlier — right before they found out he'd been covering up the fact that Cinderella and Aaron Charmé were missing. How convenient for the man looking after Carpale's throne while they completed their long-interrupted honeymoon. "I'd bet my life that he's directly behind Donner's curse returning — and my powers being taken away. And if he's wielding charms to do this, there's only one way to stop him. We need three pureblood fairies. A triad. It's the only way to get enough power to counteract a charm."

A triad. The whole thing sounded so medieval, so involved. But as Ruby put it, fairy magic had become so watered down over the generations that even a pureblood couldn't cast an effective locator spell these days without assistance. Turning rags into gowns or evaporating from one place to another was one thing, but dark magic was entirely different. In order to combat an ancient charm, Dawn would have to find Elmina, the reclusive fairy who changed her death curse into a sleeping curse three centuries earlier; Rapunzel would have to confront Grethel, the woman who abducted, raised, and then abandoned her; and someone would have to bite the bullet and ask Donner's mother to be their number three. The chosen trio would have to come together, join hands, recite some centuries-old spell to block whatever enchantment was surrounding Donner and his son, and summon every ounce of magic between them to break it. Then they would use their remaining powers to locate and retrieve the Charmés, swiftly separating Angus from the throne.

Rapunzel had called the whole thing ridiculous and pushed for a much more *human* solution: A search and rescue mission for Cindy and a public relations campaign against Angus. Only they didn't have any proof. It would be his word against theirs, and the monarchies just didn't command the same respect that they used to. Plus, who were they to tell the world's most iconic pureblood fairy how to battle magic?

"Hey there little man," she whispered, simultaneously wanting and not wanting to wake him up. Maybe if he were asleep when the nurse came to take him, she'd let him stay. "I don't think you understood anything all those people were talking about earlier — at least I hope you didn't — but just in case, I want you to know that it's going to be okay. There's no way I'm letting anything bad happen to you. None of us are. You just focus on sucking that hand of yours and shedding that umbilical cord stump. Mama's got everything else covered." She smiled, almost convincing herself that what she'd just said was true.

She flinched as the door opened and the older of her two nurses waltzed in.

"Well, aren't you two a picture?" she said, balancing a tower of blankets and two additional pillows. Dr. Frolick promised to keep the implausible birth secret for as long as possible without losing his job, but he'd still needed someone to help with the delivery. And when she finished her shift, he had to call in a second. He chose this one because, as he put it, "I can't be here at all hours, and I'd trust her with my life."

She was probably a decade older than Belle, with a premature white streak in her otherwise brown hair and a bedside manner that warmed like chicken soup. If only Belle could remember her name.

"I don't know whether you trend toward cool or hot," the nurse said, spreading a pair of blankets over Belle's feet, "but personally, I can never have too many layers. And after the day you've had, I imagine you could use a good snuggle."

Belle continued to stare at her baby but gave a thankful smile. Was it Katelyn? Kayleigh? She was almost certain it began with a K.

She didn't dare look up as the sea foam green figure floated over to the side of the bed, hands ready to whisk her child away. There was a sudden smell of lavender in the air, then a head of dark hair nodding toward the bundle slumbering in her arms.

"Are you ready?"

Belle's jaw fell and her grip instantly tightened. She shook her head. "I changed my mind. Can't he just sleep with me? It's safer. What if someone recognizes him down there? It's dangerous. And I'm awake now. I can take care of him."

The nurse gave her a gentle smile, placed a pair of glass vials beside the bed, and explained that: a) there were sixty other babies in the nursery, b) she wasn't going to let him leave her sight, and c) it's important for new mothers to rest their first night after giving birth.

"C-sections aren't to be taken lightly," she said. "Especially ones that yield sixteen-pound magical babies. You need time to recover. I'm sure Dr. Frolick explained that."

Belle pulled back a bit. Yes, Dr. Frolick had explained that — just as he'd explained that Donner's hormone levels were off the charts and her baby was growing faster than the line for ice cream during an August heat wave.

"Sixteen pounds?" she repeated, glancing down at her belly. The number was incomprehensible. Sure, she'd had a few panic attacks on the scale in the last few weeks, but how on earth had she made room for a sixteen-pound baby? "What's average? Like ten?"

Judging from her expression, the nurse didn't know whether this was a genuine question or a joke.

"There's no average," she said, kindly. "Each baby's different.

And while sixteen pounds is quite large for a baby who's more than a whole trimester premature..."

Belle watched her lips carefully, hoping for reassurance that it really wasn't *that* bad.

"Well, if we measure by development instead of birthdate, I'd call him closer to four months old. And that puts him right at average weight."

"I thought you said there was no average," Belle said, seeing right through this failed attempt at emotional charity. The nurse immediately turned to pick up a clear bag filled with fluids. "But hold on a second. Are you saying the baby you people pulled out of me last night is actually four months old?"

Nurse K turned back around, hung the bag on the IV pole, and motioned towards the baby again.

"Do you see how he opens and shuts his hands while sleeping? Babies don't do that until at least the two-month mark. Newborns tend to keep tight fists all the time. And giggling doesn't usually happen until three or four months."

Belle focused on his hands as if she expected them to sprout wings or sing to her. Did that mean she'd already missed four months of motherhood? She'd already lost the first sixteen weeks of newborn cries, smiles, and cuddles? She felt instantly angry, and sad, and guilty.

But then another question popped into her head, replacing those feelings with outright panic: Was that the end of his growth spurt? Had her twenty-three-week-old fetus catapulted through time as a one-time act of self-defense and was now going to stop? Or would he continue growing at an unpredictable rate until they found a way to break his father's curse?

She shook her head, feeling a sudden pressure in her throat. "It's already going too fast."

An awkward silence fell as Belle saw the nurse shift in her peripheral vision. She cursed herself. She wasn't supposed to cry until everyone was gone—everyone including strangers and infants.

"Tell you what," she heard as a soft hand pressed into her shoulder. "You cuddle with the little guy for a few more minutes while I get everything ready. Then I'll take him to the nursery. And after you get a full seven hours of sleep—no cheating, your vitals are right here on the screen—I'll bring him back as soon as he wants to eat. If you're up for it, maybe we can work on nursing. I think Dr. Frolick said that was part of your birth plan."

Despite the ironic use of the term "plan" for her situation, Belle felt herself perk up. In addition to the bonding and the health benefits and the rapid weight loss she'd read about, she needed to breastfeed for one supreme reason: because her mother hadn't. And until a few hours ago, her greatest fear had been turning out like her.

"That sounds great," she practically cooed. "Thank you. I was a little worried Dr. Frolick wouldn't want me to nurse."

The nurse's head tipped. "Well, that's just silly. Why would you think that?"

Belle bit her tongue. Dr. Frolick couldn't have spoken more highly about the woman standing over her, but how much had he told her? Did she know about Belle's plan to hide her baby with Snow if the hospital kicked her out before the outside world was safe? There was no point in taking chances.

"Oh, I don't know." Belle shrugged, glancing at her phone. She had a sudden need to speak with Gray. To find out whether he'd scoured every inch of the Phoenix rubble yet and found Donner's rings. She needed to know … if her baby wound up miles away with her friend on the other side of a river, would she be able to conjure that magical tunnel she was so desperately counting on? "I shouldn't question Dr. Frolick. I just got the impression he thought I was too fragile to try earlier—or maybe too drugged up."

The nurse laughed and tapped the saline bag dangling over

the bed. Then she turned just enough for Belle to glimpse the second half of her nametag.

"Well you *are* still fragile," she said, uncorking a soft-tipped syringe, dipping it into one of the vials, and squirting it into a second branch of the IV tube. "But nothing in your system now will harm the baby in eight hours, so don't worry about that."

"I thought you said seven hours," Belle said. Then, feeling suddenly looser: "Karen, right?"

"It's Kirsten, actually," the nurse answered, turning so that her nametag was in full view but then looking swiftly away. Her shoulders hunched forward. "I used to have a sister named Karen," she added, "but not anymore."

"Oh." Belle said, wanting to disappear into the bed. Every thought she had was suddenly slipping through her fingers. "I'm so sorry. I—"

"It's fine," Kirsten said, still studying the wall. "But that reminds me. Does your little guy have a name I should be using? Or is it just Baby for now?"

The question was completely reasonable, but still took Belle by surprise. She'd mentally bookmarked loads of girls' names in her travels—*Charlotte, Allison, Caroline, Emma,* to name a few— but boys' names just didn't strike her the same way. She'd always liked *Timothy.* And there was something sweet about *Benjamin.* But were those too ordinary for a future king who entered the world in a blast of fire, blood, and magic? Was a tribute like *Phoenix* too cheesy? Was it bad that her son had been alive for an entire day and still didn't have an identity?

"I … I don't actually know," she said, feeling an uncomfortable burst of anxiety. "Am I a terrible mother already? I didn't expect him for another four months. I only found out it was a *him* a couple days ago. I—"

Then she stopped. A cold wave of serenity suddenly rolled through her veins and spread all over her. Kirsten gave her a quizzical, then satisfied, look.

"It's okay," she said. "It's a big decision. My youngest was Pumpernickel until an hour before discharge because my husband said he was basically a loaf of bread that cried and pooped." She laughed. "My sister gave me a book that really helped, actually. I'll bring it to you."

Belle thanked her, then looked at the empty vial on the table. She watched mindlessly as Kirsten crossed the room, wheeled the clear, rectangular bassinet over to the bedside, and dimmed the lights.

"What did you put in that IV?" Belle asked, too calm to argue as this friendly stranger scooped the baby right out of her arms.

"Is it helping?"

"Helping?" Belle repeated. How could she explain that a giant marshmallow hand had suddenly reached down from the clouds and smoothed out every wrinkle on the underside of her skin? "Yes. Pretty sure."

"Good." Kirsten held the bundle close to Belle's face. "Now say goodnight, mama."

Belle rubbed her nose against his and inhaled him one more time. "Goodnight, angel. Sleep tight. Mommy loves you so, so, so, so much."

As Kirsten lowered the baby into the bassinet and adjusted his blanket, Belle began to feel as if her pillow was floating on top of quicksand. She heard something in the distance about labeling him "Smith," but was already starting to drift off.

Her first impulse was to fight it. With sleep came dreams. And after everything she'd experienced and everything that was still hanging over her like an anvil on a fraying thread, she could only expect nightmares: The Phoenix burning down all over again. A baby being ripped from her stomach. Donner morphing into a magical beast and roasting Gray alive.

"See you in eight hours," Kirsten said.

Belle shook the drugs away long enough to give her words a narrow but clear path. "Seven hours."

"Of course," Kirsten chirped. "Just testing. Now get some rest. Dream of baby names."

Belle felt her insides jolt. "Wait," she called out. "How much time do I have to name him?"

She heard a generous laugh covering up an exhausted sigh. "There's actually no deadline in Marestam. But if you can't decide by the time you leave the hospital, why would things be any different a week later?"

Belle nodded, her eyes sinking again. She had a point.

"Don't worry," Kirsten added. "It'll come to you. If it doesn't, you can have Pumpernickel."

Had Belle not been medicinally glued to the bed, she might have hugged her. Instead, she yawned and asked Kirsten how many kids she had.

"Two girls," Kirsten rattled off, "seven and five. And a boy. My little man. He's three."

The room was almost completely dark now, but Belle could hear the smile in her voice.

"Two girls and a boy," Belle repeated, her words barely a whisper and her eyelashes dipping in and out of view. "That sounds perfect."

She listened as Kirsten rolled the bassinet past the wheeled eating tray and the outdated media screen, and then stopped at the door. With the overhead lights off, the sterile room seemed a little less bleak. With some window treatments and a floral bedding set, she thought, it might even make a decent hideaway. Maybe she didn't need Snow after all. Maybe she could convince Dr. Frolick to make up some reason why she'd have to remain in the hospital—under quarantine—for weeks. Months. Even years.

"Kirsten?" she asked, behaving like a toddler terrified of being left alone. "What do you think of Rye?"

"What? The bread?" She heard her voice grow closer "Do you want rye toast in your breakfast order?"

Belle smelled lavender again and felt the bedspread tighten along her sides. She couldn't remember the last time she'd been tucked into bed. Had she ever?

"No, the name." Her mind was still fighting to stay awake, but her body was hoisting an enormous white flag. "Short for Ryan but spelled like the bread. Pumpernickel made me think of it. I mean, it might be more poetic to call him Phoenix or Ember under the circumstances, but…"

She heard a small breath of amusement. "I like Ryan. I think it actually means little king. But you should sleep on it. Decide when you don't think your pillows are actually clouds."

Belle nodded — or at least she nodded internally — and asked Kirsten if she would tuck in her baby as well.

"I will," Kirsten assured her, flipping off the final overhead light. "But only if you fall asleep in the next five minutes."

"Okay," Belle murmured as her eyelids fell one last time and her head hit the bottom of the quicksand. "I just want him to be happy. And safe. That's the most important thing."

"He will be," she said as a slice of light poured in from the hallway, then faded away. "You'll make sure of that."

Chapter Two

RAPUNZEL

Rapunzel leapt onto the concrete and slammed her door so hard, it triggered the alarm three cars over. She felt the metal and fiberglass frame shudder behind her, and wished it would collapse right on the spot. She could picture it now: a thousand shiny little pieces of Ethan's second favorite thing littering the floor, turning the Taaffeite Towers parking garage into a skating rink and knocking down her perfume-laden neighbors and their teensy-weensy purse dogs. At least that would be amusing.

"Babe!" Ethan called as she hustled toward the stairs. She bit the inside of her cheeks but didn't turn to look. He was lucky she hadn't swiped his keys and left him stranded at the hospital … or the Phoenix … or the bottom of the West River with weights strapped to his ankles. But there was no way that liar was getting a conversation out of her; he wasn't *that* lucky.

"Babe, I'm begging here," she heard again as he jogged up from behind. "I'm an ocker. A wanker. I deserve to spend the rest of the year on my hands and knees." Her heels clopped harder. A few months ago, she couldn't imagine being this mad at someone from Stularia—not with that loose, bouncy accent, which made even self-degradation sound sunny. "Come on," he begged, his words spraying out in all directions, glancing each corner of the garage and shooting right back at her: a 360-degree assault. "You can't stay mad at me forever. Grethel told me that if I broke my promise—"

"I know." Rapunzel gritted her teeth and pulled ahead of him again, shoulder-checking a young couple struggling to walk and kiss at the same time. The female was wearing stilettos, a tiny over-the-shoulder purse, and raccoon eyes. She'd probably met the guy a few hours earlier at a club downtown, and was bringing him home to uncover the few parts of her that weren't already on display. Rapunzel grunted an automatic apology but kept walking—away from a world they had no idea was on the verge of collapse.

All she wanted to do right now was crawl into bed—alone—and sleep until the past few days became nothing more than a faded memory. She wanted to forget the hours she'd spent pacing the hospital floors praying for Belle to wake up—not to mention the afternoon of mental and emotional counseling that followed.

Perhaps she should have left it at that. Perhaps she should have gone home when the hospital staff kicked her out, rather than sticking around to plan with Snow, Ruby, and Dr. Frolick … or schlepping over to the Phoenix because she needed to see the damage for herself and she wanted to make sure Gray didn't kill himself digging through a still smoldering crime scene for Belle's rings.

But what's done was done. She would have been exhausted—mentally, physically, and emotionally exhausted—either way. At least the extra exploits had helped keep her mind off of Ethan's betrayal. Now, however, as the night sky began to lighten and a young woman puking near the vestibule reminded her that it was still the weekend, all that distraction was gone.

She held her breath as she passed the woman and three of her eleven sisters (all of whom lived two floors below Rapunzel with a father who howled at them every weekend for breaking curfew) and pounded the vestibule door open with her palm. She smirked as it crashed shut behind her—nicking Ethan somewhere on the way.

"Thanks for that," he grumbled a few seconds later as he lurched into the elevator. She hadn't pressed the button to close the doors faster, but she had no plans to hold them for him either.

Aware that nothing exiting her mouth right now could be good, Rapunzel bit her lip and panned the granite floor, the bamboo panels, and the glass ceiling with the frosted tile inlay. Then she yanked out her keycard and rammed it into the control panel. Penthouse A. Prime real estate with a rooftop veranda and unbeatable view of Carpale Castle. She'd fought tooth and nail to snag it a few years ago, but would trade it for a cardboard box today if it meant Cinderella, Belle's baby, and the rest of Marestam would be safe.

As the elevator ascended, she saw Ethan rubbing his elbow and tried to tune out his repeating apology. A few words might have changed since it started almost twenty-four hours earlier in Belle's hospital room, but the song was generally the same.

I know where to find one, he'd said when Ruby put out a call for three pureblood fairies. *Her name's Grethel. And she'll help if Rapunzel asks her to.*

Rapunzel had taken some time to process this. She remembered feeling suddenly heavy and tilted. She'd felt the words go through one layer at a time. Land mines coated in silk before the inevitable explosion. She remembered telling herself that there was no way Ethan could know where to find Grethel. They'd been over it a million times. They'd had multiple screaming matches on that very subject. He'd asked her to trust him. She had.

No. It had been an extraordinarily long day. She assumed she'd heard him wrong. But then she felt a strong hand slide over her shoulder and squeeze. She heard Ethan whisper something about having no choice, about Grethel swearing him to secrecy. At that moment, the queen of lightning-fast wit and high-speed love affairs began moving in slow motion.

It wasn't until she saw Belle's face—clenched and ashen with her brown eyes twitching—that the silk finally pulled away and Ethan's words caught fire. Her emotions splintered off and ricocheted in a thousand different directions. She'd wanted to grab his collar and throttle until the buttons popped off. She'd wanted to curl up in the tiny linoleum bathroom and cry. She'd wanted someone to stroke her hair, lie with all the good intentions in the world, and tell her everything was going to be okay.

But her face had betrayed none of that. She'd kept her cool until they all worked out a plan to save the people they loved and the strangers they lived beside. She'd kept her cool because Marestam General Hospital, on the worst night of Belle's already tortured life, during what could quickly become the final days of the entire royal system, was neither the time nor the place for a lover's quarrel.

Her apartment, however, was a different story.

"I wanted to tell you," Ethan repeated as the elevator climbed to the forty-first floor. "I had no choice."

Rapunzel scoffed out loud without intending to. There was always a choice. Belle had chosen to believe Ruby's theory and say goodbye to Gray, whose love for her was as pure as Donner's was selfish. Rapunzel had chosen to bite her tongue in the end, and now wondered whether things would have been different if she hadn't. Ethan had chosen to hide the truth from her, repeatedly, a crime that historically meant a one-way ticket out of her love life. Just standing next to him now was unprecedented. Getting into his car after she knew he'd lied to her? Unheard of. Allowing him back into her apartment? Inconceivable.

But she needed Ethan to take her to Grethel. And to save Belle's baby. And to set every private investigator in Ellada on the top-secret search for Cinderella. In the grand scheme of things, her romantic dilemmas just didn't matter.

"Get it together, dammit," she muttered to herself as the elevator jerked to a stop and the doors peeled open.

"What?" Ethan shoved a firm hand through his hair. Each salt and pepper piece flattened and then bounced back up again. His eyes were both wide and wrinkled at the same time. "What did you say?"

Rapunzel bit her lip and drank in his terrified look in her peripheral vision. Everything about him was tight—from his balled fists to his clenched shoulders to the deep, crinkled space between the eyes she refused to catch. The words hadn't been directed at him, but why should she clarify that? He deserved to dangle for a little while.

"Nothing," she said, stomping off the elevator and landing directly on her polished cherry floors. She was just wishing she had a front door to kick open, when a deafening howl stopped her cold and a monstrous, furry freight train came barreling around the corner. Rapunzel jumped behind Ethan and dug her fingers into his collarbone. In all the commotion, she'd completely forgotten that Nathan, the inn's now unemployed concierge, had dropped Beast off after the inferno. He was the Phoenix's only four-legged refugee, surviving on visits every seven to eight hours from Gray and the building's superintendent.

"Beast!" she shrieked, in a tone no one should ever use with a hyperactive canine. "Beast, you scared the— No! Ahh!"

Rapunzel screamed as the giant dog reared up in excitement and knocked his former roommate flat on her back.

"Beast! No!" She shoved both elbows over her face, struggling to deflect the barrage of hot, leathery dog kisses. "Beast, I said no!"

Rapunzel was seconds away from losing it, when she heard something hit the floor a few feet away. The dog immediately lunged for it, then returned to drop a snot-covered rubber bone on her chest. She cursed in disgust and scrambled to her feet, going out of her way to avoid taking Ethan's outstretched hand.

"Hey!" she hollered, shoving the hair from her face and throwing her arms out as if to create an invisible bubble around herself. "Everybody just needs to back the heck off and give me a minute to breathe!"

She regretted her tone almost immediately, but couldn't say it wasn't effective. Both man and animal obeyed instantly — one shrinking away like a scolded puppy, the other impersonating a statue but sweeping the floor with his long, silver tail. At first, Rapunzel didn't know whether to scream or laugh. Then, for some reason only the universe could possibly understand, she spotted Beast's empty bowls in the kitchen and wanted to burst into tears. All she could think about was Belle lying in that hospital bed. Belle having to give away her baby. Belle's beloved rescue dog wasting away in her selfish friend's apartment.

She swallowed hard but couldn't shake the massive pressure building behind her eyes. Then she took off for the kitchen, where she could hide her face behind open cabinet doors and dangling pots.

"He needs to eat," she commanded, brandishing her pointer finger like a baton. "Poor thing's already traumatized. Then we leave him alone for hours and come home arguing with each other?"

She shook her head while Ethan stood back, mystified by this sudden change. Then she dropped to her knees and unearthed a bag of kibble from behind some pasta boxes.

"Come here, buddy," she cooed. "Your mama left this here when you guys moved to the Phoenix. It might be a little stale but…" She shrugged. "Well, I've seen you eat poop."

She dropped three scoops of the tiny brown circles into an

aluminum bowl, set it down by his paws, and then filled another one up with water. The dog wagged his tail but didn't even approach the food.

"Go ahead, bud," she said. "Eat up." When he still didn't lunge for it, she started moving her arms like a traffic cop in the direction of the kibble. "Eat. Up." She waited, then bit her lip. He should be starving.

"Come on," she half-whined, crouching down to his level. "This was perfectly good for you a couple months ago. Are you mad at me or something? Look. I'm sorry we left you alone for so long, but the hospital doesn't allow dogs and … well, I sent visitors, didn't I?"

"Tough audience," Ethan piped up behind her.

The amusement in his voice reignited the urge she'd had in the hospital to strangle him. Instead, Rapunzel rolled her eyes and gave Beast a few quick pats on the head. The tops of his eyes arched up, turning them into lopsided triangles. "Plus, we had to go by the inn and see how bad it is." Beast's head rocked side to side, in time with every other word. She knelt all the way down and scratched the side of his neck. "It's pretty awful."

His head cocked again and let out a barely audible whine.

"Yeah, I guess you already knew that. You watched it happen firsthand. You must have been terrified."

Beast repositioned his feet and licked his chops.

Rapunzel leaned in so that her cheek rested against the side of his head—which felt surprisingly silky. "She's fine, by the way," she whispered, wondering whether she should mention the baby. "I guess I should have mentioned that first. Belle's going to be just fine."

At the sound of her name, Beast's head immediately jerked towards the elevator and his front paw swung onto Rapunzel's knee. Maybe he did understand. Maybe Belle wasn't completely insane to think a dog could distinguish one two-legged caretaker from another.

But half a second after this life-altering thought crossed her mind, Ethan sauntered over, gave the dog two quick pats, and said, in a deep, commanding voice, "OKAY."

Right on cue, Beast lunged forward, sending the kibble, the bowl, and Rapunzel scattering across the floor.

"Hey, what gives?" she yelled. "Beast, I thought we were having a moment!"

She leered at the dog while mindlessly allowing Ethan to help her up. Then she pulled violently away and shot him the angriest look she could muster. She'd completely forgotten that Belle had trained him not to eat until she gave a command word, as if that was really where the gargantuan jumping bean needed discipline.

"A little warning would have been nice," she snarled at Ethan while grabbing a martini glass. Then she swung open another cabinet, studied a jumble of half-empty liquor bottles, and paused. Was it wrong to start drinking before sunrise? Even if she had been up for forty-four hours straight? Even if she added a little orange juice? She stifled a yawn and closed the doors. "I need sleep," she decided.

Ethan yawned and stretched toward the ceiling. The hem of his shirt rose a few inches above his belt, exposing what Rapunzel knew to be an excellent set of abdominals. "Now that's a spectacular idea," he said, slipping his hands around her hips. He was wearing the same cologne he'd worn the day she met him, after the sculpting class she'd taken with Cindy. That was the day her friend revealed—mistakenly, thank goodness—that she believed her husband was having an affair. Rapunzel knew deep down that Aaron would never do something like that. Just as she knew Ethan would never deliberately hurt her. But deliberate or not, he *had* hurt her.

"We're both knackered and it's turning our heads to mush," he murmured into her ear. "What we need are a few decent hours of shuteye and after that, everything will look—"

"Glad you agree," she said, repelling his advance with a flat palm. "You can take the guest room. I'll see you in a few hours." Ethan's smirk tumbled, followed by his eyebrows. "You mean ... Are you serious?"

Rapunzel stared back as if he had ancient symbols tattooed on his forehead. He removed his hands, gave a tiny nod, and backed away.

"Okay, you're serious."

"I am," she said. "And in the morning, you should probably pack."

He stumbled. "Pack?"

Rapunzel braced for an explosion. But instead, Ethan's voice seemed to collapse inward, the word trickling off his lips while his face showed the perfect mixture of pain, fear, and desperation. She swallowed the urge to comfort him.

"You can't possibly mean that," he practically whispered. "After everything we saw today? How quickly everything can be taken away? Rapunzel." He stepped forward again, reaching for her hands. She moved aside. "Rapunzel, I love you. Would you really toss that aside because I hid a secret that would have killed us?"

"Ha!" She crunched Beast's bag of kibble closed and shoved it back into the cabinet. "Telling me how to find Grethel would have *killed* us?" Her tone was as excited as his was gentle. Beast immediately scampered behind Ethan and attempted to tunnel beneath his legs. "Don't you think that's a bit of an exaggeration?"

She was spinning around in circles now: scrubbing Beast's bowl; slamming clean utensils into their drawers; picking up, then putting down, then picking up a half-empty handle of vodka. Then Ethan caught her in his arms and her fury came to a crashing halt. She looked away, trying not to see him, not to smell him. But it was too late.

"No, I don't think that's an exaggeration," he said, as sure as if she'd asked whether it was raining outside. "I know Grethel means a lot more to you than you want people to think."

"Don't," she warned, trying to squirm away.

"I know it," he repeated, holding her in place. "And believe it or not, I understand it. She was the woman who raised you. You never got closure when she dumped you in Carpale and disappeared. But you seem to forget what she's capable of."

Rapunzel tried not to look at his face, but it didn't matter. She knew where all of his scars were. She knew what Grethel had done to him. He held her closer to his chest and reached out to twist a small swath of her hair between his fingers.

"Don't get me wrong. I'm grateful to her for making things right in the end," he said. "I don't know how much longer I would have made it if I had to spend the rest of my life blind and alone, wondering whether you knew what happened to me but unable to tell you."

"You could have told me."

"No, I couldn't," he said, rolling his eyes toward the ceiling. "Hey, remember me? I'm blind and stitched together now, but you sorta swore to run away and marry me. That promise still stands, right?" He shook his head. "No. I couldn't be a burden to you. So of course I said yes when Grethel offered to fix me so long as I kept her whereabouts a secret. I didn't ask her why, and you have every right to be angry at me for it." She felt his hands clench against her back, then loosen. "I'm angry too. I'm angry that she put me in that position. I'm angry that right now I have to make the choice I never wanted to make in the first place — losing you again or —" He swallowed, hard. His breath became suddenly slow and deep. "Or becoming that burden all over again."

Dammit, she thought. How could she possibly stay angry after a confession like that? Almost reluctantly, she let a little of her weight lean into him, then looked up. She could see the red growing around his eyes.

"Do you really think she'd do that?" she asked. "Do you really think she'd undo whatever spell she used to fix you just because you told me how to find her?"

He unclasped his hands entirely and let the space between them grow. "Do you really think she wouldn't?"

"Yes." Rapunzel turned away and opened the liquor cabinet once again. "Yes. I mean no." She shook her head, slammed the doors, and emerged empty-handed. "I mean I don't think she would make you blind again. My childhood was full of empty threats. Stay away from the window or I'll board it shut. Clean up your mess or I'll turn you into a chair. Finish your potatoes or it's no dinner for a month."

"That's different. I know she wouldn't hurt *you*. But I'm —"

"Exactly." Rapunzel's hand smacked against the counter as Beast raced out of the room. "Look. You told me that Grethel scoured the world looking for you, right? And that she restored your sight as a way to make amends to *me*. Right?"

Ethan sucked on the insides of his cheeks and nodded.

"So, don't you see? That means it doesn't matter whether or not she cares about hurting you. It only matters that she cares about me, despite what the teenage version of me wanted to believe. And if she wants me to be happy, I find it extremely hard to believe she'd make me miserable just because you broke some asinine promise."

Ethan's lips rose into a small smile on one side. Then the other.

"What?" Rapunzel snapped.

"You just said losing me would make you miserable."

Rapunzel felt her breath catch in her throat. The floor became suddenly mesmerizing.

"Yeah," she stammered. "Well." She needed to shake this ooey gooey feeling away. She needed him to stop looking at her the way he was looking at her. She panned past his outline and stared out the window. The sun was almost up now. It was casting some sort of fuzzy halo over Carpale Castle. "Well, feeling responsible for someone else's blindness would make anyone miserable."

She struggled to swallow every emotion as he leaned back against the bar top and pinched the bridge of his nose. That had been a cheap shot—one that played on all his deepest fears. And she hadn't even meant it.

"Do you want me to leave?"

Her stomach tightened at the question. She was angry, yes. Hurt, absolutely. But she didn't want to lose the only person capable of hurting her to such a degree—the only person she'd let in deep enough to do so.

"If you want me to go, I will," he said again. "Because whether you believe it or not, your happiness is the most important thing to me." He waited, and then added, "I just always hoped I was a part of that."

Rapunzel's mouth opened, but she didn't know what to say. They'd fought about a lot over the past month—about Grethel, about marriage, about the orientation of the forks in the dishwasher—but it always subsided after a few hours. In the end, nothing seemed important enough to cause a fracture. Even now, her heart was telling her that hadn't changed. Her head was the one causing the problem.

"I'm going to bed," she finally said. "We can talk about this later." She saw him jolt all over. "I have a million things to do tomorrow—or, ugh, later today—and I'm about to topple over."

"What can I do to help?" he asked.

"You can tell every investigator you know in Ellada to look for Cindy and Aaron," she said. "I told Belle I'd play my part in Ruby's ridiculous triad plan, but I know what happens when all your eggs are in one basket."

"No problem. I can—"

"And you can entertain Beast while I'm running errands later."

"Sure. We'll —"

"And you can start packing your stuff." She watched carefully as the space beneath his nose instantly wrinkled and his face began to melt. Satisfied, she added, "I'm not confronting Grethel on my own."

Ethan's face lit back up. He cleared his throat, straightened up a little, and rolled up his sagging sleeves.

"When do you want to leave?" he asked, suddenly on a mission. "Just say the word. I'll take care of everything."

Rapunzel paused to draft a quick mental list. The insurance company wanted to meet with her that afternoon. She'd promised to bring Belle some decent clothes and a few comfort items. She had to return Nathan's fifteen hysterical voicemails. She had to find someone to walk Beast while they were away.

"How long will we be gone? More than seven hours?"

"Well," Ethan said, rubbing the back of his neck. "The flight's almost twenty-four hours, so —"

"Twenty-four hours!" Rapunzel shrieked as Beast sprinted out of the room again. "I figured she wasn't in Marestam, but I was betting on a road trip over the Pastora border. A ferry to Eresyn at the worst. Where the heck are we going? The moon?"

"No," he said, suddenly fingering a scratch in the counter. "But if you drilled a hole through the earth and came out on the other side … that's pretty much where she is."

Rapunzel's brain shut down for a moment. Drilled a hole through the earth? But that's how Ethan always described where he was from.

"Are you trying to tell me that Grethel is in Stularia?"

He sucked on one side of his lip. The desire to kill him came rushing back full force.

He nodded and pulled his sleeves back down.

"Was she always in Stularia?" Her mind was suddenly on overdrive. "Am *I* from Stularia?"

Ethan let out a long exhale. "I mean, I don't know where you were actually born, but ..."

"Wow," she said, floored as to how he kept that from her. Even if Grethel had put a gag order on her own whereabouts, how could Ethan have withheld what he knew about *Rapunzel's* past? About her identity. About all the questions she had and the holes she felt and the —

Oh, right. He hadn't told her because she'd never asked. She'd kept an impenetrable iron box in the back of her mind containing the parents who gave her away, the woman who raised her, the tower in which she spent eighteen years, and the people who used her when she first landed — alone and in total shock — in Carpale.

"Buy the tickets for Monday," she decreed as Beast came lumbering back into the kitchen.

"Tomorrow? Will do," Ethan chirped before sweeping her into a blitzkrieg kiss and apologizing for everything one more time. "Now what do you say we get that shuteye?"

"Sure thing," she said, flicking his chest and then pushing him away. When her head stopped spinning, she saw him give Beast a hearty scratch on the head and bounce toward the stairs that led up to her bedroom.

"Not so fast," she called after him, feeling like the coals in the center of a bonfire. He instantly twirled around and hung off the banister sporting an uncharacteristically juvenile grin. She flashed a similar one right back, then she pointed towards the hall and sent Beast up the stairs in his place. "The guest room is that way. Extra pillows are in the closet."

❧

After brushing her teeth, washing her face, shutting out the sun, and fluffing a makeshift dog bed in the corner, Rapunzel slid beneath the sheets with a sigh and took out her journal. She knew sleep would be impossible if she didn't bleed some of her feelings out and sop them up with paper. But even after filling eight pages about Belle, Marestam, Angus, Cinderella, Donner's curse, Ethan's deceit, and Grethel, she still couldn't get comfortable. She tried every position she could think of and every pillow she could find. She just wasn't used to being alone.

Cursing, she sat straight up and switched on the light. Ethan was just a staircase away, but she couldn't possibly give in this quickly. Allowing him to stay under the same roof was bad enough. He'd lied to her. Regardless of what he thought Grethel would do to him, that one fact remained.

True, he had been keeping his word. That was honorable. And if he truly believed Grethel's threat, he was right now sacrificing his own happiness in order to save everyone else's.

Ugh. All the rationalizing just made her want to scream. This is exactly why the old Rapunzel didn't compromise when relationships got too complicated. She just chucked them away like a dirty bandage. She never had to feel the mental and emotional anguish that went along with "gray areas" because she'd never allowed them in. It made her wonder whether it was possible to be carefree and independent without dying alone. Or were these things mutually exclusive?

She punched the pillow. Seconds later, Beast's hind leg began to spasm against the floor. He followed this up with a series of sleep whimpers and a deep, quivering exhale. Rapunzel chuckled and watched his massive silver chest rise and fall for a few minutes. He looked so peaceful in his sleep. Adorable even, with his front paws in an almost dainty crisscross position and his bottom ear splayed out over the wood. She was starting to understand why Belle took so much comfort in him.

He whimpered again and she wondered what he was dreaming about. Hiking through the woods with Belle, probably. Or chasing a squirrel. Or maybe he was having a nightmare about what happened at the Phoenix the other night. Poor thing had no idea what was going on. Or maybe that was to his advantage.

"Hey," she whispered, overcome by emotion. One eye popped open to look at her but the rest of his head stayed still. She was pretty sure his expression, in human terms, could be translated as, "What the hell are you waking me up for, lady?"

"Beast," she said again. "Are you comfortable down there?"

This time his head lifted and both eyes opened wider.

"I've got lots of space here if you want to come up."

He was on his feet immediately.

"Wow," she laughed, moving the pillows around to give him room. "Guess I still got it, ha?"

Beast shook his entire body in agreement—head all the way down to his tail—and then placed his snout on the mattress. She was just about to wave him on up, when she recalled all the times she'd chastised Belle for doing the same thing.

"Now Beast," she said, leaning down so that their noses practically touched. "If I let you up here, it's a one-time thing, okay?" Nothing. "No one finds out about this, got it? Not Ethan, not Gray, and especially not Belle."

The dog shuffled his paws, rearranged his snout, and sighed.

"Good enough," she said, smacking the sheets with her left hand. "Come on up. Okay!"

Before the last syllable was entirely out, the massive pile of fur leapt up, circled a few times, and plopped down with his head on top of her knee.

Rapunzel smiled, rearranged him a bit, and then wrapped both arms over his silky fur. Ordinarily, she wholeheartedly disapproved of letting anything with four legs sleep on an adult human's bed. But there was something reassuring about having him there with her—and she had a distinct feeling that he felt the same way. After all, Belle had cuddled with him almost every night since she rescued him. She would have wanted this. And who knew what other horrors were waiting for her in the coming days? Giving her dog this tiny bit of normalcy—albeit in a strange bed, in a different kingdom, when everyone was supposed to be waking up — was the least she could do.

Chapter Three

SNOW

To say she was excited went against everything Snow White stood for. She was the Zen queen, after all. She was the live-and-let-live guru, the advocate for both enormous hearts and tiny environmental footprints, the only one among her friends who believed in healing energy vortexes. She genuinely cared about strangers and wanted everyone to find deep, lasting inner happiness. So how in the world, after comforting Belle through the unthinkable for hours, did she feel her lips curling upwards as she rounded the bend towards home?

Snow forced them back down and unlatched the gate she'd built by hand out of reclaimed barn wood. She pushed it open, stepped onto the walkway, and stopped. Something was telling her to be still for a moment, to take note of where she was right now and pay her respects to everything that lay behind her.

She didn't know how Griffin was going to take the news. After all they'd been through, the very word "baby" was not something to be tossed around lightly. In the White household, those four letters sat in the same box as "capitalism," "authority," and "taxes."

Snow still remembered the first time she sat him down and

broke the big news: "We're going to be parents!" They were in the living room (the only real social space in their two-bedroom cottage) and he'd stayed in shock for a full minute. Then he'd leapt to his feet, performed a red-faced sun salutation, and scooped her into his arms. Unfortunately, more news followed a few weeks later ... and four more times after that: "Dr. Frolick said it's non-viable." "The heart stopped beating." "They didn't see a sac." "It seems my mother's poisoned apple did more damage than we thought." And finally, just a quiet shake of the head and a hushed, "No."

The day they decided to adopt was the day they decided to wipe the slate clean. They felt hope again. Then, even better: Three baby boys. Three! Three poor little triplets who'd been orphaned and needed a loving home. Within days, the second floor was cleared out and a trio of cribs sat in the corner, awaiting assembly. Griffin covered all the walls with a zero-VOC paint and found a white glider made entirely out of recycled materials. Snow gathered two dozen stuffed animals — eight for each crib — and contributed the artwork. She spent days painting four different iterations of the same oak tree standing guard in summer, autumn, winter, and spring. It was based off the giant shade tree in the center of their yard.

But then came the rampion brownies gaffe, the public relations fiasco, the Monarch Morality Movement, the microscope on Snow and Griffin's lifestyle, and those four little words from Home Adoptions: "Unfit to be parents."

Being asked to take care of Belle's son now was an honor — but it was also dangerous. It was like giving a paraplegic legs for one day and then taking them away again. It was like offering a beggar one day in the life of a billionaire, and expecting him to just walk away smiling when it was all over. But what choice did she have? A friend in need was a friend in need. And the way that baby had cuddled into her while they were waiting for his mama to wake up ... well ... Snow would just have to be careful.

That's all.

She gave the front of the cottage one last look before heading to the door. The style was quirky and cute on the outside, with a rounded front door and flared gables, but rugged and simplistic within. Most of the decor had been repurposed, and there were hardly any knick-knacks. Wherever they could have fit a portrait on the wall, they cut out a window instead so they could get a better view of the forest and the gardens they both loved to tend. To put it simply, the cottage was everything the residence of a king and queen wasn't supposed to be — at least in the minds of everyone outside of Tantalise.

Griffin was cross-legged on the carpet when she came in, but had his arms around Snow before she even removed her boots.

"How's Belle?" he asked, the top of his half-bald head glistening.

Snow hugged him tighter. "She's shaken up."

Griffin removed his glasses and let out a sigh of disbelief. He was a man of few words, but she never needed them.

"But she'll be okay."

He stuffed both hands in his pockets and watched her remove the cropped jean jacket and knee-high boots.

"Did you have any trouble?"

"Not at all," she said, forgetting all about the wig in her purse. With all the hostility aimed toward them following the rampion incident, she'd decided to ditch her usual organic peasant blouses, slap on some lipstick, and at least try to blend in with the rest of fashion-forward Marestam for a little while. "Belle didn't even recognize me at first."

Griffin's lips drew into a flat line as his focus traced the floor. "I guess that's what you wanted."

Snow shrugged and placed her purse on the table. He still disagreed with her theory that it might be better to just fall in line the way society wanted them to. It was a complete reversal, after all, borne of desperation and the sort of deep, maternal loss even a man as sensitive as Griffin could never fully understand. But if wearing high heels and enforcing Angus's laws and even moving back into Tantalise Castle like "normal" monarchs encouraged their critics to back down ... if staying on the path helped fill those cribs after all ... it was worth it.

"There's hot water if you want tea," Griffin said as she fell into the corner of the sectional and pulled her feet off the floor.

"Thanks, dear. I'm okay for now but..." She trailed off and flashed an irrefusable little grin. "Would you mind maybe rubbing my sinuses a little?"

Three seconds later, her head was in his lap and his pudgy fingers were digging heavenly little circles into her temples. She was waiting for the right time to tell him the news, when he forced her hand by mentioning that he'd found a stash of unsmoked rampion in the back of a shoebox while she was gone. "Just, you know, if you needed to take your mind off every—"

She was on her feet before he could even finish his sentence. Was he serious? After everything that vile weed had cost them? "Griff! Are you kidding me? After everything we've been through? Do you really think I even want to *look* at rampion again?"

Griffin fidgeted on the cushion for a minute, then looked at her like a dog caught in a sea of shredded toilet paper.

"I just thought..." But he trailed off, not wanting to finish his sentence. Did he really think that since they weren't going to be parents anymore, they could just toss responsibility to the wind and continue behaving like his glassy-eyed philosophy students?

"Belle's baby is alive," she said, too kind to let him suffer for long.

"I know," he said, rubbing the bridge of his nose. "You said she was fine. That's great."

"No," Snow said. "He's *alive*. He's breathing air. He's out of her body. And she doesn't want anyone to know yet because she doesn't think it's safe."

Griffin opened his mouth and then shut it. "Well, as much as I like to believe in the overall goodness of humanity, she's probably right."

Snow nodded but was a little caught off guard. She'd expected a lecture about the dangers of paranoia, and how the loss of trust leads to the breakdown of humanity. "Okay. Good. So, she wants us to take care of him until it is. Safe."

She closed her mouth and watched his face carefully. There was an unusual mixture of shock, disbelief, mortification, fear, and sadness. He pressed his thick hands together and clapped them beneath his chin, as if his head was a lollipop balancing on his two tallest fingers.

"Are you sure you want to do that?" he finally asked.

Snow's head tilted as she focused on him and tried to process such an unexpected question. "What do you mean? Belle is a dear friend and she needs us. Of course I want to help her. Don't you?"

Griffin closed his eyes, took a long, deep breath, and expelled it slowly. He was definitely holding stress in his shoulders.

"Of course I want to help her," he said. "That isn't even a question. I suppose what I should say is are you sure you're *ready* to do that? After everything we've been through, are you sure you can handle playing mother to a baby who'll one day go back to someone else?"

Snow clenched her jaw and tried to visualize something peaceful. She wasn't angry that he doubted her ability to stay unattached. She was angry that he knew her too well to stay quiet while she made a selfish, irresponsible decision. She was angry that he knew exactly what was going to happen.

"I'll be fine," she said. "And I'm not going to be playing mother, as you put it. Belle has some magical ring that'll let her pop in and out as if she's in the next room. At most, we're glorified babysitters."

Griffin searched her eyes as if they were tiny polygraph machines, showing her heart rate spiking every time she lied.

"I'm just looking out for you," he said, pulling his hands apart and pushing himself up from the couch. "I don't want to see you get hurt again."

"I won't," Snow said, giving into his hug while making a mental note to buy outlet covers for the baby's safety. And sterilization bags for his bottles. Oh, and probably a standalone freezer—so they had a place to store a few months' worth of breast milk. "Promise."

The Marestam Mirror

Diamond Ropes and Velvet Cake
By Perrin Hildebrand, King of Gossip

THE sins have been tallied, the violations weighed, and there's a good chance the King of Braddax will spend the rest of his days behind the thrice-fortified walls of Marestam Central Prison.

Carrying a mandatory minimum sentence of twenty-four and maximum of seventy-five years, Donner's official indictment (which will be formally read at the arraignment hearing on Tuesday), includes one count of arson; nine counts of third degree assault with a deadly weapon; one count of second degree assault with a deadly weapon; one count of first degree assault on a pregnant person with a deadly weapon; and one count of carrying a weapon without a permit.

Wait, you might ask. What's with all the weapons? Good eye.

The prosecution can thank the Magical Security Committee for that one. Late yesterday, just hours before the king's official indictment was released to the press, the newly convened MSC voted to change the legal definition of "weapon" to include magical powers. If this holds up in court, Donner's unborn child could be crowned King of Riverfell before it even takes its first breath.

Either that ... or according to the head of the political science department at Braddax University, the public could depose their current ruler before Belle pops, thus eliminating that monarchy altogether. "It's a slippery slope if I ever saw one, but this is an unprecedented situation. There's a reason Marestam is the only constitutional polymonarchy in existence right now—and that's because it's an extremely delicate dance. If the people lose so much faith in one monarchy that they want to see it fall, it's almost guaranteed that the others will follow. Even the most revered among us have skeletons."

It looks like the people of Braddax could have a very difficult decision to make.

The good news for the blue bloods: Parliament alone can't vote to depose a sitting monarch. They must put it to the public, as a referendum.

The bad news: Public opinion of the monarchies was at an all-time low in July, when forty-one percent of citizens said they would consider switching to a Parliamentary republic. (Source: UKM Polls) Add to that Donner's rampage and the growing Monarch Morality Movement and, well, let's just say I wouldn't put any money on which of the Charmé kids will inherit the throne in a few decades.

IN ALL the hubbub over the chaos in Braddax, yesterday's column neglected to mention one of the most unexpected corporate mergers in the last century. Tirion Enterprises, the billion-dollar international real estate giant founded by Hunter Tirion, King of Regian, has announced a definitive merger agreement with Perdemi-Divan, the world's second largest producer and distributor of alcoholic spirits, beer, and wine.

"The combination of Tirion Enterprises and Perdemi-Divan is a strategic step that unifies two great companies in the entertainment and lifestyle industry," said Liam Devereaux, CEO of Perdemi-Divan. "Joining forces with Tirion Enterprises marries our established distribution networks with innovative and aggressive global practices to create a whole new, preeminent echelon in the current luxury game."

What does that mean for us? I have no idea. The impetus was hidden somewhere inside an inch-thick legal document that gave me a migraine five sentences in. But as a shareholder of both companies, I think a champagne fountain in the lobby of every Tirion resort and country club is a good place to start.

Chapter Four

DAWN

At three a.m. in the kingdom of Regian, while most people were either asleep or slumped over a bottle, Dawn was hunched on the bathroom floor, scrubbing the toilet in her bathrobe.

She hadn't intended to do it. She'd only intended to take a shower in the hopes that it would make her feel better, and that maybe Hunter would come home while she was in there. Maybe she'd see him lounging on the living room couch when she came out, wrapped in her towel. Or maybe—just maybe—he might hear the water, push back the curtain and join her, forgiving everything she'd done without saying a single word.

But then she saw a spot the cleaners had neglected. And instead of a husband and makeup sex, all Dawn had were deep red lines on her knees and six feet of Selladórean guilt on her mind.

"Everything I believed in has come crashing down," Hunter had said, almost a full day earlier, while leaning limply over the crystalline evidence of her betrayal—love notes and fiber optic petals and part of a turquoise pendant that no longer fit its other half. "I'm going to need time."

Time. The word played on a constant loop in her head, taking on a different meaning with each iteration. Did he need time to heal? Time to let her stew? Time to call his lawyers and initiate divorce proceedings?

Dawn pumped the sponge too hard and too fast in her fist. Yellow soap bubbles fizzed out the cracks between her fingers, bubbled over her wedding ring, and slid into the suede cuffs on her sleeves. The soft pink fabric resisted for a moment but then embraced its dark side with a ravenous thirst, bleeding into a wild shade of red that would probably dry with permanent water spots. It was amazing how quickly something so pristine and delicate could tarnish.

Dawn's hand froze as she heard something ping in the kitchen. She let the sponge go and stretched her ears. Hunter had been gone for almost a full day now, not including his thirty-second return while she was putting the kids to bed, when he'd zipped in like a toy on a plastic track, grabbed his wallet and a fresh sports coat, and disappeared again. His only words, "don't wait up," would have been cliché if they were directed at anyone else. But considering his wife's condition—that is, her biological inability to sleep after being comatose for three centuries—Dawn really couldn't do anything *but* wait up.

One minute passed, then two, before she accepted that the pinging sound had probably been the refrigerator replacing the ice she'd taken for her vodka.

After their confrontation, all Dawn wanted to do was cry, scream, and guzzle vermouth until all the shame turned fuzzy and the fuzziness faded to black. She'd even considered swallowing seven boxes of sleeping pills (remnants of a night she wanted to forget) to see if they had any effect. She wondered, if she could just slip back into that coma, would Hunter forget all the horrible things she'd done? Would he kiss her back to life again and start over—if his kiss was even what had broken her curse in the first place?

If it wasn't for her children, she'd have nothing to lose in trying. But in addition to being a selfish, cheating wife, she was also responsible for two amazing little humans. She needed to keep it together to greet Morning when she came home from her sleepover, and to treat Day's bloody elbows when he returned from his. She had to lie through an excruciating smile when they asked where Daddy was. She had to make sure they felt safe, secure, and loved. And she had to accept that if they didn't feel this way, it was entirely her fault.

Another ping rang out. Louder this time. The front door clicked shut.

Dawn sprung off the floor immediately, her knees taking the grooves between the tiles with them. With that one sound, all of the questions she'd had seconds earlier — where had he been? who was he with? did he still love her? — scattered off screen.

Her feet came to an abrupt halt the moment she clapped eyes on him, but the rest of her body kept trying to lunge forward. "You're back," she chirped, arms still swinging.

Hunter was standing beside the fridge, catching cold, filtered water in a glass. She thought she might have seen his head nod about half an inch. It was a start.

"I was just cleaning the bathroom."

Another nod? Maybe a full inch this time?

"How was your walk?" she asked, edging forward. "Have you eaten? I can make you something if you want."

This time Dawn was positive she saw his head move, but it was a cringe at the suggestion of her cooking. Unlike Belle, who made desserts worthy of an expo, or Cinderella, who'd puréed her own baby food for all four of her kids, Dawn could barely broil a grilled cheese without setting off the smoke alarm.

Hunter gulped down the water and pushed it back for a refill. Dawn decided to try again.

"The kids were asking for you," she said.

Bingo. Hunter pivoted and panned slowly from her bare feet

all the way up to her bright red flyaways—though he somehow avoided catching her eyes.

"What did you tell them?" he asked, turning a blank stare to the water glass.

She parted her lips to reply, but his accusatory inflection tripped her up. Did he really think she'd badmouth him to their children?

"I just told them you were working," she said, feeling two inches tall. "It wasn't really a lie because if I had to guess where you actually were, that's how my money would go."

Had Dawn's eyes not been glued to him, she might have missed the right side of his mouth rise a fraction of an inch for a split second.

"Where you'd put your money," he corrected, unable to ignore her misuse of modern vernacular. He placed his glass on the counter.

"Right." Dawn nodded, for once welcoming his critique. But he'd neither denied nor confirmed her theory on his whereabouts. What if he hadn't been working? What if he'd spent the past twenty-four hours seeking comfort from another woman? What if he'd hiked over to Davin's mansion and socked him in the jaw? What if he'd gone to Angus Kane and tried to cancel the merger with Perdemi-Divan even though it meant losing Selladóre? She knew better than to push him right now, but—

"So, you were working, then?" Her voice was small, desperate. She felt like a child asking why Mama didn't kiss Daddy goodbye anymore.

Hunter responded by unbuttoning the top of his shirt and moving toward the bedroom. He must have stopped by a clothing store. Dawn was almost certain he was wearing a quarter-zip sweater when he left that morning, and she didn't recall him changing when he returned to grab his keys. For some reason, she found this reassuring. Retail therapy was better than someone else's bed.

"I'm tired," he said, maneuvering around the couch. "Gonna hit the hay." He glanced back at her—just for a second—and added, "That means go to sleep."

Dawn's heart skipped a beat. Was he joking with her? Was that an olive branch?

"I know what it means," she said, trying to tease back with a know-it-all tone.

But instead of continuing the banter, Hunter scowled and sucked his right cheek inward. "Whatever," he said in a tone she knew all too well. "Just trying to help. No need to get snappy."

Dawn opened her mouth to explain, but knew he'd just see it as being combative. She was in a hole now, and if she didn't carefully plot out every move, it would cave in around her. She balled her fists and took a slow, calming breath before following.

It took precisely fourteen steps to reach the bedroom, and when she finally crossed the threshold, Hunter was lost somewhere in his closet. At the sight of their mattress, Dawn already felt the dirt falling around her feet. Watching her words was one thing, but what about actions? Should she just stand there? Should she leave? Should she join him in bed?

Her thoughts began sparring with each other. On one hand, he'd said he was tired. So she should just back off and let him get a good night's sleep. Right?

But then again, he'd come home knowing she'd be there and knowing she'd be awake. Maybe what he wanted was to receive some affection—no more tears or pleading, just kisses.

Was *this* the olive branch she needed?

Did he want her to come to bed?

Did he want her to leave?

How was she going to survive if this constant uncertainty became her new normal? If every insignificant move turned into a three-page mental debate?

"I'd like to do something with the kids this afternoon,"

Hunter called from the closet, breaking through the muck and making her feel suddenly buoyant.

"They'd love that," she half-squealed before recalling the most painful part of their confrontation earlier—his insinuation that Morning and Day could really be Davin's biological children—born nine and a half months after a three-century incubation. She didn't think he could possibly actually believe that, but the fact that it even crossed his mind showed just how far she'd fallen in his eyes. Still, she decided to take a chance. "We'd *all* love that," she added.

A few seconds later, he emerged wearing black athletic shorts and an oversize T-shirt instead of his usual bare chest and boxer briefs. Even if it was the middle of winter, she knew he'd overheat in that. She heard the message loud and clear. Don't touch me.

"Great," he said, yanking the covers back and propping two pillows behind his head. She watched him fiddle with his cell phone for a few minutes before reaching for his light. "I have to be up in a few hours for a meeting with—"

He stopped, grimaced as if there was a tart taste in his mouth, and then mumbled something about the merger. The look on his face made Dawn want to curl up and disintegrate. Not only had her infidelity torn his heart into pieces and crushed everything he believed about his home life ... but in choosing Davin, she'd also set fire to his only productive means of distraction: work. Work was now the six-foot, bronze-skinned, hazel-eyed personification of her betrayal.

"Anyway," Hunter said, opting to skip the details entirely. "I'll think of something I can do with the kids in the afternoon. You should use the time for yourself."

"Oh." Dawn nodded. She wasn't invited. Okay. That was okay. Time, remember? "A new children's museum just opened in Riverfell. I've heard good things."

"Maybe," he said, reaching for the bedside lamp. "Oh, and

before I forget, I need you to be at Selladóre at ten thirty tomorrow."

Dawn tensed. Selladóre? Was he planning a romantic brunch or a public execution?

"Okay," she swallowed, not even daring to ask why. "Should I wear anything in particular?"

"Parliament wants to announce the change of ownership at that amphitheater they just built. I guess it was supposed to be unveiled Saturday, but they canceled it after Belle's attack." Dawn bit her tongue. So, Hunter's plan had worked. He'd managed to get Angus Kane's grubby hands off her homeland by offering him a stake in the Perdemi-Tirion merger. "I guess Angus wants to make some big show about Selladóre finally going home to its rightful princess—his words. As if it was his grand idea the whole time."

Dawn deflated inside. So, public execution it is. "If that's where you need me to be, that's where I'll be," she said.

"Right," Hunter murmured, letting out a grunt that essentially said, *Too little, too late.* Then he pulled the top pillow from behind his back, slammed it into the middle of the bed, and submarined beneath the covers. He rolled over so that she was now staring at his back, but she could see him watching her reflection in the two-inch slit beneath the shade.

"And yes," he added, answering the question she didn't dare ask, "*he'll* be there too. Just act normal please, if you can restrain yourself. The public might start asking questions if you suddenly start showing interest in what I do for a living—or with whom I conduct business."

The words were a swift kick to the gut, but all she could do was stand there and take it. She had no right to punch back.

"Hunter, I told you. Davin and I are over. I—"

"Please," he barked, still facing the other way. "Please, I really don't want to rehash it right now."

She nodded as a thick silence descended and seemed to pulse

for a full minute, as if the walls were actually breathing around them. She saw him raise his hand to his face and bow his head into it. His shoulders rose, gently. The next time he spoke, his voice was much softer — a pat compared to the preceding slap.

"I just need to focus on getting through the next few days, okay?"

Dawn murmured her understanding.

"But I can't do that with you tiptoeing around like a guilty child waiting for the storm clouds to pass. It only makes things worse."

Dawn opened her mouth as if to debate this, but then pulled it shut.

"Just be yourself. Please. Go shopping tomorrow while I take the kids, or get your nails done. Just don't be wearing that guilty, desperate mug when I get home. And when Parliament makes the announcement, just smile, wave, and pretend that you actually want to be there. It's nothing you haven't done a hundred times before."

The sides of Dawn's face felt completely hollow as she nodded, returned to the hallway, and shut the door gently behind her.

Had she not felt so angry, and guilty, and worthless, she might have laughed at the ridiculous turn of events. For eleven years, she'd been outraged at Parliament for refusing to make Selladóre a legitimate kingdom. She'd been sick to her stomach over its exploitation, over its rebranding as a tourist attraction and federal revenue stream. And for eleven years, she'd blamed Hunter for not fighting hard enough to stop it … only to find out that's all he'd been doing for just as long.

On paper, the transfer of her homeland from government rule to a company half owned by the husband of its rightful princess should have been cause for celebration. It should have been a reason for Dawn and Hunter to pop a bottle of champagne and laugh about all the misunderstandings that were finally in the past. But it didn't seem like much of a victory. Angus Kane still had at least one finger on it—more if Davin was secretly in his pocket.

Dawn had a horrible feeling that Hunter was just a pawn in a game that started way back when she was still sleeping—and she would do everything she could to fix it.

Chapter Five

BELLE

After seesawing between glorious slumber and bloodcurdling nightmares from midnight until the first, very unwelcome, rays of sun, Belle awoke to the sound of something popping at the foot of her bed.

She assumed it was Kirsten coming in, as promised, to give Belle her first crack at nursing. Or perhaps it was Rapunzel getting an early start on the day because she'd kicked Ethan out of her apartment and was lonely. Or maybe it was Gray, sneaking in to hand her the rings or explain why he returned to the Phoenix that night. Or maybe—

"Unless you're making love beneath a waterfall at sunset," someone said, "I highly suggest you let go of that dream and open your eyes already. That's the only case in which making your mother-in-law wait this long is appropriate."

Belle's entire body spasmed. Her eyes shot open. "Hazel?"

Hazel Wickenham gave an insincere, one-sided smile and tossed her platinum blonde hair off her shoulders. She was looming a few feet from the bed, arms crossed in a way that made them appear to be floating on top of each other rather than resting. She was inspecting Belle's massive spread of flower arrangements, a glittery pink wand poking out from her cleavage.

"Are you aware that you look remarkably like a porcelain doll while you're sleeping?" she asked, smirking again. "No wonder my son always thought you were so fragile. Isn't that so like a man? Always assuming we're delicate, brainless creatures without the capacity for deceit."

Belle jerked up to a sitting position so fast, the IV tube yanked a good inch off her forearm — bringing the skin and vein with it. She immediately covered it with her right hand, expecting blood to spurt everywhere — the bed, the floor, her mother-in-law's white single-strap bathing suit with its matching sarong.

"Deceit?" Belle repeated as Hazel sashayed forward, smoothed the edge of the bed, and perched just below Belle's elbow. She looked like the stick-legged bird Belle used to watch clean hippos at the Braddax Wildlife Park — only far less benevolent and with a significantly larger chest.

"You poor thing," she cooed, shaking her head and completely ignoring Belle's previous remark. "Had a rough night, didn't you?"

Belle's jaw dropped as Hazel cupped it between her perfectly manicured fingers.

Was she serious? Had a rough night? This was her opening line? How about, "So sorry my lunatic son went off the rails, burned your home to the ground, and almost murdered you and my unborn grandchild?"

Grandchild. Belle spun toward the bassinet as a rush of cold panic flooded her insides. How was she going to keep Rye a secret if Hazel saw a slumbering infant in her room? How was Belle going to stop her from proclaiming his existence to the world in an effort to secure the Braddax throne from federal seizure? How was she going to—

Belle's mind suddenly stopped racing. The bassinet wasn't there. That's right. Kirsten had taken him to the nursery. But she could still roll in with him at any moment.

Hazel furrowed her brow and then followed her gaze. "Can I reach something for you?" she asked, analyzing the empty corner. "Or are you expecting company?"

Belle shook her head. She needed to shoo her guest away as quickly as possible — without arousing suspicion.

"What are you doing here?" she asked. "You know there's a warrant out for your arrest, right?"

"Arrest?" Hazel laughed and dismissed this with a jingly snap of her wrist. "Let 'em try. One snap of these fingers and I'm back on Avalon with a mango daiquiri and a ravishing young pool boy massaging my … well, anything I want, really." She paused, tempted by her own words, and murmured something about waiting. Belle watched as she drew the sparkly stick from between her breasts, stretched it out into a full-sized magic wand, and gave it a flick. Half a blink later, a frosted hurricane glass appeared in her left hand. She tilted the spiral straw forward to offer Belle a sip, then tugged it swiftly back. "Whoops. Sorry. I always forget about the whole alcohol and pregnancy thing. But you've only got a few more months, right? Just hang in there. It might seem hard to imagine now, but it actually will be worth it."

As usual, Hazel's voice hopped around as if she was singing a nursery rhyme — one that had been played a few too many times.

"I never doubted motherhood would be worth it," Belle said. There's nothing she wouldn't give up for her child. Not love. Not freedom. Not her life. Not even her morality.

Hazel patted her leg through the waffle print blanket. The weight and the warmth of her hand was surprisingly comforting, as if the two women actually shared some sort of connection now — not just as women, but as mothers too. But Belle knew better than to let this catch her off guard. She knew that, unlike Penny's mother-in-law who rarely bothered to veil her criticism, Hazel was a pro at sweet-talking her adversaries. "You've had a tough road," she said, moving her fingertips in tiny concentric circles and listing all of Belle's misfortunes: Her merchant father's bankruptcy and subsequent snowball of disgrace. Her mother's decision to leave the whole family rather than face the social demotion. How scared she must have been when bestial Donner took her prisoner—even though it ended up being "the best thing that ever happened" to her. Her five-year struggle to get pregnant, and then her own sister seducing her husband. Hazel clicked her tongue along the roof of her mouth and gave a heavy sigh. "I don't blame you for running away. Goodness knows I wanted to catch a train the first time I caught *my* husband fooling around. But then I realized that being Queen was worth..."

Belle closed her eyes, not eager to hear Hazel rationalize her son's behavior again. She inhaled long and slow through her nose, and then exhaled through her mouth. She imagined walking through the trees with Beast—a meditation technique Snow had taught her over the summer—and even visualized a baby carrier this time as well. Its occupant was covered in a muslin blanket and fast asleep, despite the leash constantly jerking in Belle's hand.

The sound of her phone buzzing yanked her back to reality. She grabbed it, switched the volume to mute, and placed it face down on top of her belly. Hazel's left eyebrow rose.

"Well, it was really nice of you to check in on me," Belle said, feigning a yawn, "but I'm feeling—"

Hazel's harsh laugh cut her off. "Oh, honey. I'm sorry," she said, taking another sip of her drink, then setting the glass on the bedside table. "Did I give you the impression that this was a friendly visit?" Hazel's tone suddenly had a sharp edge—as did the rest of her. "You obviously haven't checked the early morning news yet. But we'll get to that. First, I need to know how my grandchild is doing."

Belle propelled up in bed and shoved out her belly just in time for Hazel to clap her palm over it, displacing her phone in the process. It was a weird thing to admit, but she'd always been good at giving herself a believable fake pregnancy bump. During her first couple years of marriage, she used to do it in changing rooms before buying any new clothes—because the plan had been to have lots of babies and to have them immediately.

"Call me old fashioned," she said, "but I don't think it's a good idea to store electronics on top of a developing baby's head."

"Oh, of course," Belle said, stashing the phone under her pillow. "I'm usually very careful about that stuff. I eat all organic and grass-fed, walk every day, and don't take any medications unless absolutely necessary." She paused to let Hazel look around. She wanted to make sure she understood what Belle was getting at—that two seconds of cell phone radiation was nothing compared to the traumatic experience Donner had provided. "Well, I usually do, anyway. Hopefully a few days of hospital food and immobility won't do him too much ha—"

"*Him?*"

Belle cursed herself as Hazel slammed her hands together in simultaneous shock and glee. She hadn't meant to give even that much information away.

"Yeah well," Belle hawed. "Dr. Frolick said it was a really close call," she added, not wanting her main point to be forgotten—though judging from the stars in Hazel's eyes, it already was. "Good thing he's a strong little guy."

"Of course he is," Hazel half-shrieked. Belle felt the mattress bounce as she hopped off the bed and began circling the room. "Strong like his father. I knew it! I *told* Donnie he was going to have a son. He didn't believe me, of course. But mothers always know, don't they?" She swung around, her back to the window. The sun was fully up now, and the sky was a vivid robin's egg blue. "How did he react when you told him?"

Belle opened her mouth several times before successfully spewing out some words. "I was going to tell him Friday, but..." she said, expecting Hazel to fill in the rest.

Instead, the egotistical, middle-aged diva stood back and skewered her with her bright blue eyes. Desperate for any escape, Belle spotted the nurse's call button in the corner of her eye and had the sudden urge to push it — as if a third party might scare the fugitive pureblood back to her tropical island. But it was too risky. She could arrive with Rye in tow. If only she was cooler under pressure, she thought while tilting a water bottle between them and drinking as slowly as humanly possible.

"What?" Belle finally snapped, pulling the drained bottle away and summoning the teenage attitude she never really had. "It's not my fault I lost consciousness halfway through your son's visit."

Hazel's chin drew in fast, as if the words had physically struck her. "No," she said. "I can't blame you for Donner's outburst. It was impulsive, stupid, embarrassing, juvenile, and one hundred percent selfish."

Belle's cold stare wavered.

"But I can blame you for lying to me."

Belle repeated the word — "Lying?" — but even she could hear the uncertainty in her voice.

Hazel marched back toward Belle's bed. Only rather than perching on the mattress like before, she grabbed one of the orange plastic chairs and dropped into it. Then she grabbed the seat and scooched forward, the metal legs screaming along the floor.

"Yes. Lying." She pitched forward, filling Belle's air with a mixture of rum and sunscreen. "You know that Donnie's curse is back. Don't you? You *know* that's why he acted like that. You know he would never physically harm you. And he'd never, ever even *risk* harm coming to that baby. He's ... difficult sometimes. I'll admit that. His father was a terrible role model.

But that's not as bad as a dead role model. And poor Donnie had to grow up with both."

Belle's eyes fell. Bringing up Donner's childhood was a low blow, but it worked on her every time. Perhaps this was because she'd wanted to be a mom for so long. Perhaps it was because she knew how it felt to grow up with one parent gone and the other self-destructing. And even though the world had known Varek Wickenham as a womanizing, over-the-top Neanderthal, she knew that to his son, he'd made up half the universe.

"I didn't know for sure that his curse was back," Belle lied, peeling her sheets down and then immediately pulling them back. Her legs were dying to move around, but her stomach wasn't ready to make a full appearance—yet another reason to remain in the hospital for as long as possible. "I mean, I suspected it might be. I'd like to think he wouldn't have tried to kill me if he was in his right mind. I know he's an insecure asshole who covers it up by acting like an egotistical prick, but…"

She trailed off, waiting for Hazel to either shut her up or explain the smug look carved all over her face.

"What?" Belle finally asked, uncertain she wanted to know the answer.

Hazel sucked her cheeks in and ran a nail along her plunge neckline. "Do you think I'm an idiot?"

Belle hesitated before giving a barely convincing, "Of course not." She swallowed. "Why would you say that?"

Hazel sighed and shifted her weight. "Because I received a very strange call from Ruby Welles a few hours ago, trying to recruit me for some magical mission to break Donner's curse." Belle said nothing as Hazel flattened her palm to examine her cuticles. Oops. "Did you know about this?"

Belle's jaw seemed to be glued shut.

"Listen," Hazel continued, lowering her hand and giving Belle a little space, "I don't trust that sanctimonious 'last remaining pureblood' fraud as far as I can throw her — even if I can throw her quite a distance. So if you're involved in this, you'd better start talking. Otherwise, I'm telling her thanks, but no thanks, I'll handle my son's problems my way. And trust me, she's not going to like my methods."

Belle rubbed her lips together. In five years of marriage to her son, she'd never taken Hazel the least bit seriously when it came to the general public. She'd always seemed more lipstick-stained-wine glass than gavel. But when it came to her family, she was a lioness.

"What is it you want to know?" Belle asked, pushing herself up higher on the bed. It was a simple movement, but with the blanket and the IV tube and the hospital gown, the whole action just seemed so … incriminating. "Ruby believes Donner's curse is back and she's trying to break it. It's pretty straightforward."

"But why?" Hazel asked, spinning on her sandals and pacing the room. "Why the hell would she care what happens to my son? She detests him. There's something she's not saying, don't you think?" She halted to decapitate one of Belle's roses. "Well, speak up. Telepathy isn't one of my powers, believe it or not."

Belle did a few quick calculations in her head. If she told her that Donner's curse had transferred to the baby, Hazel might ask too many follow-ups. And she didn't seem to know that Ruby's powers were gone too. She must have withheld that information from Hazel for a reason.

"Umm," she began, flexing her toes beneath the blanket and staring at the window. The weather was perfect for a walk with Beast. Poor guy, all locked up in Rapunzel's sterile apartment. It was so unnatural for him. "Well, you know how obsessed Ruby is with keeping the monarchies intact."

Hazel reached the bed in three giant strides. She hooked both hands on her hips and tilted forward. "So?"

Belle stared back for a moment, then looked away. She'd hoped Hazel would fill in her own blanks and make life a little easier. After all, Angus had control of two kingdoms and was calling for Snow to leave Tantalise too. Anyone could see that the monarchies were in danger.

"So Ruby thinks Angus Kane used some sort of magic to bring back Donner's curse," she said, screening each word carefully. "And he did it because he wanted the throne ... which he now has."

Hazel didn't move for a full five seconds, then squinted as if she was trying to sharpen the features on Belle's face. She felt a chill zigzag up her back.

"That doesn't make any sense," her mother -in-law said, her fingers flapping against her elbows again. "Angus doesn't have powers. And what does breaking his curse have to do with saving the monarchies? His son is next in line and it's your separation that caused all this. Belle, if you want my help, tell me the truth."

Seeing no other choice, Belle opened her mouth to give Ruby away. But barely two words in, Hazel tossed her hands in the air and commanded her to stop. "No, never mind. No more stories," she said, her tone suddenly a bit more jovial. "I already know the answer, anyway."

Belle didn't know whether to smile back or prepare for an offensive. "You do?"

"Of course I do. I'm a woman too, after all. I get it."

Belle's head tilted the way Beast's did when he was trying to process human speak. "It's pretty transparent, actually. I just wanted to hear you admit it." Holding back a smirk, she leaned close enough for Belle to make out all the cracks of foundation on her cheeks. "You still have feelings for him," she said, pausing to let the words sink in. "Don't you?"

Belle's lungs seemed to pull apart and suck in every last square inch of air. It was ridiculous, but it was exactly what she needed—a lifeline that kept Rye far below his misguided grandmother's radar but still guaranteed her help. The question now: did she want to take it?

"After all," Hazel continued, making up Belle's mind for her, "there's no point in breaking the curse that gives my son superhuman strength ... just so he can be secured in a jail cell for the next thirty years while the mother of his child takes another lover, and his son grows up without a crown." She paused to smile. Then she locked those two blue lasers on Belle again. "I'm sure as a future mom, you'd agree."

So that was her game. Hazel wanted assurance that Belle would stand by Donner in the future. Well, she could stand by him as an ex-wife, too. And as she'd decided earlier, she'd do anything for Rye; telling a bold-faced lie was only the beginning.

Seeing no other way, Belle let out a giant sigh and told her yes. She'd guessed it. Even though Donner's sins against her numbered on the epic, she just couldn't get past the idea of her happily ever after, which was supposed to be with him. She just needed him to stop being so controlling. And egotistical. And unfaithful.

"Sometimes I still imagine me and Donner and our children at the castle," Belle said, channeling Beast's dinnertime eyes and trying not to regurgitate in her mouth. "It's the reason we were going to try again. The reason he came over that night. But I just don't see how that can happen while he's cursed."

"Oh, of course you don't," Hazel said, mirroring her daughter-in-law's tone and sliding onto the bed again. Belle poured it on thick as Hazel reached up and ran her fingers along her cheek. "I knew you'd get sick of all that stressful inn nonsense sooner or later. Independence is good for some people, like your friend Rapunzel. Sure, you can sit around in sweatpants all day eating ice cream, you don't have to shave every day, and you can go to bed without being physically accosted. But eventually, those sweatpants start to lose their appeal and the warmth of a furry companion just isn't the same as a big, strong man, is it?"

Belle struggled to come up with an answer. What had she done? "So, you'll be part of the triad?" she asked, holding her breath.

Hazel smirked and glanced out the window. Then she grabbed Belle's hand, gave it a one-two tap and a fierce squeeze, and bounced to her feet. "Now, no more dwelling on the past. We're gonna snap this curse, break Donnie out of jail, and whip him back into the prince you always dreamed about. How does that sound?"

"Umm, great." Belle hesitated. "But when you say break Donner out of jail—"

"Oh, sorry. Poor choice of words. I'm not a felon—registry debacle aside. Stripes don't look good on me. But now that I know how you feel, I think you'll agree that the best hope for Donnie is for the woman he attacked to come out calling for his forgiveness. Assure them you're standing by your man. Blame magic. Confirm what the world already suspects and blame his curse. Heck, condemn the way I raised him, for all I care. Just get my son out on bail and try to help the public see that he's not a monster. He's just had a tough life."

Belle felt suddenly sick to her stomach. Or was that her soul trying to flee the auction block?

"If you can do that," Hazel continued, hoisting a polka dot beach bag over her shoulder and draining the last of her daiquiri, "I'll stay far away from you and Marestam until it's time to break the curse."

Belle nodded but couldn't help interpreting that as a threat. If she didn't hold up her end of the bargain, Hazel could pop in on her (and Rye, and Gray) at any moment.

"Do you really think my forgiveness is going to make any difference?" she asked. "From what I've been told—which isn't much, since everyone seems to be on strict orders to keep me as in the dark as possible—the public is livid."

"Oh, they are," Hazel replied. "But you're carrying their

future king and they respect you. They'll listen."

Belle was starting to panic. "But Angus isn't just going to walk away from Braddax. Didn't you hear what I said? He's on some sort of magical power trip and — "

"Also true," Hazel cut her off. "But power isn't the same as influence. And I'm supposed to be under the impression that this triad business will take care of him. Am I not?"

Belle had nothing left to say. Hazel had her cornered.

"So, what exactly are you suggesting I do?" she asked.

Hazel smiled and loosened her neck as if she was standing in the center of a rose garden, smelling something enchanting from all sides.

"Well, you saved him once. In the dark, empty corner of an enchanted castle," she said as a newspaper popped into her hands. She placed it on the bed. "You can do it again. Only this time, it's going to be right out in the open, on the front page of Marestam's least deplorable newspaper." Belle's entire body froze. What had she gotten herself into? "A front-and-center feature about the Wickenham's secret and the victim calling for absolution. Matilda Holt's idea. I believe you know each other."

Belle stared straight ahead but saw nothing. Her brain was suddenly three months behind her, on the steps of this very hospital, giving the story of the century to a masculine woman with a *Mirror* neck lanyard and a surprisingly warm disposition. Well, if she had to sell her soul to a reporter, it might as well be her.

"Glad we're on the same page," Hazel said. "She'll give you all the details at the arraignment."

"The arraignment?" Belle needed a paper bag, pronto. "I'm not going to any a — "

"Oh yes you are," Hazel cooed. "I've already pulled the necessary strings. Judge Ford has agreed to let you speak, and they're moving the whole proceeding to the hospital so you won't have to worry about traveling. That's how much the people respect you." She lifted her empty glass into the air in a one-sided cheers. "Oh, and one more thing. The longer you hang out in this hospital bed, the worse it's going to look for Donner — and you seem remarkably healthy minus the eye bags. I can't imagine a strong woman like you needing any more than four days here." She paused, the rest of her threat coming out through her eyes. "Now get some rest. Stress from the mom transfers to the baby, after all."

Belle sat there, stunned, as Hazel disappeared. A few seconds later, a knock sounded at the door and Kirsten waltzed in pushing a rumbling bassinet, squeezing a book of baby names beneath her arm, and praising what a beautiful, bright September morning it was shaping out to be.

Chapter Six

ANGUS

Two mornings after Belle's attack, the Prime Minister of Marestam stretched his way out of bed, kissed his mother's picture, and steeped a giant cup of gotu kola tea. His bones ached even more than usual, but his heart was a glowing ember. Despite the odds and the obstacles and the bats-out-of-hell chances, everything was working out according to plan — with a few, generally fortunate exceptions.

Angus had fully expected his physiological meddling to cause a public relations fiasco — the kind that inspires rallies and calls for immediate impeachment — or, in this case, dethroning from a completely undeserved position in the first place. He'd imagined that Donner's surging hormones might cause a paparazzi-magnified meltdown, launching him into a paranoid rampage during a massive public event or during a talk show interview gone completely awry. But setting his estranged wife's home business ablaze, endangering the lives of a half-dozen innocent tourists, putting Angus's own niece into a coma, and nearly killing Belle and her unborn child? Well, that was beyond even Angus's wildest dreams.

"You gave him too much," he could hear his mother saying.

"You're not a pharmacist. You should have been more careful. If Kiarra dies as a result of this revenge quest, can you really say it was worth it?"

The career politician's eyebrows drew so close together, they appeared to overlap. His first impulse was yes, it would still be worth it. For you, Mom. For those who wronged you. For everyone who has ever been cast aside because their blood contained no magic, no royal lineage.

Angus always knew Donner had some magic—sixty-one percent, to be exact. But he'd adjusted for that. The anabolic steroids he'd been injecting through the corks of his anonymous "Whiskey of the Month" gifts shouldn't have had such an intense effect, even with that final dose multiplied. There must have been something else at play. He just wasn't sure what. Nor was he sure that it mattered. At the end of the day, what's done was done. There was no point questioning whether the ends outweighed the means, or how he could have possibly overcalculated. All that mattered now was how close he was, after all these years, to fulfilling his promise.

Chapter Seven

RAPUNZEL

Rapunzel wanted to turn around the instant her foot crossed the threshold of Cribs and Cankles. The store was a pastel nightmare, with stuffed animals lining the ceiling, music that somehow crossed elevator jazz with lullabies, and an invisible sensor that giggled when the front door opened. Throw in a temperance band and she'd officially be in hell.

"Baby dust to you!" a woman sang from behind a rack near the far side of the store. She was standing on her tiptoes, sorting through a dozen variations of the same empire-waist, bow-beneath-the-boobs sweater.

Rapunzel flashed a quick smile and made a beeline for the nursing bras. She didn't want to be rude, but chitchatting with a maternity store associate was the last thing for which she had time — or energy — right now. Perhaps if she'd gotten a little more sleep. But Rapunzel's sunrise slumber had lasted a whopping three hours, after which she'd tossed Beast into Ethan's room and rushed off to meet with a rubbernecking insurance agent at the Phoenix. By three o'clock, her phone was filled with photos of Beast — catching tennis balls in Capitol Park, jumping on a hot dog vendor in midtown, getting a bath at a spa on Fifth

Avenue—as well as a screenshot showing an afternoon flight from Marestam to Stularia the next day. *All booked*, the accompanying message said. *How are you making out? Let me know if you need help packing, etc. Do you have someone to watch Beast while we're gone? P.S. We're having a blast. If all dogs are this much fun, we should highly consider getting one.*

Rapunzel had stared at the phone for a good five minutes before deciding on her response, which consisted of two words and completely ignored the last statement. He had a lot of nerve suggesting they take such a monumental step now. Evidently, he'd already put the whole betrayal thing behind him. What next? A damn wedding ring at the bottom of her morning coffee?

"Ah, that's our best-selling nursing bra," the saleslady said, creeping up behind her with a smile that made Rapunzel want to throw up. According to the stork-shaped tag on her shirt, her name was Shirley. "For you or a friend?"

Rapunzel twirled around, her hand still clutching a beige contraption with a few too many hooks and far too much fabric. At least it only had two cups.

"Oh, a friend," she said as Shirley's eyes grew two sizes. She turned away immediately, but it was too late.

"Oh. My. Goodness," she heard as the woman's bulb nose darted back into her view. "Rapunzel Delmonico?" Rapunzel winced as Shirley's hands clapped together and her voice climbed two octaves. She wasn't sure what was more nauseating: the overhead fluorescent lights, the oscillating music, the overpowering scent of peppermint potpourri, or the hurling pitch of this woman's voice.

"Oh my gosh you must be here for Belle! The poor thing! I couldn't believe it when I heard! But thank goodness she and the baby are okay." She paused and slapped her hand around Rapunzel's wrist. The bra's left strap snapped from its hanger. "The baby *is* okay, right?" She held her breath, desperate for the inside scoop.

Rapunzel paused for a moment. Perhaps doing Belle's shopping herself hadn't been the best idea. Perhaps she should have sent Ethan instead.

"Yes," she said as the woman finally exhaled, blasting her customer with hot coffee breath tinged with … was that vodka? Shirley's bony fingers flapped against her collarbone. "Oh, thank goodness. There's nothing more sacred than our children. Sacred, priceless, the point of all existence. Honestly, if we can't protect them, what good are any of us?"

Rapunzel just stared. It was the sort of statement that would have sent her raging a few days ago, insinuating that everyone without children, whether by choice or circumstance, was good for nothing. That they were expendable, selfish, a waste to the species. But instead, she simply nodded, plucked up a handful of different nursing bras in what she gathered to be Belle's post-pregnancy size, and headed for the register.

"Oops," the woman said, confiscating the bras and giggling as if Rapunzel had just tried to wipe her face with a jockstrap. "I think you're underestimating a bit. The Queen's still got four months of growing before she pops, right?"

Another nod.

"Then trust me, you're going to need a bigger cup. Those puppies are going to swell up like a Saint Bernard caught in a beehive by the time she really needs these."

A tiny taste of vomit reached the base of Rapunzel's throat. She checked her watch. Hospital visiting hours ended at nine o'clock. It was already six, and she was only halfway through her to-do list. She didn't have time to convince Shirley that she was wrong.

"I'll just grab a bunch," she said, scooping half the rack into her arms. "Better safe than strapped, you know? Ha, strapped. Get it?" She hated herself at the moment. "You can explain your return policy on my way out."

Chapter Eight

BELLE

"She totally played you," Rapunzel said before dropping an overstuffed duffel bag on the hospital floor and demanding that Belle "hand over that scrumptious ball of baby goodness this instant."

Belle quickly covered up and obeyed the request with a hesitant smile.

"Oh, I've been waiting all day for these cuddles," Rapunzel sighed, sweeping the baby to her chest and tapping his itty-bitty nose. He let out a merry squeak, pushed his bottom lip out with his tongue, and flailed all his appendages at once. "Someone should seriously bottle this feeling up and pour it into the world's water supply. There'd be instant peace on earth. Honestly. How can anyone hold a grudge with a bundle of innocence like this in their arms?"

Belle knotted the top of her hospital gown—a paper-thin pink thing with more laces than she knew what to do with—and slithered off the bed. "Do you really think Hazel played me?" she asked, struggling not to hover.

Rapunzel made a tiny noise, possibly a pop of laughter. Then she flashed a look that left absolutely no question. "Unless you left something out of that panicked, twelve-minute voicemail," she said, cooing the words while swaying back and forth and making faces at Rye, "would you even believe me if I said no?" Belle frowned and hoisted up the duffel—or at least tried to. She nearly toppled over from the weight but somehow managed to pitch it onto a threadbare floral armchair by the window. What the heck was in there, foundation stones salvaged from the fire?

"Ugh," she groaned. "I just didn't know what to do. She was threatening to let Donner's curse stand, and I didn't want her to know about Rye. She didn't buy the whole Angus-has-bigger-plans story, and Ruby must have kept her situation from her for a reason."

"Yeah," Rapunzel half-snorted. "The reason being pride and ego. Can you honestly tell me you trust Ruby after everything she put you through? I'm still having a hard time following her lead on all this. That woman always has an angle and she'd do anything to protect her perfect fairy image."

Belle rolled her eyes. She'd heard Rapunzel's anti-Ruby speech a million times already. "Well, whatever the case, I was about to tell Hazel all about Ruby's powers when—"

"When she played you."

Belle pursed her lips but knew she had no leg to stand on. The more she thought about it, the more it seemed likely that Hazel had bluffed her way to recruiting Belle as Donner's most steadfast defender. But selling her soul was worth it to keep Rye safely beneath her wing for as long as possible.

"Anyway," she said, aching to change the subject. "How are you doing with the Grethel thing? And the Ethan thing? Are you guys … still together?"

A few beats went by with no response.

"Please. Don't hold back just because you think I'm dealing with worse," Belle said. "I don't have a monopoly on bad days, and the last thing I want is everyone feeling sorry for me."

Rapunzel either didn't agree or was too busy playing with Rye to answer. He was batting at her nose the way a cat would bat at a ball of yarn. After a few seconds, he let out a series of sounds that were a step above crying but not formed enough to be considered babbling.

Belle hung back and blinked a few times, as if trying to capture the image on a mental camera. In isolation, it was a perfect moment—her best friend rocking side to side with her new baby in her arms. The two of them socializing in the hospital where she'd just given birth. Her baby staring up at his future godmother with eyes the size of bottle caps, struggling to say "hello" but not quite sure how to work the mechanics of his mouth.

Yes, in isolation, it was perfect. Belle just had to avoid the urge to zoom out. She returned her focus to the duffel.

"What's in the bag?" she asked, already pulling back the zipper.

Rapunzel continued rocking and, with a sugary voice better suited to a nursery rhyme, listed everything Belle had been craving since she regained consciousness almost forty hours ago: socks that didn't bunch up around her heel; soap that actually lathered; soft cotton T-shirts; yoga pants; fresh underwear; a hair dryer; peppermint toothpaste; a bundle of design magazines so she could start mentally rebuilding the Phoenix; and even a jumble of nursing bras, still on their hangers.

"Wow. This look complicated," she said, surveying one of the bras. She'd never seen so many straps and hooks on a piece of lingerie—minus the time she had to borrow Rapunzel's negligee. "And you actually set foot in a maternity store? I'm impressed."

"Yeah, that was an adventure," Rapunzel said. "If you don't like any, please just give them away. I never want to set foot in that place again."

Belle rolled her eyes and tore the tag off the yoga pants. Then she leaned against the bed and threaded both legs through at once. She instantly felt her humanity return—along with some warmth, a little mobility, and a smidgen of self-respect.

"Only you could look at a maternity store and see something wicked," she said, even though there was a time when she thought the same thing—for completely different reasons. "I think they're some of the happiest places in the world. If we can't rebuild the Phoenix for some reason, maybe that should be my Plan B. Everyone's so hopeful and full of life in those places. They know something amazing is coming—even those who went through hell to get there."

"I didn't say they're evil. They just scare the crap out of me." Rapunzel's hand flew up to her mouth as she looked at Rye. "Sorry, they scare the flowers out of me."

"Why?" Belle asked before spotting a turquoise bag deep inside the duffel. She recognized the color immediately. It was from her absolute favorite baby store in the whole world.

"Why?" Rapunzel repeated, her tone mystified. "Because if I ever tie a bow under my breasts, I don't want it to be because I no longer have a waist."

Belle laughed, snatched up the bag, and scurried over to the bed with it. "What if that's what Ethan wants?" she asked before pouring its contents all over the sheets. A jumble of baby socks and pajama suits and pocketsize sweatshirts tumbled out. "Oh my gosh these are adorable!"

"Those are just a few things I picked up," Rapunzel said, nose-diving into the change of subject. "Royalty or not, he needs a few things that actually fit him. The teething rings are all made of food grade silicone. And I thought the three-month stuff looked a little small, so I went with six."

"Oh, they're perfect!" Belle screeched, her hands shaking from overexcitement. It was like Christmas morning—only better. For days, her poor little munchkin had been forced to wear the same undersized kimono shirt, white knit booties, and striped skull cap. Kirsten had been kind enough to bring in some six-month onesies, but attempting to slide that delicate little head through the neck hole nearly gave Belle a nervous breakdown. Plus, with no baby shower, no birth announcements, and no recollection of even going into labor, this was the first "normal" new mom moment she'd had. "They're just perfect!" she said again, holding up a tiny orange fleece pinned to miniature cargo pants. She threw her arms around Rapunzel and then began explaining each item to her baby. "And bigger is better anyway. Gives him time to grow into them."

And there it was. The zoom. Belle wasn't having a normal moment with her normal child right now. Her newborn baby wasn't just unusually plump. He didn't just so happen to tip a tier on the standard clothing size chart. He'd developed at an unnatural rate because he'd been cursed, and no one knew how that would play out. No one knew when the slightly baggy six-month clothes would be bursting at the seams—in three months or in three days?

"Can I hold him for a sec?" she asked, spreading the outfit on the bed and turning her back to it. Carefully, she slid her fingers beneath the warm bundle of flesh, shifted him into her arms, and wilted over him like a day lily at twilight.

"You're right," Belle said, smiling as Rye's tiny, warm, baby body melted into her, breathed with her, clung to her because— for no reason other than instinct—he knew she would love and protect him. "There is absolutely no better feeling than this."

"Sit," Rapunzel commanded, clearing the duffel from the armchair and patting the cushion. "Be a mom. I'll put this stuff away."

Belle thanked her, but preferred to stand and sway. "He likes it when we dance," she said, gravitating toward the window while singing him to sleep. She was finally starting to feel at ease again, when Rapunzel pulled out a beautiful polka dot dress that had "going home outfit" written all over it. The sight slapped her across the face.

As much as she missed Beast and Gray and the great outdoors, the last thing she wanted to think about was leaving Marestam General—not before someone broke Rye's curse or Angus was in jail or she had one magical ring on her finger and another in Tantalise. But in reality, Dr. Frolick only had so many strings he could pull, Snow was already putting finishing touches on her nursery, and Hazel was expecting her to cartwheel out the front door as soon as possible.

"Beast is doing well," Rapunzel said, nudging her friend back to reality. "But he definitely misses you."

"He does?" she asked, accidentally jerking her arms. A pair of heavy eyelids bounced apart. She stroked Rye's cheek with her thumb and watched them slowly droop together again, then gave Rapunzel a look advising her that they had a sleepy baby in their midst. Carefully, she crossed the room and laid him into the bassinet, silently wishing he had something nicer to sleep in. Then she dimmed the lights a bit (as if he hadn't just fallen asleep in full fluorescence), and returned to hear how her other child— her furry, gigantic, crazy child—was doing.

"I miss Beast too," she said, opening herself wide open to Rapunzel's ridicule. "I know being a pet owner isn't really your style, but I really appreciate you taking him in. Knowing he's in a familiar place makes this a little easier. You didn't happen to take any pictures, did you?"

As expected, Belle received a dramatic head dip and a long, slanted stare that essentially said, *Really? Did you seriously just ask me that?* But then Rapunzel's lips curled up on the sides and she removed a phone from the front of her tight, coral slacks.

"There might be a few," she said as a huge, silver snout popped up on the screen.

Belle snapped it up and beamed at a picture of Beast curled up on his old bed—the first one she'd ever bought. It was comically small for him now, but she kept that thought to herself as Rapunzel began narrating. In less than one day, Beast had evidently gone shopping on Fifth Avenue; played catch in Capitol Park; whittled a giant tree branch down to chips; feasted on a human-grade rib eye steak; and maybe, judging by the sheets and the speed with which the photo disappeared, slept in Rapunzel's bed. Seeing this did more for Belle's morale than any medicine ever could have. She'd been picturing the poor guy moping around Rapunzel's apartment with his head down and tail between his legs, wondering what happened to all the trees.

"Ethan said he was very popular in midtown," Rapunzel said. "I think he knew it too, the way he pranced along with his tail high like a flagpole and his head up. Do people usually stop you to tell you how beautiful he is?"

Belle laughed. "All the time. He's a good looking puppy. Sweet too. People who like dogs can see that."

Rapunzel shrugged and looked away—away from the knowing smirk spreading across Belle's face.

"By the way," Belle said, ready to debunk the whole pet-aversion thing once and for all, "where's Beast sleeping during his stay at—"

"Ugh!" Rapunzel said, shoving her hands into her monstrous canvas purse. "I knew you saw it. Yes, I let him sleep on my bed this morning. It was a one-time thing. I was lonely and he just looked so pathetic—curled up on that booster that's half his size now, with those puppy dog eyes and—" She paused and pulled out two manila folders. "Well, it's not like he understands what's going on so…"

"So, you wanted to take care of him as best as you could," Belle finished her thought, trying to keep her satisfaction to a manageable level. "Maybe there is some maternal instinct in you after all."

Rapunzel rapped the folders on the bedside table and deposited them next to Belle's phone. "Don't even think it."

If Belle's smile stretched any wider, it would probably have torn her face in two. But then a word spiraled back at her: lonely. "Wait," she said. "Why were you lonely? I thought you said Ethan was still around."

Rapunzel let out another grunt, then began fishing through her bag for something else.

"There's wine in the closet if you're looking for booze. Compliments of Hazel the Terrible."

But Rapunzel shook her head and pulled out a pen instead. She dropped it on top of the papers.

"You need to sign these for the insurance company."

"Already?"

"Yes, already. High profile case like ours means publicity for them so I think they want to move as quickly — and generously — as possible, which is fine by me. The sooner we get these in, the sooner we can put all of this behind us and rebuild. We *are* rebuilding, right?"

Belle looked up. Their eyes locked for a split second that felt somehow heavy. That hadn't even been a question ... until it was phrased as one.

She fumbled for her words. "I mean, I thought so. Do you not want to?"

"Heck yeah, I want to!" Rapunzel hollered, then immediately slapped her hands over her mouth. Her eyes grew wide as a coughing sound emanated from the bassinet. They both froze and waited for a cry, but none came. Finally, when the coast appeared to be clear, Rapunzel peeled her fingers from her face and whispered, "Of course I do. I already have a bunch of inquiries from businesses that want to help. And we need this, remember?"

Belle recognized an urgency in her tone that usually preceded a pep talk, but she was in no mood for a lecture on forward progress and inner strength and not letting Donner win the war.

"Of course we do," Belle said, flipping through the first folder. She nodded, scribbled her signature a few times, and handed it back to Rapunzel. Then she picked up the next one. It was significantly thicker. "This too?"

Rapunzel grinned, probably because she'd dodged the question about Ethan for a second time. "No, that's homework."

"Homework?"

"Well, I figured we could use the fire as an opportunity to fix some of the things we did wrong last time."

Belle frowned. "Did wrong? What do you mean? I loved everything about the Phoenix. It was perfect. I mean, sure, if we'd had an unlimited budget, I might have separated the main house and added a few honeymoon cottages. Maybe used more low maintenance materials, or ... but, come on, overall I think it was just perfect. I mean it. Why are you looking at me like that?"

Rapunzel gave a slanted, devious smirk. "Just open the file."

She shrugged and laid it on the rolling serving table on which she'd enjoyed her blueberry pancake breakfast, chicken salad lunch, crusted salmon dinner, and chocolate brownie dessert — all accompanied by gelatin in various shades of green. On the top of the pile sat an email from a contractor in downtown Riverfell. Belle skimmed through the first few lines about sympathy and loyalty and "supporting the people worth supporting." Then she froze.

I'd consider it an honor if you'd allow us to help rebuild the Phoenix at cost.

She read it three more times before looking up. "At cost?"

Rapunzel smiled. "That's what it says. There are a ton of others just like it. For plumbing, landscaping, carpentry, design, catering, you name it. Even people who want to make gift bags for future guests."

"Really?" Belle dropped onto the edge of her bed and began flipping through the papers. She saw a few names she recognized: Regian Roofing, Majestic Electric, Twelve Brothers Remodeling, Always and Forever. She looked up. "Isn't Always and Forever run by the woman who did Cindy's birthday party?

Kimberly … Kimberly Epson?"

Rapunzel's smile plummeted. She must have misheard her. "You remember," she tried again, plucking the message out to give her partner a better look. "This is the woman who made that beautiful bracelet for Cindy out of her mother's old jewelry. And organized that whole party. Aaron had nothing but fantastic things to say about her."

Rapunzel stared blankly back at her, then reached for the paper. "Oh yeah," she said.

"Well, I'm sure her heart is in the right place, but what's a jewelry designer gonna do—bedazzle the concierge desk?" She let out a nervous laugh. "No, I'll just send out a reply thanking her but—"

"No!" Belle said, pulling the paper back. "I admire the heck out of that woman. I can't remember seeing Cindy so happy. It was as if she got her mother back somehow. And you know who else Kim Epson is, don't you?"

Rapunzel's shoulders jumped. Her green eyes widened. She glanced from Belle to the window and back again. Then she shook her head. "What do you mean *who else* she is?"

Belle squinted and studied the floor, as if trying to dig deep into her memory. "Kim Epson," she said, her voice barely a whisper. "You know, the Epson family." Rapunzel's face was blank. "Her sister was murdered by that horrible serial-killing husband." She leaned in and lowered her voice even further, as if her words could somehow affect Rye's dreams. "You know, Blue Beardsley. I think she was number three. Karen Epson. She had a son, too. Poor kid. Can you imagine?"

Belle watched as a strange look drifted over her friend's face. Confusion, probably, though it bore a strong resemblance to relief. Rapunzel held her tongue for a few seconds, then said she vaguely remembered hearing something about that. "It's a horrible story," she added, her tone oddly cool for such a serious subject. "But look at that pile. We can't take everyone up on their offer. Too many cooks in the kitchen and all." She reached for the paper again, but Belle deflected her hand and shook her head.

"I completely agree," she said, stowing Kimberly Epson's letter safely back in the folder and approaching the window. It must have just started raining, because while the headlights and marque signs below gave off a fuzzy glow, the streets were still bustling. "But we might need her help designing chandeliers, or planning our second grand opening. Now would you please stop being so elusive and tell me what's going on with you and Ethan? I'm pretty emotionally invested in your relationship so..."

She trailed off and watched her friend's reflection in the window. After a few seconds, Rapunzel's frown started to soften and she moved to the empty space beside Belle.

"Ethan and I slept in separate rooms last night," she finally said. "I didn't know what else to do. He lied to me, which should be the end of it. But the thought of losing him gives me this awful, suffocating feeling in my chest. I honestly don't know what to do. I've never been in this situation before."

"Do you think you're going to forgive him?"

They caught each other's eyes in the window. "I don't know. Maybe. Probably. Should I?"

"I'm really not the best person to ask for relationship advice," Belle said, reluctant to say too much. She'd blamed herself the first time Rapunzel and Ethan broke up, after Letitia's anniversary gala. She really didn't want any part in round two. So instead of saying, *I think he was trying to protect you*, she hopped into the passenger seat and asked, "Did he give you an explanation?"

It must have been the right question, because Rapunzel flew into an instant tizzy, ranting about Ethan's fear of Grethel, fear of losing his sight again, fear of losing her, fear of burdening her, and so on.

"Why can't I find a guy like Gray?" she asked, wearing a path in the floor. "Seriously, a man psychologically unafraid of anything? Want to trade?"

Belle let out a puff of air but refused to turn the spotlight on her and Gray. She wouldn't know where to begin.

"The killer," Rapunzel continued, "is that I totally understand everything he did."

"You do? So isn't that your—"

"I understand all of his reasons, and I probably would have done the exact same thing."

"Then what's the—"

"But what kills me is the fact that he lied about it so *well*. He's a good liar. And I don't like feeling this vulnerable with someone who's a good liar."

Belle sucked on her cheeks a bit, unsure whether to remind her that this shouldn't have been a new realization—that Ethan had lied about his identity months ago, when he pretended to be someone completely new to her life rather than the bloke who failed to save her from that tower years earlier.

"Ugh!" Rapunzel let out an enraged grunt and stomped the floor. "I love the bastard, but ugh!"

Belle swallowed her laugh and decided not to dwell on the fact that Rapunzel Delmonico had just announced that she was actually in love with someone. She knew exactly what love could do to a person's sanity. Plus, if Rapunzel was approaching forty-eight hours without sex—possibly even longer—she was already teetering on a very dangerous emotional precipice.

"So, did he tell you where Grethel is yet?"

Rapunzel stopped dead in her tracks, whirled around, and stared at Belle so fiercely she felt a chill. "Yeah. And you're gonna love this," she said, crossing her arms, spreading her feet wide, and holding her breath for dramatic effect. "Grethel's top secret location is all the way on the other side of the world … in Stularia. We're flying there—the two of us—first thing in the morning."

"Are you worried?" Belle asked.

"Worried?'

"About Grethel?"

Rapunzel gave a slow, half-hearted nod, then shook her head. "Not as worried as I am about facing my third celibate night in a row." She uncrossed her arms, looked at her watch, and scooped up her bag. "But anyway. I really should get going." She gave Belle a giant hug, but there was something a little rigid about it. "Airport check-in's at noon and I still have to pack. But first—" She held one finger in the air, scurried to the door, and opened it to reveal two more bags. "Just a few more goodies for the little guy."

Belle's jaw dropped. "Oh my gosh, you're going to spoil him rotten."

"Eh, well. Consider it amends for not throwing you a baby shower. Not yet anyway."

Rapunzel swung both bags onto the bed and undid the zippers. A mountain of toys and books gushed out. Thank God Rapunzel hadn't visited before Hazel showed up. "He's probably too young, but they say you should read to babies as early as possible. And these are all good ones—my favorites as a kid. Yes, Grethel read to me. Only the best for our little … say, does he have a name yet?"

Belle squinted. She really did like Rye. It was unique but still familiar. It had a strong sound. And according to the book Kirsten had brought in, it did mean king.

"I'm working on it," she said. "But what do you think of Rye?"

Rapunzel's eyebrows arched together. "As in the bread? It's okay. So long as kids don't connect crybaby to Rye-baby. You have to consider that stuff too."

Belle opened her mouth to argue, but then changed her mind.

"Oh, one last thing," Rapunzel said, spinning on her heels

and lifting a velvet pouch from her purse. "You're going to think I'm crazy, but I swung by the prison to see if I could charm my way into the evidence locker and nab Donner's ring."

"Are you serious? You're nuts!"

"Yes, and already acknowledged." Rapunzel smirked and jiggled the bag until a silver bracelet slipped out. "But no such luck. Not with the evidence locker and not with his zip-top bag of belongings." She looked up and gave a reassuring smile. "But it's okay. Gray will find them. He won't stop until he does."

Belle sucked on her cheek. "You said that already." She nodded towards the bracelet. "So, what's that?"

Rapunzel shrugged and guessed that it was supposed to be a gift from Donner to Belle the night everything went haywire. "Want it?" she asked, extending her hand.

Belle recoiled and held up her palm. "No way," she said. "You take it. Or throw it down a garbage disposal for all I care. His days of dressing me up are over."

Rapunzel gave a proud smile, zipped the bracelet into her purse, and pulled Belle into one last embrace. "I really do need to run," she said, giving Belle strict instructions to stay in the hospital for as long as she wanted ("screw Hazel Wickenham") and to say as little as possible during Matilda Holt's interview. "Talk about rebuilding the Phoenix," she said. "Talk about how pretty the leaves are this time of year. Talk about how you can't wait to put on decent looking clothes again *in four months*." She sucked her cheeks in and narrowed her eyes, as if this next statement disagreed with her stomach. "And if you truly believe Hazel won't help unless you publicly forgive Donner, do it in as few words as possible. You're not the world's best liar, and I have a feeling Angus will be watching everything you do like a hawk."

Chapter Nine

DAWN

Even after eleven years at Regian Castle, Dawn still wasn't sure whether it was a blessing or a curse that she couldn't see Selladóre from her balcony. In the beginning, its absence had certainly made her introduction to this new world more difficult. But as people in today's era liked to say, out of sight also meant out of mind—eventually, anyway. But in facing away from Selladóre, the glass platform jutting off the castle's east side got a wide lateral view of the Regian Woods—and, by default, of Davin.

Not that she could actually see his enchanted, cloaked estate through the trees. But she knew it was there. And at six thirty Monday morning—not long after Hunter had dragged himself out of bed, stumbled into the shower, and trudged out the door offering up nothing but a curt, "Ten thirty," reminder—this was enough.

Enough for what, she wasn't entirely sure. But there she was, nursing her coffee, leaning into the railing, and trying to identify the exact spot where Davin's mansion sat beneath the trees. This was less because she regretted her decision to let him go, than it was because she missed the excitement. She missed having a secret life that she believed at the time to be completely justified. She missed the frozen river, the branches coated in crystals, the breathtaking garden with the luminescent flowers, and the vines that hung on nothing but the air.

In the still, morning air, she thought about how tremendously things had changed in a matter of weeks. She thought about how a month ago, she wouldn't have cared if Hunter stopped trying to touch her, stopped acting as if they were actually in love.

But that was before her past came back to life. Before it stepped into the bright, unforgiving light of the present and her present stepped out of the shadows. It was before Hunter transitioned from neglectful business tycoon to doting family man, and Dawn realized she actually *could* be happy in this life — seconds before a swift wallop of reality sent it spiraling away.

Dawn jumped, then squinted, thinking she saw a flash of light coming from somewhere in the forest. Was Davin there now? Was he watching her? Had he just been upset the other night or did he truly mean the things he said: That she was selfish. That she was afraid. That she chose Hunter because he was the safer choice. That she was too damaged to gamble even for the sake of love.

She shook her head, then became aware of a warm feeling emanating from her chest. No, a hot feeling. Hot and wet.

She looked down and cursed, yanking her mug upright.

"Are you okay, Mom?"

Dawn whipped around to see her ten-year-old daughter's face peeking out from the sliding glass door. Morning took a quick look at the brown oval growing across the center of her mother's robe, scampered back inside, and returned a moment later carrying a blue dishtowel.

"Thanks sweetheart," Dawn said, smiling as she accepted the towel and pressed it into her chest. If there was any doubt that she'd made the right call, here was the living, breathing proof. "But what are you doing awake? You guys don't have to be up for another hour. Are you going in early for extra help again?"

Morning shook her head and hiked a yellow quilt around her shoulders. Then she climbed into the nearest glider and brought her knees up to her chest. "I couldn't sleep. Day's snoring."

Dawn started to laugh, but something about Morning's expression made her stop—that, and the realization that she'd never once heard her son snore. She lowered the dishtowel and sat on the other half of the glider.

"Are you okay, Mom?" Morning asked, resting a dainty little hand on her mother's.

Dawn immediately tensed up and sucked the air in, preparing for the follow-up questions: Are you and Daddy fighting? Does it have to do with that man who came to dinner? Are you getting divorced?

"I'm perfectly fine, sweetie," she said, patting Morning's bright orange curls against her ears. They sprung back out as soon as she let go.

"But what about you?" she asked, debating her next statement. "You know you can talk to me about anything, right?"

Morning scrunched her nose and shoved her face back into the blanket. Ready, set, go. "I do talk to you," she replied, the defensive tone of her voice signaling otherwise.

Dawn nodded, once again amazed that this sweet, smart, beautiful creature had come from her. She saw Morning as the embodiment of life—with her unruly hair; her cheerful, speckled cheeks; her perfectly pinched nose; and her huge green eyes, in which a tempest was currently brewing. Morning probably thought she had a magnificent poker face, but Dawn could see her worries spilling out everywhere—in her crinkled brow, her tightened lips, her drawn-in shoulders. She let a minute pass, and then asked if anything had happened at school.

Morning shook her head vigorously, as if trying to shake the curls right off her head. Dawn pried her up on one side and pulled her closer.

"Come on. You can trust me," she pressed. "And you know I can't fix it if I don't know what's wrong."

Morning crossed her arms and pulled the blanket tighter. "You can't fix it anyway."

"Are you sure?" Hair stroke.

"Yes, Mom. There's only one person who can fix it."

Dawn squinted. One person. Was it a boy? She'd suspected for some time now that Morning had a crush on Cinderella's oldest son. But she'd never actually said it. How precious. How momentous. How ... her childhood with Davin came rushing back ... how agonizing.

"One person?" Dawn repeated, hoping to coax rather than nag her daughter into divulging more information. "Well, considering I'm technically three hundred and twenty-eight years old and they say wisdom comes from age ... are you sure it's not me?"

Morning made a face—a half leery, half pitying face. Then, a couple seconds later, she looked up. Her eyebrows rose. Her lips parted but no sound came out.

"Talk to me," Dawn tried again. "Even if you're right and I can't fix it, what harm is there in letting me try?"

Morning pressed her hands between her knees and leaned forward. Dawn reached out to rub her palm along the top of her back. Even when her daughter was a toddler, with barely any surface area and not an ounce of stress, this always calmed her down. "You're such a beautiful, sweet, smart girl," she said. "Any boy who doesn't see that is—"

"Ugh!" Morning bounced up from the glider. It flew forward, taking her mother with it. "Is that what you think this is about? A boy?"

Dawn cleared her throat and climbed back into the seat. All of her words seemed stuck somewhere between the throat and sternum.

"Seriously Mom. Maybe that's all you cared about back when you were my age, but girls today have much more important things to worry about."

Dawn nodded. "Of course they do. I just ..." She shrugged. "Sorry, I just thought this was going to be the talk I've always heard so much about."

"The talk?"

"Yes, you know, *the talk*."

Morning stared back at her, hands on her hips and the blanket falling over her right forearm. In that moment, Dawn could see both the infant she nursed years ago and the woman she was going to become. *That's ridiculous*, she was saying with her huge green eyes. *I probably know more than you about sex, anyway. All you did to win Daddy's heart was purse your lips and fall asleep.*

"I'm not worried about a boy," Morning said, chewing on her lips as soon as the words were out. Then, an exhale. "Fine. If you absolutely must know, I'm worried about you and Daddy."

Dawn froze. She knew about Davin. Her wonderful, innocent, ten-year-old daughter knew that her mother had betrayed them and that her parents were on the verge of complete collapse. Letting Hunter take them yesterday afternoon had been a mistake. Her absence had drawn suspicion. How was she ever going to rectify this? How was she going to have the adult relationship she'd always dreamed about with her daughter? How was she—

"Everyone at school is saying you and Daddy are being fired. Is that true?"

Dawn's head twisted in a way that made her suddenly dizzy. "What? No, that's not even—"

"They say the people are turning against you and are going to vote to end the monarchies soon. They say Cinderella isn't coming back from her vacation, and Donner is going to jail, and the prime minister is going to take over all the thrones permanently. Does that mean we'll have to move out of the castle and live in a house? Can we even afford a house? Please don't tell me I'll have to share a room with Day. He farts in his sleep all the time—and on purpose sometimes too. I've smelled it. I can't live like that." Morning's voice was racing. Her face was almost as red as her hair. "I can't," she said again, shaking her head. "I can't. I—"

Dawn's arms were around her daughter before her heels even touched the floor. She could feel Morning's heart slamming through her chest as they pressed together.

"Hey," Dawn said, stroking her curls and blowing calming shushing sounds between the assurances. "It's okay. Nobody's losing anything—jobs, rooms, or otherwise." She ushered Morning onto a cushioned bench—stationary this time—and pulled the quilt back over her. "This is just what happens before elections."

Morning looked up and sniffled.

"It is?"

Dawn nodded.

"Even the unimportant ones? When it's not for prime minister?"

Dawn stifled a laugh. "Members of Parliament are still important. And there are other things to vote on each year besides people—like budgets and laws and—"

"And whether or not to get rid of the monarchies."

"No," Dawn said, suddenly in negotiating mode. "That's not on the ballot."

"Yet. It's not on the ballot yet, but the kids at school—"

"The kids at school don't know what they're talking about," Dawn blurted, with significantly more force than intended. She swallowed and inhaled. "The kids at school are only repeating what they hear their parents say, and they don't know what they're talking about either."

"But Jenny's the smartest girl in my class and even she says—"

"Morning," Dawn interrupted, hoping to settle this once and for all, "nothing is going to happen to us. You and Day and Daddy and I have many, many, many more years left in this castle." Her eyes darted toward the sky, begging the universe not to make her a liar. "And Marestam is not going to get rid of the monarchies. We're part of the Constitution. There have always been a few outliers wanting to go full democracy—just like there are people who want no government at all and people who think we should have barcodes instead of names."

Morning made a sour face, then rolled her eyes. "You're making that up. How would you even say a barcode?"

Dawn smiled and shook her head. "Cross my heart, there are people who believe that."

Morning let her weight fall further into her mother. Dawn melted like a stick of butter at the height of summer. She closed her eyes, rested her chin against her daughter's forehead, and made a solemn vow to mend her family no matter what the cost. They sat this way for a good ten minutes, listening to the birds and watching the sunrise over Regian's eastern coast. The last thing Dawn wanted was for this moment to end. But, as she'd learned too many times over the past few weeks, nothing lasted forever.

Pretty soon, she heard a door close inside and knew Day was about to nab the shower.

"Do you feel any better?" Dawn whispered, evoking an unconvincing, "Mmm hmm."

"Would it help if I let you take a bubble bath in the clawfoot tub this morning?" Dawn raised an eyebrow as Morning craned around to look at her. It was the sort of bribe she used to make when the kids were toddlers, navigating those terrible twos and treacherous threes. "If you hurry, you can soak for a full twenty minutes before you need to eat breakfast and get dressed."

Morning's bewildered look grew into a mischievous smile. "How about half an hour and I stay home today? We can go shopping in Carpale and get our nails done and have a girls' day."

Dawn smiled but shook her head. "That sounds amazing," she told her little litigator, "but I have to meet your father at Selladóre in a few hours."

"Selladóre? Again?" Morning had turned all the way around now, and was looking suspiciously at her mother. Dawn eyed her suspiciously back, before remembering that they'd visited the island together just three days earlier, under the guise of making secret inspections. Really, Dawn had just wanted company while she tried to decide what to do about Davin. It had been the first time she set foot there since her parents' funeral, however, so returning again so soon did sound a little cagey. "What for?" she pressed.

Seeing no good answer—and terrified that Morning might spot something odd between her and Davin, or between Davin and Hunter if she tagged along—Dawn kissed her daughter on the cheek and told her she absolutely couldn't miss school again. "Move now and I'll let you eat breakfast in the tub," she said. "Oatmeal with blueberries. Half an hour of bubbles. Final offer."

"Deal," Morning said, hopping to her feet and racing to the door. But the second she slid it open, she spun back around and called for her mother again.

Dawn pulled to her feet and picked her mug up from the railing. "Yes dear?"

"What do you and Dad keep looking at over there?"

"Over where honey?"

"Over there," Morning replied, raising a finger toward the northeast corner of the balcony—raising a finger toward Davin. Dawn froze. "At the woods. Is something going on there? I thought that area was protected from construction."

Dawn stumbled over a few incomprehensible words, then stumbled over her foot as she tried to continue forward. "No, I, umm." Her mind was suddenly mush. "I was just checking that side of the castle," she lied. "Your father thought he saw a bird's nest on one of the ledges."

"Did you see anything?" Morning asked, her voice suddenly full of pep.

Dawn shrugged, crossed onto the travertine tile, and slid the door shut. She could hear the shower running in Morning and Day's wing. "Nope," she said, shaking her head and guiding Morning toward the master bath. "Nothing of importance."

≈∽

The press conference at Selladóre went as well as anyone who knew better could have hoped. The ferries shuttled according to schedule. Every seat in the brand new 12,000-seat amphitheater was taken. The sun added a layer of warmth to an otherwise chilly late September day. The media, having been given embargoed press releases the previous afternoon, came out in droves. Angus Kane spoke reverently about the late king and queen, as well as the "fortitude" of the Selladórean people. Dawn smiled, convincingly, as she accepted the ceremonial "keys" to her homeland on behalf of the new Perdemi-Tirion Corporation. The crowd cheered with such force, residents of uptown Carpale reported feeling a minor earthquake. And, most importantly, neither Hunter nor Davin attempt to kill each other.

Standing between them on that twenty-first century stage adjacent to the eighteenth century square where she and Davin played as children, had been the most surreal, uncomfortable thing she'd ever experienced. But that wasn't even the worst part. The worst part was the fact that everyone with a notepad or a microphone believed it was one of the happiest days in Dawn Tirion's life. *A princess vindicated*, they said. *A people restored. A fracture stitched.*

But as the crowd broke into garrulous clumps and Dawn stood at the foot of the stage, watching Hunter and Davin pose for a few additional photos, she knew it was nothing of the sort. What Selladóre really wanted, much more than an upgraded steward, was its identity back. It wanted its royal family and its flag and its culture without the added flair of a corporate sponsor.

"So how does it feel?" someone asked, sidling up behind her. Dawn pasted on her smile and turned around, expecting to see a cameraman or a jittery reporter with a cardboard-backed steno pad. But instead, the flip of her head brought her face-to-face with the man she secretly wanted to lock in the stockades — reproductions of which were currently holding a grinning adolescent girl and a boy offering a double thumbs up.

"Oh. Hello Angus," she said, trying her best not to growl as he parked his walking stick between his shoes and leaned into it, his bony fingers covering the marbleized purple sphere on top. As usual, he was wearing a ridiculous fedora on his head and dressed as if hell was about to freeze over, in a knee-length maroon overcoat with black velvet trim. Even a woman born three centuries earlier knew his style was outdated. "How does what feel?" she asked.

Angus smirked and eyed the men on the stage. "Oh, come now," he said, nudging with his elbow, as if they had some sort of candid relationship. "Such a beautiful reunion after so many years apart. And you know what they say about true love..."

He trailed off as Dawn's bottom lip curled in and her top teeth pinned it down. A bolt of terror and anger raced up her spine and shot into all ten fingernails. What did he know? What had Davin told the man who'd discovered him during the Great Awakening on behalf of his long-deceased father's empire? What did that vindictive, social-climbing opportunist tell her greatest enemy about their relationship?

"Actually I don't know what to say," Dawn answered, feeling suddenly nauseous. "I'm not very good at twenty-first century catchphrases."

Angus sucked on his lips as if trying to clear a shard of spinach from his teeth. She thought she detected a minor shrug of amusement. "Well, people say true love starts at home, of course. That, and it never dies." His head tipped toward the stage again, toward Davin. "So you must be over the moon about getting your true love back."

Dawn made her face so hard, it probably could have cut glass. "True love is a misnomer," she replied, her words sharp and short. She kept her gaze forward—at Hunter—while the shadowy figure in her peripheral vision tilted its head. Then it pivoted ninety degrees and stared at her. "If it wasn't true, it wouldn't be love to begin with. And my love belongs with my husband."

"Of course it does," Angus said. "But certainly you can love both a man and a place."

She faltered. "What?"

"Selladóre," he clarified, though something about his tone kept her on guard. "You must be overjoyed about its return. But that's reassuring to hear about your marriage. With all that's been going on lately, I don't think the monarchies could take another rift."

Dawn grabbed a chunk of her peach eyelet skirt and balled it up in her hand. The last thing she wanted was to stand there trading thinly veiled threats with Angus Kane. She wanted to let him have it. She wanted to tell him that she knew he didn't take Hunter to Selladóre that day to scout its real estate potential. She knew he brought Hunter to break her curse while he was wafting some smelling salts under Davin's nose and whisking him away to Pastora.

But instead of launching into an emotional tirade, she put on her political face and took aim at his statement about the monarchies.

"Oh, come now," Angus said, chuckling. "Surely you've read the papers."

"I have. Braddax and Tantalise are working through some things, sure. But what's wrong with the other three?"

"Oh, my dear," he said, causing the blood to boil up to her eyeballs. "You may be able to fool the cameras with the whole out-of-place ingénue act, but I know there's more to you than that. Surely you must see that Riverfell is a civil war just waiting to happen. When in history has one brother stepped aside from the throne and been permanently happy with that decision? Carter LeBlanche may not think so now, but one day he'll regret it — especially if my niece wakes up and realizes he's given away her only chance at becoming a queen. And as for Carpale..." He trailed off as his eyes swept the cobblestones beneath them. "Well, I fear the Charmés' second honeymoon may have been a cover-up for their abdication."

"You know that's not true," Dawn snapped, immediately wanting to take it back. But the cat was out of the bag now. The mask was lowered. Guns were drawn.

Angus shifted half his weight off the cane and pressed a palm into his chest. He looked like an understudy attempting to act shocked. "Dawn," he said, shaking his head. "You hurt me. What reason would I have to make something like that up? It's terrible to think King Aaron and Queen Cinderella may have abandoned us. But frankly, the other conclusion is even worse. It's not like them to remain in the shadows with everything that's happened over the past few days. Nor is it in character for them to let weeks pass without contacting their children. Now, I've kept this from the public so as not to cause alarm, but my office has been searching tirelessly to find them, all to no avail."

Dawn swallowed and looked around, struggling to keep her anger under wraps.

"As a regular man lifted to my elected office by the people," he continued, "I understand I may not be as glittery as your comrades, born on silk sheets in towering castles, but I only have Marestam's best interest at heart. And my heart tells me the people are uneasy about their future. You, on the other hand, should be proud. At the moment, Regian is the only one that appears stable. I can only imagine what would happen if scandal overshadowed your kingdom too. If, say, the people found out you were harboring a deep, dark secret or had been unfaithful to their king." He paused, as if to let his words sink in. "Thankfully, I know you would never do such a thing. It's just not in your nature."

Dawn sucked her lip up between her teeth. Was that a threat? Was he telling her that if she defied him in any way, her affair would be the straw that broke the camel's back? That the eighteenth-century princess would drive the final stake through Marestam's heart? She needed to leave. She needed to get Angus out of strangling distance. She needed to find Elmina Goodman, tell her about the triad, and skin this upright snake before it was too late.

Muttering something about using the ladies' room, Dawn bid him a quick farewell and whipped around. Before she knew it, she was scuttling down the theatre's crowded aisles, shuffling out into the square, and sliding through a side door of the castle without catching anyone's eye. Aside from a pair of teenagers kissing beneath a portrait of her great grandmother, the main hall was empty. She tiptoed her way into the ballroom, took fifty-seven paces, and pried open a hidden door that accessed a vast network of secret passageways stretching from the basement dungeon all the way to the highest turret. At the seventh breakaway, she veered west and followed a narrow, meandering, pitch-black hallway that stopped at a windowed loft tucked inside her father's library.

Centuries earlier, this was where she'd come to hide, cry, or simply clear her head. There were books to read, a hammock to relax in, and a window through which she could watch what was going on in the square below. The only other people who knew about it were her father (who told her about it in the first place) and Davin (who often met her here in their later, less discreet years).

She was only there for a few minutes, her forehead pressed into the stained-glass porthole and her eyes closed, when the sound of footsteps made her heart skip three beats.

"Oh. Sorry," Davin said as she spun around, catching only his back as he tried to retreat right back into the tunnel. "I didn't know you were here."

Dawn hesitated for a second, then darted after him.

"Wait," she called, reaching for his shirt but hooking his waistband instead. She let go immediately, but he'd already stopped. "I need to talk to you." She felt the butterflies return to her stomach as he about-faced, his eyes panning over the hammock in the corner and the reading pillows lining the floor.

"What did you tell Angus about us?" she blurted before he could even begin to get the wrong idea.

Davin's eyes grew two sizes in an instant, then just as quickly sucked back into tiny little beads. "Are you serious?" He looked significantly more fatigued in this light than he had on stage—with all the camera flashes and that huge, pearly smile. He shook his head, looked away, pinched the bridge of his nose ... and then shook his head again. "Geez Dawn, your opinion of me really has plummeted, hasn't it? Do you really think I'd go gossiping about us to the prime minister because you chose your husband over me? What do you think I am, a twelve-year-old girl?"

"I'm sorry," she said without thinking. But then she played Angus's comments back in her head and decided the time for pity had passed. "No, I mean, I'm not saying you swapped kissing stories. But he knew about your father and when the curse was supposed to break and where to find you. It's not outside the realm of possibility to think he might also know we were more than just acquaintances in our time. Does he know I know who you really are now? Could your father have passed down stories about more than just your skill with a sword or the color of your hair? Is there any way Angus might guess we'd reconnect when you moved half a mile from my door?"

Davin sucked on his cheek and rounded the loft again with his eyes. Then he gave a soundless answer, which Dawn didn't need words to interpret.

She felt her left knee buckle a split second before Davin clasped her arm.

"Dawn," he said as she regained her footing. "Please just … put yourself in my shoes for a second."

She gritted her teeth and recalled his accusation Friday night about being unable to see beyond her own problems.

"I wanted to go back for you as soon as I got my wits about me after the curse broke. But I was miles away in a strange land with horseless carriages and flameless lights and not a single person who knew me. I couldn't just open the door and walk there. So yes, I told the only person I knew at the time. And he told me that you were moments away from marrying a king—a rich, handsome king who was supposed to ensure Selladóre remained free. So, I made a tough decision and I moved on."

Dawn glanced at the window. The stained glass made it impossible to tell what the sky was doing, but she knew rain was expected at some point that afternoon. If it came, all the tourists would flock to the castle and start poking around. A few might even uncover the secret passage and snoop their way to this room.

"So why did you come back now?" she asked, eager to speed this up but just as eager to get all the details. "What changed?"

Davin shrugged. "A few things, I guess." She found herself leaning in, waiting for him to elaborate. "You stopped looking happy in the news, for one thing. That glimmer you seemed to have at first—even if it was just the cameras catching the right angle—was gone." Dawn shifted her weight. Not long ago, she would have laughed at the claim she *ever* looked happy in the days following the Great Awakening. But after perusing

Selladóre's timeline exhibit a few days earlier, she knew it carried some truth. "So, all of my reasons for staying away were gone. This world was no longer foreign to me. Selladóre had no hope of being free. And you looked like you were ready to walk off a cliff. That's why I came back."

He cleared his throat and loosened his checked necktie. The color matched the gold flecks in his otherwise hazel eyes. "I wasn't trying to break up a happy marriage."

Dawn felt the guilt settle over her. Davin knew as well as she did that her marriage hadn't been happy when they reconnected in the woods a month ago. Happy wives didn't spend their nights spying on handsome men from overlook points in the forest. Happy wives didn't accompany supposed strangers over invisible, enchanted walkways; beneath tunnels of diamond-studded trees; through magnificent, luminescent gardens; and into breathtaking mansions isolated from the rest of civilization. Happy wives didn't play footsie with the dinner guests while their husbands prattled on at the head of the table, absolutely none the wiser.

Davin was a good man. No matter how this played out, she had to remember that. She couldn't take the coward's way out and throw him under the bus. But at the same time, Hunter had to be her priority now. He was the victim now.

"So, you never told Angus that we reconnected?"

"Of course not," he said, crossing his arms in a way that made Dawn more than a little uneasy. "But…"

"But what?"

"But he's not an idiot."

"No," Dawn agreed, feeling her heart sputter. "Not even close."

"If I had to bet on it, I'd say he wouldn't be surprised. He's not the sort of person to forget something that could work to his advantage someday, even if it was eleven years ago. Plus, he hardly asked any questions when I wanted to build an estate in

Regian. He's actually the one who suggested that enchanted plot of land and forced the permits through."

Dawn's head whipped up at this last statement—and the sound of water pinging against the window. Then she remembered what Morning had told her that morning, about the Regian Woods being protected space. Suddenly, it dawned on her: Angus had set the whole thing up. Like Ruby said in the hospital, he was as smart and as cunning as they came. He'd been planning this for years. In bringing Hunter to Selladóre and whisking away the object of her affection the moment Dawn's curse broke, he pocketed an ace that he could use against the Regian throne whenever he wanted. He knew she and Davin wouldn't just pass like two ships in the night, or grab an isolated coffee for old time's sake and be on their merry way. He knew she was disenchanted with her life as it was—everyone did. He knew old passions would reignite. He knew that whatever happened between them, it would give him the means to kick out yet one more of Marestam's royal legs.

She needed to sit down.

"Look. Even if Angus remembers what I told him eleven years ago," Davin said as she backed into the hammock, "I doubt he suspects those feelings remained. He saw us both at Griffin's party, and he knows I have a business arrangement with your husband, but that's the end of it."

Dawn nodded mindlessly. "Sure. You're probably right," she said, her words barely audible because she knew they weren't true. Davin may not have set out to do anything underhanded, but Angus was pulling his strings. "Does that mean you aren't going to team up with him and steal Hunter's company?"

She regretted the question immediately—the stupefied look on Davin's face giving her all the answer she needed.

"Wow," he said, unable to rectify the headstrong girl she used to be with the paranoid woman she'd become. "It might be easier for you to paint me as some sort of villain here, Dawn. But trust me, it's going to take a lot more than losing you to convince me to sell my soul."

"I know that," she said, standing back up and shaking her head. "I'm sorry. I just ... I just had to ask."

"If you truly knew," Davin said, his voice cold and unfamiliar, "you wouldn't have had to ask. I took this deal because my company needed it — because it was the right move. Your husband is the one who wanted Selladóre negotiated in somehow. He's the one who agreed on giving Angus that four percent stake. I could just as easily worry about them teaming up to vote *me* out. But I believe in the general decency of most people. I see we differ on that now."

"I'm sorry," she repeated as the sound of voices rose up from the first floor of the castle. She sprinted to the window. The square was packed. Umbrellas were raised. And the only thing flowing faster than the rain was the line of people shoving their way into the front of Selladóre Castle.

"You should go," Davin said, nudging her toward the passage. "I'll wait a few minutes, then head down through the kitchens. We shouldn't be seen together ... not alone, I mean."

"Okay. I'll go out through the east drawing room," she said, the escape plan kicking in like second nature. "It's closer to the bathrooms in case I need an alibi."

Davin nodded and, for a split second, a flicker of amusement crossed his face. Perhaps this reminded him of old times, with her evading her mother and him evading whatever girl was chasing him that week. He lowered his gaze to the parquet floor. In the silence, she felt a bit of their old comfort returning — their childhood comfort, before puberty and curses and duplicitous politicians messed it all up.

She flashed him a sad attempt at a goodbye smile before scrambling back into the darkness. She'd neglected to ask if he had any idea where Elmina Goodman might be hiding, but the answer was most likely no anyway. Evidently, the reclusive pureblood hadn't felt today's spectacle was worth breaking her quarantine. Dawn couldn't blame her.

She only made it a few steps when the sound of shoes and voices forced her to peel off into her father's study—or what used to be her father's study, anyway. Now, instead of a clutter of animal heads and beer steins, it contained only a fireplace, a few places to sit, and an old mahogany desk holding two books and a marble bust of her father's favorite philosopher—whose name neither she nor history ever remembered. She held her breath as a pair of giggling kids passed by, then carefully ventured back outside.

Hunter was waiting in the ballroom when she emerged, both hands in his sport coat and eyes glued to the ceiling. He looked like a man who'd just returned from war and was nervously awaiting his next orders.

"You okay?" he asked as she appeared, a bit of genuine concern seeping out with the contempt.

"Fine," she chirped, feigning a shy smile. "You know ladies' rooms. Always a line."

Hunter nodded but kept his eyes straight ahead. Their hands brushed twice as they walked, but he made no effort to take hers.

"How do you think it went today?" she asked, struggling to make conversation as they exited the castle, huddled beneath his umbrella, and headed toward the ferries. Being this close to him made her uneasy for more reasons than she could count.

"It was fine," he said as a crowd of people shuffled by, moving erratically to avoid the puddles. "Thanks for coming."

Dawn perked up. A thank you? "Of course," she said, before realizing he'd been talking to the tour group heading in the opposite direction. She scowled and increased her pace. How long was she expected to take this?

Hunter increased his pace as well. "Is something else on your mind?"

She rolled her eyes to the side. If only he knew. What *wasn't* on her mind? "I just can't stand these publicity events," she said. "You know that."

"I know. But you just got your kingdom back. Doesn't that make you a little happy?"

She grabbed his hand and stopped. "It does," she said. "It is. Thank you. I'm sorry. I just wish my parents could have been here. Or Elmina. I thought there was a chance this would have drawn her out."

A clump of Hunter's golden hair peeled off in the wind. He pushed it back with his whole hand and looked at her. "Maybe she was, you just didn't see her," he said, attempting to temper what he couldn't fix. "She is a pureblood fairy, after all. And you know she likes to keep a low profile."

Dawn started to give a half-hearted smile at his effort, but then realized he was right. She'd forgotten purebloods could change their appearance. Perhaps she *had* been there. Perhaps all Dawn had to do was ask loudly enough. Or perhaps that just proved she would never, ever find her. She would fail Belle, fail the triad, and fail Marestam in general.

When they finally reached the dock, Hunter handed Dawn over to a pair of men in black suits with squiggly wires coming out of their ears. He said he had some business to finish on the island, but they'd make sure she got home safely. Oh, and don't hold dinner.

As the ferry pulled away, Dawn felt a million emotions swell up inside of her—every one of them awful. Watching the water stretch before her and the walls surrounding Selladóre shrink, she thought about how trapped she and Davin used to feel inside of them. She thought about how desperately they wanted to know what lay beyond, and how badly the adults wanted to stop them.

"Beautiful, isn't it?" an old man asked as he slipped into the molded plastic seat beside her and adjusted his scarf. His "Selladóre Gift Shop," tote overflowed with postcards, guidebooks, brochures, and a strange wooden toy that was absolutely not historically accurate. "Congratulations on finally getting it back from the government who so politely pilfered it. I'm sure it'll fare much better under a billion-dollar company half run by your husband."

Dawn squinted, unsure how to respond. It was the most insightful thing she'd heard all day—assuming she wasn't imagining his sarcastic tone.

"So, what do you think?" he asked, pulling out a postcard and pressing it into her hand. One of Hunter's bodyguards made a motion to come forward, but she pushed him back with her eyes.

Dawn tilted her head. "What do I think about what?"

He gave her a sly sideward glance and—unless she was seeing things—winked. "What would *you* prefer, a grisly truth or a pleasing deception?"

Dawn opened her mouth but didn't have an answer. She looked down at the postcard. It showed a touched-up image of Selladóre from the middle of the river—almost exactly where they were right now—lit up like a rainbow as fireworks exploded overhead. "That's a tough question," she finally said, looking back at the stormy sky and the overgrown walls of the real Selladóre. "But if given the choice, having selected wrong in the past, I suppose I'd go with the former. Even a comforting deceit only lasts for so long, and mourning its absence makes the truth even harder."

The man nodded and smiled. "Well said," he replied, the skin around his neck bunching up against his collar. He had an odd-looking birthmark at the back of his left jawbone. "It takes some people a lifetime to figure that out—or longer."

They sat in silence for another two minutes, then he pushed his palms into the edge of his seat, sighed, and wobbled to his feet again.

"Where are you going?" Dawn asked as he hoisted the canvas bag to his chest.

"Oh, my dear. Appreciate the days when you can make a twenty-minute crossing without needing to use the facilities."

She smiled and held out the postcard, but he held a flat palm up and shook his head. "Keep it. Please. I meant to get five for each grandchild but made a slight miscalculation. They'll be even more thrilled to know the Queen of Regian and Selladóre has something I gave her hanging on her refrigerator—or, you know, sitting in her trash bin. No hard feelings."

Dawn chuckled and wished him a pleasant day as he disappeared back into the cabin and below deck.

She didn't look at the card again until she was in the back seat of the limo on her way back to Regian Castle. She started at the realization that he'd written something on the back. Had he given her the wrong card? Was this a message his grandchild would never receive?

Then she looked closer ... and gasped.

I hear you've been looking for me, it said. *Please meet me on Thursday, ten o'clock, at Sugar Showers, 1456 Bellview Blvd, Regian. Oh, and bring your sweet tooth. Auntie E.*

Chapter Ten

BELLE

"Really, I can walk on my own," Belle said, craning her neck around so Kirsten could hear her. "You know I'm capable. And I don't need a babysitter."

"I know you can. And you are. And you don't," her nurse replied as the wheelchair rolled through the corridor — one long, monotonous road of speckled nylon, bound on both sides with walls the color of cream. "But hospital policy says those feet don't touch the ground till you're outside our walls or in your room. So unless you're planning on checking out any time soon, you should just get used to being carted around. I would say it's the royal treatment, but…"

She trailed off, leaving room for Belle to give a sarcastic laugh or shake her head at the hokey joke. But humor had no place in her thoughts right now. That's because her wheelchair was going to start slowing down any second now, and Kirsten was going to make a sharp right turn into the Harold Charmé Conference Room (named for Aaron's great uncle, a Marestam General radiologist for forty-seven years). And when that happened, Belle was going to come face to face with Donner for the first time since his violent, maniacal rampage four days earlier.

She pumped her fists beneath the blanket and tried to steady her heartbeat. She had no idea what to expect. She hadn't been to a courthouse since she was a child, when her father was filing for bankruptcy and her mother was filing for divorce. And although she'd overheard the word being applied to her father many times back then, she'd never even witnessed a "criminal" trial before—let alone been a part of one. Her knowledge of these types of proceedings were limited to television shows and sad, lonely photos on the front page of the *Marestam Mirror*.

She couldn't help but wonder: Would Donner be wearing an orange jumpsuit? Would he be shackled? Would Gray be there? She hadn't seen him since Saturday, and he was an eyewitness, after all. What about anyone from Riverfell? Would Carter dare leave Kiarra's bedside for twenty minutes to catch a glimpse of the man who put her there? Or would that be too emotional? Would the lawyers try to make Belle cry or enter her baby bump as Exhibit A—demonstrating just how tragic his rampage could have been?

The left side of the wheelchair squeaked as Kirsten slowed to turn and the nearest painting—a basket of pale blue irises— angled out of view. Belle clutched the blanket as she stopped at a closed door with a thin vertical window.

"V.I.P. coming through," Kirsten sang, pushing the door open and causing two dozen heads to whirl around. The man guarding the door nodded first toward Kirsten, and then at her cargo. He was wearing a plain black suit with a striped black tie and matching black earpiece. Belle was surprised he wasn't wearing sunglasses too—until she saw them sticking out of his chest pocket.

Bypassing the center aisle, Kirsten wheeled Belle to the right side of the room. Ivory molding wound around the entire space, just like in the hallway. But rather than a comforting shade of yellow, the walls were painted a cool, sterile gray. In the front, a single chair sat behind a long, narrow table facing two smaller tables and five rows of chairs. The audience contained an assortment of men and women with overstuffed briefcases at their feet, veteran journalists shooting the breeze, and rookie reporters scribbling wildly into their notepads.

Belle recognized Matilda Holt right away. She looked exactly the same as she had on the steps of Marestam General several months earlier — frizzy brown hair, sharp eyes, and a laminated press pass strung around her neck. But there was something different about the way she carried herself — something confident and self-assured. Perhaps that's what happened when unknown beat reporters landed a story as big as Belle's pregnancy.

She'd liked Matilda back then. If she hadn't, she would have dropped her pregnancy bombshell on someone else. But now, all she saw when she looked at her was her arm-twisting mother-in-law, and all she felt was pressure.

"Please rise for the honorable Judge Kendall Ford," a strong voice called, causing a clump of lawyers in the first row to disperse — and unblocking Belle's view of the defendant. Her breath stopped as she took him in. He wasn't wearing an orange jumpsuit. She couldn't tell if there were handcuffs around his wrists. And if it wasn't for Donner's massive frame, sunken shoulders, and apparent obsession with the carpet, she might not have discerned him from any of the other men in designer suits.

"Good morning," Judge Ford said, resting her elbows on the table and lacing her fingers into a dainty but calculated arch. She was a fierce looking woman with a silver pen holding up her corkscrewed brown hair. Belle recognized her from the papers. She'd made headlines years back for holding a twelve-year-old boy in contempt and jailing him for four hours. "I imagine most of you know who I am and how I conduct my courtroom. But for everyone else, please don't mistake my informality for weakness. I may ignore a few rules of procedure here and there."

Her hands spread apart as she panned the conference room and explained that it wasn't customary to move a criminal arraignment for the convenience of a witness. Nor was it customary to even *have* a witness at an arraignment. "But nothing about this trial is customary." At this, a few of the prosecutors snickered, turning Judge Ford's rhythmic voice into ice. "Forget that at your peril, Mr. Garrett. Respect me, and I will do the same. Act out; show up late; avoid a question; speak, snicker, or so much as sneeze out of turn … and you will find yourself counting floor tiles in a prison cell. Make no mistake, *I* wear the crown in my courtroom. And don't let the cushy chairs or pretty artwork fool you. Be it on Capitol Boulevard or in a hospital conference room, so long as I hold the gavel, this is still *my courtroom.*"

Belle clenched as Judge Ford narrowed her eyes at Donner and asked about waiving his right to have the full indictment read. He was standing now, but still in a vacant trance. The half of his face Belle could see was surprisingly clean, and his dark hair wasn't dangling over his eyes the way it had been in recent months. It was a classic Noel Madison move. The go-to defense attorney for the stars, whose teeth shone as brightly as his bleached dress shirt, had probably figured a dapper Donner Wickenham might counteract the perception that he was more beastly monster than human being.

But not even a full-body spa treatment and the finest wardrobe in existence could conceal what Belle saw when Donner finally looked up and gave her a clear view of his eyes. There was no confidence to be seen. No outrage over being ordered around by an unmarried female with no royal title. None of that typical self-assurance that told the world he was better than all of them, and would end up getting off scot-free. All she saw in those black, tortured eyes of his was shame.

Belle hated herself for the wave of pity that immediately crashed over her. He'd nearly killed her, after all. No. More than that. He'd nearly killed the innocent child she'd wanted more than anything in the world. Cursed or not. Husband and father or not. Those facts remained.

"Mrs. Wickenham?"

Belle twitched as the judge called her name and everyone but Donner turned to look.

She twisted a bit in her four-wheel prison and thought about telling Kirsten to make a run for it. Screw Hazel's "deal." She'd help break Donner's curse even if Belle didn't testify on his behalf, wouldn't she? Worse come to worse, she could tell her about her grandson. In the end, which was worse: Allowing Hazel to thrust Rye into the limelight, or swallowing what remained of her pride and giving Donner yet *another* chance?

"Yes, your honor," Belle replied, attempting to look as regal as possible in her rolling chair. "But it's Ms. Middleton now."

Judge Ford frowned as a dozen pens began to scribble. "I don't see here that you're divorced."

"Oh, we're not," she said. "But we've been sep—"

"Mrs. Wickenham," she said again. "I understand that you've been briefed as to the reason for your input today. This is not a trial. You are not under oath, but your cooperation here will reflect upon your credibility as a witness, should you be called as a witness at your husband's trial down the road."

Belle nodded.

Judge Ford whispered something to the bailiff, then summoned her forward with her hand.

Kirsten promptly pushed the wheel lock up with her foot and charged forward. Belle felt like a pig being carried to the slaughter as she squeaked past the prosecution's table, halted in front of the judge, and rotated to face the audience—and Donner—head on.

Their eyes caught for a half second before pulling away. But two breaths later, as the judge flipped through her notes in silence, Belle's eyes returned. So did his.

I'm so sorry, she imagined him trying to say. But that was the old Belle again — the old Belle who was so forgiving, so easy, so naive. She shook her away and refocused on the judge. Finally, the papers stopped shuffling and the questions began.

Question one: Was she here of her own free will, with no coercion or manipulation?

Belle swallowed hard, then said she was.

Question two: Was Donner present at the Phoenix on the night of the incident?

"Yes," she replied, hoping all the questions would be this easy. "Yes, he was."

Question three: If released on bail, in her honest opinion, would Donner pose a danger to himself or to others?

Belle thought for a moment. She didn't want to look at him again, but couldn't help it. His reaction to the question might help her answer. And in her honest opinion, he looked like someone who would await his trial in the basement of Braddax Castle — possibly chained by his own hand to the cellar wall.

"I don't think so," she said, following Rapunzel's advice to talk as little as possible. The pens took off again.

"How can you possibly say that?" the prosecutor hollered.

"Objection!" declared Donner's lawyer.

"Sustained," agreed Judge Ford. "I haven't set a date for the trial yet, Mr. Garrett. This isn't the time for cross-examination. At least not by you." She cleared her throat, intertwined her fingers and focused on Belle once again. "Now, Mrs. Wickenham. Given the charges and what you experienced Friday night, what makes you so sure the defendant is not dangerous? Let me remind you that nothing is being decided right now except the wisdom of setting Mr. Wickenham free on bail. You simply need to convince me one way or the other on that point."

Belle's heart was beating so fast, she feared it might take flight any minute. Between the wheelchair and the wide-open room and the lack of a witness stand, the only way she could feel more vulnerable was if she was stark naked. Ironically, aside from Kirsten, the greatest comfort she could find came from Donner.

Their eyes locked once more, and this time she didn't let go. She swam in them, needing to know whether it was him or the curse that lost it the other night, needing to know whether he would lose it again.

Suddenly, the scribbling reporters disappeared. The pearly white teeth faded away. The crinkling of papers and shuffling of chairs and hum of the air vents dissipated into nothingness. All that remained was Belle and the man who both tormented and loved her—for better and for worse. The man who, to her, was gentler as a beast and more beastly as a man. He was a lost soul from the moment she met him, always struggling to make up for something—his appearance, his impurities, his inability to father a child.

She couldn't blame the neglect on the reemergent curse, or the repression. The curse hadn't made him hop into bed with her sister and then skewer Belle's reputation while she grieved. But deep down, she believed it *was* the driving force behind what happened Friday night—much more than jealousy towards Gray or the fear of losing his family. Sure, he would have taken a swing at Gray even without magical interference. He might even have broken his nose—or his arm. But he would have backed down after a quick pop of anger, just like he did at Letitia's party four months earlier.

Belle continued to stare as Donner pressed his lips together—two light pink pillows with a line carved down the middle—then let them spring apart. His dark curls shook ever so slightly as he clasped both hands together and leaned forward onto his table. The metal from his handcuffs clinked against the wood, and she thought about how he'd always wanted to introduce them into their foreplay.

I always wanted to break out the handcuffs with you, she could hear him thinking, *but this wasn't exactly what I had in mind.*

Why couldn't you just be good? she thought back, knowing this was happening entirely in her head. *Rich. Powerful. Gorgeous beyond description. The perfect fairy tale prince. But so, so troubled. So dark.*

As she focused, one of his curls fell, obscuring his left eye. He didn't bother to shake it off. She felt her throat tighten.

"Mrs. Wickenham?" The judge's tone was impatient. Donner leaned back in his seat, shackles in his lap. "Do you two need a room or would you mind answering the question?"

Belle panned the audience again. None of the Riverfell royals had come out. Nor had Gray.

"I'm sorry," Belle said. "What was the question again?"

All eyes focused on her. Pens clicked expectantly. Cameras prepared to flash.

Judge Ford sucked her cheek inward. "I said it's easy to sit there and release a potentially dangerous man to the public knowing you'll be safe behind the walls of this hospital, with thirty-five floors of guards between you and the outside world. What are your plans for r—"

"Oh," Belle interrupted, prompting a soul-melting scowl from the woman in charge. "Sorry. I expect to be discharged tomorrow afternoon." A deep breath came. Then a frigid, camouflaged panic. "Does that make a difference?"

෪෬

No sooner had Judge Ford's gavel smacked the wood than Belle was zooming back down the hallway, hanging onto both the armrests and Kirsten's promise that she'd get them back upstairs before the media caught up.

"I know a shortcut," Kirsten huffed, her breath already short. "We can take the staff elevators. There's one just around this—"

"Belle!"

Kirsten gasped and sped up, taking the corner like a twelve-year-old with a shopping cart. But her pursuant was about ten years younger and fifty pounds lighter. Belle heard her name again, then pant legs scraping together. She saw the flash of a neck lanyard. A press pass. Frizzy brown hair. The chair screeched to a halt.

"Wow, you never get tired of running, do you?" Matilda Holt gasped, wilting over her. She was clutching a notepad, which gave Belle an instant feeling of déjà vu—only instead of Second Avenue, they were in a hallway. And instead of being secretly pregnant, she was ... secretly not.

"Wow. You have no idea how happy I am to see you," Matilda continued, mistaking their one previous encounter for a lifelong friendship. "I was so scared when the news broke Friday night. But I knew you'd be okay. She's stronger than she looks, I said. Delicate but rock hard, I said. And now here you are, once again showing the world how much better you are than that brute in there. But really—forgiving him like that? After what he did? How did you come to that conclusion?" Matilda paused, waiting for an answer worthy of the front page. Waiting for Belle to contradict everything she'd just told the judge.

But Belle wasn't in the mood for granting exposé interviews at the moment—even ones that had been prearranged by a devious, conniving fairy. She was too busy coming to terms with what she'd just promised. She was too busy trying to figure out how she could still be there for Rye if the sun rose tomorrow and Gray hadn't yet found those rings.

"Are you going to breastfeed?"

Belle balked at the strange question. "Excuse me?"

Matilda lowered her notepad. "Too personal? Sorry. I thought you might prefer to open with baby plans." She leaned forward and lowered her voice. "Hazel did talk to you about the interview, right?"

"She did," Belle replied, giving an apologetic smile. "But I'm sorry, I—"

"Dr. Frolick is expecting to see her at ten o'clock," Kirsten interrupted, adjusting her grip on the wheelchair. "Perhaps you can arrange a time to talk after her discharge."

"Oh," the reporter said, her eyes bouncing up to meet Kirsten's but her face still pointed at Belle. She looked confused. "Okay. But my editors are expecting an exclusive interview."

Belle tried to sweeten her voice. "And you'll get one. Just—"

"Today?"

Belle smiled but made a fist beneath her blanket. The other reporters were going to come flying down that hallway any minute, and it was clear Matilda wasn't going to back down. She'd tasted the glory of a front-page scoop and she wanted it again.

"How do you account for your husband's curse coming back after all this time?" Matilda tried again, hijacking Belle's full attention. "Do you think it's because of your separation? Do you blame yourself at all for what happened Friday night? What do you say to those who believe you should be prosecuted for keeping Donner and Hazel's powers a secret? If the monarchies fall, how much of that do you and Donner take responsibility f—"

"The monarchies aren't going to fall," Belle snapped, her head spinning.

Matilda smiled and circled something in her notes. "So, you don't deny the rumors about Donner's curse being back."

"Look," Belle said, giving Kirsten the eye. "Matilda, I'm happy to speak with you after I leave the hospital, but—"

"Where? When?"

Belle ignored the question. "But for right now I'd appreciate a little—"

"I know about your baby."

Belle froze. She felt the entire universe suck in at lightning speed and then freeze in a bubble around them—holding on for the final implosion.

She forced a laugh, but not before her eyes began blinking twice a second. "What are you talking about?" she asked, trying to sound unfazed. "What do you know?"

Matilda looked around, then leaned in to answer. But before she could get a word out, a trio of voices sent all three women into a silent panic. In one fluid movement, Kirsten grabbed both the reporter and Belle's chair, pushed them into a storage closet, and shut the door.

So much for acting nonchalant, Belle thought as her chair bumped into a group of covered bassinets with giant circular holes on each side. She recognized them as neonatal incubators. Cinderella's youngest, Gregory, had spent nineteen weeks in one a few years ago. He'd arrived five weeks premature, and Belle had never seen her friend so terrified. She and the rest of the girls took turns sleeping at the hospital and planning outings so Cindy and Aaron would never be alone and their three other kids would never be idle enough to wonder what was going on.

As everyone squeezed in between the incubators and a mountain of cardboard boxes, Belle couldn't help but think about her own son. Incubators were miraculous for infants born after barely twenty-six weeks of gestation. But Belle had barely made it to twenty-three. Without the curse, he wouldn't have stood a chance. Talk about irony.

Matilda cleared her throat and looked around. "Well, I'm either on to something or you *really* hate talking to the press," she said, tapping the side of a box labeled "sterile gauze."

Belle tried to soften her stare of contempt as she whirled her head around. Matilda had seemed so nice back in May. What happened? Give a girl one big story and she becomes a bloodthirsty addict?

"Look," Matilda said, lowering her voice and turning away from the door. "Don't ask me how. I value my sources. But I know you're having a boy and he's been measuring off the charts."

"Off the charts in what way?" Belle took a steady breath and crossed everything she could — fingers, toes, brainwaves. "Is the *Mirror* soliciting prenatal approval ratings for the election? How does that work? What's next, a delivery room spread in *Maxistam*?"

Matilda cracked a disapproving smirk and shook her head. "Please don't make this any harder than it has to be, Belle. I know he's growing like you've been eating steroids for breakfast every morning. I know he was measuring thirty-three weeks last Thursday — you know, when your coworker rushed you here for 'food poisoning.'"

Belle cringed. She didn't want to relive the night she and Gray finally kissed. It was two minutes of bliss followed by days of heartache. And for all she knew, it was also the trigger that bought her husband's curse back. Allowing herself to fall in love might have knocked her hope for a better life to the ground — and Gray's refusal to let her go had set the remains on fire.

Finally, Belle pushed herself out of the wheelchair and straightened up on two wobbly legs. "Matilda," she said, suddenly wary of the entire hospital — Kirsten included. Matilda had gotten her information somewhere, after all, though at least she only seemed to know about the curse — not the birth. "I understand you think you have a huge story here, but I can promise you an even bigger one if you just hold off for a little bit."

Matilda crossed her arms and squinted. "How big and how long?"

Belle smiled. "The biggest one Marestam has ever seen."

Matilda hesitated. She bit her bottom lip. She shifted her weight. She surveyed Belle once, then twice, then a third time.

"It involves kidnapping and magic and subterfuge and every level of government — all the way up to the prime minister's office," Belle added, laying it on thick.

Matilda's lips curled involuntarily, but she forced them back down. "An exclusive?"

Belle nodded. "Of course."

"How long a delay are we talking here?"

Belle thought for a moment. Assuming Rapunzel found Grethel right away and Dawn took—what? a week to bring in Elmina?

"Ten days," she said.

"Three."

Belle cringed, but what choice did she have? "Five," she said. "Five days and I'll hand you a story that will redefine Marestam forever."

A cluster of voices passed by the closet as the reporter thought. "Okay," she finally said. "I think I can hold my editors off for a few days. But they're going to need something to tide them over."

Belle sucked on the inside of her left cheek and locked it between her molars. She sat back down and wracked her brain for another juicy secret, but they were all too intertwined to spill. Ruby's lack of magic would require a massive explanation, and even telling her about Gray would jeopardize Hazel's involvement with the triad. There was only one that would work—as much as it gutted her.

"What if I told you that Snow White was going to be a mother after all?"

Matilda snickered. "Sure. Maybe when this Monarch Morality movement dies down, but—"

"No. I mean now," Belle said. "I don't know all the details, but someone finally came to their senses. She's getting a baby boy. A sweet, adorable baby boy."

Matilda's lips spread wide. Her eyes lit up as she stared at the far wall. "Redemption at the hands of a child," she said, already brainstorming headlines. "That's a great story. I always rooted for her, you know. When's it happening?"

Belle took a deep, shaky breath, and made a mental note to call Snow immediately. "Tomorrow, I think. But you should contact her to be certain."

Matilda rapped the air with her pen. "Bingo," she said. "Fair trade—so long as I have the biggest story Marestam has ever seen coming down the pike. Your words."

Belle nodded as Kirsten sidled back to the wheelchair and spun it around. "You will. So long as you don't breathe a word of what you know about this little guy"—she tapped her empty belly—"to anyone."

Matilda looked down, then to the side, and nodded. "Of course," she said, her voice rising half an octave. "Mum's the word from here on out. Coast is clear. Good luck with the discharge tomorrow. Talk to you in five days!"

Chapter Eleven

RAPUNZEL

Rapunzel rolled her head along the edge of her seat and stared out the window. The coarse fabric disagreed with her skin. The thick pleather piping jutted uncomfortably into her left eye. And there was a putrid stench of something — stale cheese mixed with antibacterial hand gel, perhaps — that made her want to stop breathing all together.

After languishing in the airport for hours, fielding delay after delay from the never-ending storms, Ethan and Rapunzel finally boarded Sandman Flight 425 a few minutes before midnight. At one point, roughly seven hours into their twenty-hour flight from hell, she actually wished Ruby was sitting beside her instead of Ethan. Magically impotent or not, the fairy's perfume-soaked hair might have neutralized the air. That, and her boundless negativity seemed much more appealing at the moment than Ethan's exhaustive efforts to pretend nothing was wrong.

But from where she sat, absolutely everything was wrong.

For starters, where were the bottomless champagne glasses? Where was the hot tub? Where was the aisle wide enough for all sorts of physical acrobatics — with some extra headroom for flinging clothes? Where was the smug millionaire with the capped teeth, private jet, and easy out clause?

"They must have given you kids seats by mistake," she murmured, struggling to cross her legs without getting them stuck. "I'm going to have a permanent dent in my knee. There's, like, two inches of space here." Grunting, she finally grabbed one foot with both hands and shoved. It hit the tiny porthole window then finally dropped down, causing her elbow to lurch back and jab Ethan's left bicep. "And that's another thing. Do they think people's arms are half an inch wide? This is negative elbowroom. This is inhumane." She glanced at the microscopic vodka bottle shoved into the flimsy plastic cup on Ethan's tray table, and let out one more grunt of disgust.

"They're economy seats," said her *travel companion* — as she'd specified for two flight attendants, the security official, and the guy who brewed her latte at the gate. "First Class only had one spot under such short notice, and I figured you'd be just as disappointed. No mile-high hot tubs in my lifestyle, love. Wish I could say otherwise."

"It's fine." She plucked a magazine out from the seatback pocket, flipped past forty uninteresting pages in one breath, and hurled it back. Then she focused on the tiny washed out media screen in front of her. On it, a swaying cartoon airplane was gobbling up yellow dashes that stretched more than ten thousand miles, over two oceans and an entire continent, to the giant island realm of Stularia. She'd never been there, but knew its size was deceiving. While Marestam could fit inside its water-locked borders almost a thousand times over, only a fraction of Stularia was actually inhabited. That left more than two million square miles of untouchable land, perfect for hiding a reclusive fairy with no need for societal convenience. No wonder Rapunzel could never find her.

"So, what's the plan?" she asked, not eager to converse with Ethan but even less eager to sit in uncomfortable silence. "Do you have an address or something? Should we bring a housewarming gift? Does she know we're coming?"

"Funny," he said, popping an almond into his mouth.

"Which part?"

He gave her a sideways glance and held it as his back molars cracked down on the nut. "I don't have an address. They didn't have eye of newt in the gift shop. And judging by the fact that I can still see that scowl on your face, I'm guessing she doesn't know we're coming."

"I'm not scowling," Rapunzel said, catching an involuntarily glimpse of another passenger's screen two rows down. A teenage girl with headphones was watching some trashy news program about the Wickenhams. It had probably been spliced together while Belle was bleeding out in the emergency room. The producers had probably hoped she'd die so they could up the ratings.

She chomped down on her cheeks but couldn't take her eyes away as a bunch of headlines flooded the screen: *Donner pleads not guilty to attempted murder, gets out on bail ... Belle to leave hospital Wednesday ... Parliament questions future of the monarchies ... Crackdowns on magic cause uproar ... Kiarra Kane: The trial of the century's wild card.*

Rapunzel's chest rose and fell so fast, she could feel her bra pulling away from her shirt.

"God, I hate the media," she said. "I can't believe I used to be part of that. They're just a bunch of nosy, blood-thirsty bullies who slap up whatever headlines will start the most fires."

"Then stop looking at it," Ethan suggested, tilting forward to obscure her view. "They don't even know what they're talking about." His eyebrows rose a little, then he leaned closer to her and whispered, "They're just desperate to know what happened, and you already do. Don't get caught up in all the packaging."

"I know," she whispered back, shaking her head at the glittery talking heads and their cattle audience. "And you're right." He tipped back in surprise, unblocking a photo montage of Belle dancing with Donner on her wedding day; Belle telling a *Mirror* reporter about her pregnancy and Donner's affair; Belle and Rapunzel toasting to the Phoenix B&B at its grand opening; and Donner being hauled away in a police cruiser with the Phoenix in flames behind him. "But do they *really* have to do that?"

A few heads turned their way as Rapunzel's voice jumped over the appropriate airline din. She slid quietly down into her seat. She hadn't really expected to hop on a cross-world economy class airliner without being recognized at all, but she'd hoped to hold off until landing.

Sure enough, after this outburst, the woman sitting directly across from Ethan began rubbing the back of her neck in a poor attempt to disguise her staring right at them. "Excuse me," she finally cooed, leaning over the aisle and dancing her fingers across Ethan's arm. Rapunzel lunged for her porthole. She pressed her forehead against the glass and willed herself to fall asleep. Instead, she heard, "Aren't you Ethan Wilkins? William's son?"

Rapunzel let a tiny chuckle slip out as she heard him fumble for an answer, then take on a million questions about his father's upcoming wedding and the mental state of his soon-to-be stepbrothers. She often forgot that Ethan was technically a low-level Stularian royal (even though it had caused her such anguish initially), and that his dad was going to be Penny's father-in-law in a few days. What a small, funny world it could be, she thought as it occurred to her for the first time that if she married Ethan, Penny and Rapunzel would be sisters-in-law. Not that she had any intention of legally binding herself to anyone … but a lifelong relationship of the non-contractual kind was still on the table.

Rapunzel rolled her forehead against the cold glass and tried not to chuckle as Ethan's admirer extolled Prince Carter's "epic love story sacrifice." The naiveté made her want to ram her head through three layers of plexiglass. Instead, she stared out into the pitch-blackness and wondered how in the world she'd gotten here. Not that it was particularly amazing how quickly her life had changed. She knew all too well that the world could wake up on any given morning and decide to topple over. The amazing thing was that she'd *let* it change. After the initial resistance, she'd actually sat by and allowed *love* to cap the frayed wires in her brain ... to turn her into the maiden in a nauseatingly epic love story ... to convince her to do the one thing she'd never done with a member of the opposite sex: forgive.

She must have dozed off for a while, because the next time her eyes opened, the darkness had morphed into a blanket of puffy, turquoise clouds, running into a huge orange sun in the distance. The horizon flushed green and blue, and the morning light cast a rosy glow into the otherwise miserable pod chugging its way through the atmosphere. There was something therapeutic about it, as if it was happening for her eyes only while everyone else's were clamped shut or buried beneath a sleep mask.

She did a quick survey and noticed that unlike the dead fish across the aisle, Ethan was sitting straight up with one elbow on the far armrest and the other one tucked against his side. She smiled, assuming he'd purposely kept the middle armrest clear in case she decided to use it. Something about this action, combined with his innocent sleeping face and the fact that they'd hardly touched each other in days, gave her a sudden need to be close to him. She missed wrapping her fingers around his arm and hugging it like a child would hug her favorite stuffed animal. She missed pressing her head against his shoulder, and feeling him stroke her hair. She missed the smell of his skin. She missed hearing him joke without that grating edge of uncertainty he had now — as if worried she might take offense.

She missed his warmth, and his taste, and how well they fit together right from the start. She missed —

She catapulted back to the window as Ethan began to stir. The clouds were simply white now, with a slight pinkish tinge and a cobalt band running between them and the predictably golden sun.

"Oh shoot. Did I miss the sunrise?" Ethan's breath tickled the back of her neck as he leaned over, his hand instinctively resting on the top of her back. Rapunzel didn't answer. She steadied her breath and forced her eyes to remain shut. He waited, then leaned so close, his stubble caught the hair cascading over her ears. "I know you're not asleep, love."

Love. She felt a tiny spark and pressed her lips together to absorb it. She waited a beat, then slowly lifted her lids and began stretching — first her hips, then her legs (as much as she could in the space allowed), and finally her arms, one of which hooked around Ethan's outstretched neck. She froze, suddenly unsure what to do about the still sleepy eyes staring back at her, or the pair of parted lips just inches from her own.

She needed him. She loved him. She wanted to grab his face and jump all over him that instant, save for the huge psychological boulder holding her back.

"How did you sleep?" she asked, pulling away and catching her breath just as the cabin lights clicked on and the intercom dinged. The question came out more formal than she'd intended, but what's done was done.

He nodded, twisted so that he was facing forward once again, and rubbed both palms fiercely against his forehead. "Like a baby. You?"

She shrugged and thumbed the indent on the tiny plastic window shade. "Fine. But you still haven't answered my question."

Ethan grabbed his bottle of water and pulled the cap off with one twist. "What question is that?"

"Grethel. How are we finding her? What are we doing when we land?"

He paused with the bottle perched just over his lips. His eyes stared forward. "Oh. Right." He tilted his head back and started to chug. As she waited, the plane seemed to come alive around them. Blanketed lumps rose up and stretched their arms to the ceiling. Full bladders summoned every other row to the miniscule bathroom. Foil bags crunched as a flight attendant floated by holding an extra-large trash bag. Overhead bins clicked open. The smell of fresh coffee wafted through the cabin.

"You do have a plan, right?" she pushed. "You have at least some idea where we're going?"

Ethan nodded, with far more enthusiasm than warranted, and held up one finger. Then he finally lowered the water bottle and let out a satisfied sigh. "I do," he said, dumping the container into the passing trash bag and thanking the flight attendant with a wink. Rapunzel grimaced. "The only thing is ... well, Grethel isn't actually *on* Stularia ... per se."

Rapunzel lurched in her seat. "What do you mean?" she shrieked, then immediately reeled it in. "What do you mean she's not on Stularia? Why are we going there then?" She sucked in all the air she could and clenched her teeth. "And where the hell is she?"

Rapunzel watched his eyes pan from the blank screen in front of him, to the top of her shoes, to the notch in the center of her collarbone. Then she heard him explain that last time he heard, Grethel was living on an uninhabited island a few miles *off the coast* of Stularia. Rumor said the place was cursed, so he was going to have to bribe someone at the docks to take them there. It wasn't the worst answer she could have imagined, but nor was it ideal.

"Okay," she said. "But what time is it going to be now when we land?"

"It'll be late afternoon," he said, bouncing his hands between his knees. "Which is why we need to spend the night." And with that, Rapunzel's frown started to force its way up.

"Oh we do, do we?" she said, suddenly picturing a short but luxurious stay in an ocean-side resort. They could make up under the stars. They could share piña coladas and watch the sunrise. That way, her first visit to Ethan's homeland (which she'd envisioned many times though would never admit it) wouldn't be completely ruined. "And I suppose that was just a happy accident?" Her voice was teasing, but sensual. It felt good to show that side again. "A late landing, a cute hotel, drinks and a little dinner, and all of the sudden we're all made up?"

"Well..."

She reached out and flicked the pocket on his maroon T-shirt. He bit his lip and rubbed the back of his neck.

"No, of course n —" "That sounds perfect."

Their eyes locked and then flew in opposite directions. "Wait, what?" they asked at the exact same time.

Ethan pounded his hand through his hair, simultaneously confused and worried by her sudden romantic interest in him.

"Umm," he stuttered for a moment. "Bollocks."

Rapunzel's claw fell limp over his pocket, which was now almost the exact same color as his cheeks.

She pulled back. "What?"

"Well," Ethan said, flattening out his shirt and shaking his head. "I mean, you said you wanted space. And I grew up here. I couldn't *not* tell them I was coming."

Rapunzel steadied her breath as the intercom chimed again and the pilot announced Sandman Air's final descent. "Tell who?" She bore down on the words while her finger bore down around the armrest.

Ethan swallowed. "My sister lives twenty minutes from the airport. It's on the way to the coast anyway and I haven't seen her kids, my nieces and nephews, in ages. You'll love them."

Rapunzel felt herself beginning to panic — not because she

didn't care about meeting Ethan's family, but because she did. And on the hunt for Grethel, while Marestam was crumbling and their relationship was threatening to capsize, was definitely not how she'd wanted it to go down.

"Won't we see them at the wedding next weekend?" she heard herself blurt out, immediately aware of how awful it sounded. Judging by the way Ethan's mouth opened and curled up in the center, he was aware of it too.

"No," he said, chewing the word like a slice of stale bread. "Elisa doesn't want to take everyone out of school. But it wouldn't be the same in a formal setting anyway, especially for the kids."

There was that word again: kids. It reminded her of Ethan's text message suggesting they get a dog together, and of Belle's comment about Ethan possibly wanting children. But children inferred marriage, and he knew she despised the institution. *Everyone* knew she despised the institution. He still brought it up every month or so, as if to retest the waters, but he always respected her decision in the end.

"How many kids are we talking here?" she asked, envisioning her one night in Stularia surrounded by a room full of wailing, shoving, tantrum-throwing toddlers. "And how old?"

She heard his breath get heavier as he turned to fully face her. "Look," he said, holding both hands up as if she was a bear and his skin was coated in honey. "I should have run it by you. But it's free room and board and I'd really like for them to meet you. Plus, you seemed to be so smitten by Belle's baby that I thought—"

"I'm not good with kids," she interrupted before he could say something they'd both regret. "I've told you that."

Ethan's face fell. He rotated again to face the front. "I'm sorry I didn't tell you," he said, eyes dead ahead. "If you'd rather get a hotel, that's fine. I can pick you up in the morning. You've made it pretty clear that I'm just your travel companion, anyway."

Rapunzel felt a lump the size of an in-flight pillow in her throat, and an even bigger one in her stomach. Arguing about his lie was one thing. She'd been the victim there, and it was entirely her call to forgive him or move on. But this was different. Somehow, even though she was simply reiterating a preference he'd known from the very beginning, she felt guilty about it.

"It's fine," she finally said, pinching her lips and punching her screen back on. A photo of Belle appeared beneath the headline: *Protective wife or criminal liar: What did Belle know?* She groaned. "You're right. We didn't come here to get drunk at a beachside hotel. If your sister's on the way, we should see her. I'm exhausted anyway."

"Do you mean that?"

She nodded, yanked her journal from the bag stuffed beneath her seat, and shoved her entire body back up against the window.

"Thanks for understanding," he said, his tone more than a little sour.

"Sure thing," she replied, pressing her pen into the paper and waiting for the negative energy to release. Maybe she'd write a public service announcement about how falling in love was detrimental to your health. Maybe she'd list the qualities of her ideal man and see how Ethan measured up. Maybe she'd write down everything she wanted to say to Grethel. Or maybe she'd just stare out at the clouds, imagining that one person's problems are just blips on an air traffic control radar. Needles in hemlock forest. Grains of sand on an abandoned Stularian beach.

~∞~

"Leila, watch out! Hands off! Porter, for goodness sake, leave the candles alone. You're not gonna be happy if you burn your fingers. Camilla, I swear, if you touch the dog's water bowl one more time, I'm going to—well, I'm probably not going to do anything to be honest, but just leave it alone. That's a big no-no."

Ethan's sister shot Rapunzel a frazzled look as she swiped an aluminum bowl from a two-year-old, sidestepped a cartwheeling first grader, and slipped on a minefield of discarded board books. Not missing a beat, the toddler promptly leapt on top of her mother and began singing, in a tiny squeak of a voice, "Mama fall. Mama fall. You okay Mama?"

"I'm okay," Elisa Wilkins howled, bear-hugging her daughter and writhing with her on the carpet. "But I got you now! Tickle monster's here!"

Rapunzel pressed her lips into what she hoped would resemble a smile, then continued stirring her ginger tea. She'd barely said a word to Ethan since they got off the plane—or no meaningful words, anyway. She was angry all over again—mostly at him, partially at herself, and then back at him all over again for making her mad at herself.

"Last chance for that turn-down service and silk pillow," he'd said as they wound their way through customs and waited for their bags. "Personally, I'd rather spend some quality time with the family I never see while I can. But if luxury is still what's important to you, even after everything we just experienced with Belle, there are loads of five-star resorts along the coastline. I'm happy to pick you up in the morning."

One shuttle and a twenty-minute car ride later, his words were still burning circles in her head. Of course she knew people were more important than luxury. Maybe the stress of almost losing Belle was the very *reason* she needed a little mindless relaxation. But what had he meant by "still?" The sexual escapades, the wining and dining, the image-ballooning attitude ... those things were never truly important to her. She'd used them as a barrier—but a barrier he'd knocked down months ago. She thought he knew that. She thought they had an understanding. She thought they were one of those couples she'd always mocked but secretly envied—the ones who could beat the linguistic crap out of each other and still remain madly in love, who told each other everything but never at the cost of respect, who blurted things out before thinking and were automatically understood. That was how true love and "happily ever after" was supposed to work, right?

"So. Bait or birth control?"

"What?" Rapunzel looked up as Ethan's sister slid down beside her and threw most of her torso onto the table.

"Bait or birth control?" Elisa propped her head up with one hand and flicked it in the direction of her children. Rapunzel stared, slightly dumbfounded, as her lips rose up on one side and then parted to give a teaser peek at her teeth. It was the only part of her anatomy that confirmed she and Ethan were related. Everything else—the tight blonde curls, the freckles, the stick-thin appendages—could have belonged to a total stranger. "I always wonder what people think when they see my little monsters," she continued. "Is it 'Oh, I want one,' or 'Thank all that is holy those things belong to someone else.'"

Rapunzel gave an insecure laugh and fingered the bracelet she'd procured from Donner's things at Marestam Central Prison. She understood why Belle didn't want to take it, but it was quite dazzling—a flawless platinum chain interspersed with pink gold squiggles and pea-sized rubies. Rapunzel just couldn't bear seeing it go to waste.

She winced as she heard Elisa clear her throat. Back home, the sun would be long gone by now, those curfew-breaking sisters would be sneaking out of her building to dance at the nightclubs, and Rapunzel would be cuddling up with either Ethan or a silky-eared canine. But she wasn't at home. She was halfway across the world, nursing this relentless motion sickness with ginger tea in a four-season porch surrounded by blinding sunlight and an army of pint-sized nutcases.

"Is that helping?" Elisa asked, nodding to the tea. "I get nauseous when I fly, too. Ethan used to call me 'Crinkles' because whenever we went on family vacations, I'd have to breath into a paper bag the entire way. Until I started threatening to throw up on him, anyway."

"I'm fine," Rapunzel said, though it wasn't even remotely true. She never got airsick, not even pole dancing on a private airbus during an emergency landing. It was probably just stress and jet lag. Not that the sugar-high circus was helping. "So, you've really got your hands full, huh?"

Elisa laughed and repositioned her camisole, as if she had anything to reposition it on. "They're good kids," she said, reaching for a bottle that looked like a beer but was really just cream soda. According to Ethan, his sister ran a completely dry household because her ex-husband liked to get sopping wet. Rapunzel understood the mentality, but didn't believe it for a second. There had to be a nip or two around here somewhere, at least for emergencies.

"They haven't seen their uncle in six months, so..." Elisa paused, as if she wanted Rapunzel to sympathize—or apologize—for her brother's choice of residence, "they've got a lot of pent-up greetings to get out. It really is a shame they can't get together more often. He's so good with them. Don't you think?"

In all honesty, Rapunzel hadn't thought about that at all. But she peeled her fingers away from her aching temples anyway and eyed the trail of discarded books that led from the kitchen to the living area. Ethan was crossed-legged between the couch and a ransacked bookshelf, reading to a five-year-old girl with strawberry blonde pigtails. She couldn't hear what he was saying, but the little girl's face absolutely radiated as he traced the words and pictures across each page and helped her to sound them out. She looked so tiny in his lap, but so ... perfect, as if that scene should have been on the cover of a magazine somewhere or included in a time capsule and shot into outer space. Rapunzel watched for at least three pages, trying to understand the strange feeling warming the center of her chest, until Ethan looked in her direction. Her eyes instantly zipped back to the tea.

"He's good with most people," she said, downplaying Elisa's question—both the spoken part and the inferred. "Is it usually this chilly in September?"

"He's always been great with kids," Elisa said, completely ignoring her attempt to change the subject. "I keep telling him to move back to Stularia, but it's like asking a rock to soak up water. He must have something really special keeping him there."

Rapunzel gave a quick nod, then picked up her mug with both hands and disappeared into it. She wasn't used to having sober conversations with her boyfriend's relatives. She felt like a dead frog, splayed out for a bunch of overachieving pre-meds on the dissection table.

"Sorry." Elisa scratched at her soda label and laughed again. "I'm babbling, aren't I? Really have to work on that. I just miss my little brother, that's all. And now that our father's marrying that Marestam Queen—"

"Letitia," Rapunzel filled in, as if she didn't know the name of her future stepmother. "And I don't think she'll be queen when they actually get married. I think Logan and Penny's coronation is first. Letitia's the sort of woman who wants to be the main event, not an opener."

"Right." Elisa took a long slug of her soda, then dropped it back on the table. "Sorta-Queen Letitia. Anyway. At this rate, maybe I should disown my birth country and move to Marestam too. Find out if the streets are really 'paved with fairy dust' and all that jazz."

Rapunzel glanced at Ethan again. How long was that damn book? This conversation was going from plain old uncomfortable to hostile, fast.

"I guess that's just the way of the world now. No one marries the girl from down the street anymore. Not with planes and computers and — actually, you *are* from Stularia, aren't you? Sort of. Maybe you'll convince each other to return to your roots after this little getaway. Maybe there's hope for my kids having cousins nearby after all. Gosh, I'd love to see that. Ethan was born to be a father."

Rapunzel's spine cracked as her shoulder blades magnetized together. Her mug cracked against her teeth. What did she just say?

"What about you?" Elisa leaned even closer. She smelled of cinnamon with a hint of vanilla — or was that the cream soda? Either way, it gave Rapunzel the sudden urge to vomit.

"Oh, I definitely wasn't born to be a father," she joked, crossing her arms and kneading the table with her elbows. She panned the room, praying to see something she could use to change the subject — a lamp flying through the air, a kid springing off a couch, a bottle of milk spray painting the wall. But of course, the very moment she needed them to be devils, Ethan's nieces and nephews were perfect little angels.

Finally, the corners of Elisa's lips stretched apart and she hoisted her torso off the table. "Well, you must be tired from your trip. I won't be insulted if you want to take a catnap, or just head to bed early if you need it. From what I understand, you've got an early morning and another long day ahead." Rapunzel furrowed her brow. Was she being politely told to go away? Did she particularly care at the moment? "Your room's just up the stairs on the right. Towels are in the closet. Bathroom's across the hall. If the door isn't locking, pull the handle up a bit as you close it. Dinner's at six o'clock if you're up for it — or breakfast at seven thirty sharp. Do you like eggs?"

She did. But before she could answer, Elisa twisted around and announced, in a voice worthy of the opera, that AUNT Rapunzel needed some peace and quiet so it was time to play outside. For about two seconds, all noises ceased. Rapunzel could not only feel her heart pounding against her ribs — she could hear it too. And then, just as quickly as it had come, the silence gave way to a cacophony of cheers, shouts, and pipsqueak demands — bubbles! swings! slide! bikes! — as the horde spilled into the yard and Ethan flashed her a small, distant smile goodnight.

The Marestam Mirror

Diamond Ropes and Velvet Cake
By Perrin Hildebrand, King of Gossip

AFTER five days locked behind the impenetrable walls of Marestam General Hospital, Belle Wickenham will finally be released today. I believe this calls for a full-hearted, deep-bellied, "Huzzah!" At least for a moment.

With four months left in her pregnancy, the Phoenix in ruins, and Braddax Castle acting as Donner's electronically monitored home-away-from-jail (yes, he was released last night on $100,000 bail, in typical Noel Madison, attorney to the stars, fashion), I'm just dying to know where the estranged queen plans to live out the remainder of her rotund weeks. Sure, she's got that die-hard royal sister circle of which we're all insanely jealous, but think about it:

• Rapunzel has a brand-new roommate of the carnal variety.

• Cinderella is thousands of miles away, sopping up the culture and evading an increasingly frustrated press on Honeymoon Part Deux. (Seriously, if we don't see a picture of them sipping mojitos on an Elladan beach soon, I might start to worry.)

• Penelopea still lives with her mother-in-law and is probably having hourly panic attacks about her upcoming coronation.

• Snow has somehow gotten her hands on a screaming infant and will be focusing on him 24/7. (Plus, she lives hours away from any decent birthing centers should Belle continue her recent streak of hospital visits.)

• That leaves Dawn. And let's be honest, no one wants to witness *that* marriage at work on a daily basis.

So, unless our sweet Belle has a secret boy toy to shack up with (perhaps the kind that could send a rich, rock-solid, narcissistic monarch completely off his rocker...) your guess is as good as mine.

SPEAKING of screaming infants, Rapunzel Delmonico was spotted stocking up on maternity and baby clothes this weekend at Cribs and Cankles in midtown Carpale.

"She said it was for the Queen of Braddax," explained storeowner Shirley Templeton. "But she was extremely frazzled and the items she selected simply didn't add up. I'm not saying she's in the family way or anything—though goodness knows that would be a precious, life-changing gift for a woman like her. I'm just saying you might want to keep an eye out. I have a sixth sense when it comes to babies. Always have."

Keep an eye out I will, Shirley. Always do.

HURRICANE season officially arrived on Monday, bringing winds and rains heavy enough to delay flights, disrupt a Selladórean press conference, and turn the Riverfell Palace throne room into a swimming pool.

According to official reports, the damage is considerable. And with the combination coronation/wedding slated for Friday (or, as I like to call it, the Royal Coronedding), this is causing heart rates to skyrocket all over Riverfell.

Says the newly dubbed king-to-be, Prince Logan: "We're exploring all of our options right now, including the possibility of changing venues. My mother has been looking forward to this for a long time—as have Penny and I. The people of Riverfell are expecting a celebration on Friday, and I will do everything I can to ensure they are not disappointed."

For the sake of Logan, his crown, and the people who've been backing him for decades, I hope he's right. Who knows what could happen if the grand event gets pushed back a week—or even a day?

After all, it only takes one second for someone to pop out of a coma.

TONE-DEAF protesters continued to condemn both the monarchies and Parliament's recent security crackdowns this week—the latter including an uptick in spontaneous search-and-seizures, as well as rumors of MSC confiscations disguised as burglaries.

Sporting a sign reading, "Tyranny!" one man accused Angus Kane of vilifying the monarchies in order to cut them off and create one overarching throne for himself. He called particular attention to Parliament's statement late Friday that it would send troops to Tantalise if the Whites didn't abandon their throne (rhetoric from which it has since backed down). "If he can force his way into the private home of a monarch and tell them how to live, can you even imagine what he would do to ordinary people if left unchecked?"

A dozen feet away, a woman hoisting the same message but wearing a Monarch Morality Movement T-shirt, said the monarchies had no place in modern society. "They're nothing but a bunch of nepotistic tyrants, living their reckless and selfish lives, keeping each other's secrets with no consideration for the people who could get hurt," she said. "Aside from the Charmés, I can't even remember the last time any of them did something to better my life. It's finally time to let them drown. Bring down the crowns!"

Shiver.

Chapter Twelve

BELLE

Belle had never seen anything so amazing in her entire life. To call him perfect—regardless of what any doctor's chart said—would be like describing the aurora borealis as "pretty." From his pursed little lips to the chubby fingers that constantly curled around her own, he was everything she'd ever wanted. In the instant they locked eyes ... the instant Snow whispered those unbelievable words: *he's yours* ... Belle knew that for the next sixty years, her heart would be crawling, or walking, or barhopping outside of her body. She knew she would be vulnerable as only a mother could possibly be. She knew she would do everything in her power to protect him. She'd give up everything to ensure that he grew up happy, healthy, and safe. Even if that meant sacrificing ... what?

Everything? Too vague.

Her freedom? Absolutely.

Her friends? She loved them dearly, but yes.

Her life?

The latter would give her pause—but not because she wouldn't gladly take a bullet, a lethal injection, or the most excruciating disease known to man if it meant keeping her child safe. No. It would decimate her because then he'd grow up without knowing how much she loved him. He'd have to navigate this crazy world without a mother to be there for him unconditionally, to regale him with stories before bed, to kiss away his boo-boos, and to lift him up when he discovered that hearts could break.

Belle knew firsthand how hard this could be—having that sort of love for a short period and then having it stripped away with no explanation. She'd spent most of her adolescence wondering how her own mother could have abandoned her children—even though their father messed up; even though they had to trade their lavish manor house for a cramped cottage in the woods; even though someone else came along and promised to keep up the lifestyle to which she'd grown accustomed. She still could have had a relationship with her kids. She could have moved down the block. She didn't have to disappear off the face of the earth. And now, finding herself in almost the exact same position two decades later, her mother's actions still seemed unfathomable. In fact, the only thing Belle's parenting books hadn't prepared her for was the intensity with which she would love her baby. She couldn't imagine this could ever change. But then again … it was her mother's blood that coursed through her veins. And to a degree, she was seconds away from doing the same exact thing.

"Just remember that this is only temporary," Penny assured her as they watched the sea of people spilling out on the streets below. From what she heard, it stretched ten blocks south and filled the entire east side of Carpale.

"The only thing harder than leaving my baby is having to pretend it's a cause for celebration," she said as Penny wrapped her arm around Belle's shoulders and rubbed the pocket of Rye's tiny flannel shirt.

"This is an adorable outfit," she said, pasting on a huge smile and then glancing toward the window. "And they're here because they love you. If anything, take comfort in that."

Belle choked back another wave of tears, not that she really had any left to shed. They'd been coming for almost twenty-four hours now, ever since she returned to her room after the arraignment. She knew Penny had a point. She knew that the people waiting below — with their cameras and their homemade signs and their flowers — meant well. They just wanted her to know that the baby she carried had a special place in their hearts too, and that she would always be their "hero" — as one woman put it — if not their queen. But knowing this didn't make it any easier to smile through the most emotionally gutting day of her life.

"We can go whenever you're ready," said Penny, who'd offered to be Belle's chauffeur in light of Rapunzel's absence and her preference that Gray stay off the media's radar for as long as possible. She was surprised that they hadn't already started asking questions about him — a handsome bachelor "groundskeeper" who just so happened to be front and center during both of her trips to the hospital — and wasn't eager to push her luck. "There's no rush, of course," her friend added. "You take as much time as you need."

Belle nodded and thanked her, even though she knew it was a lie. In the fifteen minutes since her arrival, Penny's phone had chimed almost as many times as Belle had blinked.

"How's Letitia taking all this?" she asked, snooping over Penny's teal cashmere shoulder to catch a massive group text with the entire LeBlanche clan. "I'm sure she expected her wedding to be saturating the news this week. Instead it's a brief mention on page two, not including the news about the flood. Believe me, I'd trade places with her in a heartbeat."

"Well, she's certainly not happy about it," Penny said, fingering an angry reply into her phone. It was answered two seconds later with three more chimes. "But I've definitely dealt with worse. Maybe with everything else that's going on, she's finally realizing that she isn't the center of everyone's universe. Or maybe she's just relieved that I can't take Logan away from her once we're glued to the throne."

As if sensing Penny's frustration, Rye began to squawk and squirm in Belle's arms. Then his furry little head shook from one side to the other and an entire fist flew into his mouth.

"Is he hungry?" Penny asked, finally dropping her phone against a pumpkin orange ballet skirt.

"Maybe. But let's try this first," Belle said, laying him under a fabric mobile in a play gym Kirsten had brought from home. She cooed and "shushed" to him while winding up the music box. "Hey. See the elephant? Ooh. And what's that? A monkey? Do you know what the monkey says?"

Rye giggled and kicked his legs as she attempted to imitate a monkey. Then he yanked off his sock, rolled onto his stomach, and tried to eat a chunk of crinkly fabric that dangled off the mat.

"I could watch this all day long," she said, not taking her eyes off him for a second. She almost added, "I'm going to miss this," but she didn't—partly because saying it out loud wasn't going to change anything, and partly because she was still hoping for a miracle. When the music stopped playing, she cranked the dial fourteen times until it started over. Then, about halfway through, she did it again.

"You said Gray found the rings, right?" Penny asked, the concern in her voice undeniable.

Belle nodded. Yes, Gray had called her around three o'clock that morning to say he'd just uncovered the remains of a jewelry box—and in addition to a handful of charred gold and silver pieces, there were two chunky platinum rings with red diamonds that appeared to be completely unscathed. Charms. Indestructible to everything but magic, just like Ruby had said.

She'd actually missed the call, but he left a voicemail and she decided against calling him back. He sounded exhausted, for one thing, and almost an entire week had passed since they confessed their feelings for each other. If she closed her eyes, she could still hear the crackle of the fireplace, feel the tension in the air, see the way his eyes — all wide and stormy — seemed to pulse in time with her heartbeat. Just thinking about it now made her heart curl up a little inside her chest. She'd never felt such passion before Gray. She'd never wanted anything with such ferocity before (except perhaps a child, but those feelings were completely different). In that moment, when she debunked his whole "I can't fear" story because he *feared* losing her, she'd felt as if not kissing him would be on par with not breathing. If she didn't let her feelings out — and if he didn't say he felt the same — they might consume her like a uranium core, decaying for eternity.

So, she did. And it was absolute heaven for a full fifteen minutes — until her baby started growing at an excruciating rate and *Ruby* told her that returning to Donner was the only way to save him.

"Are you sure he's not hungry?" Penny asked as Rye replaced the crinkly piece of fabric with his fist again.

Belle deflated. "He is hungry," she acknowledged, feeling both angry and ashamed at the same time — the exact combination of emotions she'd seen on Donner's face at the arraignment. "I'm just stalling because this might be the last time I get to feed him for a while."

"Why? Can't you pump?"

"Yeah," she said, glancing over at her stuffed duffel bag. "I can. I will."

"So, you can just give the bottles to Snow and she'll use them whenever you can't be there," Penny said, still glued to her phone. "Right?"

Belle wiped her eyes and scooped her baby back up into her arms. She'd had the exact same conversation with Snow a few hours earlier, when she called to get Belle's instructions on diapering, feeding, burping, sleeping, singing, bathing, teething, reading, and all over mothering. But it wasn't the physical act of nursing she was worried about losing, it was the emotional one. It was something she didn't expect Penny—or Rapunzel, or even Snow—to understand. But there was something, oh, celestial about burrowing up with Rye and connecting with him in such a profound, intimate way.

"I mean, if you have the rings, isn't it just like he's in the next room?" Penny continued. "Only instead of walking through a regular door, you'll be walking through a magical one." She glanced up long enough to blink. "Sorry. Letitia's leaning toward moving everything to Selladóre Castle, but there isn't enough space. So, she's going through the guest list with a fine-tooth comb and—"

She looked up again, read the look in Belle's eyes, and immediately tossed the phone onto Belle's bed. "I'm sorry," she said, shaking as if a hypnotist had just snapped his fingers in front of her face. She crossed the room and gave Belle a huge butt-out hug so as not to squish the baby. Belle hung onto her and pulled her closer, repositioning so that Rye was well out of harm's way. "Just tell me what you need. Anything. Are you still planning on staying at Rapunzel's? I should stay with you. How about that? We'll swing by the Phoenix, pick up Beast and some pizzas, and have a girls' pity party. The secret mommy and the reluctant queen. I'm sure Rapunzel won't mind if we break into her liquor cabinet."

Belle laughed through her tears and pulled away. "That sounds great, Pen. But you've got so much to do. Your coronation is in three days."

"It's fine," she said as the phone chimed again. She tried to disguise her flinch by jiggling Rye's tiny sneaker socks, but Belle wasn't convinced.

"I really appreciate the offer," she said. "But Beast can keep me company and, like you said, I'll probably be walking through magical doors all night anyway."

Penny twisted her mouth and stared at Belle as if she was a cryptogram in need of solving. "Okay," she finally said. "But consider me on call, at any hour. I've been spending most nights digging into Angus Kane anyway, just in case the triad needs an extra boost. Did you know his mother used to work at Braddax Castle?"

Belle shook her head. That was weird, but she wasn't sure how that really helped with the mission to break Rye's curse.

"Well, he did. Before Donner was in the picture, but I still find it a little fishy. Plus, you know, the lawyer in me." She shrugged and forced a laugh. "I may not have magical connections like Rapunzel and Dawn, but that doesn't make me useless."

"Oh, Pen," Belle said just as Rye began to pull at her breast. "You're never useless. You're the one who found that loophole in Donner's prenup and—"

"Yeah, but then I screwed it up by sitting on the details."

"It's okay," she said, losing her focus as Rye began to lose his patience. "But do you mind giving us the room for just a few minutes? I don't think I can hold him off much longer, and I kind of want to..."

She trailed off, unsure how to describe her emotional need to shove her boob into Rye's mouth.

"Cherish the moment?" Penny filled in. "Not a problem. Take as long as you want. When you're ready—" She grabbed her phone off the bed. "Just holler."

⌖

Belle held her breath as she stepped out of the car and saw the scorched bones of the Phoenix for the first time. It was a reaction that came partly from shock, but primarily from the overwhelming smell of char in the air. When she finally inhaled, a thick cloud of grit slammed into the back of her throat and clawed its way down.

"Wow, that's pungent," Penny said, shielding her mouth with an orange ikat scarf.

That's the smell of my life eroding, Belle thought, too stunned to actually speak. To her, the whole scene looked less like the site of a fire than of a hurricane—followed by a gas leak that sparked an explosion that led to a raging inferno.

Not a single wall remained. The concrete beneath the stone veneered steps climbed their way to nowhere. In all directions, the wet, charcoal ruins of her former life saturated the grounds. The parking lot, which she'd declined to pave in deference to Mother Nature, now disappeared beneath a blanket of ash. The gold and purple sign they commissioned from the former front door hadn't made it. Nor had the porch, the second floor, or the garden oasis Gray had created during his first days here—excluding the fire pit, of course, which stood in all its glory. And where there once was a border garden lined with colorful annuals, there now sat a berm of black rubble and a bright yellow line of "Crime Scene" tape—simultaneously the only unscathed object and the only one that didn't belong.

Belle felt like a ghost, haunting her yet-to-be-discovered grave and assessing the life she'd left behind. Perhaps that's what was going on. Perhaps she'd actually died in the fire and all of this was just the void between consciousness and eternity. Or perhaps this was all a dream, and all she had to do to wake up was find her body buried somewhere beneath that mound.

"I really don't think that's a good idea," Penny called as Belle dragged her feet through the ash and pushed the tape skyward. "I'm sure that line's there for a reason. What if things are still smoldering? Maybe you should wait for Gray and—"

Belle closed her ears and dipped under. She had to see the damage for herself, and she was just as happy (if not more so) to do it alone. She'd already passed the first three stages of grief—shock, denial, and anger—at the hospital. The guilt stage officially started this morning, as she packed for Rye's open-ended excursion to Tantalise, and bargaining ... well, bargaining had always been there. In a way, it was what got her into this mess to begin with. If she'd just listened to Ruby at the outset — not tried to bargain with the universe for trivial things like independence, freedom, happiness — perhaps the curse wouldn't have gotten this far. Or perhaps it truly was all Angus Kane's fault and nothing she did mattered at all. Either way, what's done was done. Acceptance. Stage seven. She could skip depression.

Her first few steps on the other side of the tape were steady. She had this. Everything under her feet right now could be replaced.

Her foot slipped on the base of a frying pan. Junk.

She looked down and realized she was standing on the stove. Replaceable.

Her new porcelain sink drowned beneath a mountain of debris, including a shattered mirror and two iron bookends from the guestroom above. Trinkets.

She looked up. Beneath the peach glow of a mid-sunset sky, the whole thing could have been so poetic: a sentinel chimney and three surviving stairs, shadows harkening back to a time when hope still existed.

Belle continued to walk the rooms, covering twice the real estate with everything on one level, for at least twenty minutes. She saw the fireplace where the whole battle began. She saw fixtures from the lounge and the bathroom beside the front desk. Her heel landed on the tarnished service bell, which responded with a sad, spiritless clink. At times, it seemed like the thousand-degree flames had operated with no rhyme or reason whatsoever — pounding some items beyond recognition while leaving others almost intact — chunks of defiance in a sea of defeat.

Her gloom retreated for a moment when she discovered the safe untouched, but it contained only a few legal documents and a guest's camera. Crammed beneath it sat a box stuffed with magazines and notebooks she'd used when designing the inn. To her astonishment, only the sides had been scorched.

It was this discovery that finally gave her the strength she needed to step over the threshold of what used to be her bedroom. Maybe the bins filled with baby clothes had been shown the same mercy. Flames rose, right? Maybe the box under her bed — with her father's letters, her grandmother's broach, and the corduroy bear that survived all four of Cinderella's hyperactive kids — had gotten lucky.

But then she saw the crumbled crib rungs ... and the melted mobile ... and the mutilated, black quilts that now hung like tissue paper over the destruction ... and she realized the denial stage wasn't even close to being over. Nor was anger. Or shock. And she was just toeing the edge of depression.

Suddenly, the contents of her stomach started to churn and a sickening feeling washed over her. Her ears began to scream like boiling lobsters as she doubled over, spilling her last hospital meal all over the hideous chrome collage Donner had brought just a few minutes before the world ended. She thought about crumpling to the floor and crying. She thought about curling up inside the sandstone shower she loved so much and waiting for Gray to come find her. She thought about picking up every solid, moderately heavy object she could find and bashing it against the chimney until her anger looked every bit as devastating as Donner's.

But it was getting dark. Snow would be arriving in Tantalise any minute now and Belle wanted to be there to get Rye settled. So with all the strength she could muster, she pushed herself back up, hoisted the box of magazines into her arms, and clopped back down to the parking lot.

Penny's car was still there, its headlights illuminating the crime scene all over again, but no one was in it. Belle dropped her souvenir on the hood and followed the ashen tracks down to the only other place she could be—Gray's cabin.

"Find anything?" Penny asked, pulling back the door before Belle's knuckles even touched it. Her olive complexion looked unusually pale in the moonlight—at least Belle wanted to think it was the moonlight. She didn't want to live the rest of her life under a cloud of pity.

"Not really," she said, stepping inside. "And please don't look at me like that. I'm fine. There's nothing up there that can't be replaced. The only thing that really matters is on his way to Tantalise, sucking his hand and wondering what happened to—"

Belle's tongue skidded to a stop as the rest of her sentence rear-ended it.

She hadn't seen Gray for days—only days—but turning the corner and catching sight of him did something startling to her insides. He was looking the other way, tucking a fleece blanket into the corners of her favorite armchair, and draping a second one over the back just in case. She could have stared at him for another hour. Silent. A fly on the wall. No expectations or explanations or questions. Smelling the onions and tomatoes simmering in the kitchen. Feeling the heat rising up from within her and hearing the fire crackling inside the wood stove.

It seemed absurd to think she'd been more prepared to see her home in ashes than to face the man who'd stolen her heart. But then again, it wasn't. The Phoenix was gone no matter what she did. Sure, she had the power to recreate it. But at the end of the day, nothing she did could reverse what had happened. She couldn't stand by those stairs to nowhere, ring her neutered bell, and wish it all back. Her only option was to accept it.

With Gray, however, the options were as endless as the questions. She hadn't prepared for this moment simply because she wasn't sure how. She didn't know whether to blame him for provoking Donner or apologize for bringing him into this mess. But more importantly, she didn't know who she would see when he finally turned around: the flippant, cheeky drifter she first met in the woods; the sweet, chivalrous man who'd taken care of her and talked her down when she was borderline suicidal; or the dark, tortured soul so convinced he was unfit for happiness that he blocked himself from feeling at all.

She was still debating what to say when Penny's cell phone tore through the silence like a colicky baby in a church.

"Shit," Penny snarled just as Gray looked up and the room shrank three sizes. "It's Letitia. I'll be right back. Gotta take this."

Belle might have murmured something in return, but she honestly wasn't sure. She was too busy staring ahead, a hostage to the figure standing in front of her.

Gray was wearing jeans, as usual, and a dark blue Henley with the sleeves rolled up. She saw his breath speed up as he straightened his legs and looked at her. She had a sudden flashback to that afternoon in the rain, with the flat tire. She recalled how the water soaked through his shirt and she realized lean was not the opposite of muscular. She felt her breath catch as he ran his hand through his thick, brown hair, and one side of his mouth began to curl.

"Hi," she said, her voice like that shredded quilt back in the nursery.

"Belle," he said, the same way he'd said it that evening as they dried off beside the fire. It had that same soft longing. It was still half sigh, half question. But this time, she locked her eyes on his and answered.

"Gray," she said.

His eyebrows shifted like a sideways "S" and then flattened. His front knee flinched. He opened his arms and charged forward as she prepared to be scooped up into his arms. But something changed in him mid-stride.

"It's so good to see you," he said, plunking both his hands on her shoulders. She automatically tightened. He ran his thumb against her cheek and gave a hopeful smile. But his eyes didn't follow through. His eyes looked sadder than ever. "You must be starving. I made that stew you like. Beef this time." His hands slipped away. "Sit. I'll bring it to you."

And then he was gone. The air inside Belle's lungs went stagnant. Pots and pans clanged in the kitchen. Penny tapped her shoulder and said something about velvet shoes and a cobbler. Could she take Belle to Rapunzel's now? Was Beast ready to go?

Beast? The word sparked like a stick of phosphorus, dissipating the mental smoke and forcing the air to recirculate. She flew into the kitchen.

"Where's Beast?" She squeezed the counter. Gray looked up, one hand wrapped around a pasta bowl while the other fisted a ladle. Belle's started to flutter. "Rapunzel said you were taking him. Is he here? He usually greets me at the door. Or is he— Is he mad at me for leaving him? Did —"

"Deep breath," Gray instructed before heaping two large scoops into the bowl.

But Belle kept going. "Where is he? Did you tell him I was coming to get him today? He's always on alert. If he didn't hear my voice, he definitely would have heard the car door or the engine or —"

Gray's one-sided smirk made her want to fling the stew all over him—piping hot, right from the burner. She stomped forward. Their eyes caught. And there it was. In that moment. With his amusement over her mania, his refusal to diagnose the worst before it came to be, and his serenity neutralizing her rage. There was normalcy.

And then there was a bark.

She looked at Gray.

A second bark.

She about-faced and ran, as fast as her overtaxed legs would carry her. Out of the kitchen. Past the living room. Down the hall.

By the time her fingers hit the doorknob, the barking had been replaced by a slow, heart-wrenching whine. She laughed.

It sounded nothing like a baby's cry, but to Belle it had exactly the same effect. *Let me in*, it said. *Take care of me. Feed me. Love me.* She pulled back the door. *Let me jump all over you.*

Before she hit the floor, she saw a huge silver tail, two massive front paws, and a wide pink tongue that could have served twice as much stew as Gray's ladle. There was fresh dirt, hot breath, sharp nails, and the most exuberant greeting she'd ever received in her entire life.

Chapter Thirteen

RAPUNZEL

"Ethan is an amazing uncle, but he was born to be a father."

"No one marries the girl from down the street anymore."

"Uncle Ethan and Aunt Rapunzel."

From the moment she slipped out of her travel clothes to the minute she rolled off her mattress the next morning (right over an empty, Ethan-sized indentation), Elisa Wilkins' words played on a never-ending loop inside Rapunzel's head.

Her vision of the future had changed a lot since Ethan came back into her life. *She'd* changed a lot. But her opinion on marriage—that faithfulness should come from the heart rather than a legal contract or a diamond cuff—really hadn't. And children? Dear God. That idea only crossed her mind once every twenty-eight days. And by some stroke of divine luck, it never lingered.

"Just relax," Rapunzel told her reflection, all hazed up below a smiling decal reminding her to *Wash your hands, Flush the potty, Brush your teeth.* She considered finding a pen and adding *Shut the door,* a skill which Ethan's nephew had yet to grasp, but didn't want to be rude. So instead, she closed her eyes and tried to give herself a pep talk. "Take a deep breath," she said. "You're getting all worked up over nothing. This is what family does — they meddle. Ethan knows exactly who you are."

She nodded, a self-convincing nod, and then flipped her head over to tackle her sopping wet hair. The rubber duck wallpaper disappeared, replaced by her unmanicured toes (the one thing she couldn't fit in before leaving) and a picture of a rainbow in front of a waterfall. But no sooner did she begin toweling out the dampness than another voice piped up and asked the question she'd been trying to keep down. *Ethan might know who you are*, it said. *But what if you don't know who he is?*

Three sharp taps sounded at the door. "Rapunzel?"

She flung her head back up, splattering the wall with tiny darts of water and making her feel woozy. She grabbed the vanity and hovered over a glob of green toothpaste.

"Breakfast is ready when you are," Elisa called, her voice making Rapunzel feel pressured and inadequate all over again. "No rush. But I'd hate for you to leave here on an empty stomach."

"Okay," Rapunzel called back, her mouth filling with saliva. She shouldn't have flung her head around like that. She had low blood pressure. What was she thinking? "Be down in a few!"

She didn't move again until she heard Elisa clop away and thump down the stairs. Then she threw her hair up into a sopping wet bun and lunged for the toilet.

∂∾∾

"Smells delicious," Rapunzel lied as she ambled into the kitchen and darted straight for the coffee machine.

"Good morning!" five kids and Ethan sung from the table — the latter sporting an ear-to-ear grin and a lopsided chipmunk cheek stuffed with scrambled eggs.

Brandishing a spatula like a lasso, Elisa twirled around from the stovetop and plucked the mug right out of Rapunzel's hand. "And how are you this morning?" she asked, replacing her spoil with an already steeped cup of ginger tea.

Rapunzel stared at it for a second, grateful for the forethought but also a little disappointed. "Thanks," she said as her hostess winked and turned back to the stovetop. "I'm fine. Sorry for missing dinner though. I really didn't expect to sleep for fourteen hours." She surveyed the counters, unsure where she'd left her cell phone. She'd resisted the urge to call Belle earlier because of the time difference, but it was just about dinnertime there now. And with Donner out on bail, she needed to make sure her friend was okay.

"No worries," Elisa said, flipping an egg with gusto. "You must have been exhausted. A lot of people don't understand how draining it can be ... but I've been there." Elisa looked up and smiled. "Traveling, I mean."

"Yeah," Rapunzel replied, eying a tiny upper cabinet in the corner. It was probably hiding all the booze. "Hey, do you mind if I get your wireless password? The last bit of news I saw about Marestam was on the plane and—"

"Oh, we don't have Internet," Elisa said, giggling as if Rapunzel had just tried to brush her hair with a fork. "Nothing good there. But if it's news you're hankering for, you can always grab a paper on your way to the docks. Right, Ethan?"

Rapunzel sucked the side of her lip and turned toward the window. She was either learning how to cope or approaching a breaking point, because this was suddenly getting comical. No Internet access. No booze. Five kids and a relationship analysis from her boyfriend's only sibling. And now a newspaper? An actual, folding broadsheet made from tree pulp? Did the *Mirror* even sell those anymore? And did they export to Stularia?

"Sure can," Ethan sang, dunking a chunk of bagel into some hollandaise sauce and swirling it around his plate. "But we should head out soon. It's a half-hour drive and—"

"No!" the children shouted, instantly abandoning their plates and leaping on their uncle.

"Don't go!"

"What about the playground?"

"Don't you like us?"

"Can't you stay? You and Punzel can have my bunk bed. Pleeeeease!"

Only Camilla, who was strapped down with a five-point harness, remained seated. "Egg," she commanded, sliding her plastic plate towards Ethan and pointing to an empty corner.

He laughed and dutifully obeyed, selecting one egg and half a muffin and carving them into bite-size pieces. "How can I possibly refuse you?" he asked, flicking a glance up at Rapunzel, but swiftly lowering it when he saw that she was looking back. His lips fell too, from that wide-open smile to a tight, slim line.

"Here you go, sweetie. Now I have to help Aunt—to help Rapunzel find her phone. Be right back."

Only he wasn't right back. It took ninety minutes of scouring before they finally found her phone—stashed inside a saucepan in the pantry, along with Ethan's.

Elisa blamed it on Porter at first, but a quick interrogation exposed the true culprit as five-year-old Rebecca.

"Don't go," she pled through bright red eyes. Then she latched onto Ethan's leg as if she was a barnacle and he was disintegrating on the ocean floor. "Pleeeeease."

Rapunzel might have rolled her eyes at the embarrassing display, had it not been for the tiny little sniffling sounds coming from that pipsqueak of a creature. And her face taking on the same strawberry tint as her hair. And the watery rim in Ethan's eyes as he dropped to his knees and so engulfed her with his arms that she disappeared entirely.

Shit.

"Come back soon, okay," Elisa said, pulling Rapunzel close and then analyzing her at arm's length—as if confirming a purchase before swiping her credit card. "I mean it. You're welcome anytime."

"We will," Rapunzel said, hoping her eyes followed through. "Thanks for putting us up."

"Maybe you can return the favor sometime. Or, you know, just move here." She winked. "We offer compulsory playmates and unlimited free babysitting."

"Allllrighty," Ethan swooped in, curling his arm around Rapunzel's waist and pulling her hip against his. "If I keep looking at these adorable faces, I might never leave. Chin up, Becs. You'll see me in a couple months, remember? I promised you a sandcastle and I fully intend to honor that."

Rebecca beamed through her bloodshot eyes and looked straight at Rapunzel. "You too?"

"Umm." Rapunzel wavered. She didn't know what to say. She didn't want to disappoint the seven sets of eyes boring into her but—

"What? I'm not enough for you now?" Ethan joked, bending down again and wiping Rebecca's cheek.

After a few more tears, another round of hugs, and a one-two tap on the rental car horn, Rapunzel and Ethan were back on the road, en route to find Grethel.

"So what time is the ferry?" she asked as the neighborhoods transitioned to highway and the boisterousness of the Wilkins' house disappeared. She fumbled for a charging cable and jammed the adaptor into her dead phone.

"The ferry's whenever we get there," Ethan replied, his tone sending a chill down Rapunzel's back.

She shot him a look of surprise. "Are you mad at me?" He said nothing but repositioned his hands on the steering wheel. "Look. I'm sorry I wasn't thrilled about meeting your family. I just wasn't ready for that yet and—"

"No, that's not what I meant. There *is* no time for the ferry. We have to ask around to see if someone will drop us off on

Blood Island. It's not a typical route. No one goes there." He shook his head and squeezed the bridge of his nose.

Rapunzel could tell he wanted to say something else, but was holding back.

She stared out the window, noticing for the first time the orange clay along the roadside, the brightly colored beach huts in the distance, and the strange, bulbous baobab trees that resembled giant wine bottles covered in bark. It was a beautiful landscape. If only she felt as beautiful in it.

"Okay," she said, ignoring the fact that Ethan never told her Grethel's island was uninhabited — or that it was called *Blood.* "But I really am sorry about how I acted on the plane, and if it took me a little bit to warm up to them." She waited for forgiveness, but none came. "I wasn't feeling great though and … well anyway, your family seems great." She was struggling. "I'm glad it all worked out in the end."

She flinched as Ethan let out a tight, staccato laugh.

"What?" she shot back.

He shook his head. "Sorry, but I wouldn't call pouting at the table for half an hour and then going to bed 'working out in the end.' You hardly gave them a chance."

Rapunzel's entire body pulsated. "Is this because I didn't promise Camilla we'd build sandcastles in December? I thought she was joking. I mean — "

"That was Rebecca. Camilla's the baby," he said, merging seamlessly into a rotary and just as seamlessly pulling off. "And December is summer in Stularia — not that it should matter. She's a little girl. You could have just said yes."

"Well how was I supposed to know summer is — "

"And you didn't take a 'little bit' to warm up to them. You didn't warm up period. You didn't even try." He brushed his palm against his cheek, calling attention to the gash that still remained from his encounter with Grethel almost twenty years ago. "You took one look at the kids and tightened up like a snake around a kangaroo. Which frankly, considering how much you seem to adore Belle's son, I just don't know how to take. Is it just my family that sickens you or—"

"They don't sicken me!"

Ethan started to reply, but clapped his jaw shut and focused on the road again.

Rapunzel followed suit, unable to say anything else because she didn't believe he was wrong but didn't know how to explain her feelings, either. Something about seeing his family had sent her into fight or flight mode—and she'd chosen the latter.

They spent the rest of the drive in silence—save for the beep of the horn, the clacking of the turn signal, and the grunts of frustration caused by a complete lack of service on her phone, which only caused her anger to deepen. What if Belle needed her? What if Donner had escaped his babysitters and went after her? What if he'd relapsed into full beast-mode, gone on a rampage through Capitol Park, and set Braddax Castle on fire? Or what if Ruby had discovered another way to break the curse and didn't need Grethel after all?

"Here we are," Ethan announced, grimly, as the car knocked to a halt and he stomped down on the emergency brake.

Rapunzel looked around, expecting to see cruise ships and tourist shops and hordes of passengers carting around giant suitcases. Instead, she saw dirty old trawlers, heaps of empty fishing nets, and a dozen scruffy looking men dressed in tank tops and rubber overalls.

"Market's over there," she heard Ethan say in a tone that made her feel like a schoolgirl—but not in the sexy way. "You get your newspaper and I'll find out who's going near Blood Island."

There it was again: Blood Island. But before she could ask for clarification, he was out the door and waving to a group of men as if they were old college roommates.

The "market" (simply dubbed *Whatcha Need* by a spray-painted piece of plywood), was a dilapidated shack with three squat aisles, a case of rotating hot dogs, some sort of slush drink machine, and a teenage boy with a toothpick in his mouth, mud-crusted boots on the counter, and an actual tube television set. Had she stepped back in time?

"Hi," she croaked, pasting on a smile. "I'm looking for a newspaper."

The boy raised a hand and pointed towards a rack on the other side of the store.

"Thanks," she said, feeling more than a little slighted. He could have at least looked up.

She flipped through the newspaper rack like a child searching for a rookie broomball card. *Early Morning Enquirer, Stularian Journal, Wallabie Gazette.* Nope, no *Marestam Mirror.*

"Excuse me?" she called, as a toilet flushed behind a crooked bathroom door. Taking the clerk's head bob as an act of acknowledgment, she continued. "Do you carry any newspaper from the United Kingdoms of Marestam? The *Mirror* perhaps or even the *Post*? I'm visiting from there and — "

"Marestam? You're in Stularia," he said, scraping his boots together. Rapunzel cringed as globs of mud fell onto the counter.

"Well, I know that but — "

"We carry Stularian papers."

Rapunzel stared back at him in complete disbelief. "Okay. Then can you tell me if any of these papers cover international news?"

No answer. She stomped forward, ready to go all old-timer on this delinquent and give him a piece of her mind. To pluck that damn toothpick out of his mouth and slash the coin-sized holes dangling from his ears. To find out just what was so damn important about that boob tube that he couldn't even look a customer in the eye and —

Then she saw it, the same channel she'd been unable to avoid on the plane. Only this time, the headlines were different: *King of Braddax jumps bail. Manhunt underway. Royal jet missing.* She was so consumed with fear and guilt that she barely heard the bathroom door shut behind her, or the heavy footsteps lumbering down her aisle.

"Maybe I can help," said a man's voice. She looked down to see a tall and extremely broad shadow at her side. "I just came from Marestam."

"Oh, thank goodness," she said, preparing to bombard this stranger with questions. But as soon as she began to turn, the shadow came into focus and she lost all ability to breathe.

"Beautiful morning," said Donner, cupping a black-banded coffee cup in his gigantic hands. "And beautiful bracelet, while we're at it. How've you been?"

The Marestam Mirror

Diamond Ropes and Velvet Cake
By Perrin Hildebrand, King of Gossip

BREAKING NEWS!

Lock up your daughters, folks! Don't let small pets outside! Donner Wickenham has given Marestam's Finest the slip!

According to Guard Chief Toby Kind, officers entered Braddax Castle at eight a.m. this morning when the king failed to check in at his appointed time. But instead of a surly detainee, they discovered a perfectly intact ankle bracelet (a message from mommy dearest?) and a missing sports car. Further investigation revealed that the royal jet was also missing from a rented airplane hangar a few miles down the road.

"Right now, we cannot ascertain whether the king has fled Marestam entirely or is hiding somewhere within our borders," Chief Kind told a clamoring press this morning. "Needless to say, we have every department in both our and surrounding realms working on tracking him down, and we will be activating several of the MSC-backed surveillance measures that Parliament passed on Monday. We understand that some of these might cause minor inconvenience, but appreciate the public's trust that everything we do, we do for their own protection. Residents are also being asked to exercise extreme caution outside their homes, and to report any suspicious activity to the Marestam Guard. Rest assured, we will track down this threat and any accomplices together."

Chapter Fourteen

BELLE

Moments earlier, Belle was sitting outside on a checkered blanket, scooping up mashed strawberries with a baby spoon while Beast ransacked a field of wildflowers in pursuit of a hurled stick. In the cloudless sky, the sun hung bright and warm above them. The branches swayed overhead. The corner of Rye's periwinkle blanket fell across her left knee. And while she couldn't quite make out who had thrown the stick, Belle knew it was someone she cared for. She knew because she could feel it: Sublime peace. Warmth. A comfort and a happiness unlike she'd ever encountered before. A feeling that this was where she truly belonged.

Then the camera inside her dreams panned left, and the child beside her came into focus. Blue eyes. Brown hair. A chain of dandelions wrapped around his chubby toddler hands.

"For Mama," he said, holding the necklace out proudly.

Belle felt something melt inside of her. "Oh, thank you so much, sweetheart." She placed the strawberries in her lap and reached out carefully. She didn't want to lose a single petal. "What a wonderful—"

"No," Rye said, pulling the necklace away as soon as she

touched it. He held it against his chest and looked around. "For Mama. Where Mama?"

The pain hit on both sides of Belle's heart. She opened her mouth to ask what he meant by that. *She* was his mother. *She* was Mama.

"There Mama!" Rye squealed, lighting up and pointing to another figure sitting down to join them. Snow.

Belle felt something wrap around her heart and squeeze. Dream Snow pulled the dandelions over her head as Belle glanced down. Something wasn't right. Suddenly, the strawberries in her lap multiplied by the thousands and gushed like blood all over her dress. When she looked up again, the toddler with the dandelions was gone. Instead, there was a teenager. A brown-haired, blue-eyed teenager with dots of acne across both cheeks. One blink later: a young man with a block jaw and stubble.

Belle brought both hands up to her eyes and shook her head. The whole world began to swirl and shake in front of her. She heard someone in the distance shout her name, just as her chest erupted in fire and her eyelids ripped apart.

"Belle? Belle, wake up! Are you okay?"

The voice belonged to Gray, who was standing directly over her. His hand was clamped around both her arms, as if he was trying to pull her back from something that refused to let her go.

"Belle," he said again. But he still sounded miles away. The pain was drowning it out. Then his palm flattened against her cheek, siphoning away just enough to yank the world into focus.

Beast was at full attention beside her, frantically licking his mouth with eyes wide as saucers. She murmured something inaudible. A momentary flash of relief cracked across Gray's face and he leaned closer. "You were crying in your sleep," he said. "And you're hotter than a bonfire in August."

Belle pushed herself up on her elbows. Her shirt—the same one she'd left the hospital wearing yesterday—was soaking wet.

She was shivering, despite Gray's diagnosis, and her chest felt like it was being crushed into a cube at an impound lot.

She flung the covers aside and raced to the bathroom. Beast sprinted after her, chasing the invisible assailant, but she shut him out with the door.

"No," she said, fumbling with her buttons and hoping she was imagining the excruciating pain and the rock-hard boulders that were hanging off her chest. "No no no no no."

How long had it been since she emptied? She remembered Beast arriving. Penny leaving. The stew. She'd passed on the wine because she'd intended to breastfeed as soon as she heard from Snow. She remembered waiting, and waiting, and waiting for the call, which seemed to take forever. She and Gray had passed the awkward hour like teenage lovers one year after their summer fling. All the pieces looked the same, but on the whole, there was something different between them–and neither one knew how to respond to it. She remembered him testing the waters with small talk that only tapped each big topic once, the way a zoo animal might test its cage for weaknesses–one quick tap and if it didn't give, on to another section.

The ring was already in her fist when Snow finally called, blaming traffic for the delay. "Then Rye woke up as soon as we got on the ferry," she'd said, "so I had to feed him a bottle. I'm sorry. I know you wanted to feed him yourself, but I couldn't bear making him wait all that time. Thank goodness he dozed off right after, but he's still sleeping now. No problems with the room or the crib or anything. The poor thing must be exhausted. He doesn't know what's going on, but I think he knows it's something big."

Something big. Belle couldn't help but picture Snow wearing an ear-to-ear smile as she said this. Nor could she help but scowl as she heard it. They both assumed he'd be up within the hour to eat again, and Snow promised to call her as soon as that happened.

Belle remembered feeling disappointed and a little woozy. She hadn't been able to kiss Rye goodnight. She hadn't gotten her evening cuddles. She'd felt empty, inadequate, alone. She recalled shooting Gray a weak smile and then folding herself into a ball on the armchair. But then Beast had pattered over and tried to unfold her, shoving her limbs aside with his snout until finally giving up and resting it on her thigh.

"You've still got one baby here," Gray had said with a laugh, before standing up and declaring that she was in no condition to be alone. "Penthouse or cabin. You can have the bedroom while I take the couch. You decide, but I'm not leaving you."

She'd argued for a few minutes — partly in fear that Hazel would find out and partly distressed by his assumption that she'd want them in separate rooms — then gave in. "Cabin. Beast will be happier," she'd said, neither denying nor declaring that she would be as well.

She should have pumped a little before climbing into bed, but Rye was supposed to be up any minute and she didn't want to scam him. She could take a little bit of pain, she remembered thinking seconds before her head hit the pillow.

Only it wasn't just a little bit of pain, she now realized, huddled in front of the bathroom mirror. Her boobs were the papier-mâché balloons she used to make as a kid — soft on the inside, hard as plaster on the outside, and ready to pop any second. She slung her sleeve back to look at her watch. Six o'clock. She'd gone more than fifteen hours without either nursing or pumping. Why hadn't Snow called?

"Belle?" Gray said through the door. "What's wrong? Beast is worried sick out here." On cue, she heard his big wet nose smacking the doorknob. "Can I help?"

Were it not for the pain, she might have found the whole situation quite amusing. Here she was, holed up in her wannabe lover's bathroom, cradling her breasts like they were newborn puppies, while her dog tried to break down the door because he thought she was being attacked—just like he thought the mailman was really a covert assassin who occasionally delivered treats.

"Can you get my bag, please?" she pled between clenched teeth. "And my phone?" Then she leaned into the sink and tried to remember what her books said about manual expression. Pinch then out? Pinch then in? In, pinch, out?

Her lids came together as she tried to concentrate. In, pinch, out. In, pinch out. In, pinch—

"Woops!" she heard. Her eyes shot open as her purse dropped onto the bathroom floor and the door slammed shut behind it. She yanked her shirt closed and caught the thin, vertical glow of the living room just before it disappeared.

"Gray!" she shrieked, absolutely mortified.

"Sorry! So sorry," he repeated, at least five times, through the wooden door that suddenly seemed paper-thin.

"I'm fine. I'll be fine. I just have to call Snow and probably Doctor—"

She jumped as her phone started singing and Snow's face popped up.

"Belle?" Snow's voice sounded ridiculously calm—sleepy even.

"What happened? Is everything okay? I just woke up. Did I miss your call? Is Rye all—"

"I can't believe it, but he slept through the night. I guess the Tantalise woods are more peaceful than a bustling, mid-town hospital." Belle tore a hand towel off the bar and twisted it into a ball. "Anyway, the little guy sure is hungry so you should hurry up and—"

"Two seconds!" she hollered, hanging up before she was even finished speaking. "Be right there!"

Moving as if she had a rocket strapped to her back, Belle shoved her buttons back together, high-stepped out of the bathroom, grabbed the hideous chunk of metal that would take her to her baby, and jumped back into bed. Then she slammed the ring onto her finger, spun the diamond inward, squeezed her pillow as if it was Angus Kane's neck, and closed her eyes.

Then she waited. After a few minutes, she stopped hearing Beast's nails rapping against the floorboards. She thought the air felt different. She thought she heard a cry. In one fluid motion, she opened her eyes, flung the covers back, and threw her feet over the side of the bed. But rather than landing on Snow's eco-friendly cork flooring, her heels hit polished red oak. Rather than seeing Snow's wicker loveseat and the towering aloe plant in the corner, she saw Gray, jaw half-open, and Beast, sitting nobly beside him with his head cocked almost parallel to the floor.

She must have done it wrong.

Without a word, she closed her eyes again, squeezed the ring, and pictured Rye—his bright blue eyes, his dark fuzzy head, his tiny fist jammed into his mouth.

Nothing.

She cursed and catapulted the pillow across the room—an action that caused her ring hand to ricochet across her chest, slashing her inflamed nipple. She wailed and doubled over. Her boobs were on fire. Her baby needed food. And this damned, stupid, magical booty call ring wasn't doing its job. Why wasn't it doing its job?

"What's wrong with this thing?" she screamed, wanting to fall to pieces but knowing she didn't have that luxury. Gray twitched, unsure whether to answer or pretend he wasn't there. Beast had already fled into the kitchen. "You found both rings, right? And Snow has the second?"

Gray nodded and said Griffin had picked it up earlier that day.

"Then why won't it work?" she begged, dropping onto the edge of the bed and letting the floodgates open. "I have to take care of my son. Why can't one thing in my life work?"

Slowly, Gray tiptoed forward, lowered himself beside her,

and wrapped her in his arms.

Maybe she was doing it wrong. Maybe she needed to actually fall asleep for the magic to take hold—though that would be a pretty stupid waste of a charm. Maybe the universe just didn't want her to be happy. Maybe she was doomed to turn out like her mother no matter what she felt inside. Maybe *she* was the one who was cursed, not Donner.

"Maybe the universe is trying to tell you something," Gray said, reading her mind.

"Yeah," she said, laughing through her tears. "I think it is. I think it's showing me a huge middle finger and trying to tell me f—"

"No," Gray said, pulling her tighter but hiding a smirk. "Maybe it's trying to remind you that you're a person too."

Belle looked up. "What is that supposed to mean? Of course I'm a person."

"A person who needs to take care of herself too," he clarified. "You're making yourself responsible for the entire world, Belle. You keep choosing total misery rather than yourself."

"Yeah well, I'm only one person and—"

"And it's that thinking that makes people fall in love with you—that made me fall in love with you when I was convinced it was physically impossible." His hand landed on her knee. She stared at it. Something concrete in this big, confusing, magical mess.

"Now I know you want to take care of your baby, but you have to take care of yourself as well—inside and out. You can build a castle out of the strongest steel known to man if you want, but if the foundation's falling apart, it won't last a year. I wouldn't be surprised if that's why the ring isn't working. What was it Ruby told us in the hospital the other day? Magic has a mind of its own sometimes?"

"I just want to help him," Belle said, even though she knew he had a point. "I'm his mother. If there's one thing Rye's supposed to be able to count on right now, it's me. And I'm failing him."

"You are not." Gray's voice was gentle but firm. "You've given him more in four days than most mothers are asked to give in four years."

"Yea. I've given him a curse, a new mom, and a freakishly small nose. Go me."

"Hey," he said, drawing her face toward his by the chin. His eyes pulsated inside of hers as he emphasized every word. "Snow White is not his mother. She's a good friend, but she'll never be his mother and everyone who matters knows that. *He* knows that." Belle sniffled and gave two quick nods—more because she wanted him to stop than because she agreed with him. "And your nose is not small. It's perfect. Like a button."

She smiled. Only he could make her smile at a time like this—even if it was fleeting.

"Yeah, well, my button-nosed baby is probably crying his eyes out right now because he's starving," she said, rising to her feet and reaching for her phone.

"What are you doing?"

She took a deep, resolute breath. The words were going to hurt as much as her chest. "Telling Snow to feed him another bottle," she finally said. "I'm going to see Dr. Frolick and will be there as soon as my body allows me to be."

∂∘⟨

By the time the elevator hit the thirty-fifth floor, her chest was still on fire but everything else shivered beneath a down coat and one of Gray's fleece-lined flannels. He'd insisted on coming with her, but the last thing she needed was for Hazel to see them together in the newspaper and realize prison wasn't the only thing standing between Donner and that big happy family.

"Belle!" she heard the moment her shoes hit the tile. She clenched instinctively and swung around, expecting to see a flood of reporters rushing towards her, pens hoisted like lances in some medieval joust. Instead, she saw a few orderlies, a man swimming in a cloud of Mylar balloons, and Kirsten.

"Belle," she called again, clopping towards her with a little boy and another woman in her wake. She was wearing tan sneakers and an open trench coat over her periwinkle scrubs. "What in the world are you doing back here so soon?" she asked as the groups converged. "Don't tell me you missed the salmon cakes and lime gelatin. Why aren't you cuddling up with that li—" She raised her eyebrows and caught herself. "—with that pregnancy book you were trying to finish? Is everything okay?"

Belle gave a flustered smile and eyed the other woman, who was struggling to keep hold of her son's hand.

"Oh, where are my manners?" Kirsten finally said, tugging on her companion's elbow. "Belle, this is my sister, Kim, and my nephew, Jasper."

The woman gave her a distracted wave, then did a double take and shot straight as a flagpole. "Your Majesty," she said, prompting a speedy correction from Belle. She was nobody's majesty anymore, nor did she want to be.

"We were just headed to lunch," said Kirsten. "If you like tuna melts, there's a diner three blocks over that makes the best on the planet. You're welcome to join us ... if you're free."

Belle started to decline but was cut off when a woman sped between them and almost sideswiped the little boy. "Whoops, sorry!" she called back, hardly slowing down.

Kirsten frowned, then ushered the group away from the elevator. When they stopped, a few feet from a display stand filled with public service brochures and hospital schedules, Kim was still staring.

Belle pulled her coat a little tighter. "Oh, no. I'm fine. I just..."

Kirsten's eyebrows moved in opposite directions. She just what? Needed a medical plumber because she'd neglected to breastfeed the infant that's still supposed to be in her belly?

Couldn't survive even twelve hours as a mother without hired help? She brushed her hand out to indicate it was nothing. "I just thought I might have left a piece of jewelry here, that's all. But—"

"Oh no," cooed Kim, one hand on each of the boy's shoulders. Belle looked at her for what seemed like the first time. She was small and pretty, with long brown hair, a swirly tattoo on her wrist, and the sort of face that seems instantly familiar. "We can help you look. We don't have reservations or anything, and I'm a big—well, I don't know if fan is the right word but—supporter of yours. What does it look like?"

Belle rubbed her hands together while trying to send a telepathic S.O.S. to her former nurse. Then she realized she was rubbing Donner's ring. She propelled her left hand forward and laughed. "No, it was this. Sorry. I thought I'd lost it, but I actually found it stuffed between the seats on the ride over. Go figure." She rolled her eyes and pointed to her right temple. "You know what they say about pregnancy brain. But while I'm here I figured I'd say hello to everyone." She laughed again, but this time the reverberations traveled straight to her chest. Instead of cringing, she channeled the pain into a ridiculous, ear-to-ear smile.

"Oh, then you should definitely join us," Kirsten said.

"Yes, you should," Kim echoed. But her voice was suddenly cooler. And her eyes were glued, uncomfortably, on Belle's hand.

"Actually," Belle said, spreading both hands over her exaggerated belly, "I really should see Dr. Frolick while I'm—"

"That's an interesting ring," Kim interrupted. "Do you mind if I ask where it came from?"

Belle's head automatically listed to one side. "It's ... It's my wedding ring."

"Really?" Kim said as her son slipped away and started plucking health pamphlets from the display case. He looked to be about six years old—or early grade school, anyway—and had bright blue eyes just like Rye. He could have been Rye in a few years, really—or a few months if they didn't break the curse soon. Maybe that's why he'd already slept through the night. "Sorry, I'm just interested because I used to have one exactly like it."

Belle's throat caught. Kirsten's sister had one of Donner's booty call rings? She felt sick all over again.

"Well, I shouldn't say *I* had one, exactly," Kim continued, glancing at Jasper as he picked up a brochure about the dangers of UV radiation. Poor kid. He had no idea his mother was a home wrecker. "It belonged to my sister."

"*Our* sister," corrected Kirsten, who seemed instantly—almost guiltily—obsessed with her sneakers.

Kim nodded and looked away to watch her son again. Her hair parted a bit to reveal a second tattoo, this one with on the back of her neck—three circles. No, three stars.

"Anyway," Kim said, coming suddenly back to life. "Her ring disappeared a few months ago. It sounds crazy, but I think someone stole it from my house." Kirsten made a protesting noise but Kim waved her off. "I'm telling you. I never leave my bedroom windows open. There are no screens and I only have one air conditioning unit. But a few days before I realized it was missing, I came home to an open window. The bush underneath looked a little tousled too."

"I'm still convinced you just haven't looked hard enough."

Kim narrowed her eyes. "No, it's gone," she said, her voice straining a little. "I never wore it anywhere."

Belle shook her head. She was two minutes late for her appointment and needed medical attention stat. But something told her she needed to stay—something more than morbid curiosity. Perhaps it was the sudden pain in Kim's eyes. Perhaps it was the fierce anger in Kirsten's. Perhaps it was the way they both seemed to sink into the little boy collecting tri-fold glossy treasures a few feet away. Either way, she was in no way prepared for the tears that would flow from her next, seemingly simple question to Kim: "How old is your son?"

He was almost seven, they said, but he wasn't her son. Kim was raising him but Jasper was their nephew, born to their other sister shortly before her husband strangled her to death and stashed her body in the attic—along with his previous two wives.

Belle's chill turned into frostbite as she began to connect the dots. Everyone had heard of Blue Beardsley, the serial killing husband who'd murdered his first three wives and faked their disappearance. It was the trial of the century just before Belle met Donner, back when she was living as her sisters' punching bag in that tiny little cottage. Sometimes Julianne would whisper the details of the murders to Belle as she fell asleep—so that she couldn't find peace even in her dreams.

Then Belle remembered something else—something about her first night at the hospital, calling Kirsten by the wrong name. *I had a sister named Karen*, she'd said, *but not anymore.*

Karen Epson, yes, that was the name of his third wife.

Belle blurted a million apologies without thinking. Then she brought a hand to her mouth and panned from Kirsten to Kim, whom she now recognized as Kimberly Epson, the woman who'd planned Cinderella's thirtieth birthday gala and offered to help restore the Phoenix. "I didn't realize." She looked at Kirsten. "I didn't know your last name."

Kirsten pressed her lips into a sad, closed smile. "Don't worry about it. It's not something I like to advertise."

Belle nodded forcefully. "Of course. I'm sorry."

"For what?"

"For dredging up something like that. I didn't mean to—"

Kirsten's hand landed on Belle's shoulder, just as Jasper came bounding back into their circle, holding a jumble of brochures with both hands. "It's not like we don't think about her every day," she said, softly. "But she's still here, in that amazing little man there."

Belle nodded. It was a beautiful thought. But "that amazing little man there" was also the product of the psychopath who'd murdered their sister. She wondered if they ever saw parts of him in Jasper, too. Either way, these women were living saints. She opened her mouth to say as much, but decided against it.

"I'm hungry," the boy called out, pulling on his aunt's sleeve. "Can we get lunch now?"

Kirsten smiled and looked at Belle. "I'm telling you, best tuna melts ever. Our treat."

"Can I take a rain check?" Belle asked, still a little shaken by their revelation—and a little ashamed. She'd been so obsessed with her misfortunes that she'd failed to see her blessings. Her pain, both emotional and physical, was nothing compared to theirs. She could still hold Rye, even if it took her a little longer to reach him. Suddenly, she no longer saw her problems in a vacuum. Suddenly, her problems were manageable.

She leaned over and put both hands on her knees, wincing through the pain. Jasper gave a shy smile and hid halfway behind Kim's leg. Then he peeked out, brought his right hand up to his forehead and started twisting his eyebrows—first the hair, then the skin. It was a nervous tic that she'd seen before, though she couldn't remember where.

"What have you got there?" she asked, pointing at his fistful of pamphlets. "Do you have something to keep them in? I'd hate for you to lose your treasures all over the streets of Carpale."

He inched out a little further and looked up at her with those huge blue eyes. Belle wondered if they came from his father. She smiled and fished a zip-up diaper pouch from her purse. The diapers slid right out, without Kim noticing.

"This looks like just the right size. And look, it's brown, just like a real treasure chest."

"Wow," the boy exclaimed, venturing all the way out from

behind his guardian. Belle held it open for him as he stuffed it full of brochures. Then she helped him zip it up. "Wow," he said again, tracing the neon green stars.

"Now what do you say when someone gives you something nice?" Kim said, laying a hand on his shoulder.

Jasper looked straight at Belle again. "Thank you."

Belle opened her mouth to say it was nothing. But before she could, he launched forward, arms wide, and wrapped his arms around her like an octopus bringing in its prey. It was too much weight for her, in her hunched over position, and the both of them went down instantly.

Kim screamed. Jasper laughed. Kirsten raced around and hoisted Belle back up by the shoulders.

"Oh my gosh are you okay?" Kim asked, her eyes wide and her hands shaking. "I'm so sorry. He's been acting very strange lately. Sorry, not strange. Energetic. Intense. Must be a growth spurt or something. Jasper, you can't just go jumping on people like that! Especially pregnant ladies! Kirsten, is she okay or should we get a doctor?"

"A doctor?" Belle repeated, wiping the tears from her face. "No, no, I'm fine. These are tears of laughter," she lied.

"But what about the baby?"

Belle stopped wiping and dusted herself off. "Oh, I do worse than that to myself all the time. Don't worry." Kim's mouth slanted a bit. "But I'm going to see Dr. Frolick anyway, so I'll see what he thinks. No worries, little man. Never apologize for a hug; you never know how badly someone needs one. Now you enjoy that tuna melt."

A few moments later, Belle was standing outside a bright yellow door with a pink frosted window. She'd been there a hundred times. But there was something a little surreal about today. It was as if she could see, or feel, the hundreds of previous iterations of herself in this exact same spot. Years of trying to have a baby. Years of that emotional roller coaster. Sometimes she'd come in brimming with hope, spouting off lists of symptoms and signs and "feelings" that it worked this time and she was pregnant. Other times she'd arrived wearing the colorless face of death, pummeled into devastation and convinced that her body was a wasteland. She'd never have a baby. Nothing would work. She didn't have the emotional strength to keep on fooling herself.

But today, she stood there as a mother. There was a second little version of her ten miles away on Tantalise. Yes, her situation was still far from ideal, but maybe there was no such thing as ideal. At least they were both alive. At least she could be there for her son, even if no one else knew who she really was for a while. At least her wish had finally come true, even if it did come with a few unfortunate conditions. As a grown woman, she should know that they always did.

Chapter Fifteen

RAPUNZEL

Rapunzel hesitated as she stepped onto the ferry, ten steps behind Ethan and a few uncomfortable inches from Donner Wickenham. She opened and closed her fist along the peeling rail, but her left foot didn't want to follow the other onto the slimy, filthy fishing vessel that stank of guts and seaweed.

"What's the holdup?" Donner asked, blocking her escape like a cinderblock wall. "Foot stuck to the dock? It's no yacht, but the sooner you hop on, the sooner you can get off." He paused, giving his double entendre time to sink in. "I'm sure you're familiar with that idea."

She whipped around and leered at him. If the stuff churning around in her stomach decided to head north, she knew exactly where to aim. "Look," she snapped, still unsure why he was here. "I don't know what your sociopath mother told you, but Ethan and I are perfectly capable of finding Grethel on our own. So why don't you just fly your little jet back to Marestam, go back to your castle, and enjoy your undeserved luxury while everyone else does the work for you? I'm sure you're familiar with *that* idea."

Donner's smug smirk doubled in size at the vitriolic wordplay. "I think you're forgetting I'm a fugitive now." His eyebrows lifted a half-inch, as if asking whether that sort of danger turned her on.

"Ugh. Just tell them you had too much to drink and accidentally activated the autopilot or something. Maybe they'll cut you a break." His smile grew even larger. "Or give mommy dearest a call during her sober hours. I'm sure she'd have no problem twisting Belle's arm again and painting you a halo."

Donner's eyes shifted to the side as his smile descended. "What's that supposed to mean?"

Rapunzel grunted in disgust, pushed herself off the railing, and stomped onto the boat. Ethan was standing in the cockpit talking to the captain, while three men in rubber overalls shared a parting smoke on the bow. One had holes in his earlobes wide enough to see through, one had a beard braided down to his chest, and one looked like he should have retired decades ago. The first two nodded towards her, then towards each other, then flashed her the creepiest smile she'd seen in weeks.

She scurried over to Ethan and latched onto his arm. "Do you think he knows how to swim?" she asked, gesturing toward Donner. "Or should we tie an anchor to his waist when we toss him overboard?"

The corner of the captain's mouth rose, but Ethan gave her nothing. How had *she* become the one pining for forgiveness?

"How far away is the island?" she asked, louder.

Ethan's arm jerked a bit between hers. "About an hour. Right, Captain?" he said, not even answering her question directly.

The captain, who looked like he was still in high school, squinted toward the increasingly cloudy sky. "Just about," he said. "As a bird flies, your island's 'round sixty-five minutes due east."

"Think you can handle that?" Ethan asked, patting her on the head but removing his arm in order to do so.

"Yeup," the captain continued. "But thanks to the delay—we've been having spots of engine trouble here'n there—our schedule's sayin' to head northeast first and then swing 'round.

Don't you worry though. We'll want to hit the best fishing waters afore deadlight." He looked directly at Rapunzel. "That's early evening feeding—just afore twilight, when all the fish come out'n we try to snag 'em afore the sharks and other sea creatures. So we'll have you folks on that island right around fourteen hundred hours." He turned to spit on the floor. "Oh, and afore I forget, the life jackets are under a hatch on the starboard side over there. That is, assuming ya'll don't change your minds first."

He winked at Rapunzel and then leaned in. She doubted he'd showered in days, but plugged her nose and tilted closer anyway.

"Like I told your boyfriend here, they don't call it Blood Island for nothin'. Some say it's cursed. Some say it's booby-trapped. Some say there's..." He shook his head and gave a condescending chuckle. "Well, there are lots of strange ideas about it. No refunds a'course, but I feel it's my duty as an honorable Stularian seaman to let you know. Now, you're welcome to stay above deck so long as you ain't in the way, but there's a table downstairs with some cards and a bathroom for the lady. If you need help with the flusher, I'll be right here" — he paused to wink and run his hands over the wooden steering wheel—"manning my giant helm."

Rapunzel stood there for another minute, jaw slightly agape. Then Ethan moved in front of her—actually looking into her eyes this time—and assured her that there was nothing to worry about. "This boat may not be pretty," he said, "but it's sturdy. We're not going to capsize in any shark-infested waters. And all those strange stories he's talking about are just Grethel trying to keep people away. You know that, right?"

Rapunzel did know that. She couldn't care less about Captain Creepo and his fear-mongering superstitions. Her fear came from something much more real—and far more disturbing. She panned slowly around, looking at the men with the rubber overalls ... at Donner, lurking in the middle of the boat with his *Whatcha Need* coffee and no handcuffs ... at the tiny hole in the floor that led to a tiny table and a toilet that might not flush and probably hadn't been cleaned in years.

"Am I miscalculating," she asked, "or did he just say we're going to be on this boat for the next four hours?"

This time, Ethan laughed. His chiseled face angled to the side and his eyes — a million compacted flecks of green and brown — sparkled against the white clouds above. If she'd meant to be funny, she might have latched onto this as an offer of peace. But she hadn't. And seconds later, when the boat motored up and the stagnant air turned into a slightly less putrid breeze, the opportunity for reconciliation sailed away on it. Ethan soon followed.

She cracked her back in frustration.

"So that's the man who tamed the wild Rapunzel." Rapunzel scowled at the sound of Donner's voice directly behind her.

"Look," she growled, almost poking his eye out with her fingernail. "If we're actually doing this, I don't want you talking to me unless I ask you a question. Got it?"

He raised both hands in mock surrender. "Whatever you say, boss. Though from what I just saw, if you aren't talking to me, you're not going to be talking to anyone for the next four hours." Their eyes remained locked as Donner raised his cup and took a long, drawn-out sip of his coffee. "Just to be clear, that was a question, right?"

Rapunzel's teeth slammed together. Donner tossed his cup into a mound of garbage and crossed his arms — black sleeves rolled up to the elbows and a giant watch with red flecks instead of numerals. He leaned against the exterior of the cockpit, bent one foot behind him, and swooped a few inches toward her. His wild black waves smelled like a Fifth Avenue salon, but his stubble said he hadn't shaved in days. Amid all the darkness — his hair, his clothes, his eyes — that bright white smile almost made him look like a decent human being. Had he been a complete stranger and had she been pre-Ethan, all of this sparring might have ended below deck, with the two of them out-rocking the ocean.

"Come on," he pled, slipping on the second syllable. "Give me a chance. It's going to be a long ride, and I think both of us could use some company."

Rapunzel wanted to punch him in that square, chiseled jaw of his. How dare he talk to her as if they were friends? How dare he try to catch her off guard with some fake desperation in his voice and that phony sadness in his eyes? Looking at him now, it was no wonder Belle stuck with him after his monster hair molted. It wasn't fair for the devil to have so much sex appeal. He should have had boils on his face, no hair, and five extra layers of fat instead of muscle. Suddenly, his first curse made perfect sense.

"Look, I'm not asking for us to be besties," he said. She pressed her eyes into slits and glared out at him. "Just, you know, pull back a bit on the hatred."

"Hatred?" Rapunzel crossed her arms with such force, she nearly lost her breath. "Hatred doesn't even begin to cover it. You burned down my inn and almost murdered my best friend. Try loathe, or detest, or—"

"I thought Cinderella was your best friend."

Her jaw dropped mid-sentence and hung there. Was she even supposed to respond to that? "Not that it's any of your business, but I can have two best friends. Just like you can try to have two wives."

"Hey, I might not have been an ideal husband in the end," he said, "but I still know Belle better than any of you."

"Now that's the exaggeration of the centur—"

"She always felt like the outsider of your little group. She thought Dawn and Snow were aloof, and the rest of you treated her like a child."

Rapunzel shuffled uncomfortably in place. "Yeah, well. She *was* a child until she grew a pair and got rid of you. Now she's a butterfly — a kickass one. You were the cocoon she was suffocating in for the past five years."

Donner parted his lips and froze, as if letting the jab fully sink in and dissipate. Then he dropped back a bit and looked her straight in the eye. "You have no idea how sorry I am for the way I treated her," he said. "But even *you* have to know I'd never hurt her."

"Ha!"

"I'd never *physically* hurt her if I had any control over my actions. You know about my curse. I couldn't contain it that night, and it nearly cost me everything. But I'm not here for myself. I'm here because I don't want our kid paying for my mistakes. You have to believe that. Belle respects your opinion more than anyone's now."

Rapunzel felt her hostility soften a bit, but continued to glare. She was gearing up to rip into him further when something he'd said came back and tripped her up: *I don't want our kid paying for my mistakes.* Did he know about Rye or was this a trick? She shuffled uncomfortably in place. "Who told you about—" She stopped and bit her lip. He could have been talking figuratively. Neither he nor Hazel were supposed to know about Rye. "What do you mean you don't want your kid paying for your mistakes?"

Donner stared at her for a few seconds. Then he looked at the sky, let out a long, deep breath, and finally settled his gaze on the moldy, splintering deck. When he finally spoke, it was in a raspy, disbelieving whisper. "So, she was telling the truth."

"Who?" Rapunzel blurted, instantly afraid she'd said too much. "What do you mean?"

Donner shook his head. "Some reporter. Matilda Hart — or Holt. She grabbed me before the arraignment to get a comment about my curse coming back and spreading to my unborn child."

He swayed to the side a bit, then regained his balance. Rapunzel gave a tiny smile of relief over the word *unborn*. At least that part was still a secret. "What?" Donner barked, his huge, black eyes growing red. "How is that possibly amusing?"

"It's not," she said, gazing into the distance. The harbor was just a speck on the horizon now. The captain was propped up behind the helm. The crew was scattered around the deck, and Ethan was with Pippi Longbeard in the very back, winding a rope around a peg. She watched him for a good twenty seconds, but he never looked her way. "It's not," she said again. "I'm sorry. It's just..." She trailed off and tried to shake her senses back. "It's okay because we're going to fix it."

Donner gave a quick, appreciative nod. In that one moment, Rapunzel saw the face of a wounded child, convincing himself that yes, he was a big boy and he was going to be okay. Then she saw Ethan in her peripheral vision. He was looking her way. Seeing an opportunity, she ran her hand up along Donner's rock-hard bicep and gave a sympathetic smile. He flinched in surprise but didn't pull away.

"You know, you're right," she said. "If we're going to be stuck on this boat for the next four hours, we might as well call a temporary truce. What do you say? Interested in checking out that poker table downstairs?"

"Really?" he blurted, then immediately cleared his throat and struck his usual domineering male specimen pose. "I mean, absolutely. But if you really want to make lover boy jealous," he added, lowering his voice and glancing toward Ethan, "we should make it strip."

Rapunzel leered at him and glanced toward the tiny hole that led to the ladder that led to the cabin beneath the boat. On second thought, perhaps descending into a tiny space with a devastatingly handsome man with bricks for arms, magical powers, and no control over his off-the-chart hormones wasn't the best idea. But then she caught Ethan looking her way once more.

Maybe what her boyfriend needed was another reason to get his blood boiling—and, if the tide so turned, rescue her for real this time.

෨ൟ

After seven hands of five card draw, Rapunzel was still confident that Ethan would fly down that ladder any second to reclaim her. He would apologize for being stupid, and she'd apologize for being aloof, and they'd go on to get Grethel together.

After fifteen hands, she was beginning to worry.

But after sixty-plus rounds of poker, three hours of meaningless banter with Donner, and no sign of the man who'd loved her through attempted murder but apparently drew the line at being bad with kids, she was furious. She was just about to march up there and give him a huge piece of her mind when three firm stomps sounded at the top of the ladder.

"We're approaching," Ethan shouted through the hole. "You two should think about coming above soon."

Rapunzel stared, bewildered, at her royal flush. What was *that*? "You two?" He hadn't even said her name. Her fingers went rigid and then curled slowly into a fist.

Donner smirked and traced his fanned out playing cards with the tips of his fingers.

"What?" she snarled, jerking forward in the tiny pleather seat and then slamming back again.

"Oh nothing," he said, pulling two new cards from the deck. "I just recognize that feeling."

"What feeling? There's no feeling." She curled her fingers again and tossed two pretzels into the pile. She was *not* talking about this with Donner. "It's fine. I'm fine. Call, raise, or fold?"

His thick lips rose to one side as he placed the cards face

down between them. "No, it's not fine," he said. "You just think I don't know anything about relationships."

Rapunzel exhaled sharply through her nose and slapped her cards in the middle of the table, face-up. The pile of pretzels she'd been using as chips spilled over. "That's actually not true," she said, launching to her feet and stomping over to the ladder. "I think you know loads about relationships. Just like an exterminator knows loads about mice. How else would you be so good at killing them?"

Donner scowled and followed her. "I'm not as bad as you think I am."

Rapunzel's laugh reverberated through the tiny cabin as she spun him out of view and threw her foot up on the first rung with such fury, it careened right off and crashed onto the floor. When she spun back around, she saw Donner's eyes glowing red. His eyebrows had descended into a deep, wide "V," and he seemed to have grown ten inches in an instant. In the blink of an eye, his fist rose up and slammed into the table so hard the entire boat shook.

Something inside her began to shake, too, and she heard shouting from above deck. What if he caused the boat to capsize? What if, in provoking the cursed monster, she triggered another rampage and somebody died? That would be on her. What had she been she thinking?

But just as she was about to make a run for it, Rapunzel watched Donner close his eyes, lower his face, and take three slow, bottomless breaths. As her hand gripped the ladder, he raised his chin and appeared to be muttering something to himself—something about control. The boat continued to shake for two excruciating, white knuckle minutes. Then, finally, it stopped. Donner's fists steadied. His eyes opened, no longer red. And when he looked at Rapunzel again, it was as if nothing at all had happened.

"Can I ask you a question?" he asked, pressing his hand into his forehead and tearing at his right eyebrow. What a strange tic. "Do you think Belle could ever forgive me?"

Rapunzel went to answer, but as soon as her lips parted, she felt something other than words trying to come out. Suddenly, her mouth filled with saliva. Her eyes flew wide. She spun back around, zoomed up the ladder, and was bent over the portside rail just in time to revisit Elisa Wilkins' scrambled eggs.

A few seconds later, she felt someone pulling her hair up and behind her. "Let me guess," Ethan said as a soft hand ran along her back. "Too much of Donner's cologne in too small a space?"

Rapunzel's chin collapsed against her knuckles, which were still white against the railing. Her legs and arms trembled. She appreciated the help, but hadn't yet gotten over their argument in the car. "Is this really what I need to do to get your attention these days?"

Silence.

Then another voice: "Are you okay?" It was Donner, a clump of tissues in his massive hand. "Here. I didn't see any paper towels."

"Thanks," she muttered, accepting the tissues but keeping her eyes on Ethan. He opened his mouth to say something but couldn't seem to find the words. Then he pulled a faded orange life vest from a wooden crate and held it out. She couldn't even count all the buckles, pouches, and snaps. It was Belle's nursing bra on LSD.

"That's really not necessary," she said, holding up her hand. "I may be a little woozy, but I'm fully capable of walking around on a beach without drowning."

"I'm sure you are," Ethan said, tossing the vest at Donner and making some comment about them not carrying "monstrously huge" size. Rapunzel readied her tissues. She didn't like where this was headed. "But we're not getting dropped off on the beach. There's a razor-sharp reef surrounding the island that a vessel like this can't navigate. Lucky for us, it isn't shallow enough to hurt swimmers."

"Swimmers?" Rapunzel blurted, feeling woozy again.

Ethan nodded, handed her the vest a second time, and then turned to look at Donner. "You at least know how to doggie paddle, right?"

Fifteen harrowing minutes later, the trio washed up on a beach with powder-fine sand set at the base of a small, craggy mountain.

"So, where to?" Donner asked before anyone could even catch their breath.

"What?" Ethan gasped, still doubled over with both hands on his knees. "You mean after spending all that time as an animal, you can't sniff her out?"

Rapunzel heard the skirmish start but frankly didn't care enough to stop it. She was too busy shoving the sand around with her shoes and peering into the tree line that began a few dozen yards away. The branches seemed to twist and jut off in nonsensical directions, as if completely immune to the call of the wind or the sun. The bark was all gnarled, with patches of dark purple moss and bright turquoise lichens. The white sand seemed to sparkle gold as it approached the emerald water. And the air — there was something familiar about its smell, or its taste, or the way it flooded into her through every pore, as if she'd been suffocating all these years without it.

"Beautiful, isn't it?" Ethan said, pulling up beside her and unbuckling her soaking wet life vest. "Welcome home. I guess."

"Marestam's my home," she said before floating forward mindlessly, letting her arms slip from the vest as he held it. As she stepped into the forest, she heard Donner order Ethan to move out of his way, but again, didn't even bother to look back.

Home, she repeated, stepping around a bush with glowing white flowers. Home? How could this possibly be home? She wasn't born here. She had no friends here. She'd never wished it a teary farewell on her way off to college. It had never invited her back for holidays. This was as much her home as was the roach-infested apartment her first "employer" allowed her to sublet when Grethel dropped her in Carpale without a dime to her name. But that didn't take away from the fact that, yes, it was beautiful. And calming. And despite the way she and Grethel parted all those years ago, something about it made her feel … almost … happy.

Forgetting all about the quibbling men behind her, Rapunzel continued to wander. Soon, the beach disappeared entirely. The trees grew denser but the glow of the sun didn't seem to fade. In fact, it seemed to intensify. Perhaps it was leading her toward something. Hopefully, it was something good.

She finally stopped to look around when she reached the base of the mountain. Her traveling companions were nowhere to be seen and there was no path at her feet—just white wooly grass, needle-thin trees, and a steep, craggy slope leading—well, she wasn't exactly sure where. She felt like the marble in the center of a pinball machine, oblivious as to where she was headed but not concerned enough to ask questions. She just knew something was compelling her forward. No, upward.

"Why are we following her?" Rapunzel heard in the distance as she bent down to double-knot her sneaker. She'd made the mistake of hiking in ballet flats once before, with Belle, and was glad she'd come prepared this time. "Does she know where she's going? Who's in charge of this ramshackle—"

She heard a loud thrashing sound, followed by a series of curses.

"Geez, mate. Do you have feet in those shoes or boulders?" Ethan said, bringing a smile to her face. It was good to hear that bouncy sense of humor again—even if it wasn't meant for her. "And she's going exactly where she needs to go, mate. She just needs to remember."

"I'm not your *mate*, buddy," Donner snarled back. Another stumble. A flash of black between the trees about ten yards back.

And then silence. Rapunzel froze at the base of the slope, unsure whether to go back or push forward.

Then she heard Ethan's voice again, only a few yards away now. "Like I said, she knows where she's going. But keep up. I don't want to lose her."

Rapunzel smiled at this statement, and then began to climb. After about twenty minutes, the rocks flattened out and gave her a chance to rest. The treetops were far below her now, replaced by pockets of orange and yellow wildflowers. The sun was just starting its descent into the ocean, painting the horizon with a breathtaking orange glow and glistening off the water.

It made her think about Belle, who loved watching sunsets from above the rest of the world. She'd tried to take Rapunzel once, in the Braddax Hills, on the day they wound up encountering the Phoenix and the feisty old lady who lived there. That was just a few months ago, but it seemed like a lifetime. Rapunzel had just broken up with Ethan. Belle had just adopted Beast. Rapunzel had stumbled along like a baby deer trying to walk for the first time, while Belle looked like a professional hiker, with granola bars and water and a backpack full of everything they needed to survive—that is, until Rapunzel marched off, the sun went down, and they wound up lost in the darkness.

Crap. She looked around now. Sunset meant the beginning of evening, and she had no desire to share some sort of makeshift shelter with Ethan and Donner in the middle of nowhere. Let alone try to figure out the bathroom situation.

"Ethan!" she shouted, lumbering toward a pink-toned boulder with a cutout that looked like it would fit her derriere perfectly. "I'm up here. It's going to be dark soon, so we should stop and talk about—"

She turned the corner and stopped. Her head dropped back. A few dozen yards behind the boulder, one side of the mountain shot straight up and was smooth as glass—with no ledges, no outcroppings, and no footholds. Only it wasn't flat. It bulged all around. A cylinder. As if some mythological giant had picked up a lighthouse, sliced it in half from top to bottom, and slapped it against the side of this mountain.

It wasn't gray, as she remembered, but overgrown with purple moss. And rather than stretching into the clouds, it probably reached thirty feet—no taller than a standard single-family house in Braddax. The only thing she seemed to remember correctly was the bundle of brambles and thorns that loomed at the bottom. They hadn't changed much at all—aside from now being stained with poor Ethan's blood.

She turned around at the sound of heavy footsteps and hushed bickering.

"That's it?" Donner grunted, examining the tower with his arms crossed. "That's the monstrous, inescapable tower you were imprisoned in for all those years? What's with all the flowers? It looks like something from a fairy tale—and not the scary kind."

Rapunzel leered at him, just in case he was under the impression that a bundle of tissues and a few rounds of poker made them friends.

"You shouldn't believe everything you read," Ethan explained, traipsing up between them and dumping the waterproof backpack he'd bought off a member of the crew. At least their phones were safe, not that they worked all the way out here. "Maybe she wasn't as desperate to escape as the stories say she was." He pulled out a water bottle, flipped the top, and handed it to Rapunzel.

"Thanks," she said, letting their fingers touch as the bottle passed between them. She didn't mind Donner's assumptions. No one but Ethan had ever bothered to ask if there was another side to the whole kidnapped-girl-from-the-tower story.

"So now what?" Donner asked, marching toward the razor-sharp barricade and peering between the thorns. "Is there a doorbell or do we have to sit here while you grow thirty feet of hair?"

Rapunzel rolled her eyes. There was a difference between using a few magical hair extensions in place of rope, and hoisting a stranger up a tower by your scalp. Her head throbbed just thinking about it. "Even if that part of the story was true," she said, "it wouldn't do us much good down here. Now would it?"

Donner made a face, then turned to analyze the tower again. The first twenty feet of rock looked slick as ice, but after that, a series of tiny windows spiraled their way up, leading to a bulbous wraparound deck and several larger windows.

Ethan looked at Rapunzel. "Any ideas?" he asked.

Rapunzel shrugged. "If Grethel didn't even want *me* coming, she's not going to be very happy to see three of us. Especially that over-privileged Neanderthal over there," she said, gesturing toward Donner. "She sort of hates men."

"Ha." Ethan ran his palm over the scar on his cheek. "Sort of?"

Rapunzel gave the ground a tiny smile and kicked her foot a bit. "Yeah, and you're one of the good ones." She felt the air between them loosen a little. "We have to tread carefully. She's like a terrified rabbit."

"Yeah," Ethan laughed. "A rabbit that can break your neck with a twitch of its—"

"Hey!" Donner suddenly hollered, flapping his arms and staring up. "Grable!" Rapunzel's eyes grew three sizes as Ethan sprinted over to shut him up. "Or whatever your name is," he called, shoving Ethan back as if he was nothing. "Witchy lady!" he hollered again. Ethan lunged again and grabbed his shirt. "We've come a long way with a big problem and—"

Silence fell suddenly as Ethan's fist collided with Donner's jaw. The men instantly shot apart, one shaking out his injured hand, the other cradling his chin.

Rapunzel watched, mortified, as Donner's eyes lit up again.

His chest puffed out. His eyebrows descended, just as they had on the boat, and he appeared to swell up in all directions. With a mighty grunt, he ripped a fist-thick branch off the nearest tree and stomped toward Ethan, who immediately threw both arms up as a shield. She screamed as he reared back, rounded up, and torpedoed the branch two inches over Ethan's head and into the tower.

Rapunzel shook as it cracked into a dozen jagged pieces and plunged into the bramble below. Ethan lowered his arms and panned from the bramble, to Donner, to her. The same questions flew through their minds as the cursed, magical maniac stood several yards away from them with his legs wide apart, eyes on the ground, and fists still pulsing. He looked as if he was trying to stop his heart from thumping its way out of his chest, but wasn't having much luck. He was grunting, and flinching. He was a man at war with a second personality.

"Hey, calm down," Rapunzel said, raising her hands and inching forward. "Breathe," she commanded, her voice strong and calm. "Just like I saw you do on the boat." She laid her fingers on his arm. He flinched but didn't pull away. "No one here wants a fight. We're just trying to help you — and your child. He needs you." Donner grunted but let the air in. "Belle needs you." She saw Ethan watching on the side, but her focus remained on Donner. His eyes bore into hers. The red began to fade. "Show her you can beat this. I want to tell her you beat this."

Slowly, Donner's hands fell to his sides and he backed away. Rapunzel turned to Ethan in triumph. Had he seen that? She'd just prevented a magical disaster.

But rather than looking proud or relieved, Ethan looked as if the branch had actually hit him — smack across the face. His jaw hung open. His eyebrows fell. His eyes jerked from Rapunzel to Donner and back again.

Shit. Her mind flashed back to the boat, to her attempt to

make him jealous, to her three hours below deck with Donner. She thought about his swipe on the plane about her old life. But still. No, he couldn't possibly think —

"I'm going to find some firewood," Ethan grumbled. His face was white as the sand back on the beach. "If Grethel was home, she would have reacted to that. There's no sense in all of us twiddling our thumbs here, waiting for her to come back without preparing for nightfall. Like you said, it's going to be dark soon."

"I'll come with you," Rapunzel said, charging forward.

"No." Ethan shook her away before she could even reach him. "Stay with him. Keep each other company. Maybe you can find a way in." He looked at Rapunzel for a split-second and then marched away, weaving a little to both sides before vanishing around the bend.

A full minute passed before she felt Donner pull up by her side.

"Firewood?" he repeated, his voice like nails on a chalkboard to her now. "Not that it's my problem, but what are the chances that was just an excuse so he could be al — "

"Oh, just shut up and help me find a way into this place!" Rapunzel snapped, spinning around and tossing her hands toward the sky. "Maybe there's a secret door I never knew about. Or a ladder. Or even a freaking note saying, 'Out to dinner. Be back at half past six.'"

One side of Donner's mouth rose in amusement. But the other half stayed flat, almost disclosing a little guilt. "I'm on it," he said, pushing his sleeves toward his elbows and wandering towards the tower.

I'm on it, Rapunzel repeated as she began circling the tower, studying it from the bottom up. What a piece of work he was. A master at getting under a girl's skin. And *not* — despite his looks — in an enticing way. No wonder Belle had such an identity crisis while they were together. One minute, he was sympathetic—maybe even sweet. The next, he was either a sarcastic ass or a raging, dictatorial bully. Curse or no curse, when it came down to it, Donner Wickenham was a child who genuinely wanted to help but had a short temper and narcissistic tendencies. That's what Belle must have seen in him—the propensity for good if he worked at it, even if the opposite was more natural.

"Found it!" she heard from the other side of the tower.

She rolled her eyes immediately, expecting another sarcastic quip. But then she heard the same proclamation again, and saw Donner sprinting over as if he'd unearthed the next clue in a kindergarten treasure hunt.

"Found what?" she asked.

"Stairs!"

She leered at him as he grabbed her arm and started hauling her towards the rock. "Grethel doesn't need stairs," she said. "She's a pureblood fairy."

"Yeah, well, maybe she put them in after you took your magical hair away," he said as they approached the spot where the tower stopped curving and connected with the floorboard-flat rock. "Just in case."

She gnashed her teeth together and yanked her arm away. "For one thing, she banished me. I didn't leave. And seriously with the hair again? She only used that a handful of times when she was sick and her powers went a little haywire."

"Touch it," Donner said, positioning her so that her nose was inches from the stone.

"What do you mean, tou—"

Suddenly, he pulled her back and flung her towards the wall. She screamed. Her hands flew up to soften the impact, but ... but none came. She flew through the stone like a gnat through a window screen. And in front of her now: stairs.

"What the heck?" she said, running her hand along a narrow, spiral railing as her gargantuan companion slipped in behind her. She looked back to examine the hidden entrance. Had this always been here? She drew her foot up and placed it on the first step. Then she put her weight cautiously on the next and began to climb. She said nothing for the first twenty steps, and was hopeful Donner would do the same.

"So," he said on step twenty-one, "if there's a door at the end of these stairs and we actually make our way in, is this going to be a happy reunion? Or should my priority be finding something to use as a shield?"

Rapunzel's bracelet rapped against the railing. It was a fair question, but she honestly didn't know. All she knew was her stomach was churning and if these stairs didn't come to an end soon, she might decide to turn around and go back home.

"Got it," he said, translating her nonexistent response. Then, a few seconds later: "What about Ethan? Are you worried this quasi-mother of yours might try to kill him again?"

"Please," she said, her voice curt and piercing. She wanted him to stop asking questions. She wanted him to stop trying to get into her head. They weren't going to be friends—today or any day thereafter. They were putting up with each other because they shared a common interest, and that was as far as it would ever go. "I don't want to talk to you about Ethan. Or Grethel. I barely even talk to my closest friends about either. Please, let's just get inside this tower, grab our second fairy, and fix Belle's—fix *your*—son. Okay?"

Donner grunted something in reply and stayed quiet for the next few steps. But just as she reached a narrow landing with an iron-framed oak door, she heard him mutter, "And people think *I'm* the damaged one."

She spun around so fast, she almost lost her balance. "What?"

"I'm just saying. I've always wondered how things would have turned out if I grew up with a better role model, or if I didn't spend a year blocked off from the world like a monster. But you did that for eighteen years. No wonder you go through men like pairs of socks. You don't have the slightest idea how to trust."

"*Excuse* me?" The air was suddenly on fire. She was finding it difficult to breathe. "Ethan's not upset because I have trust issues. He's upset because he pissed me off and I stayed mad at him for too long. And because I didn't have a slumber party with his nieces or do his sister's toenails."

"Wow." Donner shook his head. "That's the attitude he gets after everything he went through? For going blind and almost dying, all because he fell in love with you? You know, most guys would curse the day they met a girl like that and never speak of her again. But this sap not only found you, he came back *here* with you — to the thorns that split him in half. Do you think a semi-committal guy would do all that for a fling? This poor sap is in it for the long haul — kids, marriage, holidays with his parents — and that scares the crap out of you. *That's* why he's upset, because you still haven't brought down that wall." He slapped his hand against the stone to illustrate his point. "And at this point, you probably never will."

Rapunzel blinked. Twice. Three times. Words piled up in her head but tumbled away the instant she tried to catch them. He didn't know what he was talking about. He was guessing. Donner's authority on relationships was downright comical and Ethan wouldn't have blathered about something so personal while they were walking together — would he? She felt a wave of panic wash over her. The tower of stress was building and she wasn't going to be able to keep it up very much longer. She needed to get out of this stairwell.

She spun around grabbed the handle with both hands, but it wouldn't budge. Her sneaker flew into the door as she throttled her entire body like a half-naked cheerleader in a horror flick. Finally, she dropped her head back and opened her mouth to scream. But the next sound to enter the stairwell wasn't a scream at all. It was a crisp, tiny but unmistakable click. Then the doorknob turned.

Chapter Sixteen

DAWN

Sugar Showers sat between a shuttered computer repair shop and a laundromat in Hobbs Hill, a decidedly unhip neighborhood halfway between the Regian Woods and the northern coast of the kingdom, after the East River bent horizontal and before it officially dumped into the sea. It was squat, drab, and downright desolate. And on this drizzly, dreary morning, Dawn wondered why she'd once told Hunter not to let Tirion Enterprises barge in and "mess with it."

"Right here," she said, scooting to the edge of her seat and pointing to a narrow storefront with a black awning bearing bubbly gold letters.

"Got it," Christophe sang, flipping on his blinker despite the empty street and pulling into a spot a few doors up. "Strange place for a latte. Who are you meeting again?"

"Just a friend," Dawn said while unbuckling her seatbelt. Then she smiled. Christophe was a Selladórean native and had worked for her father once upon a time. He was the only royal driver she trusted to keep her excursion a secret—not that Hunter seemed to care how she spent her time anyway.

For going on five days now, she'd seen her husband more on

the news than in real life. He was always there: posing, smiling, shaking hands. No one suspected that his heart was in pieces and his marriage threatened to follow. In fact, were it not for a few concrete signs of existence—a drawer left slightly ajar, an empty whiskey tumbler in the sink, the toilet paper torn outside of the perforation—Dawn may have thought he'd already gone.

She'd contemplated telling him about Elmina, and the triad, and all the things she'd intended to tell him days ago. But the full story would have included Davin's connection to Angus Kane and the ramifications that had on her "awakening" via Hunter's lips. It would have included her suspicion that Hunter wasn't one in a million so much as he was one in the right place at the right time. Or even worse, that he was handpicked to be there not by fate or the universe, but by Angus.

So, she didn't tell him. She couldn't bear to watch any more affection drain from those eyes that had once held so much. It was hard enough watching his smile fall every time he walked through the door and saw her there. She knew she deserved to be punished. She'd betrayed his trust on a monumental scale. But she was finding it harder each day to paste on a positive attitude, when he gave no signs that it mattered at all. She knew the kids needed it. She knew doing otherwise would give Hunter even less incentive to take her back. But everyone had their breaking point, and lately, she'd found herself wishing he'd just toss her into the street and be done with it. At least then, she could tell Christophe to just keep driving—north, outside the borders of Marestam entirely, until they reached a shoddy motel where he could leave her, never to be heard from again.

"I'm already late, so I'd better head in," Dawn said instead, crushing the handle of her purse in her fist and opening the door. "If it's any good, I'll bring you back a muffin. Blueberry crumb, right?"

Christophe grinned and gave her a shallow, two-finger salute.

Dawn's boots clacked as they hit the sidewalk, averting a mound of black garbage bags lined up along the curb. The walk was too short to bother with her umbrella, so she pulled her hood up and snuggled into her collar—blocking both the cold rain and the sweet, rotting stench of trash day.

The storefront was impossibly narrow, with a tiny window displaying a single cupcake, a diet-sized sliver of blueberry pie, and a chalkboard sign reading "Welcome" in faint, white letters. She opened the door slowly, expecting to hear a jingle of some sort, but there was nothing. There was only the low hum of a radio and a disembodied voice chiming in at random intervals from the kitchen. Well, if Elmina was going for discreet, she nailed it. How had she even found this place?

Dawn hovered by the door for a few seconds, then edged in. The bakery was long and claustrophobic, with three small white tables and a beige counter with low-backed bar stools in alternating pink and orange. To the right of the cash register, three coffee dispensers sat beside a mountain of paper cups. To the left, a glass case displayed a mouth-watering collection of brownies, tarts, pies, scones, muffins, and all kinds of cookies on a sea of white paper doilies. Why on earth hadn't these been in the window?

Dawn was admiring the chocolate-coated squares with the rainbow stripes, when the door to the kitchen swung open and a pretty young woman with caramel-colored skin and tight black curls appeared.

"Well, hello and welcome," she sang, smearing her hands on a dishtowel and floating behind the counter. "Lovely day for a treat. Nothing brings on the sugar cravings like a dreary autumn morning, does it? Except perhaps a dreary winter morning, I suppose. But then no one wants to venture more than ten feet from their fireplace, so it doesn't help me much." She let out a bubble of laughter and threw her long, lanky arms on top of the display case. She was tall and thin to the point where Dawn doubted she actually ate anything she sold. "So, what's your pleasure? Everything's fresh this morning, the coffee was pressed at dawn, and if there's something special you want but don't see, just say the word. I've got a few tricks up my sleeve and have yet to make a pastry that wasn't worth the wait."

Dawn eyed the woman for a moment, unsure how to rectify her delicate, pretty exterior with the garrulous, overconfident empress that appeared the moment she opened her mouth. At a loss, she lowered her eyes to the muffins. They really did look delicious. But would it be rude to order something before Elmina arrived? This is when a handbook of modern-day etiquette would come in handy.

"Umm," Dawn said, glancing toward the door. "I'm actually meeting someone, but she seems to be late too." She looked back again, then fiddled with her watch. Elmina's note had said ten o'clock, not ten fifteen, but she wouldn't have come and gone this quickly—would she? "Do you mind if I just sit for a few minutes?"

The woman's youthful smile plummeted as she dropped her dishtowel on the counter. "Two dollars a minute for loitering. For the first ten."

"Excuse me?" Dawn said. "The first ten what?"

"Minutes. Minutes eleven and up are five bucks a piece. And the wireless is password protected. This is a bakery, not a free place to hide till the rain lets up."

"Oh," Dawn said, pressing her palm against her collarbone. "No, I'm not hiding. I really am meeting someone. An old friend of my parents. I didn't miss her, did I?"

The woman smirked and leaned forward over the counter. "What does this old friend look like? Young? Old? Pretty?"

"Old," Dawn blurted, rocking on her knees a bit. She hadn't seen Elmina for over ten years. "I mean not *old* old, but old*er*. Like sixty-something by now. And short."

"Short and plump?"

Dawn jumped. "Yes!" she called. "Well, probably. I don't know what she's been up to over the last decade so I can't say that for sure but…"

She trailed off. Judging by the scowl growing across the young woman's face, *she* couldn't say for sure either — whether to kick Dawn out on her royal tuckus or start calculating her loitering bill, that is. Dawn reached for her purse.

"Okay. You know what? I'll have a tea while I wait," she said, the words rushing together. "Medium please. Green if you have it."

Another stare, then a gruff grab of the kettle and a tea bag. "Two dollars."

Dawn's head fell to the side as she pulled out her wallet. "Is that two dollars for loitering or two dollars for the tea?"

The woman smiled but gave no answer. She had bright amber eyes and an unusual birthmark between her left earlobe and her neck — as if the world's smallest bird had landed on a permanent inkpad and somehow waddled onto her face. She'd seen something like it recently, but couldn't remember on whom.

"Two dollars for the hot water and sack of herbs. Make it two fifty and I'll throw in a scone. Nothing goes better with a rainy day than a scone. I highly recommend vanilla orange. Your friend might appreciate one too. They're big hits with the elderly and overweight."

"She's not — " Dawn started to correct her characterization of Elmina, but decided why bother? As recent events proved, she was incapable of filling any holes she dug by mistake. She only made them deeper. "I'll take two of those, sure. And a blueberry muffin. Thank you."

Dawn glanced at the door again as the woman plucked a sheet of orange wax paper from a drawer and scooped up two vanilla orange scones and a blueberry muffin. She dropped the latter in a box and the former on two plates while Dawn watched, shifting her weight like her kids during the potty training years.

"One for you," she said, sliding the treats across the counter. "One for your driver. And one for the buxom old fairy you're meeting."

Dawn's face knocked back a few inches, followed by her feet. She hadn't said anything about a fairy.

"How —" Dawn began, her insides starting to quiver. What if that note hadn't been from Elmina at all? What if Angus had written it? What if any second now, Davin was going to burst through that door followed by the paparazzi — checking on a tip about the Queen of Regian meeting with her Selladórean lover? "Did I say I was meeting a fairy?"

But rather than answer, the woman laughed and rapped her index finger against the counter three times. On the third tap, the blinds snapped shut over all the windows, blocking out what little natural light there was. Dawn spun around as her heart flew into the bottom of her throat and the chandelier above them flickered.

"Oh relax," she heard next. "I'm not going to hurt you. This isn't a kidnapping." Dawn nodded but continued to clutch her purse like a shield. "But seriously, where's your sense of adventure? Where's your curiosity?" The woman snapped her fingers as if having a eureka moment. "Oh, that's right. You never got those magical gifts because I had to save your life instead. Tell me, if you had to choose now, would you prefer bravery and moxie or grace, dance, and song?" The woman shook her head. "Beauty, I can understand. Like it or not, looks come in handy in this world. But as for the others ... did those frivolous old bats expect you to sing an operetta while juggling atop a unicycle too?"

Dawn's bottom lip fell open, but singing a juggling operetta actually seemed easier than finding something to say at the moment. This twenty-something bakery girl was talking about the so-called "gifts" a group of fairies bestowed on her as an infant: grace, beauty, dance, song, and a bunch of other ridiculous qualities intended to make her more marketable to some unnamed prince three hundred years ago.

Dawn looked at the woman's birthmark again as she gave a bored sigh and raised both hands to the ceiling. She then closed her eyes, turned her palms inward, dropped them quickly to her hips, and disappeared—but not in the traditional sense of the word. As her arms fell, the pretty young woman fell with them— at least fourteen inches—and plumped out on all sides. Her tight skin loosened like the pleats along Dawn's brow. Her upturned nose doubled in size and bumped out in the middle. Her glossy black curls morphed into a wiry brown mess that looked speckled with confectioner's sugar.

When the transformation was complete, Dawn was staring at the fairy her parents had treated like a member of the family. The fairy who took their daughter's death curse and turned it into a three-hundred-year nap. The fairy who had woken up with Dawn and the rest of Selladóre, but abandoned them when they needed her most.

"Oh, shut your jaw," Elmina ordered, her lips pulling up at the sides. "I wouldn't have teased you like that if you'd shown up on time. Now, what do you need?"

Dawn continued to stare. Then she looked at the food. Was she still talking about pastries?

"I heard you were looking for me the other day," Elmina clarified, plodding out from behind the counter and covering the nearest table with the scones, Dawn's tea, and a mug of black coffee. "What do you need? Let's talk. Or do you want me to change back into Alliana? She *is* easier to look at, I'll give you that."

Dawn closed her eyes as tightly as she could, then reopened them. "Who's Alliana?" she asked, despite the many far more important questions whizzing around her brain.

"Alliana's the girl who offered you the fifty-cent scone. She's my, umm, alter ego." She plopped down into an orange chair and winked. "One of them, anyway."

Dawn stared at the scones. She could see the slivers of orange rind popping up all over the place, as if they were struggling to rise up against the dough and fly into space. What was Elmina talking about? Had she lost her mind? Is that why she'd disappeared? What other reason could she possibly have for cutting off all ties, opening up a third-tier bakery in a rundown part of Regian, and making up "alter egos" like some sort of magical schizophrenic?

"I'm not crazy," Elmina said, cupping her mug with both hands. "If that's what you're thinking."

Dawn froze. There were so many things she needed to ask her, and to tell her—about Angus Kane and Donner's curse and Belle's baby and the triad and the Charmés. But when she finally found her voice, her words had nothing to do with any of that.

"Was it true love's kiss?" she blurted, grabbing the second chair by the back but not sitting down. "Was it Hunter's kiss that broke my curse or did you construct it to expire on a certain date three hundred years later?"

Elmina stared ahead, then asked how "true" the love could be between a comatose woman and a man she'd never met before.

"Then why three hundred?" she blurted, all of her most deeply buried questions pouring out at once. "Why couldn't you have put me to sleep for five? Or ten? Or just long enough for Jacara to die and her spell along with her? Was my life really worth more than the hundreds of people who died either during the curse or right after? And how could you just abandon us? How could you abandon me? My best friend was gone and my parents were dead and the whole world was different. You couldn't have even left a phone number? You know, just in case I felt like razoring myself or my mother-in-law attempted to cook me—which, in case you hadn't heard, she did."

Dawn jerked the chair and glowered, causing her tea to topple over. "And now I find out that all this time, you've been a few blocks away baking cookies in some hole-in-the-wall pastry shop? Disguising yourself as some pretty young waif so you could sample all you wanted and never gain an ounce? What were you—"

Her fire started to sputter as the spilled tea spread to the left side of the table and poured over the edge. "How could you—"

The years of isolation rushed back up from their crevices. "Why did you abandon me like that?"

Finally, the silence hooked over them like the crest of a wave. Elmina didn't move for a full minute. Then she tossed two napkins over the yellow-tinged liquid and traced the rim of her coffee mug with one finger. She closed her eyes and let out a hiccup of a laugh.

"What on earth is funny?" Dawn demanded.

Elmina's head shook from one side to the other. "Do you know how old I was when you were born? Twenty-six. I didn't even know how to cast spells without a wand yet."

Dawn narrowed her eyes. "You can cast spells without a wand?"

Elmina shook her head and laughed again. "Child, you may have been born in the eighteenth century, but you really have no idea how much things have changed in the past three hundred years, do you? You were too busy chasing after that Lima boy and torturing your poor mother to pay any attention. What people call a pureblood today is like a newborn fairy in our time. Even the strongest of them can only transport themselves when they evaporate. And the non-purebloods can't cast spells at all; they basically just make things hover. Thank goodness Jacara— that's the nutjob who cursed you in the first place—"

"I know who she is," Dawn snapped, her shock quickly turning into anger.

Elmina's eyebrows rose. "Okay. Well anyway, if *she* was

around today, with all these mortals and a handful of so-called fairies with their watered-down magic..." She shivered to illustrate a point. "Well, she'd have the world in chains. She was the most powerful fairy in a time when magic was a thousand times stronger than it is now."

"What does that have to do with anythi—"

Elmina clacked her mug against the table and leaned forward. The cap of her apron ballooned open like the rim of a basket. "So, to answer your question, Miss Ungrateful, that's why it took three hundred years for my rookie spell to change hers. She cast a spell to kill you; I changed a few lines to make you sleep instead. But overriding someone that powerful isn't like frosting a cupcake. And your parents *really* wanted you to see your eighteenth birthday." She leaned back and nibbled on one side of her mouth. "You're lucky I managed to cast it at all without making you explode. Bits of baby all over the throne room and my head on a stake. Would that have been more to your preference, Your Majesty?"

Dawn loosened her grip on the chair but remained standing. In hindsight, perhaps her line of questioning had seemed a little bratty, but her lack of tact didn't negate her point. Yes, letting her die would have broken her parents' hearts. But she would rather have died than destroyed thousands of lives the way she did—both from that century and this one.

"Listen, it was certainly unfortunate that people died during the Great Sleep," Elmina said, failing to hide her cringe at the contrived moniker. She stood up to grab two dishtowels and an assortment of cookies from the display case. "That was never my intention." She continued speaking as she cleaned up the rest of Dawn's spill and placed the cookies on the table. "But back then, the life of a princess *was* worth more than those in the kingdom she presided over."

Dawn stared at the rainbow cookies but remained grounded. "It wasn't right."

"I didn't say it was right," Elmina said, her tone suddenly softer. She sat down and took a jelly-filled crescent for herself. "But it was a different time. And it wasn't your choice. You were an infant. No one can blame you for it." She paused and looked Dawn straight in the eye. "No one *does* blame you for it."

Slowly, Dawn slid into the chair she'd been clutching, picked up a rainbow cookie, and turned it over in her palm a few times. She had simultaneous urges to cry, disappear, and give Elmina a giant hug. She'd never expressed these regrets to anyone. She'd never had the opportunity.

"And as for abandoning you," Elmina continued, her tone suddenly sharper. "The only reason I'm here is because I *couldn't* abandon you."

Dawn's response to this was immediate and scathing. Half a mile away or half the world, she said, turning the chocolate-covered rainbow into mush, Elmina had most definitely abandoned her. "The last time I saw you was the day I buried my parents. You showed up, gave me a hug and a pat on the head, and then disappeared. I had no one. You have no idea how depressed I became. How bad things got."

"Oh, I know how bad things got." Elmina shook her head but didn't raise her eyes. "And just because you didn't see me doesn't mean I wasn't there."

Dawn squinted and thought about Alliana. Then she thought about the old man from the ferry. He had that same birthmark on the back of his left jaw; that's where she'd seen it before. How many other faces did Elmina have? A castle guard? A ticket salesman? The coach of Day's broomball team?

"I've been here this whole time—watching you mourn a past you couldn't change, clapping as you cut ribbons with a man you so obviously despised, and pretending I didn't see you shacking up with that cocky little twerp you always followed around like a minstrel groupie."

Dawn's eyes and mouth flew open simultaneously. Her chair

screeched across the floor as she jumped to her feet. "What? Are you talking about Davin?"

Elmina scoffed and rolled her eyes. "Ugh. Yes. Daaaaaavin," she said, drawing his name out the way Dawn might have as a teenager. "Your parents would be so disappointed in you."

"How do you know about—"

"Like I said, just because you haven't seen me doesn't mean I haven't seen you."

"But," Dawn started, then shook her head. "Why all the theatrics? Why hide? The people of Selladóre needed someone like you to look up to when they lost my parents. You brought them here, but then you disappeared. You abandoned them. You…"

Dawn trailed off as Elmina's gaze grew more and more penetrating. She interpreted it as a mixture of disbelief and disgust.

"They needed someone like me?" she repeated. "Or someone like you?"

In that moment, the shop became so silent, Dawn could hear each individual raindrop as it pelted the windows. She lowered herself carefully back into the seat. She had no argument. Elmina was right.

"I may have *looked* different," Elmina said, twisting the knife, "but I was *there*. I was on the ground helping the people whose lives I destroyed. I wasn't sulking in my ivory tower, lamenting my marriage to the king who thought the sun rose and set with me, or the two beautiful children I never would have had were it not for the curse. I'm not the one who abandoned them."

Dawn pulled her lips over her teeth and examined the floor. The events of Friday night and Saturday morning came storming back at her. Davin had called her a selfish princess. Hunter said she'd been blinded by her own bitterness. They'd both implied that Dawn had been so obsessed with her own problems that she couldn't even recognize anyone else's. And now here she was, beating her own grievances to death when she should have been recruiting Elmina to help Belle, and Cindy, and all of the innocent people in Marestam.

"You're right," she said, her voice barely a whisper. Then, louder. "You're right, Elmina. I was scared and bitter and I shut down when Selladóre needed me the most. I wished I'd just died when I was supposed to, and all those people went on to live and die when they were supposed to. But that's not what happened, and I should have just sucked it up and moved on."

Elmina stared, dumbfounded, for a minute. Then she got up, waddled behind the counter, and returned with two plates, two forks, and a gigantic slice of blueberry pie. Good God, how much sugar could this woman ingest?

"Something tells me we're going to need this," she said, unfolding a napkin for her lap. "In case you haven't figured it out yet, I'm my own biggest customer."

Dawn didn't move at first, but eventually pressed her lips together, picked up the fork, and scooped a tiny blue sliver up towards her mouth.

"And would you still rather have died than lived?" Elmina asked.

The pie halted two inches from Dawn's mouth. It was a surprisingly difficult question, but—

"No," said a voice she vaguely recognized as hers. Then, with more conviction, "No. I don't. Because if I had, Morning and Day would never have existed. And despite everything—" She paused for a moment, but decided not to elaborate. "I don't want to lose what I have now." Elmina's head craned to one side. "But that's not why I'm here. I don't need you to solve my problems, but I do need help solving someone else's—a whole bunch of people's actually. Pretty much the entire realm's."

Elmina's eyebrows rose. Her head followed.

Dawn started at the very beginning, with Donner's affair and Ruby's misinterpretation of what Belle's independence would do to all broken curses. Then she told her about Belle's baby, Angus Kane, the Charmés disappearance, and the need for Elmina to take part in Ruby's triad. When she was finally finished, Elmina stared into space for a couple minutes, then shuddered like a bird after a heavy rain.

"Wow," she said. "Okay. That does sound like a problem. But I have to caution you against following Ruby Welles too closely."

Dawn lowered her fork. She had no great love for Ruby, and Rapunzel absolutely hated her, but Cindy always gave her the benefit of the doubt. "What do you mean? I don't really think Ruby's the—"

Elmina cut her off with a grunt. "This is what happens when amateurs overstep their authority. You're all looking so hard at the forest that you're not seeing the trees."

"What's that supposed to mean?"

"That magical rulebook, for example. The one you think said all broken curses would come back if Belle left Donner for good. Ruby's interpretation of it couldn't have been more wrong."

"But—"

"That thing was written centuries ago—back when people thought the world was flat and fairies were part demigod, part demon. Once a curse is broken, it's broken. Caput. Poof. Gone. All of the original magic goes back to the caster. Belle's reconciliation with Donner didn't stop his curse because she had *nothing* to do with it returning in the first place."

Dawn had a strong inclination to explain the whole story all over again. Perhaps Elmina hadn't been listening. Perhaps she missed something.

"I'm not saying Donner isn't cursed. But I don't think it's his old curse revived," Elmina continued, sucking both cheeks in so deep she almost looked emaciated. "I think this is a new curse entirely. And judging by the fact that only purebloods have that ability and Ruby is inexplicably powerless at the moment, my gut says that's the massive sycamore tree none of you ladies are seeing."

"But…" Dawn scrunched her face and ran both stories through her head. Then she crossed her arms. "Ruby said Angus used a charm to both take her powers away and to curse Donner. Are you saying that's not possible?"

Dawn recognized Elmina's expression immediately. It was the same look she used to give Morning when she was a toddler, spouting out ridiculously naive and adorable thoughts all the time—like the belief that the moon had a boo-boo whenever it was less than full.

"Magic isn't like a layer of sunscreen you can just wash off. It's much more formidable and complex than anyone—including me—can ever understand. The ability to remove another fairy's magic isn't just a rare power, it's almost unheard of." Dawn gripped her thigh with her fingertips. Elmina stood up and began clearing the dishes. "Do you want to know what I honestly think?"

"Of course," Dawn chirped, though she wasn't entirely sure.

"I think Ruby cursed Donner because she just couldn't handle the thought of her version of 'happily ever after' falling apart. That's where her powers went. Belle and Donner are icons. Beauty and the Beast. A front-and-center part of Marestam's history. For someone like Ruby, their demise is akin to the Seven Wonders of the World toppling over one by one. It's the beginning of the end. All she needs is the Charmés to follow, and her world is officially over. I'm not saying she misread that ridiculous rulebook intentionally. But when she realized her prophecy wasn't coming true—meaning Donner wasn't growing fur and Belle wasn't racing back into his arms to save the world—she fulfilled it herself. And it opened a box she wasn't powerful enough to close."

Dawn let this theory seep in and roll around a bit. She thought about how awful Ruby had looked at the hospital—all frizzy and red-nosed and sneezy and unfashionable. Then she shook her head. "I'm sorry but … but I don't think so. Ruby's a mess without her powers. She wants them back, desperately. And I don't love her, but I don't believe she'd hurt an innocent child to get her way."

"Nor do I. As much as I dislike that dogmatic diva, I don't think she's evil. Misguided, absolutely. Dangerous, you bet. But not evil. Like I said, even *I* can't understand all of magic's nuances. It isn't all abracadabra and true love's kiss. It's unbelievably powerful. It's finicky. It's dangerous. And most of the time, it's completely unpredictable."

Dawn scooted forward, unable to believe she was even entertaining this idea. Were she and her friends really that blind — or that biased against Angus Kane?

"But if that's true, why all the charades?" Dawn asked. "Why blame Angus? Why not just tell us the truth and end her spell so she could get her powers back? Why send us all on a mission to recruit three purebloods for a triad?"

The dishes clanked as Elmina dropped them onto the counter and marched back, pressing both hands into her hips so she had two chubby chicken wings.

"Aside from ruining her perfect image?" Elmina asked, her voice betraying a significant level of disgust. "Because she probably doesn't know *how* to break it. Because if she's the reason Belle's baby is cursed, then the only surefire way to break it is for her to die. And if you weren't all busy searching for hermit fairies, you might figure that out."

Dawn was stunned. "That's ridiculous," she said. "That implies she thinks one of us would actually kill her if we knew."

Elmina stared at her, letting the silence direct Dawn's thoughts. Rapunzel had threatened to kill Ruby for far lesser offenses, Gray would do almost anything for Belle, and there were few if any things a mother wouldn't do to protect her child — even if it meant selling her soul.

"Ruby overstepped and is out of ideas that don't involve

dying," Elmina finally said. "That's why she wants the triad. Angus is just a scapegoat—a deserving scapegoat, but a scapegoat nonetheless."

"But..." Dawn sputtered. "But what about all those charms he's confiscated? Certainly with those he could—"

"I'm telling you, Ruby's your girl. Charms just aren't as powerful as you've been led to believe. And it's not unheard of for fairies to lose control of their own spells—especially if it was made in a fit of passion."

"But what about Cinderella's disappearance?" Dawn was getting agitated now. Her voice was getting louder and firmer. "And his move to get rid of the monarchies? Oh! And I'm pretty sure he planned for Davin and I to come back together just when—"

"Stop," Elmina said, flapping her wings. "Are you really going to blame Angus for your affair too?"

"That's not what I was saying," Dawn growled, getting up from the table and mimicking Elmina's stance. "I made a colossal mistake, but there's more to it than that. Did you know Davin's father didn't fall asleep with the rest of the kingdom?"

Elmina's hands moved off her hips and crossed in front of her chest.

"He was outside Selladóre when the curse struck," Dawn explained. "He built that whole distillery company and left instructions for his son to take it over three hundred years later. And when that time finally came, guess who was on Selladóre to tell Davin all about it?" She paused. Elmina was leaning forward now, poised to explode any second. "Angus Kane."

Elmina froze for a moment, then started muttering to herself. "No," she said, pushing off her heels and lodging her thumbnail between her teeth. "No way, it's not possible. Is it? Could he have known? After three hundred years?"

Dawn waited, silently, as the fairy paced and mumbled for a good three minutes—about Angus, about Jacara, about the Great

Sleep, and about Davin's poor father. Finally, she stopped dead in her tracks and pointed at Dawn. There was a new fire in her eyes. A new sense of urgency.

She swiped the air with both arms. "Forget everything I just said. If Angus was on Selladóre when your curse broke, he was there for a reason."

"Yeah. He was there to take Davin away."

"No," Elmina said, pacing again. "I mean, maybe initially but … if it was anyone else, I'd overlook it. But this is Angus Kane. He's smart. Viciously smart. If anyone could have figured it out, it's him."

"Elmina," Dawn said, grabbing Elmina by the shoulders and holding her still. "Figure what out?"

There was a heavy sigh, a weight-of-the-world sort of sigh.

"It's very rare that a curse outlasts the life of its caster. Usually, when the caster dies, the curse automatically breaks — like Ruby's would if she'd cursed Donner. But when I modified Jacara's curse, I inadvertently extended it. Jacara died centuries ago, but her curse lived on with mine. So, when it finally ended, Jacara's powers were released. I always assumed they just flitted into the universe somewhere since she wasn't alive to receive them. But maybe…" Her gaze fell toward the floor, then slowly rose back up to look at Dawn. "Remember how I said the ability to steal another fairy's magic was almost unheard of?"

Dawn nodded, suddenly understanding where this was going.

"Well, unheard of doesn't mean *never* heard of." She analyzed her shoes again — red moccasins with orange and turquoise beads on one end. "Jacara had that ability. Jacara would have been able to steal Ruby's powers, use them to curse Donner, and still have her own to use as she pleased. But that's just the start of it. If Angus Kane found a way to harness her magic — which is where those charms may have come in — there's one reason that you, specifically, should be terrified.

Not sure she even wanted to know, Dawn just stared back in silence. Her eyes asked the question.

"Jacara didn't just have the power to hijack magic. She could obliterate it too, and not just from that moment forward. Jacara had the ability to undo every spell another fairy ever cast. If Angus has that capability, he could undo Ruby's rags-to-riches spell on Cinderella. He could reverse history as we know it. He could obliterate the modification I made to Jacara's curse three centuries ago. He could make you—"

"He could make it so I died three hundred years ago, when I was supposed to," Dawn finished, her voice half dead already. "Got it."

Chapter Seventeen

BELLE

She knew it was a bad idea.

She'd been told, over and over again, that barring a life and death situation, you should never wake a sleeping baby. But she hadn't seen Rye for almost twenty-four hours now. If she didn't take him into her arms in the next sixty seconds, she was going to split apart at the seams.

Outside, the sun had just begun its midday descent. But in Rye's nursery, the only light came from cracks between the window frame and the shade, and from a battery-powered disc that glowed yellow, then red, then purple, then green, on a perpetual, flowing loop. It was attached to his crib and—once she got used to the darkness—illuminated every inch of his tiny, innocent face. She could see his itty-bitty nose, barely larger than her thumb, and the cherub crinkle atop his bow-tie lips. He had a new scratch on his cheek—nothing major, just babies being babies. And his mouth was partially open—the bottom lip pulled to one side by his curled but open fist.

Belle shook her head at this last observation. His hand-sucking habit was already giving him blisters. Leaning into the crib, she reached out to remove his fist when something else caught her eye. The buttons on his footed pajamas were pulling apart. Had they been that snug at the hospital? Her heart pounded a little bit faster. Was this further evidence that the curse was speeding up already? In leaving him for twenty-four hours, how much of his growth — how much of his life — had she actually missed?

Then she dipped closer and examined his clothes. All of the pajamas she'd packed for him had tiny animals embroidered over the heart. These had no animals. Snow must have bought them — from an environmentally sustainable company that only sourced organic materials, no doubt.

This realization swiftly pulled the weight of worry off Belle's shoulders. But just as quickly as it disappeared, a new one returned. A nagging feeling. A, dare she say, jealous feeling. Not only was Snow sheltering, feeding, loving, and comforting her baby ... she was rebranding him as well.

Suddenly, the desire to scoop him up and press him to her chest was overwhelming. She felt jumpy — giddy almost. She *needed* to hold him, as much as Rapunzel's parents must have needed their rampion fix. She needed to give him the one thing that only a mother could, in the way only a mother could. She needed to see and feel the relief wash over him as he latched on and realized she had returned. She hadn't abandoned him.

But Dr. Frolick had been clear. She had the worst case of mastitis he'd ever seen. She needed to start a strong course of antibiotics immediately, as well as pump or feed diligently every three hours. He'd promised that the medication wouldn't hurt Rye, but nursing was going to hurt like hell. Plus, it would change the taste of her milk and could turn him away from it forever. "Just another gift from the inexplicable world of magical perinatology," he'd said.

"Well," she whispered as she slid her hands deftly beneath Rye's fragile little neck and his tiny little bottom. "Here goes nothing."

Holding her breath, she lifted him one, two, three feet up and over the railing. She exhaled, slid into the glider, and pushed the feathery bangs away from his forehead. Five days old and he already had bangs long enough to reach his eyelashes. At this rate, he'd need a haircut every other day.

"Okay little man," she said, cringing as she opened her blouse and undid the tab on her bra. "Drink up."

He latched immediately—a genius even in his sleep. A split second later, his eyes popped open. Belle's heart skipped a beat, but then his lids fell back down and he sighed. His hand reached up and touched her, as if he was holding a bottle between his fists. Belle shut her eyes to pressure out the pain. It was the sort of pain only a mother could voluntarily bear for her children, the sort of pain her own mother would never have endured for hers.

Wincing, she bent her neck forward close enough to feel the tiny hairs on her forehead brushing into his. On the one hand, she was feeling a thousand fire-tipped arrows shooting into her chest and exploding. On the other, she was completely at peace. Full serenity. Needed, wanted, and in love with every little molecule in her—

The wailing came out of nowhere. Belle jerked up, then looked down. Her euphoric little angel was suddenly bright red, flailing, and screaming at the top of his lungs. Thinking he'd just unlatched, she tried to fix it but he pushed her away like a tiny ninja, swatting away a goblet of poison.

Belle quickly switched him around and tried the other side. The quiet only lasted two seconds this time.

"What in the world is going on?"

The overhead light blasted on as Snow raced in and asked the very question that was spinning around in Belle's head.

"I ... I don't know." She stood up, seeking answers from Snow the way she'd sought them from Kirsten at the hospital. "I was trying to feed him and— Well, Dr. Frolick said it might taste a little different but I never imagined—"

"What might taste a little different? When did you get here? Did you wake him up?"

"No," Belle said, the questions colliding in her head. "I mean, yes. Sort of. Griffin let me in. He said you were out walking. I took the ferry here because the ring wasn't working. I just had to see —"

"Let me take him," Snow said, grabbing a towel from the dresser and holding out her hands.

Belle's first impulse was to pull Rye closer and back away. Who was in charge here? Who was the mother? Why was she trying to justify stopping by to see her own son?

"Belle," Snow said, jerking the towel and glancing pointedly at her chest. "Let me take him while you clean up."

"Clean up?" Belle squinted, then crinkled her lips. Of all people, she wouldn't have pegged Snow as a nursing-makes-me-queasy kind of girl. But then she looked down and realized why Rye had gotten so upset. It wasn't just a shift in flavor. It was a change of Biblical proportions. Instead of white or even yellowish milk, she'd been feeding him blood.

Belle gagged, swiftly trading Rye for the towel. "Dr. Frolick said there might be a little blood, but this is— Gah! I'm so, sorry, sweetheart!"

"He's fine," Snow said, bouncing and swaying her way to the door. "I'll just give him a bottle for now. I mean, if that's okay with you?"

Belle looked away and shut her eyes. Her entire face crinkled inward, but she appreciated being asked. "Yes," she said. "Thanks Snow. Sorry I didn't call before showing up. It's been one of those days."

Snow shot her a maternal smile and shifted Rye to her shoulder. "You never need to call. Consider this room just an extension of wherever you are. That's what we decided at the hospital — whether you get here by ferry, magical ring, or dragon. You can explain everything else downstairs."

Once Belle was cleaned up and emptied (manually — talk about endurance), she joined Snow in the great room — so named not because of its size, but because it essentially encompassed the entire first floor.

"Why don't you just stay here?" Snow asked after Belle updated her on the ring, the mastitis, and her unplanned sleepover in Gray's cabin, "If you want to continue nursing, you can't possibly go back and forth every three hours by ferry. Honestly, that would be more suspicious than you just packing a bag for a few days. If anyone asks, you can say I offered to be your nurse while you recuperated."

"So, say you're taking care of both an infant and an injured pregnant lady?" Belle shook her head and quipped, "That's believable."

"Fair enough. Then we can say you're getting in some practice before *your* baby arrives."

Belle pondered this idea as she tucked a receiving blanket around Rye. He was in a vibrating napper, ogling a pair of monkeys dangling above it. "That could actually work," she said, before tilting her head and eying the cardboard mountains lining the entire back wall — refugees from Griffin's office-turned-nursery. "But no." She shook her head. "You don't have the room. I've put you out enough already."

"Put us out? Nonsense! We love taking care of Rye. Griffin hardly used that office anyway. And don't forget, we changed that into a nursery months ago."

Belle pressed her lips together and sank further into her cushion. She hadn't forgotten. How could she? Snow was the only one of her friends who had any understanding of what she'd gone through, waiting years and years to conceive a child. Being devastated over and over again but somehow finding a way to keep hoping. Only now, Belle felt like the prisoner who'd been pardoned at random while Snow still languished behind the barbed wire walls.

"There's just something remarkable about having a baby around," Snow was saying. "Trust me, Griffin feels it too. Last night the two of them were playing peekaboo and he was just laughing and laughing and — "

Belle's head jerked to the side. "Last night? But I thought you said Rye fell asleep in the car and didn't wake up till this morning. How was Griffin playing with him last night?"

Snow's hands plummeted back into her lap. "Well. Okay. He did actually wake up for a second. But really it was only while we were transitioning. Griffin entertained him while I put on a fresh diaper and PJs. I was going to call you after that ... but he nodded back off before I even finished the swaddle."

Belle was staring at her knees when Snow's right hand spread over them. "I'm sorry. I should have called anyway."

Belle swallowed the lump in her throat and bent over the napper. She picked up the blanket, bundled it around Rye, and pulled him into her lap. Then she grabbed a green teddy bear from the floor and nuzzled it into his chin.

"It's okay," she said, thinking about poor Karen Epson and the two additional cribs Snow had removed from Rye's nursery and stored out of sight. As bad as things were for her, they could have been worse. "I'm here now."

"Yes," Snow said before standing up and proffering some herbal tea. "Decaffeinated, of course. Although ... if you're not going to nurse for a couple days, you can probably spring for regular."

Hearing the question in her friend's voice, Belle took a huge, slow breath, and relayed exactly what Dr. Frolick had told her. "So, it's safe," she concluded. "But I never want to hear him scream like that again — especially not because of something I did."

"I completely understand," Snow replied, filling up the kettle. "You're probably afraid that if you keep trying, you'll turn him off for good, too. Even when it's all cleared up."

Belle nodded.

"Okay then. How's this?" Snow buried her head in their tiny

freezer. "I have nine more bags of your milk here, so that's …"
She paused to count on her fingers. "One and a half days' worth.
Maybe two. Do you think it will clear up by then?"

Belle shrugged. "The antibiotics are for four days, but maybe.
It'll at least be better."

Snow slipped back onto loveseat.

"I really don't want to wean him," Belle added, pulling Rye
tighter and closer than—well, almost tighter than when she said
goodbye to him at the hospital.

"You won't have to."

"But what if it's not even my milk that's the problem?" Belle
said, her voice beginning to quiver. "Maybe he just likes bottles
better now that he's had one. I've heard that can happen. Five
days old and he's already done with me—"

"Stop it."

Belle's upper and lower jaws collided. She'd never heard
Snow use that tone before. It was assertive. It was commanding.
It was … slightly to moderately impatient.

"There are nine bottles left. We'll give him three over the next
twelve hours and you can try again tomorrow morning. If that
doesn't work, we'll do the same for the next twelve hours. I'm
sure it'll get better by then." Snow sighed and looked away. "I
know what you're thinking. That it's the only thing no one but
you can give him right now, but it's not true. You're his mother.
Only you can give him that. I couldn't replace you if I tried."

Belle nodded and sniffled herself into a smile. "Thanks
Snow."

"Don't mention it. Now let me get that tea. And then you can
tell me how you wound up staying with Gray last night instead
of at Rapunzel's. I don't know what was going on between him
and Ruby at the hospital last week, but he seems like a good guy.
Passionate too—I like that." She paused and let out an
uncharacteristically sly grin. "And can I say absolutely
gorgeous?"

Belle smiled and rubbed her nose against Rye's. He giggled and tried to bat it with his tiny fingers. "He is a good guy," she replied, feeling surprisingly sure of her words. Then, just to Rye: "Even if he did used to call you a gremlin."

Rye stopped for a moment, as if insulted by what she'd just said. Then he let out a screech of laughter and resumed thrashing.

భా

The call from Dawn came just in time: Elmina was on board; their theory about Angus was plausible; and Belle got to be the first mortal to experience evaporating with a fairy in the twenty-first century.

"Thanks again for the ride," Belle said as she and Elmina Goodman materialized outside Gray's cabin. She felt like she'd just fallen nine hundred stories in a glass elevator. "It takes at least two hours to get here from Snow's house taking the ferry."

Elmina laughed, said two hours was a gross understatement on "that rickety old boat," and told Belle she was happy to help.

"From what Dawn told me, you've had a rough few days," she said as Belle swished her foot through the fallen leaves and hoped her ring would work tomorrow. She didn't want to call Elmina every time she needed to travel between Braddax and Tantalise. And she didn't know how many more trips she could stomach.

"Pretty spot," Elmina said, ignoring the mountain of rubble a hundred yards away. The sun was entirely set now, but the sky still had a bright, steely glow. "It's nice to know there are still a few pockets of wilderness in this concrete jungle—even if they are just thrown in here and there."

Belle nodded and inhaled the crisp, early autumn air. The smell of dirt and decomposing leaves traveled deep into her lungs and diffused throughout her body. She hesitated to say she enjoyed the smell of autumn even more than spring. It was sort of like proclaiming she preferred death over new life. But to her, there was always something fresh about this time of year. It had always felt invigorating. Like the grand finale at a fireworks display, it was Mother Nature's last hurrah—an opportunity to show off its brightest colors before the world hid away for winter.

At least that's how it used to feel, she thought, as the smell of wet tree bark faded into the stench of five-day-old, stale campfire. Or, to be more accurate, Phoenix fire.

"Are you expecting someone?" Elmina asked as a pair of headlights turned up the drive.

Belle squinted. The headlights lit up square, not oval, and they had a slightly blue tint.

"That's not Gray's car," she said, her instinctive reaction one of concern. It could have been Penny or the insurance agent or even Rapunzel back from her trip. But the negative possibilities seemed far more likely: Donner, Angus, a reporter, one of her siblings, a lunatic fan, or just a member of the public eager to help but destined to cause more harm than good.

"Elmina, you should go," Belle blurted as the car rolled towards them. "And quick. With all these new laws about magical people, we can't take any chanc—"

Her words stopped the second she swung around and realized she'd been talking to herself. Two beams of light centered on her chest as the car came to a stop.

"Angus," she half-shouted as the back window rolled down to reveal the prime minister's sunken face. Her voice was ten times cheerier than warranted. "What are you doing here?"

The old man's needle-thin lips grew at both ends, but his teeth remained hidden. His eyes panned both her and the space around her. "I actually came by to see how you're doing. And to apologize for not paying you a visit at the hospital. As you can imagine, things have been quite busy over at the castle, but I still should have found the time."

Belle nodded but clenched her fist at his reference to Carpale Castle as if it was his, not Cinderella's.

"It's a dark time for Marestam," he continued. "What with this new magical threat and the hesitance toward the monarchies. The people are frightened. But thank goodness you're okay. And the baby…"

A few seconds passed before Belle realized these last three words weren't meant to be a statement, but a question. Certainly, he'd read the papers. He must have heard the news reports claiming that her unborn baby was safe. Did he doubt them?

"Yes, thank goodness," she sang, pushing out a sigh of relief and bringing both hands up to her belly. "Thank goodness. We're both fine. I'm so sorry about your niece."

"Thank you. Kiara is actually my wife's niece, in the interest of full disclosure, but has been like a daughter to me nonetheless. I like to think that's why she took on my name. Goodness knows it wasn't for the wealth." His lips grew again, almost cynically. "Anyway, I'm very glad to hear you are well. If there's one thing the people need right now, it's hope. As a matter of fact, that's part of the reason I came to see you. When you weren't at Taaffeite Towers, I was a little worried — especially with that crazy husband of yours being — "

"You went to Rapunzel's apartment?"

Angus cleared his throat. "Yes, I assumed that's where you'd be staying, under the circumstances. I hope I didn't overstep."

Belle hesitated a moment, then brushed the air with her hand. She didn't want him thinking Gray was anything more than an employee. "No, of course not. I'm lucky to have such powerful friends looking out for me. I've actually been going back and forth between here and Taaffeite Towers. There's just so much to do and — " She forced a laugh. "Well, call me delusional, but I'd like to have the Phoenix rebuilt by the time this bump becomes an actual baby."

Angus nodded in what seemed like approval. "I wouldn't expect anything less."

"Yeah," Belle said, instantly clamming up.

"Well, I won't keep you. It's almost dark and I have the State of the Realm Address in an hour." His eyes analyzed the trees behind her again. "Are you alone?"

"Yes."

"Well, please do be careful. Like I said, the people need hope right now, and with all that's been happening, I think you're the monarch to look up to now." He paused to let this sink in, then offered to provide her with a government security detail or an escort back to Carpale.

Belle gracefully declined and pointed out that she no longer considered herself a monarch—and no one else should either. Angus gave this comment a one-sided smile, tipped his head, and said that's precisely why it's so fitting. "Looking forward to seeing you at Prince Carter's coronation Friday," he added before ordering his driver on, "assuming it actually happens."

Belle waited a few minutes after the brake lights disappeared, then scanned the trees for Elmina and sauntered cautiously up to the front door. She was just about to knock—though the cabin technically belonged to her—when she heard a familiar bark in the distance.

"Come on!" she heard Gray shout from somewhere in the trees. "You do know I can't throw it for you if you never let me have it, right buddy?"

Belle felt her lips stretch wide as two figures emerged from the tree line—one prancing on four legs with a giant stick in his mouth, the other running beside him and struggling to pull it loose.

As she slipped around to the back of the cabin, the laughter in his voice brought a flood of memories to the surface. This was the old Gray—the bouncy, carefree drifter with a childlike love of life and no imperiled love interest to bog him down. She thought about their very first meeting—how he'd destroyed his car to avoid hitting her renegade dog; how he fearlessly flicked a poisonous snake away from them as if it was a coiled stick; how she'd wanted to send him packing immediately but Rapunzel invited him to stay.

Then she remembered waking up beside a warm fire after Ruby's badgering had actually caused her to faint, like some frail starlet in a period melodrama. She recalled the tranquilizing feel of his arms—sturdy but lean as opposed to Donner's overwhelming girth—as he carried her back into the cabin. She recalled the intoxicating smell of spiced turkey stew as she slowly regained her senses and began to open her eyes. It was then Belle began to understand why she'd felt such fierce and immediate hostility towards the complete stranger. It wasn't because she despised Gray. It was because she didn't. It was because he threw a five-foot-eleven wrench into the last-resort plan she'd been clinging to—the plan that said she could keep her baby and her business so long as she renounced romantic love for the rest of her life.

Watching him now, playing keep-away with her rescue dog but thinking it was a game of fetch, she felt all of those emotions come rushing back. Maybe this wasn't where she belonged in the eyes of Ruby Welles or her ancestors or Hazel Wickenham or the universe in general … but it was where she wanted to be. And at some point, didn't that have to count for something?

She remained in the shadows for several minutes, soaking up the happiness that came out when her troubles weren't front and center. She wanted to see Gray without the terror that came from loving someone with so many problems. She wanted to see Beast bounding through grass with his tail hoisted towards the sky like a curved victory flag, without the despondent pout that came when she was too busy or too sad or too tired to play with him.

"You'll always be my first baby," she'd assured him months

ago, after assembling the crib in the nursery nook of her bedroom. His head had been on her lap as she leaned against the butter yellow wall and stroked his silky silver ear. She remembered wondering if he understood what was going to happen. Based on the way his eyes lifted up like triangles being pulled up at the tips, she doubted it. But she'd promised him that he wouldn't be forgotten, anyway. Things would change, and there might be times when he was no longer the center of attention, but he would always be an essential part of her family.

So far, she hadn't made good on that promise. She'd fought to stay at Marestam General for as long as she could. She'd rushed out first thing this morning even though he hadn't seen her for days and was probably still having nightmares about the fire. And now she was still contemplating patting him on the head, grabbing some clothes, and heading back to Tantalise for the foreseeable future. What else could she do?

"Hey," she called as Gray finally grabbed the stick.

He about-faced and beamed, but Belle couldn't help but notice his posture become instantly more rigid—less like a kid on the playground and more like a soldier preparing for inspection. He barely made it three feet before Beast zoomed in front of him, stripped the stick from his hand, and barreled towards Belle like a runaway roller coaster on freshly greased tracks.

"Hey!" Gray yelled, picking up his heels. "Gentle, buddy! Belle, watch out for—"

But Belle was ready for him this time. Hinging at the waist, she unlocked her knees and held both hands out so she could catch his paws before they knocked her over.

"Hey buddy!" she cooed as he gained speed. "I missed—"

Her hands and face both dropped as Beast zoomed right past her, brandishing the stick in the air, and raced back to Gray. Was this payback for her disappearing all day?

Belle crossed her arms and was just about to sulk when the

dog spun back around. He threw both paws out in front of him, lifted his tail, and let out a playful growl.

Belle laughed and dropped her purse. "Oh, I see. You want to play, huh?"

Beast growled again, splayed his paws further out and raised his entire butt towards the sky. Then Belle broke into a sprint (or as much of a sprint as she could muster with her stitches) and Beast took off, galloping between her and Gray. Before long, he was in full "crazy run," as she liked to call it, when his hind legs hitched all the way up through his front legs and he essentially flew on solid ground. He wove between the humans, diving and teasing with the ball in his mouth until he'd finally carved enough figure eights to bring Belle and Gray side by side—at which point he struck a calendar cover pose and dropped the stick at their feet.

They continued to play until everything was pitch black except the stars, a sliver of the moon, and the glow from the kitchen window.

"I take it you got the ring to work," Gray said as the exhausted trio settled in by the fire—Gray on the sofa, Beast on his bed, and Belle cuddled on the floor beside him, stroking the folds of his neck.

"Not exactly," she replied, concealing her frown in Beast's fur. He gave a long, contented sigh. "I had to take the ferry to Tantalise. But Dawn's fairy was able to give me a lift back here. And by lift, I mean she waved her fingers, we spun down some mind-numbing metaphysical drain, and something spat us out here."

"She can do that?"

Belle nodded. "Apparently magic was a lot stronger three hundred years ago, so yeah. Must be nice." Her eyebrows rose. "I'm still hoping the rings will work in the morning, when I'm a little less..."

"Insane? Psychotic? Completely off your rocker?"

She gave him a look. "I was going to say upset. But sure."

Gray squinted and leaned forward. One elbow balanced on his thigh while his hand splayed out, as if grasping for answers. "So how long were you at the hospital? Do they know what's wrong?" The fear in his voice was undeniable. "Is it serious? Are you going to be okay?"

"I'm going to be fine," she said. "Dr. Frolick gave me some medication and it'll clear up in a few days. It's a very common thing for new moms. Don't worry, I won't go into detail." She kissed Beast on the forehead, pushed off the floor, and slid onto the other side of the couch. The cushion between her and Gray seemed simultaneously minuscule and massive.

She looked around the room. Gray had placed five pillar candles on the mantel over the wood stove, but everything else looked the same as it had before the fire.

"This is just weird," she said. "I don't know what's more noteworthy: the crazy feeling of déjà vu I'm having right now, or the fact that my secondhand cabin furniture suddenly feels so special."

Gray let out a small chuckle. An uncertain chuckle. Then the timer for the ravioli went off and he disappeared into the kitchen. He returned a few minutes later with two clay bowls and some rice for Beast.

"Sorry," he said, handing over the dinner. "It isn't my usual masterpiece but I didn't know whether you'd be coming back."

Belle dipped her fork in and blew on the pocket of spinach-and-cheese stuffed pasta. A puff of steam billowed off. "It's perfect," she said, lowering the dish into her lap to let it cool. "But do you mean to tell me you don't cook filet mignon and spaghetti squash pasta when it's just you?"

Gray laughed again—this time more heartily, more real. He shook his head. The dark waves tumbled towards his eyes, then back again. "Well, this is a delicacy compared to the dry cereal and eggs I survived on while searching for those rings."

"Dry cereal?" she repeated, picturing him digging through the rubble in the moonlight, never stopping to eat, sleep, or even take a proper bathroom break. "I'm sorry. I didn't think the rings would be so hard to find and — "

"Do you remember the last meal we had together before the fire?"

"Of course," Belle said, grateful for the subject change. "Takeout in the lounge. That was unusual too."

"It was an unusual day," he said, not missing a beat.

An electric buzz shot up her spine. She picked up her fork just as he lowered his.

"It was," she agreed. "It was the day I found out Donner emptied my bank account. Domineering jackass that he was — is."

Gray nodded, leaned back, and threw his arm over the back of the couch. "Yup, and you went speeding over there like a lunatic with a death wish. Do you remember pulling away while I was still half outside the car? I thought for sure you were gonna kill at least one of us."

Belle focused on the ruffled design lining each ravioli. As much as she enjoyed reminiscing, she didn't want to go much further in fear that he might remember something about that night differently. She never wanted to forget how he challenged Donner and came to her rescue, or how he looked changing her tire in the rain. She wanted to always remember the fireplace back at the inn, and the tension so thick she could have sliced it with a fingernail. And then, of course, their kiss — at least the first perfect seconds of it, before the stabbing pain and the trip to the emergency room.

"Oh, come on. I couldn't have been *that* crazy," she teased, depositing the still-too-hot ravioli between her teeth. "Otherwise you'd have been crazier for deciding to get into the car with me."

"You know I didn't have a choice," he said in a tone that sent a chill down her back.

The ravioli felt like a rock in Belle's throat as her mind flashed to Gray crouched by the side of the road, his olive-green shirt clinging to his torso as the water poured over him. She did know why … now. But at the time, she wasn't sure. She hadn't yet realized that his anger towards Donner and his concern for her meant she'd flipped some sort of switch inside of him—just as she wasn't sure what changed the following afternoon, after her first stint in the hospital. They still hadn't discussed it.

But it was time. If there was any chance for them at all, she had to know why he came back the night Donner lost it.

"What changed?" she asked, staring into the red and yellow jumble in her bowl.

Seconds passed. Beast groaned and rolled over on his bed. She could feel Gray looking at her, questioning her question with his eyes.

He pulled his arm off the back of the couch but didn't resume eating. "What do you mean?"

"The night you came back." Belle could feel him tense up again. "You knew why I went back to Donner, even though it killed me to let you go. You knew we all believed it was the only way to save my son, but you came back anyway."

Slowly, robotically, Gray lowered his head, placed his bowl on the coffee table, and turned to face her. It was only then that a new thought popped into Belle's head. "You did know, didn't you?" she asked, feeling her throat tighten. "Ruby told you. I mean, that's the reason you left to begin with. Right?"

"No," he said, pushing himself off the couch.

Belle felt all of her organs deflate. So, he hadn't left to protect her? He'd just … just left?

Gray pinched the bridge of his nose. His sleeve fell just far enough to reveal the scars on his forearm—an intricate web of blood that had oozed out and dried up years ago. "I didn't know the details about the curse," he said, "but I knew you were better off without me. Ruby reminded me of that the first night you went to the hospital. The people around me always wind up getting hurt, and I would never forgive myself if that was you — or anyone you care about."

Belle squinted, as if doing so would make what he'd just said any clearer. He'd never gone into detail about his past, but he'd told her, over and over again, that it was dark. She'd never pressed it because she knew he was a good man. The past was in the past. She didn't want him to reveal all of his skeletons any more than she wanted to reveal hers, but she wasn't an idiot. She saw how Donner's eyes jumped when he got a glimpse of Gray's arm, and how he immediately backed off. That scar wasn't from his time working on the fishing boat, or in the iron mill. It was a sign of membership.

Rather than make her afraid, however, knowing this made her pity him even more. At least newspapers eventually found their way into the trash bin. His mistakes would be carved into his skin forever.

"I left because it was the right thing to do," he said, staring at the pile of wood beside the stove. "But the further I drove away from you, the sadder and angrier I got. I felt myself becoming reckless again, so I … I came back. I thought what we had was strong enough to change things. But look at what happened. If I'd stayed away, you and Rye would be healthy and safe right now. And who knows, maybe Donner would have morphed into the perfect husband in a few years." He gritted his teeth and tugged on his sleeve. "I came back because I didn't want to picture myself without you, but with that selfish decision, I verified everything Ruby had said about me. Darkness can't keep company with light without dimming it. I don't deserve someone like you. I should have just kept driving."

Their eyes caught — defiance at first, and fear. But as the moment passed, Belle's frown began to soften. He'd just given her the only answer she really needed: He'd come back because he couldn't stand to be without her. It had been selfish, yes, but love has a tendency to do that. It makes people foolish and hopeful enough to think they can defy all the odds. He couldn't have possibly predicted what wound up happening that night—no more than she could know what would have happened had he kept driving.

"I'm glad you didn't," she finally said. "I'm glad you didn't keep driving."

Gray's mouth opened in disbelief. He swayed a little in her direction, but then shoved his hands into his pockets and looked away. Something was still holding him back, but Belle would wait—just as he'd waited for her.

"How about some dessert?" he said after a good five minutes of silence. "Frozen yogurt? Assuming you're heading back to Tantalise tonight, it might be wise get your sugar fix beforehand. You know ... considering your track record with sweets at Snow White's house."

Belle smirked at his cheap rampion brownies quip. Then her eyes panned the ceiling and her toes dug beneath Beast's warm fur. "Actually, I think I'll let Snow have Rye to herself tonight. How about some wine instead?"

One of Gray's eyebrows rose while the other fell, a move that sent a whole colony of butterflies swarming around her stomach. "Are you sure? I thought you said alcohol gets into the milk and—"

She silenced him with a wave of her hand. "I have it covered. We both deserve a night off from everything outside this cabin."

Gray agreed, albeit hesitantly, and scurried off to grab two goblets and a bottle of chianti. A few minutes later, he popped in to place these on the table, zipped out again, and returned holding a massive piece of cardboard between his outstretched arms.

"I have a surprise for you," he said, halting and balancing his cargo on his feet. "Remember that painting you had over the mantel in the lounge? The one of the forest and the seasons?"

Belle gripped the arm of the couch and refocused on the cardboard. "Yes," she said, unsure where he was going with this. She had loved that painting, despite it coming from Angus. But there's no way it could have survived the fire.

"Well, maybe the universe decided to cut you a break after all," he said, flipping the cardboard around to reveal the exact same painting.

Belle let out a pop of disbelief. "Wow," she said, getting up to inspect it. "This looks exactly the same. Where did you find it? I guess it wasn't one-of-a-kind after all. Figures."

"What do you mean?" Gray replied. "This *is* that painting. The one we hung on the wall." Belle shook her head as a chill ran up her spine. "I found it in the rubble."

She stared at it again. There wasn't a scratch on the thing. A little ash that wiped right off, sure, but the canvas was intact. Ruby's words from the hospital replayed in her head: Only magic could destroy magical charms.

"Where's the frame?" she asked, the urgency in her voice catching Gray off-guard.

He scratched his head. "I … ummm …. This is how I found it. I'm sure we can get another frame though."

So, the metal frame melted in the fire, but its canvas painting came out unscathed? Belle shook her head and started pacing the room. "It's not just a painting," she said as Beast stood up to shake. He could sense the storm coming long before Gray. "It's a charm. It has to be. There's no other explanation. That feeble old snake put a charm in my inn, in the very same room where Donner went completely berserk. Can that really be a coincidence?"

"I thought Donner went berserk because he's cursed," Gray said, obviously not following.

Belle shook her head and kept pacing. It didn't add up. It had never added up. Yes, Donner was cursed. She didn't deny that. But she'd never seen him lose control like that in the past, even at his absolute worst.

"Strange things happen in fires," Gray said as Beast scampered out of the room. "Filing cabinets melt around reams of paper that survive because they're so tightly packed. Things close to the floor only get smoke damage. Maybe this got knocked out of its frame when it fell off the wall. You can't assume its a ch—"

"You're right," Belle said, lunging forward with the corkscrew in her fist.

"Belle! What the heck are you—"

Gray jumped back as the pointed coil of metal slammed down onto the canvas. Once. Twice. Five times with gusto.

"Not a dent," she said, repeating the same move on the wine cork, then filling two goblets to the brim. She held one out for Gray, clutched the other in her fist, and tapped the air. "Looks like we've had the enemy front and center all this time. Cheers."

Chapter Eighteen

RUBY

Ten minutes after the phone call, Ruby Welles rolled off her frayed floral couch, trudged into the dark, laminate kitchen, and unearthed the bottle of Armagnac she'd been keeping for a just such an occasion. Absolutely nothing was going according to plan—not that this was much of a surprise. Nothing in her life had ever gone according to plan.

As usual, cursing Donner Wickenham had been impulsive. Selfish. A crime of passion she immediately wanted to undo but lacked the expertise. Up until then, Ruby didn't even know it was *possible* to resurrect a broken curse. Or, if that's not what happened, to cast a new one without a wand, a spell, or even the intention to do so. An earth-shattering curse by accident. Some iconic fairy she turned out to be.

The first time it happened, six years earlier, Donner was so close she could have chucked a beer bottle in the air and nailed him smack in the nose. In hindsight, that's probably what she should have done instead—though that wouldn't have given him a shot at redemption. It wouldn't have allowed him to meet someone as pure and good as Belle without sizing her up for a drunken one-night stand. And wasn't that the whole point of her abilities? To better the people who needed bettering? To save the kingdoms that needed saving? Even if they went into it kicking and screaming?

But this second go-around was just plain irresponsible. It was the quintessential result of an itchy trigger finger. It meant her previous symptoms were plain old psychosomatic. It was, if it ever went public, exactly the sort of mishap Angus needed to win his war against magic once and for all.

Ruby tapped her cup and plodded over to the window, which started at her nose and stopped just below the parquet ceiling. It was frosted around the edges with a giant stained-glass sun in the center. She still remembered the day her mother had it installed. "Just because we live in a basement doesn't mean we shouldn't see the sun," she'd said. "Watching everyone's feet all day is depressing—even if most of them do have very lovely shoes." A cheeky teenager at the time, Ruby had called it tacky and old. That description haunted her now—now that she was a sixty-year-old spinster who owned a luxury apartment but spent most of her time in her dead parents' subterranean hovel beneath Marestam's famous Western Library.

Swirling her drink, Ruby took a long, wet sip and tried to process what she'd just heard. Belle's call about the painting had been surprising, but not altogether transforming. They already knew Angus had access to all of Marestam's confiscated charms. If anything, the discovery bolstered Ruby's allegations against him. It supported her finger-pointing and her declaration that Angus was behind *everything* that was going to hell at the moment—not just the Charmés disappearance and the movement to abolish the monarchies, but Donner and his child's curse as well.

Elmina's call, on the other hand … Elmina's call had changed everything. If the eighteenth-century fairy's theory was right, taking down Angus was going to be much more difficult than Ruby originally thought. But if the triad succeeded, perhaps the extent of his betrayal could work in her favor. Perhaps the people's faith in true love and happily ever after and white knights and fairy godmothers would be restored all on its own. Perhaps, in scapegoating Angus to cover up her own blunder, Ruby inadvertently pulled back the curtain on one of history's most diabolical villains.

Still, there were almost too many questions to count: For how long before the Great Awakening did Angus know about Selladóre? Why let Hunter Tirion take all the credit for breaking the curse? If Jacara's powers really had blasted out from the broken spell like a dog in search of its master, could Angus really have caught them? And if so, could Ruby get her hands on them instead?

Feeling a sudden chill, she pulled a chartreuse cardigan off the ironing board, pushed two fluffs of graying hair behind her ears, and returned to the couch. Her eyes fell on the coffee table and the massive book that hung over the sides. The words of her parents echoed in her head each time she saw it. "One day, the Western Library will have a new custodian, and you'll be responsible for preserving Marestam's history," they'd said just a few days before their accident. They'd sat her down in this very room, with the Welles family register in the exact same spot as it was now, and explained that their vocation was more than just a job — it was a calling. It would be her responsibility to not only record the realm's greatest stories of love, courage, sacrifice, and hope, they explained, but to protect them as well. "The Marestam we know can't survive if it forgets where it came from. We are the keepers of the past, and without that, there can be no future."

Perhaps she'd taken the word "protect" a little too literally, but how could she have known? There were no Welles left to ask. There were no friends upon whose shoulders she could cry or whose ears she trusted enough to bend. There were only her beliefs, the tenets in this book, and the few words her disinterested teenage ears bothered to hear the day her parents told her everything.

When all was said and done, there was only Ruby. For decades now, behind the international media corporation, the billion-dollar name, and the faultless authoritative personality, there was only an orphaned teenage girl trying to make things right.

Chapter Nineteen

DAWN

Dawn didn't fully comprehend the magnitude of what Elmina had told her until she came home and saw her two children in the living room, hunched over their schoolwork on opposites sides of the couch. Day had his bare feet on the coffee table, brown-bottomed socks on the floor. Morning was sitting cross-legged with her back straight as a flagpole, textbook perched inches from her nose. The local news channel, which repeated the same thirty-minute program on an endless loop all day, was on but muted. There was a tall glass of water on each side table, and a half-empty bowl of popcorn on the center cushion.

If the wackadoo fairy's theory was right and magic was retroactively erased from existence, the people of Selladóre wouldn't be the only ones to disappear. Their children—regardless of what century they belonged to—would fade away as well. Dawn had to make sure that didn't happen. She had to stop Angus from committing genocide, intentionally or not, on an entire kingdom and an entire race. But first, she had to tell Hunter what was going on.

So after tucking the kids into bed, kissing their precious

foreheads, and wishing them goodnight, she poured two glasses of whiskey and joined him on the couch.

He straightened up the moment the cushion compressed, but didn't look at her. His eyes remained focused on a yellow binder filled with line graphs and stock symbols and a bunch of other things she'd never bothered to understand.

"I need to talk to you," she said, proffering the alcohol.

After a few seconds, he raised his eyes to the television, then the glass, and then, finally, to her. "No thanks," he said, sending her blood pressure through the roof. "'I'm not drinking tonight."

Dawn resisted the urge to empty the drink right onto his binder — or his head. But at least his rejection was directed at the drink, not her request for conversation.

"Hunter," she said, rotating so they were perpendicular to each other. "I know I deserve all of this cold shoulder, pulling teeth, humble pie stuff right now ... and I'm not trying to get out of it. You have every right to be mad at me. If I were holding your shoes, I'd feel the same way. But there's something I really need to talk to you about." He angled his chin toward her and raised an eyebrow — no doubt intrigued by her proper use of four modern phrases ... or at least she thought. "Please?"

Hunter's shoulders rose and the binder closed. Slowly, he pulled his right foot off of his left knee and twisted — just a little — towards her. "What's wrong?"

Dawn froze. They were just two tiny words, but their tone and his body language and the concern in Hunter's eyes made her feel as if ... well, as if some higher power had reached down and told him, *Enough. This is a ceasefire. Your wife is in pain.*

She flinched as his hand landed on hers and moved the shaking glass of whiskey to the coffee table. He didn't even bother with a coaster. Then he brought his hands back to his knees and waited.

Dawn rocked her jaw side to side a few times, as if she needed to warm the muscles before taking off. She decided to start with what happened at the hospital with Belle. She'd build on the familiar, with what he thought he already knew. After all, had he not found her memory box that night, all of this would have already been said.

He showed no emotion throughout the entire spiel. Then, when she came to a decent stopping point, he leaned forward and grabbed up his shunned glass of whiskey.

"Okay," he said. "So. To recap. The baby that everyone thinks Belle is still carrying is actually the four-month-old everyone thinks Snow White adopted." Dawn nodded. "Cinderella and Aaron are missing. Ruby Welles believes Angus somehow took away Ruby's powers and brought Donner's curse back. And the plan to fix all of this rests with Donner's mother, the witch who kidnapped Rapunzel, and the fairy responsible for your sleeping curse?"

Dawn nodded again. He was a good listener.

The liquid in his glass dropped a full inch.

"Do you have any proof against Angus? Or is this based entirely on what Ruby says?"

Dawn's nod went crooked. "You don't believe me?"

Hunter frowned. "That's not what I said. I'm just wondering whether Ruby did something to lose her magic and is blaming Angus so these three fairies will come together and get it back."

Dawn hadn't expected this, but she was prepared. It was almost exactly what Elmina had thought before she told her about Selladóre.

"Sweetheart," he said, laying a soft hand on her thigh and capturing all of her attention. "I'm not saying you and your friends are wrong. I'm just saying you can't leap to such grand conclusions on one person's word—at least not without considering other possibilities. Have you tried just *talking* to Angus? I mean, I don't doubt he would like to rule Marestam on his own, but I just don't see him kidnapping two people or endangering a child in order to do so. You know how stressful parenthood can be, especially when you're in charge of an entire kingdom on top of it. Maybe Cinderella and Aaron just decided to be irresponsible for a little while. This trip was supposed to be the continuation of their *honeymoon*, after all."

Dawn felt a familiar sting behind her eyes, but forced her body to shut it down. The last thing she wanted to do now was cry in front of Hunter. That's not the way she wanted to get him on her side.

"But if you *are* right," he continued, "once you get some proof, you won't need any magical assistance to —"

"Angus is the one who found Davin," she blurted. Hunter's jaw stopped mid-syllable. "He knew Selladóre was more than just an overgrown island, and he knew exactly when the curse was going to break. That's why he brought you. And while you were with me, he was taking Davin away to Pastora to take over Perdemi-Divan so he could —"

"Wait." Hunter's head shook like a dog with an infected ear. "What?"

Dawn flashed a smile of pity. "I know. It's confusing. Davin's father started Perdemi-Divan three hundred years ago. He was outside the kingdom when the Great Sleep started and was — for lack of a better phrase — locked out." She sucked in as hard as she could, but felt the tears starting to tip past the edge of her eyelids. Curse it. Not now. "And, yes, that means Angus and Davin had a relationship long before the merger and —"

"No, not that part," Hunter interrupted again. The skin around his eyes looked suddenly flushed. "You just said Angus knew when the curse was going to break. What does that mean? I thought I broke the curse when I kissed you."

Dawn stopped her breath, then forgot to exhale. Her chest grew two sizes.

"You did!" She lunged forward to grab his hands, but they were too busy cupping both sides of his whiskey glass ... which was trembling. "Of course you did! I don't know —"

"Because that sounds like Angus only invited me along that day because he needed someone to hold your attention while he absconded with the man you *really* wanted to be with."

"No, Hunter that's not—"

He drained his glass and pushed up from the couch.

"It all makes sense. Choose a king so her parents would push her into a marriage they assumed would save their kingdom." He dropped two metal ice cubes into the glass. "Mentor the corporate heir to ensure you've got an insurmountable foothold in a billion-dollar company." He swung the liquor cabinet open and pulled out a fresh bottle. "Then, just when people's faith in the monarchies are beginning to crumble, send the long-lost scion back here to plunge another royal marriage into scandal and make it even easier to knock the whole system down." The ice cubes crashed together as he swirled his glass. "I guess I should be grateful that you chose me in the end—or at least that you chose your crown and your children—but a scandal's still a sandal no matter how it ends." He shook his head and gulped his drink. "Well, thanks for giving me the heads up, I suppose. It's helpful to know we're stuck in Angus Kane's pocket until he decides to destroy us."

Dawn didn't know what to say. She'd been staring at all those dots for days, trying to figure out how they played into Ruby's theory. Hunter had connected them in a matter of seconds.

"Hunter, please. I—"

"Just tell me one thing," he said, swaying a little though not from the alcohol. "Was any of it real? If the kiss didn't break your curse and you only married me out of perceived obligation, was any of it ever real? Was there ever a time when you loved me at all?"

Dawn was on her feet and across the room in seconds. She grabbed hold of his hands and fell to her knees spouting all sorts of assurances that she *had* loved him … that she *did* love him … that she'd been blind and selfish and she was determined to do everything in her power to prove that she'd changed going forward.

"Stop it," he said, pulling her back onto her feet. He pressed his lips together as the skin around his eyes turned red. "This isn't a movie, Dawn. And it's not a fairy tale either. There's no grand gesture that can make everything right again, and no criminal mastermind whose defeat is going to undo what you did. The only thing that's going to fix us is you loving me, for real. You realizing that you truly want to be in this marriage, in this time, with me. But I can't make you do that. There's nothing in this world that can make you do that. Not Angus. Not Selladóre. Not even the kids. You have to decide that on your own, and you have to be sure. If you don't think you can do that, please—"

"Hunter," she said, pulling his hands to her heart. He forced himself to look at her eyes, as if he knew the truth wouldn't come from her mouth. "I've already decided. And I'm already sure. I feel like I've lived the last decade entirely in the past, and you've lived it in the future. But more than anything, I want us to both be in the present now, together. I know I can't get the last eleven years back, but I don't want to squander whatever we have left."

Dawn felt his hands soften between hers. He took a long, deep breath and exhaled. She could see the tension melt from his body as the air passed his lips and traveled elsewhere.

"There's one more thing you need to know," she said, hating herself for ruining this moment. "I found Elmina today. She thinks that when my curse broke, all of the magic that would normally have gone back to Jacara—that's the fairy who tried to kill me—actually found its way to someone else."

Hunter's eyes swam inside hers. "Someone else like whom?"

Dawn released his hands and clapped her own against her chest. "She can't say for sure. Ordinarily spells don't outlive their casters but … well, with Angus being right there that day and having access to all those charms … it's possible he found a way to contain it."

Hunter looked confused, possibly even a little amused at the audacity of it all. "Absorb it? Eleven years ago? But if that happened, why haven't we seen him turn a political rival into a frog or raze any buildings with his bare hands? The worst he's done is manipulate Parliament into extending his term limit. What would even happen if he absorbed it?"

"Well," she said, struggling to find the right words. "Elmina couldn't say whether or not he did. But *if* he did — or if *anyone* did — it could be devastating. Jacara was the most powerful fairy she'd ever seen, apparently — and that was three hundred years ago, when every fairy was more powerful than any today."

"Dawn," Hunter said, placing both hands on her shoulders and bending down so their eyes were on the exact same level. "You're skirting the question. What might happen?"

She took a deep breath, pulled in her cheeks, and shook her head. Then she dropped her face and started to cry. A few seconds later, she felt her legs moving toward the couch, the cushions press against her back, and Hunter's body lean into her side. Her heart pounded as he took the base of her chin between his thumb and forefinger, and moved it gently towards him.

"Dawn," Hunter said, taking her hand and lacing her fingers between his. "Tell me."

So, she did. And as he wrapped his arms around her like a metaphysical seatbelt and swore he'd stop at nothing to make sure she and *their* children were safe ... as he told her his company and his pride and even the realm meant nothing to him if he lost his family ... she felt their ceasefire settle into permanence.

Chapter Twenty

RAPUNZEL

The feeling hit her like a two-ton freight train on a faulty track: Home. As soon as that door opened, Rapunzel was a child again—clopping down the hallway in Grethel's oversized slippers, reading beneath the bow window in the corner, and coloring all over the driftwood coffee table Grethel was so inexplicably fond of. The giant sea glass bowl still sat in the center (though it now held wicker balls instead of candy), and the hearth still had that one disproportionate rock that stuck out an extra two inches and had scraped her legs more times than she could count.

For a moment, she forgot all about Ethan, Belle, Rye, Cinderella, and even the brooding shadow looming behind her. Being in that tower again, after ten-plus years in another world, was all-encompassing.

"Is she there?" Donner asked, as if his eyes and ears weren't twelve inches behind her own.

Rapunzel scowled but didn't answer. After that speech in the stairwell, she wasn't interested in engaging him any further. She was too busy reconciling this beautiful, transitional space with the cluttered, kaleidoscopic fortress of her memory.

At her feet, a woven jute rug spread out across the entry, which opened up to the coastal-themed living room and an eat-in kitchen with stainless steel appliances and a wide, butcher block island. But rather than being buried beneath a chaotic mess of color — sweatshirts strewn over the couch, books doubling as tablecloths, drawers yanked open and their contents spewed all over the floor, spaghetti-crusted dishes soaking in the sink — the place was spotless. Without Rapunzel, it had gone from budget daycare to the cover of a home design magazine. She'd never realized how disruptive her presence had been in Grethel's life.

She flinched as Donner cleared his throat ... twice.

"Where's the cauldron?" he asked before eyeing the staircase at the far end of the hall, between the powder room and the kitchen. "Wait. This place has more than one level?"

"It has four," Rapunzel answered, feeling a slight flow of pride followed by a strong wave of guilt. No doubt, he'd envisioned Grethel as a dreary, pockmarked, villainous old hag who lived in a one-room dungeon with animal carcasses pinned to the walls and shelves full of pickled eyeballs. It was a common misperception, but it was a misperception she'd never bothered to change — either because she was angry at Grethel or because her whole "survivor" image held a lot more water when people envisioned the worst.

But in truth, the tower in which she'd grown up was just like any other picture-perfect suburban home — just taller, skinnier, and with a more unique exterior. If memory served her right, she and Donner were standing directly below her bedroom, which sat beneath the ensuite master and a mysterious, locked room Grethel referred to as her "office." Rapunzel had spent many years trying to break in, but either the magic or the steel always prevailed. When she finally gave up, her favorite pastime became daydreaming in the rooftop garden. The flowers that bloomed there were always in season, the air was easier to breathe, and the views were spectacular. This was where she was when Ethan spotted her all those years ago—before his harness broke on the climb up and her hair (instantly ankle-length thanks to Grethel's enchantment) just managed to reach his fingers. It was where he sat and told her that the world beyond the turquoise blue horizon wasn't a wasteland like Grethel had said it was. It was magnificent, and exciting, and worth being a part of.

"Grethel?" she finally called, venturing into the living room. She ran her hand along a dusty blue pillow and tried again. No answer. Half a second later, Donner clomped over the threshold with a sigh, popped his massive frame onto the couch, and plopped his muddy feet onto the table.

"You might want to let your boyfriend know we're up here," he said, pulling a silver flask from his pocket, but tucking it back in upon spotting a glass decanter in the corner. "You don't want him thinking we ran away together and left him. Poor guy's been through enough already."

"Cut it out," she commanded, smacking his shoes off the table and continuing on to open the window. She'd have no problem spotting Ethan from up here.

"Fine. Ignore me," Donner said, getting up to inspect the decanter. "But sometimes the best advice comes from the unlikeliest of places. And even with my faults, you can't deny I've had more meaningful relationships than you have." He swished the amber-colored liquid beneath his nose, then poured two glasses and returned to the couch. "Not *more*, of course. God, you'd be hard-pressed to find anyone who could eclipse *that* record. Just more that actually meant something."

The rage started in her toes, then shot all the way up her spine and into her eyeballs. Rapunzel's fists clenched. Her insides seemed to leap forward while her feet remained firmly planted to the floor. She'd felt the exact same way a hundred times before, right here, with Grethel. But now, she also felt woozy. And a little queasy. This sudden propensity for nausea was really beginning to cramp her style. She needed to sit down.

"You know what? Fine," she said, taking one last look out the window, then plummeting into the armchair opposite the couch. She grabbed the second glass of whiskey. "We're stuck on this island until Grethel comes back so … enlighten me. What warped philosophical advice is lurking behind the ethical black hole that is Donner Wickenham's brain?"

His left eyebrow rose in surprise. "Really?" they seemed to ask without help from his mouth. Then he uncrossed his legs, leaned forward, and rested both elbows on his knees. "Like I said before," he began, "I don't know what he did to make you angry but—"

"So what makes you think you're qualified to analyze it?"

He tightened his lips but ignored her question. His eyes fell on the bracelet wrapped around her wrist—the one she'd taken from his things at the prison. "I don't know what he did, but I do know that you're incapable of separating an unfortunate slip-up from calculated betrayal. Your punishments are the same either way. And that's going to be your downfall."

Rapunzel took a swig from her glass, then shook off the sting. Grethel always did have good taste in liquor. "That's ridiculous," she said, chewing on her words. "It's not like I *want* to punish Ethan. Just like I don't want to shave my legs every day but, you know, a girl's gotta do what a girl's gotta do."

Donner shook his head and tipped back his glass, watching her through the bottom but not saying a word. After draining it, he got up to pour some more.

"I think it's one per customer," Rapunzel muttered.

He raised an eyebrow as the liquid streamed out, then tried to justify his thievery by explaining that he was a recognized whiskey connoisseur—so much so that Perdemi-Divan sent him a free batch of their bestselling concoction twice every month, purely out of respect.

"Just a thought," Rapunzel replied, "but excessive alcohol

consumption while cursed might not be something to brag about. Definitely not an opening line at your trial."

Donner's glass descended as he gave her a disparaging look. "I've barely touched the stuff for days."

Rapunzel laughed. "Good for you. How much of that is because they don't allow flasks in prison?"

His eyebrows dropped a good inch and conjoined in the middle. "This is actually my first drink since getting out. Well, technically second." He set the decanter back down. "I guess I can handle fleeing the law sober, but listening to your self-destructive bullshit is where I draw the line. You don't even realize how screwed up you are."

Rapunzel's legs swung forward as her body lurched to the edge of her chair. "I'm screwed up? Why? Because I'm a woman who stands her ground? Have you looked up the word 'chauvinist' lately?"

Donner's glass paused inches from his frown. "There are female chauvinists too, you know. Seriously, you're so deep in your own propaganda that you don't even realize you've lost control."

"My propaganda?" Her voice hit a note she'd never heard before. "What does that even mean? Where do you even come up with this st—"

"Rapunzel Delmonico, so wild and free." He let out a sarcastic pop of laughter. "You act like you're this completely autonomous, independent female force, not caring what anything else thinks. But you aren't even calling your own shots right now. Your *image* is. You're crucifying a good man because that's what *she* tells other women—like my wife—to do."

Rapunzel forced a laugh, settled back into her chair, and crossed her legs. Then she uncrossed them. Then she spun his bracelet around her wrist and folded her arms. "You're delusional," she finally said.

"Am I? One single mistake is grounds for dismissal, is it not?

I mean, so long as the perpetrator is male. And you're sticking to your own damaged advice now solely because you think doing otherwise would be hypocritical." He paused. Rapunzel wondered if he could hear her heartbeat as well as she could. "Even though in reality that makes you the biggest hypocrite of them all."

Rapunzel didn't know what to address first—the fact that Donner had just spoken with such eloquence and insight about human emotion, or the fact that he'd just insulted her to the core. She grabbed hold of the latter while struggling to ignore the scores of butterflies swarming just beneath her skin.

"Ethan lied to me," she barked back, embracing the latter. "And I have a problem when someone betrays the person who trusts them the most—male or female. So yeah, I put up a wall. It hurts like hell, but it's the right thing to do. Because it's one lie now—and I even understand why he did it. But how do I know that's the whole disease and not just one of a million other symptoms? How do I know that five years from now, I won't be holding a positive pregnancy test the same day I find someone else's red underwear in his study?"

Her words barreled down and then dropped like a horde of rocks over a bottomless gorge. In the ensuing silence, her chest heaved and Donner stared at the floor so intensely, she feared it might break beneath his feet. After a full minute, Rapunzel noticed his jaw moving, ever so slightly, as if he was mashing something tiny between his teeth.

Finally, he picked up a coaster, tossed it down on the table, and returned to the couch. "He wouldn't do that."

Rapunzel stretched forward in her chair, staring him down like a tigress waiting by the watering hole. "How do you know?"

She watched his bottom lip open, then close just as quickly. He sat back. "Because your relationship is nothing like mine and Belle's." He pushed his head back, letting it rest on the back of the couch. "Because even an ethical black hole like me can see that there's something a heck of a lot stronger than a wedding ring holding you together."

Rapunzel sealed her lips and looked toward the window. The sky had a faint, pink glow to it now. She wanted Ethan to walk through the door soon, before it got dark.

"We were never friends," he continued. "We never joked with each other or challenged each other. What she said at Letitia's party that night was true. I was a mess when she came to the castle—inside and out. I needed a savior, and she was so pretty and sweet and patient. Of course I fell in love with her. But there's a difference between true love and *truly loving* someone. She was the wife and I was the husband. And despite what you want to believe, I was a good husband for the first few years. But we were never close. Everything was always 'fine' with her—even when I knew it wasn't. If she didn't like something I was doing, or buying, or saying, she just tucked it inside somewhere and accepted the disappointment."

Rapunzel scoffed. "Beautiful and obedient with no opinions of her own? Sounds like every man's dream girl."

"God, no. Not even close." Donner rose to his feet and sliced his hand through his hair. "Do you know how many times I saw my own wife without makeup on? I can count them on one hand. Do you know how often she let me comfort her or how many times it was *her* idea to make love—and I don't mean while she was ovulating? Do you have any idea how depressing it is to live with someone who's disappointed by everything you do but too polite—or too defeated—to say a word about it?"

Rapunzel slid back onto the cushion. He was describing the exact same Belle she used to find so irritating. The old Belle. The goody-two-shoes with no emotions and a life-size doll's wardrobe.

Donner crossed the room and leaned into one of the windows near the hall. He stood this way for a few painful seconds while Rapunzel tore shards of skin from her bottom lip.

"At first, I just wanted her to let loose. I wanted her to yell at me for something. Make a mistake. Break a lamp. I wanted to know she still cared enough and believed in us enough to try and fix my faults — like she did before. But this time, she just accepted them."

Another shard of skin, but no response. When did Donner Wickenham become so ... deep? Was that why he'd fallen for Belle's sister? Because she was bossy, unhinged, selfish, and everything Belle wasn't? Was it ironic or just sad that in order for Donner to fall back in love with Belle, he'd had to make her despise him?

"Believe it or not, I get that," Rapunzel heard herself saying. "I actually do. But if that's really what you wanted, why did you insist on her dressing up like a porcelain doll all the time? All of those ridiculous dresses..."

She trailed off as Donner sighed, pinched his nose between both fingers and muttered something inaudible. Then he turned to face her. "There are two sides to every story. But look, that's not why I brought us up. My point was that if Belle and I had what you and Ethan do — so long as you stop running away from it — things would have been very different."

Rapunzel rolled her eyes. "You can't possibly know that. Life isn't that black and white. Maybe if you'd married Julianne to begin with, it would have been Belle's panties beneath that bookcase and Julianne sobbing on my doorstep at two a.m."

"I know more than you think," he snarled, his eyes suddenly darker, as if a shadow was crossing over them. "I let other people's opinions stand in my way once, and it ruined my life."

"Are you serious? You think losing Julianne ruined your—"

"Dammit, I'm not talking about Julianne!"

Rapunzel heard the roar first, then the sound of glass breaking in Donner's fist.

"I'm sorry," he said, turning his injured palm toward the ceiling but doing nothing to stop the blood. "It's this damn curse.

A lifetime sentence for one mistake."

Rapunzel's heart thundered against her ribs. She felt her entire body leaning forward, willing him to reveal one of the biggest secrets of the century—the story about who turned Donner Wickenham into a beast six years ago and why.

"If you want to know so badly," he said, scooping up the shards of glass, "just ask."

Rapunzel looked up from the chair and gave him an odd look—as if he'd just appeared out of nowhere and she didn't know what to say. Donner glanced at the couch but then retreated to the fireplace. He tossed the glass onto the wood, grabbed a stack of cocktail napkins, and leaned against the brick.

"There was someone before Belle," he said, applying pressure to the makeshift bandage. "No, there was *the* one before Belle." Rapunzel felt her eyes widen. "We had what you and Ethan have. A romance that spanned the ages, that we couldn't deny no matter what else was happening in our lives. When she wasn't around, I was a lesser person. When she was around, everything was brighter, warmer, happier."

Rapunzel migrated to the edge of her seat. She tried to picture a different Donner—younger, kinder, gentler.

"We were best friends and lovers, too." He took a deep breath and stopped. "And then someone killed her."

Rapunzel's hand flew up to her mouth. "I spiraled. I couldn't have cared less about living anymore. I wanted to be in the ground with her, but I was too cowardly to do it. So I drank myself into belligerence every night. I went to bars and started fights, hoping one might solve my problem. Then one day, some high-and-mighty fairy with no idea what I was going through took it upon herself to teach me a lesson instead of help. And before I knew it, poof! The monster raging inside of me switched places with the outside, and the rest is Marestam history."

Rapunzel stared at his shadow, transfixed. "That's ... that's horrible," she said, suddenly wanting to defend him. "That's not fair. That's exactly the sort of thing that makes people afraid of magic. Do you know who it was? Who cursed you?"

Donner's head sprung up in surprise. One side of his mouth drifted to the side as his bottom lip slowly opened ... then pulled closed again. He looked the other way and shook his head.

Rapunzel had a feeling he was lying. There were only so many purebloods known to exist. Could it possibly have been his own mother?

"Do you know who killed her? Did they ever catch him?"

Donner sucked both cheeks in and shifted his palm into a claw. Rapunzel pulled the throw pillow into her chest.

"Yes," he said, escaping into some mental dungeon from which she doubted he'd return anytime soon. "Her husband. She wasn't the first."

∂∞∾

After watching him stare out the window and twist his eyebrows in silence for a good twenty minutes, Rapunzel realized Donner had told her everything he was comfortable telling, and was going to keep any remaining secrets locked inside his vault. Perhaps that's the real reason he'd flown across the world—not to provide unnecessary help in the search for Grethel, but because he wanted someone in Belle's corner to hear his side of the story for a change.

Well, she had—and now she needed some air. A lot of air. Mumbling something about watching for Ethan from the roof, she shot a farewell glance at Donner and drifted toward the stairs.

Rapunzel knew Grethel wasn't home because she would have rushed out with either a suffocating hug or a vehement tirade. That's what she remembered most about her childhood: it was an unpredictable dance of cuddles and reprimands, of belly-laugh afternoons and long stretches of complete isolation.

At first, it was all the former. She had a mother, a mentor, and a best friend all rolled into one. She had an island paradise at her feet and a clear view all the way to the horizon. Back then, there was no such thing as deception, or bullying, or heartache. She fit into her perfect little world like a cork fit into a wine bottle. Until one day, she didn't.

Rapunzel held her breath as she reached the landing and saw her bedroom door for the first time in over a decade. It was still pink, still covered in stickers, and still held the nameplate she'd decorated with a dozen different scented markers. As she passed over the threshold, she noted that the red letters still smelled like cherry.

Inside, everything looked exactly the way it had the day she disappeared, though no dust had accumulated. Socks were strewn across the floor, but the carpet looked freshly vacuumed. The bed was unmade, the bottom dresser drawer was ajar, and … she gasped … her very first journal sat, open, on her freshly polished desk. A blue pen lay across the right-hand page.

Dear Diary, the first line read. Rapunzel cringed at the lack of originality. *I met a man today. Yes, a living and breathing man, just like the princes in those storybooks I found in G's closet. He wants me to run away with him. And I want to. I want to see all of the amazing things he's sworn exist somewhere outside of this island. But I'm scared. It took G years to admit that other people even exist beyond this island. And when she did, she made me promise never to leave. She said we're safe here. And happy. She said the rest of the world holds nothing but misery. She said that if I ever left, I'd end up just like my birth parents — desperate, selfish, and enslaved by my own hand. Perhaps even worse, she said she wouldn't be able to help me. The future has suddenly opened up but I don't know what to do. I'm supposed to decide by tonight because he's coming back to —*

It stopped abruptly. Rapunzel didn't need a play-by-play to remember what happened next. Grethel had called her down to dinner. Rapunzel, who hadn't yet learned how to camouflage her emotions, gave herself away by asking too many questions.

This led to a fight. In anger, Rapunzel had threatened to run away.

"In fact," she'd said, "When you wake up in the morning, I might be in another world entirely … on the other side of that reef you put up to pen me in."

"Reef?" Grethel had repeated, forming an expression of such profound sadness, it seared into Rapunzel's memory for the next dozen years. "Who told you there was a reef?"

Several hours later, after screaming and crying until her head felt like it might explode, Rapunzel got what she requested but didn't actually want — to be as far away from Grethel as humanly possible.

"I'm sorry, G," she whispered now, closing the journal and dropping the pen into a mug she and Grethel had made together one rainy afternoon. It said *Daydreamer* in raised blue letters and was as lopsided as it could get without toppling over. "I'm so, so sorry. I didn't really want to leave." She sniffled. The tears came fast, welling up and tipping over her lids without the slightest pause in between. She stared out the porthole window and slammed her wrist on the desk. "I never thought you'd actually get rid of me so easily."

"You think it was easy?"

Rapunzel jumped. She dried her eyes with her wrists and spun around. The figure in the doorway was slightly blurry from the remaining tears, but she knew exactly who it was. Her heart leapt up and splattered against her rib cage.

With one turn of the head, she was suddenly a child again, caught storing broccoli in her dinner napkin for an eventual flight out the window. She was a teenager, losing her ring in the liquor cabinet she wasn't supposed to touch in the first place. She was a thirty-year-old bachelorette, slumped over her journal looking at the woman who'd fed her, bathed her, read to her, sang with her, tucked her in, and one dark day decided to wash her hands of her.

"Punsy," Grethel said, though the sound was so soft, she only recognized it by the way her lips moved. The only things she heard clearly were the pounding of her heart and the rustle of Grethel's ankle-length skirt as she crept forward. It stopped halfway and waited, either out of caution or respect, but her eyes seemed to advance the remaining six feet anyway.

Rapunzel swallowed hard and looked at the carpet. She wasn't ready for this ... this what? Reunion? Rematch?

"Letting you go was anything but easy," Grethel said, rubbing a chunky silver heart dangling from a leather cord around her neck. "It was the hardest thing I ever had to do."

Rapunzel exhaled and immediately tried to shake the words away. She glanced up for just a second to see those eyes still staring back at her — those emerald green eyes with the orange ring around the pupil, the only ones that had looked at her for eighteen years straight. "You didn't *have* to," she said. "I was angry when I said those things to you. I didn't realize I was so expendable that — "

"Expendable?" Grethel rushed forward, her head shaking and the ruffles of her skirt gushing out like brown lava. "No. Is that what you think?" She stopped suddenly and knelt down, taking Rapunzel's face between her hands. "There is nothing in the world I love more than you. But this tower was built for a bitter, lonely woman with no faith left in the world. It was wrong of me to ever think I could keep you here."

Rapunzel bit back the sting and pushed her hands away. She jumped to her feet. "Wrong for who? Since when do you care about being wrong? You attacked people to keep them away from this island. This entire house is filled with things you stole — me included. You're telling me you couldn't fight the temptation to swipe someone else's coffee table, but kicking *me* out over one teenage tantrum — no problem?"

The outburst acted like a mushroom cloud, ballooning out around the room and continuing to rumble long after the initial explosion. Grethel stepped back, her shoulders hunched and her hands poised in front of her. They were significantly more wrinkled now, as if her skin was in the middle of a drought, and all of her veins seemed to jut too far above the surface. But her eyes were still intense. Her hair, while interfused with white, still looked primarily chocolate. And Rapunzel could still see a little youthfulness in her face, though it seemed to be retreating — quickly — at the moment.

"You're absolutely right," she said, her voice trembling. "I'm not a good person. I don't do what's right. That's why I'm here. That's why I have no friends. That's why the world makes up stories about how evil I am, and I don't even care. But there is one thing I do care about." She looked up. Their eyes magnetized. "You're not a coffee table, Rapunzel. You have free will. I wanted you to want to stay, forever. But eventually, forever would mean all alone. It killed me to set you free, but I had to do the right thing just that once. I had to do the right thing when it came to you."

"But ..." Rapunzel's voice felt tiny. "If you wanted me to have a life outside of here, why didn't you just let me go with Ethan?"

Grethel's lips rose a bit on both sides, then parted. "I didn't know Ethan," she said, saying his name as if she was flicking an ant. "And I wanted you to find yourself first. I wanted you to get to know the world before deciding what you wanted out of it. You spent your entire life eating nothing but bread and suddenly got a taste of pineapple. But I didn't want you eating only pineapple for the rest of your life either — not without ever trying chocolate or strawberries or steak. I mean ... I'm not nearly as eloquent as you are but ... does that make any sense?"

Grethel looked like a guilty child waiting for absolution. She wanted Rapunzel to open her arms and say, "Yes. I forgive everything you put me through. The desolation. The tears. The feeling of complete worthlessness. The men who took advantage of me because you left me with nothing and no clue how to get by. I forgive you for all of it because you were just trying to set me free, like the bird in that poem."

But that isn't what she said. Instead, Rapunzel shook her head slowly and thought about how she used her first job—fetching coffee at the *Mirror*—to research every registered magical being in the realms around Carpale. She thought about how she took freelance travel assignments featuring any destination that so much as touched a body of water. She thought about Grethel's threat to plunge Ethan back into darkness if he didn't keep its location a secret—even from her.

"I tried to find you," she finally said. "For years. I looked everywhere I could think of. Why didn't you want me to? I still could have had a life outside this island without losing you completely. We could have talked or written or visited. Crap G, you're a pureblood fairy. You could have zapped in for a nightcap and then zapped right back here in seconds. You didn't have to cut me off completely."

Grethel pressed her thin lips together and clutched the locket again. This time, it seemed to pulse with a faint white light. "There was a time I thought I could keep you here forever— when you were a baby, when you lit up every time you saw me, when you raced across the room, arms spread open, and crashed into my legs to hug them. I thought we could be best friends forever, a mother-and-daughter duo. "But you are a remarkable woman, Rapunzel, and I feared your loyalty to me would have held you back." She glanced away. "But for what it's worth, I never actually left you. I've been there for everything. The ups and the downs. The lazy, comfortable days, and the brand-new beginnings. You just didn't recognize me. You weren't supposed to. I got to see you blossom without becoming your burden."

"Burden?" Rapunzel's head shook a dozen times in two seconds. "What are you talking about? You wouldn't have been a b—"

"Punsy, I'm sick," she said, stopping Rapunzel's tongue as

effectively as a meat cleaver.

What? Rapunzel's heart instantly began to race. She could feel and hear every blood vessel in her body.

"I need to show you something," Grethel said, pulling slowly away. "It's time. I've hidden it for long enough."

⤳⤙

For years, Rapunzel imagined what could be hiding inside Grethel's top-secret office. Was it treasure? Weapons? Bodies? Did she keep a secret lover locked away in there? Was Grethel even more into bondage and submission than she was?

But when the key finally penetrated the lock and the deadbolt clacked aside, Rapunzel saw a cluttered room filled with newspaper clippings from Marestam, photos of Rapunzel as recent as two weeks ago, a bunch of machines that looked like they belonged in Marestam General Hospital, and medicine — shelves and shelves overflowing with medicine.

"You should have told me," Rapunzel said for what seemed like the fifth time since coming downstairs. A goblet of wine sat between her hands, but for some reason she didn't feel like drinking it. All she could focus on was the word "cancer" throbbing and repeating inside her head. "I could have helped. I could have been there for you."

Grethel shook her head. "All you missed out on was twelve years of nagging and power struggling."

Rapunzel frowned. "Well, I'll take that as an I.O.U." She moved her glass pointlessly along the table. This was so much harder than she'd expected. "But are you absolutely sure you can't stop it? You can't cast some kind of spell to reach inside and pull all of it out?" She thought of Ethan, who was in the living room now, bonding with Donner over their fear of Grethel and all other pureblood fairies. "Is it because all your powers are being used to power Ethan's sight? Because I don't think he'd want that. He knows how much you mean to me and —"

"That's not why," Grethel said, looking down to conceal a humble smile. "His spell isn't taking much from me."

Rapunzel tapped her glass. Part of her wanted to jump on this tangent, while another wanted to exhaust the subject of Grethel's illness until they brainstormed a cure. Finally, Grethel made the decision for her.

"The universe — or the ancestors, or the powers that be, or whatever you want to call it — considers every spell individually. Restoring Ethan's sight barely counted as a curse, I guess, because it was done to right my wrong. So I still have plenty of magic remaining. As long as I'm alive, Ethan will see as if I never threw him from this tower to begin with."

"Oh, that's great news," Rapunzel said, feeling vindicated to hear that Grethel's threat had been empty the entire time. "Because I need to ask you a favor and was afraid you'd have to take his sight away to —" She stopped, five of Grethel's words coming back to haunt her. "Wait. What do you mean *as long as you're alive?*"

Grethel took a deep breath and looked at Rapunzel. Her eyes said it all. When she died — whether from abnormal cell growth or skydiving on her one-hundredth birthday — all of her magic would fade with her. "I've been trying to transition Ethan's spell into a magical object," she said, clutching her locket again. "But I'm not strong enough to enchant it. I haven't given up though. I won't give up." She let go of the necklace and gave Rapunzel's hand a one-two tap. "Now about this favor…"

It took a few seconds for the question to break through Rapunzel's mental fog. "Oh. Right. Favor. You see, I —"

"I'll do it," Grethel interrupted.

"You'll do what? I haven't even said what it is."

Grethel eyed a five-inch thick binder she'd brought down from her office. It was overflowing with newspaper clippings and candid photos from Rapunzel's post-tower life. "If you want me to be a part of Ruby's triad in the hopes of saving your friends," she said, "I'll do it."

"How did you know about Ruby's—"

"Like I said," Grethel replied with a smirk, "I've been everywhere. You just haven't seen me."

Rapunzel then went over all the details, most of which Grethel already seemed to know. She wasn't entirely sure how to feel about this.

"There's only one problem," the fairy said when she finished. "I can be in Marestam in the blink of an eye if time is of the essence, but it's going to take more than a day for you all to get there. Unfortunately, my powers don't accommodate any passengers when I evaporate."

Rapunzel chewed her lip a bit, not eager to undo their fledgling reconciliation. "Well," she half-whispered, "can't you banish us there?"

Grethel gave her an injured look, then shook her head. "Sweetheart, in my condition, you'd be more likely to land on the top of a mountain in Vashia than in Marestam."

"Looks like you're lucky I'm here then," a gruff voice sounded from the doorway.

Both women spun around to see Donner standing there with his arms crossed, a silver flask in his hand, and Ethan behind him.

"What are you talking about?" Rapunzel huffed, not in the mood for his games. "You're not a pureblood. The only way you're going to evaporate to Marestam is if you fling yourself into the ocean and swim."

He crossed the room in three quick steps. "I don't have to be a pureblood," he said, grabbing hold of Rapunzel's wrist—and the bracelet wrapped around it. "This will get us to Belle. And it can take us both."

"Both?" Rapunzel blurted as Donner unclasped the bracelet and stuffed it in his fist. "What about Eth—"

"Any chance you know how to fly a plane?" Donner asked, tossing Ethan a set of keys and his flask.

Ethan caught them, then stared back, panning between Rapunzel and Donner with his mouth agape.

"Sorry mate," Donner continued, taking the silence as a no. "You two could use a little space anyway."

Rapunzel tried to pull away but Donner held on tight. "I'm sorry," he said again as her eyes locked with Ethan's. "But I can't face her without you."

Rapunzel's mouth sprang open to protest, but before her vocal chords even began to tremble, she saw Grethel and Ethan shrink in front of her and spiral out of sight. She found herself careening through some sort of mind-altering vortex, flying past doors and through beams of light. Her brain felt like it was going to squeeze out between her eyeballs, and her stomach was just about to explode when her body collapsed against the cold, hard ground. She heard the pre-sunrise call of a barn owl, felt grass and dirt between her fingers and saw … oh no. Snow White's cottage. The bracelet had taken them straight to Tantalise. It had taken them straight to Rye.

Chapter Twenty-One

DONNER

Donner was on guard the moment his feet hit the ground. He didn't know what he expected to see, exactly. A home nurse, perhaps? Mountains of flowers urging a speedy recovery? Belle, or that smirking miscreant of hers, lunging for the nearest sharp object?

But instead, he saw towering shadows against a dark periwinkle sky. He heard crickets chirping in every direction, a few birds summoning the sun rise, and a lone barn owl. He smelled dirt and grass and an herb garden that made him wonder whether Belle had taken up residence on an illegal rampion farm.

Then he squinted at the cottage in the distance, and noticed a veiled square of light on the second floor.

"Are we on Tantalise?" he asked, leaning down to pick up the quivering figure by his feet.

Rapunzel responded with a quick punch to his chest and a deafening reprimand. "Let go of me!" she screamed. "How could you do that? You just left him there! We need to go back. I—"

"Shhh!" he commanded, shoving his palm over her mouth

but apologizing profusely as he did it. He wasn't naïve enough to think their conversations over the past few hours had made them friends, but he did hope they'd humanized him a little. "I didn't have a choice," he said. "We couldn't wait three days for a helicopter and a plane ride. Ethan will be fine. He's probably enjoying a few drinks in peace." He slowly lifted his hand and looked around. "Now, where are we? Is that Snow White's place?"

Reluctantly, Rapunzel wiped her thighs and wobbled around a few times. "Yeah," she said, patting the white fence with her hands. "This is Tantalise all right. Home of the world's most understated palace and two monarchs who decide royal policy by consulting the stars. Why did you bring us here?"

Donner struck that iconic one-leg-bent, arms-crossed in confusion stance and dug into his thick, dark waves. The sound of his nails scratching along his scalp was amplified out here.

"She must be inside," he said, suddenly pitching forward and wrenching the gate open.

Rapunzel scurried after him. "Who? Belle?" She somehow managed to squirrel her way between him and the front door. "Why would Belle be at Snow and Griffin's house in the middle of the night?" she asked, forcing an exasperated smile that he could see right through. "If she left the hospital, she'd be at my place with Beast. I'm sure of it."

Donner leered at her. The ring — or the bracelet, now — didn't take wrong turns. "She has to be here," he growled, reaching beneath her arm to grab the doorknob.

Rapunzel stuttered for a moment, as if her thoughts were working on a delay — or struggling to make up a story. "But … but she can't be here. Why would she go here? She'd want to be close to the hospital, and the inn, and — "

She bit her tongue. Donner stopped short and loomed over her. "And what?" he said, though he knew exactly what she was about to say. And *him*. Gray. As if that was even a name. Gray, the smooth-talking, wise-cracking vagabond who didn't deserve her. Gray, the reformed gang member attempting to steal his wife and child. But that's not why he was here now. He was here to swallow his pride. He was here to show Belle how sorry — how truly, gut-twistingly ashamed — he was for what happened. He was here to hoist the white flag and give up ninety percent of what he wanted ... in hopes of salvaging the most important part.

Rapunzel rubbed her foot into the flagstone and gave a distracting smile. Donner knew instantly that waiting for her to continue would just be a waste of time. She was just trying to keep him from reaching that window.

"I just need to talk to her," he said, moving Rapunzel aside and pushing through the door. Figures the Whites would leave it unlocked. They probably didn't even believe in locks.

The house was tiny and the glow from beneath the stove vent lit his path straight to the stairs. Donner took them three by three, reaching the landing in four giant strides. Then he stopped. There was a linen closet to the left, a porthole window to the right, and a narrow hallway that rolled out a few feet and then curved. He inched down slowly, even though he could hear Rapunzel pounding along the floor below him.

When he reached the end, the pounding was replaced by singing.

"And if that diamond ring turns brass, Mama's gonna give you a looking glass."

Donner held his breath. That was definitely Belle's voice. His hands felt blindly for the doorframe, as if there wasn't enough light to guide him, and clamped down.

"And if that looking glass gets broke, Mama's gonna build you a sailing boat."

When he peered in, Belle was facing the other way. She was pacing the tiny room — the tiny nursery — holding what looked like a bundle of blankets in her arms. She looked beautiful, but what was she doing – practicing for motherhood? Had his rampage caused damage to her brain?

"And if that sailing boat turns over, Mama's gonna find you a four-leaf clover."

Just as Rapunzel raced up behind him, his throat clapped shut and his breath stopped. The linens in Belle's arms had moved. He looked at Rapunzel to confirm. The expression of defeat and worry said it all. Belle wasn't practicing her midnight feedings for when the baby arrived. She was actually caring for a baby. But whose baby? Last he'd heard, the Whites lost their adoption. He was so paralyzed with fear, wonder, and awe, that he barely noticed Belle was beginning to sway in a circle, rotating from the far wall to the curtained window to the doorway.

"And if that four-leaf clover turns brown, you'll – "

She screamed loud enough to wake the whole forest. The baby jerked in her arms and then howled. Two more sets of feet pounded up the stairs. Griffin and Snow stopped just behind the intruders, the latter waving a bat in her hands.

"What on earth is going on?" Snow shrieked. Her raven black hair looked like a raven black sheep's coat after a hurricane.

"Rapunzel? Donner? What's going on?" Griffin demanded, edging behind his wife.

At that moment, Donner recalled hearing something about the Whites finally adopting a baby. Belle must have been helping them. But this early in the morning?

"Donner?" Belle said, shielding the screaming baby from his view as Rapunzel rushed to her side and whispered something into her ear.

Donner saw her glance at the bracelet still clutched in his fist. He immediately opened his hand and extended it as if he was surrendering a dagger. "I was supposed to give – "

"Please don't," Belle said, raising her palm. "I don't want jewelry from you."

Donner's jaw opened to explain that it wasn't just jewelry – it was his freedom.

"Belle," he said, inching forward and trying to pretend they were alone. "I want to … need to … apologize. "There aren't enough words in any language to explain how sorry I am for what I did to you." His hands fell together, but he resisted the urge to kneel. He didn't want her to worry that his anguish was anything but genuine. He didn't want her to think he could be putting on a show, because he wasn't.

The truth is he hadn't slept in nearly a week. And it wasn't just the frigid cinderblock walls or the patronizing taunts of his neighbors that had kept him awake. It was the shame Everything he'd told Rapunzel back in that tower was true—he and Belle had never been each other's true love. By the time she came around, Donner's heart was shattered beyond repair. And though Belle had done a spectacular job of gluing it together, there was just no way she could replace his Karen.

Yes, she'd been married to someone else, but that man was a monster—a *real* monster—and her love for Donner was true. He should have begged her to leave him. He should have promised to make her a queen no matter what society said. He should have pissed on social convention and royal propriety and followed his heart. Had he done that, the love of his life wouldn't have become a decomposing corpse in her murderous husband's attic. Blue Beardsley. Blue mother-fucking Beardsley. Serial killing husband who deserved to be hung inside out from the rafters at Marestam Central Prison, not preserved there.

But none of that was Belle's fault. Donner had been wrong to try and change her. He'd been wrong to use her like a paper doll over which he could drape some remnants of his Karen—not that she hadn't done the same with him, in her own way. As soon as all the excitement from their fairy tale wedding faded, he could see the disappointment start to settle in. He had come with the right exterior, the right accessories, and the right bank account. But contrary to all the stories she'd read as a child, he wasn't the man of her dreams. Even before they started having problems making children, he could see that.

But he never intended to hurt her. If he couldn't have Karen, there was no one else he wanted more than Belle. She'd saved him in every way a flawed man like him could possibly be saved. He owed her everything. Standing here now, he couldn't believe the way he'd behaved with her sister. He couldn't believe he'd acted so terribly to her—more so than he'd ever acted under his original curse. It was almost as if he'd spent those months under some sort of drug-induced fog, intent on destroying everything that held him up and everyone who tried to help him stop.

"Rapunzel?" he heard Belle say, pushing the baby into her arms. She was giving him a strange look, watching curiously as his fingers tore at his right eyebrow—a nervous habit he thought he'd broken years ago. He pulled his hand down as her eyes widened. "Can you … can you take him downstairs with Snow and Griffin? I want to talk with Donner alone."

Rapunzel gawked back at her.

"It's okay," Belle insisted, nudging her toward the door. "I'll be fine."

After another minute and a few more hushed assurances, the audience retreated and Belle shut the door behind them. Donner picked a spot beside the crib, clasped the top rung, and stood there like a child waiting to be punished.

Her first move was toward the glider, where she bent over to pick up three picture books and place them on the built-ins. Then she gathered an empty bottle and two tiny blankets, which she carefully folded into squares. He watched as she did this, thinking she looked radiant but extremely tired. All of her chestnut waves were pulled over her left shoulder and secured with a tortoise shell clip. Her blouse was unusually disheveled, and one of the buttons was undone. Her mascara was slightly smudged, which probably contributed to the perception that she had sideways crescents etched beneath her eyes. This was not the overly made-up Belle he'd lived with for the last five years. This was the organic Belle he'd always wanted but suppressed by holding on so tightly to his first love. He saw that now.

Watching now as she took a calming breath and floated toward the window, Donner had an overwhelming desire to march forward, wrap his arms around her, and hold on tight. He wanted to just stand there as she nestled her head safely beneath his chin. He wanted to feel her heart thump from her chest into his. He wanted to undo everything he'd done to her over the last week … six months … five years.

But he wasn't brave, or presumptuous, enough to do it.

Finally, she spoke. "What happened?" The words were soft, as if not actually meant for his ears. "I keep playing the pieces back in my head," she said, still staring at the curtain with her back to him. "I don't understand."

Donner's fingers fell from the crib. He took two steps across the room, then stopped. Was she talking about the Phoenix — or their marriage?

"Even when you were cursed — I mean the first time — I never saw you like that. I could always get through to you. What was different this time?"

Donner shook his head as he tried to come up with the words. "I … I don't know."

The curtains shifted as Belle let out a puff of disapproval, as if he'd just given the wrong answer on a midterm. As if he wasn't trying hard enough to answer the question. Though perhaps he wasn't.

"Belle," he said, pressing his palms together. "I didn't go to the Phoenix that night intending for anything bad to happen. I swear. I was determined to be a new man for you and our baby. I was thrilled that somehow, the universe was giving me a second chance. After all I'd done. I should have known that was too good to be true. I didn't deserve it."

Belle shook her head and spun around. She pointed an angry

index finger towards the carpet.

"Then what happened?" she demanded, beating her finger at the last two words. "Why did you go from hopeful, soon-to-be father, to raging, homicidal maniac? Forget about *me*, you could have killed our child — *your* child. You know, if it wasn't for — " She bit her lip as if contemplating whether to continue. "If it wasn't for your *curse*, you actually would have. He actually would have died." Donner's head jerked up. "That's not an exaggeration, or a guess. That's a certainty. The curse is the only reason he was strong enough to — "

"Wait. *He*?" Donner stumbled in place, as if poked by the sudden flicker of light inside his chest. But just as quickly as it ignited, however, it dimmed again. Belle was glaring at him.

"Rapunzel told me you know about the curse," she said. "I just assumed Matilda Holt used a pronoun here or there when she broke the news."

"No," he said, staring at the floor. Rapunzel had called their child "he" back on the island, but Donner hadn't thought anything of it. Now, the news made him feel simultaneously elated and devastated. He looked at her belly — the belly that should have been such a huge part of his life now. The belly that should have been his favorite thing to touch and talk to over the past few months. It somehow looked a little smaller than the last time he saw her. Then again, she'd been in a wheelchair.

"It's nice to see you standing up and out of the hospital," he said. "How are you feeling?"

"Fine," she answered instantly, refusing to lower her guard. But then came the tiny crack of a window. "Tired," she added. "Overwhelmed. Scared. Angry. But grateful at the same time, and a little ashamed for not being more so."

Donner looked to the side to disguise an amused smirk. This was Belle in a nutshell. Feeling guilty for having emotions.

"There's nothing wrong with getting angry once in a while," he said, no longer able to keep the distance between them. Before he knew it, her shoulders were between his hands and she wasn't pulling away. "Or scared. It doesn't take away from whatever gratitude you feel or make you any less saintly."

She laughed—a sharp, staccato laugh that accused him of pulling compliments out of his ass. "I'm not a saint."

"Maybe not entirely," he said, letting his arms fall. "But I don't know anyone closer. How many other people would have asked a judge to be lenient after what I did to you?" She flinched, as if it wasn't extraordinary. "And now look at you. Fresh out of the hospital and you're helping out with your friend's adopted baby at six in the morning?" He looked around at the nursery. A little simple for his tastes, but cute in its own way. "You're going to be an amazing mother."

An awkward silence dropped. He bit his lip and stowed both hands in his pockets. His fingers wound through the bracelet. It was made from the stone that once sat in the middle of his ring, which had been passed to each firstborn man in his family for generations. Its magic would allow Belle to go almost anywhere she wanted in the blink of an eye, simply by clearing her mind and wishing it. In giving her this power, Donner was giving up his ability to disappear … to avoid prison … to pop in on his kid even if Belle refused to grant him visitation—since now, custody was undoubtedly out of the question.

But there was a difference between having a forced relationship with his son and having a good one. He'd decided to let Belle make that decision. It would have been a nice gesture a few days earlier, after she'd promised to return to him anyway. But now, with a price on his head and absolutely no hope for reconciliation anymore, it was the ultimate sacrifice.

"Belle," he said, clasping the bracelet in his fist, "I'd really like you to—"

"You still haven't explained what happened," she interrupted, delaying his offering once again. "What set you off?"

Donner sighed and pulled his hand out of his pocket, empty. "I don't know," he said, his voice cutting a sharper edge than he intended. But it was frustrating. Not an hour had passed without that horrible night playing and replaying in his head. He remembered every detail, every feeling, and every movement. But still, he didn't understand how he let it happen. It was as if his body had been manipulated by something else—some alien over which he had no control but that was part of him nonetheless. "I wasn't myself," he said, trying to boil all of his thoughts into a few simple words. "I'm cursed again, remember?"

"I know you're cursed," she snapped back, her fists pumping at her sides. "Everyone knows you're cursed. But the last time, I could still see *you* in there when you flew off the handle. Last week I … when I looked into your eyes, I didn't see anything I could grab onto. I didn't see anything I could use to pull you back. What was different?" She bounced on one leg and bit her lip. "Was it because of Gray?"

Donner felt the rage instantly. He snorted and pulled back, veering his head toward the crib. There was no good way to answer that question. Was he angry that a stranger had destroyed any chance he had at getting Belle back? Absolutely. Was his appearance at the Phoenix the trigger that set him off on Friday? Possibly. But was jealousy enough to fuel such a terrifying rampage? He shook his head. He was stronger than that.

"I'm not naive enough to think you'd ever come back to me now," he said. "But if I'm going to lose you, I want to make sure you and the baby are safe. I want it to be because you found a genuine happily ever after—not another beast in disguise."

Belle's eyes boomeranged toward the ceiling and back. "I know about Gray's past," she said. "Or I know as much as I need to. Scars or not, he's a good man now. He wouldn't hurt a fly now if he didn't have to. I, on the other hand, would do *anything* to protect our son. Anything. Without hesitation and without remorse. So if you're going to talk about one of us being a monster, I think you have to point the finger at me."

Donner stood in shock for a moment. So, this is the woman he'd been repressing for all these years. He felt a tiny spark of pride in his bottom lip. Then he grabbed the bracelet one more time and started explaining before she could protest.

"It's not an attempt to buy you back," he said. "And it's not an ordinary piece of jewelry."

Belle crossed her arms and looked away, but Donner thought he saw a flicker of recognition. By the time he finished explaining, the bracelet was curled up in her cupped palm and she was looking down as if it might jump up at any second and turn into fireworks.

"Is this the whole stone?"

He nodded. "The power's one hundred percent yours. This is the original stone. The master. It's not limited to one track, like yours. It can take you anywhere you want — with some caveats for private homes, same as a pureblood. But unlike a pureblood, this lets you take someone with you. Just make sure your mind is clear before you use it — easier said than done, I know, but with practice you'll be able to do that in the middle of a hurricane if you need to. And don't let Parliament find out."

"But why — " Her head shook a few times and she looked up. "Why would you give this to me? It's your ticket out of here. Everyone in Marestam is looking for you and — "

"And I could use that to start a new life, sure, but it would be a lonely one. Without my son." He paused, the word feeling wonderfully strange and perfect rolling off his tongue. "Without the people I care about the most."

Belle's pupils contracted just the tiniest bit, and he could feel her studying his eyes, his mouth, his hands. Finally, she pulled off her wedding ring and pressed it into his palm. Now it was his turn to look confused.

"Fine," she said. "I'll take the bracelet. But only if you take the ring."

Donner shook his head and started to hand it back. "You should give that ring to our son. When he's older. It will connect to the bracelet so that way he'll always have a link to you."

Belle put her hand up, refusing to take it back. "He'll always have me anyway. But this way, he'll always have a link to his father too. And if I decide I want a magical tunnel connecting us, I can always just give him the other one."

"The other one?" Donner reached up to rub the back of his neck. He thought back to a party a few months ago at Riverfell Palace, when she accused him of giving "booty call rings" to women he'd been sleeping with. As if he had some bevy of mistresses whom he summoned to his bedroom using dozens of magical rings all cut from and linked to his own. As if he was running an underground harem or giving out party favors. *Thanks for the ride. Accept this ring as a token of my appreciation.* It was absurd.

Judging by Belle's frown, however, she actually believed it. And in truth, he had created another one—but only one. It had belonged to Karen. He'd always wondered why she didn't use it when Blue attacked. But was it really worth explaining that to Belle now? Would it be worse for her to think of him as a sex-crazy philanderer or a broken-hearted pansy still hung up on a woman who died years ago?

"Thank you," he said, choosing the former and slipping the ring onto his finger. Rapunzel would probably tell her about Karen anyway, when he wasn't in the room. "But are you sure?"

Belle gave an assertive nod. "I don't want our son to grow up not knowing his father—his *real* father, not the louse they write about in the history books."

Donner felt pressure start to build behind his eyes. He didn't deserve her—even as a friend. They looked at each other for a moment longer, then he cleared his throat and said he should get going. Rapunzel and Snow were probably starting to worry, and he needed to figure out a way to get out of Marestam immediately, before anyone spotted him and called the authorities.

"Wait," she said just as he was about to move in for a hug.

He instantly jerked back. "Sorry," he said, flinging his hand through his hair. "I'm sorry. I shouldn't have — "

"There's something I need to show you," she said, opening the door and motioning for him to follow. "It won't take long."

He stood frozen for a minute and then obeyed. Through the hallway. Down the stairs. Out into the tiny living room where Griffin and Rapunzel were trying to look as if they hadn't been eavesdropping seconds earlier. Snow was leaning over a bassinet, cooing.

Softly, Belle took Donner's hand and led him over to Snow's baby. He had no idea what she was trying to do — gauge how he dealt with children?

As they got closer, he could see that it was a little boy. He had chestnut brown hair, similar to Belle's, and curly lips that reminded Donner of his father's. He wasn't red or squished, which indicated that he wasn't a newborn. But there was something about him. Donner had an odd feeling in his gut as he leaned over.

"Donner," Belle said, cupping his hand in hers. The child's eyes flew open at the sound of her voice. They were black as the grate inside Snow's fireplace. They were black as his own. "What I was saying before about the curse making our baby strong enough to … to survive the…" She stopped as his heart began to pound and his hand drifted forward. "Meet our little miracle. Four months early and with one heck of a story to tell. Donner, meet your son."

જ⁊ઝ

Donner could have scaled twenty stories without a safety rope. He could have leapt off the Prince Williams Bridge and entered the water with a gold medal splash. He could have lifted a five-ton elephant and lobbed it onto the highest turret atop Braddax Castle. Or at least that's how he felt as he waltzed his way out Snow White's front door, through two miles of trees, and down towards the island kingdom's western ferry dock.

He was in love. He was more in love than he ever had been before and ever imagined he could be again. He was a father. A secret father, sure. But a father. And what's more, Belle had *chosen* to tell him. Perhaps it was just obligation. Perhaps she just had to obey that moral advisor perpetually perched on her shoulder. But he didn't think so. He wanted to believe that something magical had happened tonight. No, not magical. At this point in their lives, "magic" was a dirty word, not a cause for celebration. What happened between them tonight was miraculous. She'd forgiven him, perhaps not with her words, but with her actions. And she'd chosen to keep him in her life — even if it had to be in secret.

It was the clemency he'd been longing for. It was the second chance he needed. It was the apocalyptic kick in the ass that would justify his becoming a better man — because there were still reasons to do so and people who cared whether or not he did.

Now, as he marched down the hill and hid his face inside Griffin's gray hoodie with the words *Love Matters* scrawled across the front, Donner saw the black void in front of him liquefy. In a matter of minutes, his future had gone from a cold, dark cell with little to no contact with his family … to a tropical island with a secret, undetectable tunnel to Belle and the son he'd always dreamed of having.

All he had to do now was get back to Braddax Castle undetected, throw some essentials into one of his bottomless trunks, decide which tropical paradise would least likely extradite a U.K.M. royal, and bribe someone to get him there. What could possibly go wrong?

The Marestam Mirror

Diamond Ropes and Velvet Cake
By Perrin Hildebrand, King of Gossip

JUST one day before Riverfell's grand celebration and three days after heavy rains turned their ballroom into a swimming pool, Queen Letitia and Prince Logan have finally moved the Royal Coronedding to Selladóre Castle. Personally, I'm more than a little disappointed. Here was an opportunity to throw the first ever all-night downtown Carpale royal rager ... but instead we get more stuffy halls, uncomfortable seats, and terrible acoustics. Plus, the three-thousand-plus guests will have to cram their way onto looping neon green ferries in order to get there. Classy.

Online coverage starts bright and early. Logan and Penelopea will take the spotlight first, priming the crowd for what promises to be another glitzy, gaudy, diamond-crusted display from her Royal Divaship, Queen Letitia.

But while my fingers are crossed for excitement, even Your King of Gossip must admit feeling a little bored by the guest list. With Donner Wickenham on the lam, Cinderella and Aaron Charmé still hiding somewhere in Ellada (at this point, I'm convinced Ruby Welles gave them a cloaking spell before they left — it would explain her lack of flare of late), and Snow White staying home with her new bundle of joy (who my sources say is both adorable and in extremely loving, capable hands — take that, Monarch Morality freaks), the only royal couple in the audience will be Dawn and Hunter Tirion. Oh goody. You'll excuse my lack of enthusiasm.

EARLY this morning, Yours Truly received a series of photographs showing Belle Wickenham and her insultingly handsome groundskeeper sharing a bottle of wine late into the evening yesterday.

Yes, you read that right, wine. And from what I saw, a lot more than a sip. So what's the deal, people? Has our esteemed Belle toppled off the wagon? Has she found a rebound man and lost all of her senses? Has she decided that gambling with her unborn baby's health is a fair price for a few hours of liquid relief? Or … and I'm falling apart as I type this … is it possible the doctors at Marestam General were a little less than truthful when they said the heir to the Braddax throne had survived its father's rampage unharmed?

Answering these questions will be my top priority over the next forty-eight hours — that and photobombing Queen Letitia without anyone having a clue.

P.S. The photos arrived with no name and no return address, which would give any honorable journalist pause. Yes, there's a chance they were doctored … but do you really wish I'd held them back? I think we both know the answer to that question, and lucky for you, I run a gossip column. I gave up honorable journalism years ago.

FOR those of you who skipped last night's State of the Realm Address, here's a quick recap: Magic is evil. The monarchies may be worse. Opinions are changing and Marestam must change accordingly. Oh, and don't forget there's an election just around the corner. Yada yada yada.

Chapter Twenty-Two

SNOW

When Snow agreed to give Belle's baby a temporary home, she had no intention of becoming the den mother for a pack of rebels seeking to overthrow Marestam's federal arm. But she certainly didn't mind. Neither she nor Griffin had ever been one for rules. And in her experience, authority just opened the door for corruption … or abuse … or mental illness with a dash of poisoned-apple filicide.

"So, what now?" Rapunzel asked as Snow prepared a tray of veggie sticks and hummus for her guests. "Do we need to find a cauldron and some dead rabbits so you can cast your spell?"

"Yeah, let's get started," Belle said, bouncing in her seat next to Hazel, who had no idea "Snow's adopted baby" upstairs was actually her grandson. "The sooner Donner's curse breaks, the better."

"Agreed." Snow nodded as she placed the snacks in the center of the table, then pulled up an empty chair. Her insides were a wonderful sort of jittery.

"Yes," Ruby said as she laced her hands together and dropped them onto the table. Her jumble of bracelets clacked against the wood. "Time is certainly of the essence.

Unfortunately, it's not actually that simple."

"Ugh!" Rapunzel groaned, scraping her chair against the floor. "Of course it's not! I knew we shouldn't have gone along with this cockamamie plan. We should have just come out with what we knew from the get-go. Sometimes simpler is just better." She panned from Grethel to Belle to Snow, seeking backup. "What do we need to find *now*, Ruby? The hair of a unicorn?"

Ruby narrowed her eyes. "For one thing, finding a spell that would break Donner's curse was probably harder than finding Grethel. So, you're welcome." Rapunzel made a face but backed down. "And secondly, it *was* that simple initially. All these three had to do was join hands, chant a few spells together, and voila! We'd have an all-human Donner, a drop of blood pinpointing the Charmés' exact location on a map, and a thirty-second glimpse into the inner workings of Angus Kane's brain."

"Thirty seconds? That's it?"

The old fairy frowned. "That's all we'd need. And we could have done it anywhere." Her voice was sharp. "But that was before we found out there could be three-hundred-year-old dark magic involved."

"The strongest dark magic you could imagine," Elmina added.

"Exactly. So now we need a little more oomph, so to speak. We need to channel as much magical energy as we can possibly get our hands on."

"More oomph?" Rapunzel's jaw fell open. "It was hard enough to find this much oomph! How are we gonna find — "

"What about the Hall of Curiosities?" Snow cut in, cracking a stick of celery between her teeth. "That's where all the charms and magical relics are, right? I mean except the ones Angus took for himself."

Ruby's outstretched hand told her that she'd hit the nail directly on the head. "Exactly," she said, giving Snow a symbolic pat on the back. "And the best time to break into a guarded tourist attraction like that is to do it while everyone's looking at something else."

"Okay," Belle said, drawing out the word and spinning her brand-new magical bracelet around her wrist. "And when exactly do you suppose that will be?"

"Tomorrow," Ruby said, plucking out a carrot stick and breaking it in half. "During the Riverfell coronation." She paused and shot the mortals a hesitant smirk. Snow felt another zap of excitement fly into her gut. Not that she'd enjoyed being hunted by her deranged mother all those years ago, but in all honesty, life had been a little ... tame since then. "*Then* we can fill a cauldron with dead rabbits and chant."

Grethel made a chastising face and laid a motherly hand over Rapunzel's arm. "Or, you know, just chant."

Chapter Twenty-Three

ANGUS

It might seem obvious to say that, as a politician, Angus Kane was no stranger to betrayal. After all, he'd risen from insignificant wretch with no influential allies to prime minister of the most influential realm in the world. He'd lobbied his office from a two-term limit to four. He'd cleaned up the streets of Carpale and kissed babies and incited record crowds to both applaud and threaten to kill him.

History would call this a testament to his intelligence and say he earned his stripes as honorably as he could. But in reality, "as he could" changed meaning at any given hour on any given day. In reality, Angus Kane's link to betrayal went deeper than any of his colleagues could possibly imagine. He was conceived because of it. He was born in the thick of it. He watched his mother disintegrate because of it. And for well over half of his lonely, bitter life, he'd been consumed by it.

Perhaps that's why his surprise visitor late Friday night didn't actually surprise him all that much. He'd sat on the front lines as husbands betrayed wives, fathers rejected sons, sisters demolished sisters, and even the best of friends sold each other out for the most rudimentary desires.

When she first popped in, Angus felt inclined to summon the Marestam Guard stationed down the hall. But he hadn't reached the highest elected office in the land by reacting as if everything was black and white, cut and dry. He knew that even the most despised adversary could offer something of value.

So in the end, Angus decided to open the doors of Aaron Charmé's private office and invite his visitor to take a seat. He would have used the throne room, but the Charmés had stopped greeting visitors there years ago, calling the venue "intimidating" and "elitist." It was one of the reasons he couldn't truly hate the Charmés — at least not the same way he hated the others: Letitia with her narcissistic extravagance. Snow with her irresponsible pacifism. The Tirions with their obsessive tunnel vision. And Donner. He hated Donner Wickenham for more reasons than he could count — for his adolescent vanity, for his presumptuous greed, for destroying an innocent woman, for overlooking everyone around him, for his last name, and most of all, for sharing half of Angus's blood without having the slightest idea.

The prime minister said barely ten words during the impromptu meeting, having learned that silence and a steely presence often work better than questions. He sat on the armchair, emotionless, holding his cane between his legs and nodding. When the claim came across that Ruby Welles had lost her powers, he started kneading into the marbleized purple sphere beneath his fingers. It had come from Selladóre, on the day of the Great Awakening — the day his plan finally began to seem feasible. There was something about it that had caught his attention, almost as if it was calling to him. So he'd lugged it back to Pastora along with a quibbling young man who, not unlike the royals, was about to inherit a fortune he'd done absolutely nothing to earn. In the following days, Angus had the stone cut and polished and placed atop his walking stick. He liked to think it gave his mission additional importance — that the injustice he sought to topple stretched back centuries. It was so much bigger than regular old vengeance.

When his visitor finally left, Angus felt like he'd caught a goose who not only could lay golden eggs, but could also level entire castles with a flap of its wings.

"I want every guard on duty by two o'clock tomorrow afternoon," he instructed the chief of the Marestam Guard as soon as Aaron's office was empty again. "Double what we've assigned to Selladóre, get me in touch with your best commander tonight, and quadruple operatives stationed around Carpale's lower east side. I just received intelligence indicating an imminent attack on the Hall of Curiosities."

Chief Kind's eyes bugged wide, exposing a thick line of white around his entire iris. "Yes sir," he replied, commenting on what seemed to be an emergency-scale response to an unidentified threat. "I'll lock down the entire area and alert the heads of the kingdoms."

"No," Angus said, maintaining the same opaque, confident cool that had gotten him this far. "Plainclothes but carrying. We need to lure them in before capture. Make them feel comfortable before we attack. And I have reason to believe the kingdom heads to which you're referring have already been compromised. In order for this operation to succeed, it must remain for Parliament's and my ears only. Please inform your commanders accordingly."

Chief Kind hesitated for a moment. "But protocol says—"

Angus parted his feet and planted the base of his cane between them. He narrowed his eyes at the man and waited.

"Of course," Toby Kind finally sputtered, gluing his arms against his sides. "Whatever you say, Prime Minister." He raised his right hand in a rigid, speedy salute. "Plainclothes. Armed. Hall of Curiosities and Selladóre. Top notch classified. You got it, sir."

Chapter Twenty-Four

PENELOPEA

"I don't know. It's a lot to swallow," Penny said, swaying slightly with a half-full glass of champagne in her hand. She and her friends were holed up in Selladóre Castle's Maritime Drawing Room (inaptly named by the government-sponsored Preservation Society) while Letitia got stitched into her wedding dress on the other side of the building. By some miracle, her mother-in-law had decided that not even Penny should see her before her grand entrance. It was a slight that gave the reluctant queen-to-be space to breathe for the first time in months. "Personally, I think Elmina's first theory about Ruby holds more water than the one about Angus."

"You do?" The shock in Belle's voice trilled over the mechanical noise of her breast pump, which she'd hidden beneath an overpriced blanket with a strap on one end. She pushed herself further up on the couch. "Penny, you think it's more likely that *Ruby's* the villain here than *Angus*?"

Penny traipsed over to a table overflowing with petite sandwiches, fruit platters, and crudités. It was shoved up against a stunning wall of windows overlooking the East River. "I didn't call her a villain. I'm just saying we *know* fairies lose magic when they curse people. We have no idea whether … what's her name again? Janetta?" She turned abruptly towards Dawn, sloshing the remaining half of her morning libation on the carpet.

But Dawn was too busy pulling at a loose red curl to hear the question. Letitia had commandeered her go-to stylist for the day, and her usual twist updo just hadn't turned out the same.

"What was the name of that maniac who cursed you?" Penny repeated.

"Oh." Dawn poked at her hair a few more times and then resumed tying tiny purple ribbons around gold boxes of truffles — last-second favors for Letitia's esteemed guests. "Jacara."

"Right." Penny gave an exuberant nod even though her head felt like a bowling ball. She'd barely slept a wink, but still managed to dream about a giant lizard in a wedding dress trying to staple a crown to her skull. "Yes. Jacara. Well, we have no idea whether it's even *possible* that Jacara's magic survived after the curse broke. Even Elmina said it's never happened before. It just seems like quite a leap based purely on the fact that Angus happened to be there the day the spell broke. Hunter was there too. Does that mean we should be accusing him as well?"

Dawn tossed a wrapped box into the pile between her and Rapunzel. "Of course not," she said, her tone slightly hostile. "And perhaps on its own, that could be seen as a coincidence. But don't forget he's been hiding Cindy's disappearance, too. And his public address the other night made it pretty clear he wants the monarchies gone. And for goodness sake," she added, almost falling off her seat, "the painting he gave Belle turned out to be a charm — a charm that *takes pictures*, judging from Perrin Hildebrand's latest column. Does all of that really seem like a coincidence to you?"

Penny tugged on the monstrous teal bow on the side of her dress. She wasn't trying to start an argument, but these days everyone was wound tighter than Letitia at a mud wrestling biker bar. She *absolutely* believed Angus was up to no good. She believed he was a greedy, conniving old man who'd always wanted to take over Marestam and saw an opportunity when the public started losing faith in the monarchies. But she had a hard time swallowing the whole criminal mastermind, stole-history's-most-powerful-fairy's-powers story. Ruby losing her self-righteous cool one day and casting a spell that accidentally wound up affecting an innocent child, on the other hand… *That*, she could wrap her mind around.

"I'm not saying he isn't up to something," she clarified, refilling her glass and popping a purple grape between her teeth. "I'm just saying he might not be the only one."

"Here, here," Rapunzel chimed in, though without her usual merriment. She was slumped down in her chair, gazing at her cell phone with a half-tied box of truffles in her lap. Her face and lips were unusually pale, and she hadn't touched a single drop of food—or drink—since she arrived. Outwardly, she blamed this on "the nauseating presence of Belle's milking machine," but Penny didn't buy it. She'd heard about Ethan—the deceit, the trip to Stularia, leaving him stranded on an island halfway across the world—but never expected to see Rapunzel so crestfallen over a man.

"It's about time someone else saw through that imperious old nutball," Rapunzel continued. She then gave a sigh and trailed off, as if the very act of talking was sapping all of her energy. "Sorry, my mind's on overload. Ethan keeps sending me these cryptic, schizophrenic messages that don't make any sense. He was an absolute disaster when Elmina brought him back—because, you know, Grethel's island has some magical force field and we had to concoct a crazy Elmina-Grethel train idea to pop over and bring him home five hours before his father's wedding." She furrowed her brow at her phone one more time, then looked up. "But sorry. That's another issue. Back to Ruby. What I meant to say is I don't trust her as far as I could kick her.

But I think Angus is just as bad if not worse."

Penny frowned. "Thanks for the help," she said, her voice dripping with sarcasm and punctuated by a hiccup.

Dawn took this opportunity to commandeer her friend's glass and replace it with water. There would be a top-shelf open bar after the wedding, but Penny still had a coronation to get through.

"Hey," Belle cooed as she switched off her pump, pulled a full bottle from beneath her cover, and frowned. Still pink. "Everyone here is under a lot of stress, but taking it out on each other is just going to make things worse. Guessing who to trust and not trust isn't going to change anything now. Hazel, Elmina, and Grethel will find out soon enough what's going on, and I'm sure they'll come to us first if Ruby's been less than genuine. So, let's let them handle it for a few hours and focus on the reason we're all here today—to support Penny. Okay?"

No one made a sound for several seconds—Penny included. While she appreciated Belle's words, she was still fairly miffed by Ruby's decision to assemble her precious triad today, of all days. Her coronation and Letitia's wedding were going to be stressful enough without a band of renegades flooding midtown Carpale with illegal magic at the same time.

As it stood, Penny had already survived three panic attacks since sunrise—one when Letitia's black roses showed up with brown along the edges; one because the special-order aisle runner, dyed to match Riverfell's flag exactly, unfurled six feet short of the doorway; and one because her brother-in-law was still at Marestam General—unshowered, wearing two-day-old clothes, and refusing to answer Logan's calls. Had her friends really wanted to support her, they would have forced Ruby to choose a different day—or at least wait until the "celebration" was beginning to die down. Like midnight. Wasn't that when magical enchantments were supposed to end anyway? Wasn't there some sort of secret universal agreement about that?

But rather than open that box of negativity, Penny forced a smile and thanked everyone again for coming to her pre-execution gathering. The coronation would begin in roughly two hours now, and the butterflies in her stomach were starting to feel more like vampire bats. She still couldn't believe it was happening—and not in the dream-come-true sort of way. No one seemed to realize that she was as much a victim of Donner's rampage as was Belle, Rye, and Kiarra Kane. Had it not been for him, Kiarra would have insisted Carter take the throne and make her his queen; Logan would have finally seen the light at the end of his mother's birth canal; and Penny would have started the life she'd always hoped for—the one that involved a white picket fence and chicken dinners that came out overcooked sixty percent of the time.

"How many of these do you need again?" Rapunzel whined, tossing two more boxes into the heap and then collapsing back into her chair.

Penny pressed her lips together and surveyed the pile. Then she surveyed her friends. Each one of them looked mentally and physically exhausted. Belle had excruciating mastitis on top of her other injuries, and was on pins and needles waiting to find out whether the triad could reverse her little boy's curse. Rapunzel was in a monumental row with the only man she'd ever loved, and she'd been traumatically mum about her reunion with Grethel. And Dawn ... well, if Dawn truly believed Elmina's theory, she could be wiped off the face of the planet any given moment—along with her children. Penny could have scraped the gloom with a hairpin.

"That's plenty," Penny lied, scooping up the thirty-something truffle boxes and tossing them into a shopping bag. "Thanks again for your help." She then reclaimed her champagne glass, circled the room to refill everyone else's, and plopped into an armchair.

"So has Ethan found out anything about Cindy?" she asked,

desperate to pull a little more life out of Rapunzel. "Last I heard, he was contacting all of his colleagues in Ellada, right? Any luck?" All she got was a quick glance of surprise followed by a headshake. "Well, like Belle said, I'm sure we'll know everything by the end of the day anyway. Between their powers and what they can draw from all of those charms at the Hall of Curiosities, it should take no time, right?" She took in all the head nods, then thought of something else. "It *is* just the three of them, I assume. It might look a little suspicious if Ruby wasn't at the wedding and—"

Dawn nodded mid-sip. "She's supposed to stay here so as to not arouse suspicion. She's not very much help to them without her magic anyway." She looked squarely at Penny. "Yet another reason why she probably doesn't have anything to hide."

"We'll see," Penny said, deciding to try something else. "Hey, how's Hunter getting along with Liam Devereaux? I never pictured him as the sharing type."

Dawn started. Her crossed leg slipped to the floor as champagne splattered over her knee. "What do you mean?" she asked, blinking four times in quick succession.

All heads turned toward her and tilted. What was that reaction for?

Penny looked around, confused. "I just mean … the merger … with Perdemi-Divan. What else would I mean?"

"Oh, of course. He's fine. They're fine." Dawn let out a nervous chuckle and stood up. She crossed the room and filled a small plate with carrot sticks and a quarter of a turkey sandwich.

"What's Liam Devereaux like?" Belle chimed in, half a second before Dawn's plate tumbled from her hand, sending miniature sandwiches scattering.

"Oops sorry!" she exclaimed, frantically wiping mayonnaise off a bunch of purple grapes. Penny told her not to worry about it, but Dawn kept going as if she was polishing an antique vase.

"He's nice," she continued. "I mean, from what I gather. I've hardly spoken to him, really. Most of those business dinners are all numbers and posturing. You know."

She let out another laugh.

Three heads nodded. Six eyes squinted. Something about her mannerisms seemed fishy.

"Dawn," Penny said, "is there something you're not telling us?"

Rapunzel leaned forward, her interest finally piqued. "Yeah. I've never seen you drop a napkin, much less an entire plate of food. What gives? Don't tell me you have a crush on your husband's business partner."

"A crush?" Dawn's chin launched up. "Don't be absurd. Davin and I are strictly — "

"Davin?" Penny interrupted. "Who's Davin?"

Dawn sputtered a few times, did a fantastic impression of a meerkat on high alert, and finally caved.

For the next half hour, Penny, Belle and Rapunzel sat with mouths wide open while Dawn — perfect little eighteenth century Dawn — told them all about the long-lost love she'd stumbled upon in the woods. She told them how she always thought he'd died during the Great Sleep. She told them about his breathtaking diamond-studded trees and fiber optic flowers and invisible frozen walkway. She told them how his return made her realize how dangerous the mind could be — how hers had recreated the past and blinded her to the present. She told them that, in the end, the man she really wanted was the husband she'd pushed away for years. And then she told them about Angus Kane's role in the whole thing.

"Wow," Rapunzel said, her cheeks finally showing some color. "I ... I honestly don't know what to react to first. The fact that you kept all this from us for months or that you actually did something immoral."

"He was the childhood love she thought died years ago," Belle said, coming to Dawn's rescue. "I wouldn't call that *immoral*. She thought he was her true love—and for good reason. It sure sounds like a fairy tale. I would have done the exact same thing."

Rapunzel's jaw plummeted. "Well, now I've heard everything."

Penny's head was still swimming. No wonder Dawn was so sure Angus was the villain here. But why hadn't he exposed them yet? "So, you and Hunter…" she said, intentionally trailing off.

Dawn gave a slightly sad, slightly hopeful smile from her seat. "I think we're getting better," she said. "When I told him about Elmina and what could happen to me and the kids if she's right, I think that took precedence over what I did."

"So he no longer thinks Morning and Day could be Davin's?" Belle's voice was sheepish, as if she didn't really want to ask but shamefully wanted to know.

Dawn shrugged. "We haven't discussed that directly, but there's no possible way they're Davin's."

Rapunzel laughed. "So, you're saying he didn't pop your cherry three hundred years ago in one of these stone towers?"

Dawn sucked her cheeks in and gave Rapunzel a scathing look. "No. Things were different when I was growing up. People didn't go straight from touching hands to ripping each other's clothes off."

"Well, sorry if our hedonistic century corrupted you, but—"

"But you can't tell a story like that and leave out the most important part!" Penny interrupted, elated by the shift in mood. "How was it? I mean, I can only imagine how amazing the sex must be after waiting three centuries!"

"Yeah, spill!"

"Oh." Dawn's eyes fell as the other women leaned in. "No. Actually. We didn't actually … do that."

Three cries of protest hollered out in unison. "What?"

Dawn shrugged. "What happened between us was bigger

than sex. Just kissing and holding each other and talking about everything we'd been through ... and then..." She looked away as her face turned bright red. "Like I said, we're from a different time."

Rapunzel fell back into her cushioned armchair with a bang. "Okay, hold on," she said, rubbing her forehead. "Not to diminish the emotional aspect of betrayal but ... well, does Hunter know you were purely PG rated?"

Dawn looked at her. Then she looked at the others, and shook her head.

The room filled with laughter. Then tears of laughter. It was exactly the sort of gossipy, ridiculous girl talk that Penny needed — that they all needed — to make it through the rest of the day.

Roughly one hour later, Logan swung by to tell them that the ballroom was filled to capacity and it was almost twelve o'clock. By Penny's calculations, after all the pompous rites and speeches, that still gave Kiarra Kane forty-five minutes to wake up and stop the whole thing. Then she could buy that perfect little house with the picket fence, four bedrooms, and space for a private home office.

"You're going to be a great queen," Belle said, reading her mind. "You and Logan are bulletproof together."

"Yeah, and if you can't stand it for any reason," Rapunzel added, "I say buy your dreamhouse and make him commute like every other working stiff in Marestam. You've sacrificed for long enough; it's his turn now."

Penny thought about this for a minute. No matter what they said, she knew things wouldn't be exactly the way she'd wanted. Even if they did manage to move out of Riverfell Palace, Letitia would always be looming over them, treating Logan like he was still in braces and Penny like she was the high school prom date who wasn't good enough for her son. But hey, a girl could dream.

"You're right," she said while raising her glass, pulling her lips wide, and hugging each of her dearest friends with her eyes. "Cheers."

১৯৩৫

At first, Penny could do nothing but stare at the far end of the ballroom. While the officiant spoke, she traced the filigree borders with her eyes and studied the massive arched windows, each one tall enough to fit one Carpale subway car on its nose. There were seven lining the back wall, for a grand total of sixty-three rows of stained-glass diamonds and seven three-dimensional rosettes painstakingly restored to their original gold leaf splendor. For something so ancient, it was quite beautiful—more so, in many ways, than the dramatic skyscrapers lining Marestam's capital, each one perfectly designed and executed to be the tallest or the strongest or (insert other muscle-flexing superlative here) edifice of its time. Back in Vashia, she'd been so impressed by those towers. She'd seen them as beacons of freedom, summoning her from the other side of the world.

But now, sitting beside her husband while a thousand strangers waited for an old man to place a golden shackle around her head, the word "freedom" took on a whole new meaning. Maybe Marestam wasn't quite as liberated as she'd thought. Cinderella had said something to that effect a few months back, but everyone had shaken it off—blaming it on hormones, or hunger from her obsessive desire to fit into a dress she'd worn as an emaciated peasant ten years earlier. While Marestam *was* light-years ahead of her childhood kingdom, there were still so many restrictions for those with magical blood, so many codes for those of royal lineage, so many barriers for those born with nothing or born with eggs instead of sperm.

It was in this moment, as her gaze fell from the rear windows to the double-thick line of police stretching across the back wall (Letitia's doing, she assumed), that Penny began to realize having a scepter might not be such a terrible thing after all. Like her friends said, she wasn't Letitia and Logan wasn't her keeper. Perhaps she *could* make a difference as queen. Perhaps she could take Cinderella's social charity work and ramp it up a notch—inspire actual, fundamental change, not just healing. Strengthen it with her schooling and her knowledge of the law. Give it claws.

She flinched as Logan squeezed her hand and rose to his feet. The half-bald officiant was teetering before them, palms spread flat as if he was checking for rain. He had wiry white hairs sprinkled along his pockmarked head, eyelids that seemed ten pounds too heavy, and a belly to rival Belle's baby bump—even when it had been real.

As Penny stood up, she felt her fake smile becoming more and more genuine. She surveyed the people sitting in the silver-brushed banquet chairs, accented with surprisingly stunning black roses, on either side of an amethyst aisle runner. Belle, wearing a suspiciously flattering maternity dress, was holding her stomach and staring into nothingness. She was sitting beside Dawn and Hunter (whose hands were intertwined, she noted, but not for the cameras) and an empty chair. Where was Ruby?

"Logan Jonathan Jean-Pierre LeBlanche," Penny heard her husband say, pulling her back before she could panic. She turned to look. The officiant's trembling hands now clutched the Riverfell crown, and Logan's eyes shone like diamonds.

Penny took a deep breath, splayed her hand across her husband's back, and purged her mind of everything not related to his joy at this moment. True, it would have meant more if they were in Riverfell's throne room instead of Selladóre's ... and if they weren't the opening act to Letitia's second marriage ... and if Logan hadn't been dubbed heir by default ... and if Carter had actually made it to his own brother's coronation. But this was still the fulfillment of his life-long dream.

Just before the old man steadied himself and began to raise the crown, Penny saw Logan close his eyes and take the same kind of breath she'd taken when she landed safely on Marestam soil so many years ago. It was the sort of breath that signaled both the end of a tumultuous journey and the start of something even greater. Penny was so proud of him. And after everything, still so in love. Even more than the white picket fence and the dog bowls and the honey-I'm-home moments, that is what she'd dreamt about most when she was plotting a way to escape that oppressive regime back across the ocean: the sort of love that wound tighter when faced with adversity and always came out stronger when the smoke cleared.

"Bless thee this crown," she heard as Logan smiled at her and bent his head.

Her stomach churned. She stopped listening to the old man's words, focusing instead on the movement of Logan's back muscles through his shirt, the love of the friends seated before her, the—

Someone's cell phone screamed out but was quickly silenced.

"Guide our new king in all of his regal duties…"

Another ring. A different phone. Penny's shoulders tensed. Logan pressed his lips together but in classic, easygoing Logan fashion, refused to look up. Finally, the officiant lowered the crown, said a few more words about making her husband wise, virtuous, and forever protected, and left it in Logan's nest of golden curls. He then took a second, smaller crown from a scarlet pillow and did the same thing (minus all the blessings) to Penny.

His fingers were still hidden in her waves when the entire room erupted into an offbeat symphony of tinny pop refrains and electronic ringtones. Seconds later, dresses and suits began shifting in their seats. People started standing. Chairs screeched out against the parquet floor. And then, just as the confused voices multiplied and took on a panicked edge, the guards stationed along the perimeter tripled up around the doors. What the hell was going on?

Within seconds, Logan had a line of guards at his side and was hunched over a cell phone with one finger in his ear.

"Carter? Where are you?" he shouted, his eyes going everywhere and nowhere at once. "You're supposed to— Yeah, it's over. You missed it. But never mind that. Something's happening. Do you— What?"

Logan pulled the phone away to examine it, then returned it to his ear. He looked confused, terrified, and livid all at the same time. But for some reason, he wasn't saying a thing. That's when Penny's ears zeroed in on one corner of the room and she plucked out three separate snippets that pulled her arm hairs up by their roots: "Magical terrorism," "Hall of Curiosities," and "She woke up."

Then, as her heart started beating outside of her chest, she heard Logan's voice again: "What? No! That's not— What do you mean can we *undo* it?"

The Marestam Mirror

Diamond Ropes and Velvet Cake
By Perrin Hildebrand, King of Gossip

BREAKING NEWS!

Warning: The following is an on-the-ground, as-it-happens, chaos-in-the-making breaking news report, folks. Flair will be lacking.

MARESTAM IS UNDER ATTACK!

Right now, I am hunkered down in the ballroom at Selladóre Castle. I'm surrounded by hundreds of coronedding attendees and their over-stuffed, over-feathered, and over-pompous ensembles. The air is thick with perfume. The bathrooms are inaccessible. And while I've never been one for higher powers, I am praying for the Marestam Guard to unblock our exit asap.

Here's what I know firsthand and from my sources on the outside. The rest I've filled in with the help of "citizen journalists" legitimized by the power of "social media." Desperate times, folks. Desperate times.

The Hall of Curiosities is in ruins after a firefight broke out between members of the Marestam Guard and three intruders. According to MG Chief Toby Kind, two of these intruders have been identified as Selladóre pureblood fairy Elmina Goodman and wanted Braddax Queen Mother Hazel Wickenham — also a pureblood. The third female has yet to be named, but reportedly showed magical abilities also consistent with pureblood status.

Logan and Penelopea LeBlanche have officially been crowned King and Queen of Riverfell. However, hospital staff and witnesses are reporting that Kiarra Kane is, indeed, awake. That's great news for Donner Wickenham, wherever he's hiding, but not so wonderful for the fledgling monarchs. According to an overwhelmed nurse who happened to be in the room when Carter told his darling what he'd done with his crown, Kiarra Kane's first words were short and to the point: "Get it back."

In response to the attack on one of Marestam's most iconic buildings, Angus Kane has declared a state of emergency throughout the realm and is enforcing a mandatory shelter-in-place order until all three suspects are in custody. He has also issued an executive order that makes anyone either harboring an illegal magical person or concealing his or her whereabouts to be as culpable as said illegal. Welcome to martial law, folks.

Chapter Twenty-Five

BELLE

Belle didn't process what was happening until she was fully out of the ballroom and jammed between a dozen members of the Marestam Guard. They were hurrying down a dark, narrow hallway with wainscoted walls, stone floors, and candleless sconces every ten feet.

"Where are we going?" she asked, trying not to trip over the boots shuffling in front, behind, and to the side of her.

"Somewhere safe," the lead officer grunted, not bothering to look back.

"Where's that?" she pushed, not sure who to trust at the moment but doubting she had a choice in the matter either way.

The whole thing had happened so fast. One minute she was watching Penny get her crown, and the next, she was being pushed and pulled in a dozen different directions as the ballroom erupted into a very unceremonious frenzy. She'd been sitting with Dawn and Hunter, but they immediately launched into some sort of private mission—first with hunched and hurried whispers, and then with Hunter yanking the nearest guard aside by the elbow.

Belle's questions then, just like now, had gone unanswered.

"Where's this safe place?" she asked again, tripping over the stone.

Still nothing. A hot rage gushed over her panic, sealing it in on all sides. She was so sick and tired of being treated like a porcelain doll—like something to be protected but not even for her sake, for someone else's. That was the old Belle. Hadn't this band of badged ruffians received the memo?

"Hey!" she hollered, as if the young man's ear wasn't inches from her mouth. He barely flinched. "Fine," she barked, stopping dead in her tracks. A thousand pounds of masculinity rammed into her from behind, taking out her center of gravity. The pack leader spun and reached out just in time to break her fall.

"What the hell are you doing?" he howled, hoisting her back on her feet and glancing at her stomach. "Someone in your situation should be more careful. That's how tragedies happen."

Belle frowned but dusted herself off. "*That's* how tragedies happen? I wouldn't have stopped short if you'd answer my damn question."

"That's classified," he said, sucking both of his cheeks inward and biting down. The hallway was dark, but she could still make out a long, bony nose, buzz-cut hair, and beady—or at least squinting—eyes.

"Classified?" Her right hand curled into a fist. "Do you realize how asinine that sounds? I'm the Queen of Braddax and I'm carrying the heir to the throne." As much as she'd been denying her title for the past four months, she had no problem using it now. "I have a right to know. Are you here to kidnap me, arrest me, or get me the heck out of here?"

The silence lingered long enough for her question to take an ominous turn. The man ran his tongue between his front teeth and his upper lip.

"You're not a prisoner," he finally said. "Protocol is to take all sitting monarchs to a safe location when there's an attack. We're under orders to bring you to the fourth floor," he said, pausing immediately as if even that vague drip of information was too much. "That's all I know. Now can we please continue moving before the prime minister thinks we lost the Queen of Braddax and its future heir?"

Reluctantly, Belle pressed her lips together and waved them onward. She still didn't know what was going on outside this hallway, but outrunning thirteen Marestam Guards didn't seem like a great idea. Plus, she was wearing Donner's bracelet. If things got sticky, all she had to do was clear her mind (piece of cake, right?) and hightail it out of there.

They walked for another five minutes in what seemed to be the backstage of a gussied-up warehouse—taking sharp, blind corners and clamoring up three sets of rudimentary, winding stairs—before finally stopping in the middle of nowhere. Belle was just about to ask the head dog if he was lost, when he reached up, ran his hand along two panels of wainscoting, and pushed.

Belle started and shielded her eyes as a column of light split the darkness, then stretched out on both sides to reveal a bright room with a red velvet couch, two armchairs, and a dormant fireplace. It was nicely outfitted, with wall-to-wall built-ins, burgundy wallpaper, and a clean mahogany desk.

"A bit small for a safe house," she said as the guards ushered her in. "Where's everyone else? Logan and Penelopea? The Tirions?"

But as soon as she turned around, a far less secret door flew open and none other than Angus Kane swooped in. "Oh, thank goodness," he said as her heart plunged into her stomach. He was out of breath and uncharacteristically disheveled— waistcoat unbuttoned, face flushed, comb-over flopped over the wrong side of his head. With his arms outstretched and the usual walking stick in hand, he flounced forward as if arriving late for Thanksgiving dinner.

Her instinctive reaction was to block him with both arms and slide backwards.

"My apologies," he said, immediately receding and offering a weak handshake instead. "I suppose catastrophes have a way of stripping away things like decorum. Please sit."

Belle hesitated as Angus held onto his cane and lowered himself shakily onto the cushion. He looked like he was pushing seventy rather than fifty years old. Halfway down, he spotted the guards. "Thank you for keeping Ms. Middleton safe," he said, using her maiden name in an attempt to butter her up. "But there are three thousand terrified people downstairs who are going to need help getting off this island in an orderly fashion. I'm sure your colleagues would appreciate some help with crowd control."

"Yes, Prime Minister, but—"

Angus held his hand flat in the air and moved it side to side. "Two men outside this door should be plenty of protection for us."

The lead guard eyed Belle one last time, then reluctantly departed. His legion followed.

"I do apologize for all the secrecy," Angus said once they were alone. "But these are dark times and frankly, I don't know who I can trust right now." He waved his hand toward the empty couch and reiterated his previous invitation.

Belle didn't know whether to expect a friendly chat or an interrogation, but she couldn't refuse the opportunity to find out what Angus was up to.

"What do you mean, you don't know who you can trust?" she asked, settling into the middle cushion and letting her head tilt slightly to one side. God, she hated pretending to be this clueless—probably because it hadn't been an act until recently. "What's going on, Angus?"

Angus plucked at the fuzz balls on the end of his armrest. Then he straightened both elbows like a cat stretching after an afternoon nap.

"What's going on?" he repeated, mulling the words with his tongue. "That's an interesting question indeed. But I'm fairly certain you know the answer to that a lot better than I do."

Belle froze as all thoughts flitted away except one: What did Angus know—or want her to *think* he knew? His upper lip thinned even further as he pressed it into the lower one, waiting for an answer. His fingers looked extra long and spindly from this angle.

"Belle," he finally said, his voice patient, not confrontational. "I know you've been through a lot lately. I know your generation has a hard time putting the greater good above convenience and fleeting pleasure." Her eyebrows pulled downward, partially obstructing her view. "But downing half a bottle of wine midway through your second trimester doesn't ... well, it just doesn't seem like you."

Belle's shoulder blades tensed as she shifted on the sofa. This was really his main concern?

"Nor does shacking up with a roaming handyman while you're still technically married—though that's slightly more forgivable under the circumstances."

Belle swallowed hard. She could actually hear the blood flying through her body as he spoke. She could feel her pulse slamming into every appendage.

"You're supposed to be carrying the last heir to the Braddax throne. I never thought I'd say it about you, but your actions could create another Monarch Morality scandal. And to put it bluntly, I don't think the Marestam monarchies can take any more of those. I think your best option now is to set the record straight."

By the time he finished speaking, Belle was in all out shock. Her limbs felt gelatinous and she was at a total loss for words. Set the record straight? What did that mean? Was that his way of saying he knew about Rye? Did he know she'd hidden him in

Tantalise? Did he know Belle was part of the insurgent group who'd just attacked the Hall of Curiosities and wanted to bring him down at almost any cost?

"Please, don't misunderstand me," Angus continued, firing more bullets while maintaining the face of fatherly concern. "I'm in your corner. I just don't want history blaming you for the death of the whole monarchical system when really you're just another one of its victims. One of its most tragic victims at that." He bowed his head for a moment while Belle struggled to understand what he was saying. "You really would have made a wonderful mother."

Belle's head whipped up suddenly. "What's that supposed to mean?" The words took on a mind of their own, spewing past her lips with no prior thought or planning. "I am a — I am going to make a wonderful mother."

Angus yanked a particularly large thread out from his armrest and balled it between his fingers. The sides of his mouth seemed to be growing. "Would a wonderful mother put her child in that kind of jeopardy for a few hours of ... how did that columnist put it ... a few hours of liquid relief? Belle, why are you lying?"

"Lying?" Belle's palms launched to either side of her hips and pressed down. But rather than blasting to her feet as intended, all she did was pin her dress to the couch and bounce against the cushion. "How dare you criticize me. You who gave me a painting that — "

"All right. All right. Perhaps *lying* is a bit severe. Let me put it another way. Why are you sacrificing your reputation — the only thing you still have left — to protect a man who's betrayed you in so many ways?"

She paused. Elbows locked. Torso bent forward. Cheeks pinched. What was he talking about?

Again, her interrogator sighed. She watched as he pulled both arms off the chair and laced his fingers over the top of his walking stick. "You aren't pregnant anymore, are you? You lost the baby during Donner's attack."

Her jaw dropped. Her elbows loosened. Still, she didn't dare make a sound.

"I spoke with several doctors. There's no way a twenty-two-week fetus could have survived that degree of trauma."

"Twenty-three-week fetus," she corrected.

He frowned, though it seemed to be more out of pity than of disapproval. "Add to that your shrinking belly, your secrecy, the slip with the wine, and it's perfectly clear what happened. You had a miscarriage but are covering it up to protect him -- either from the guilt or the prison sentence or the fact that there's no coming back from that kind of public loathing. You're suffering in silence for what? For a man who imprisoned you, humiliated you, and then tried to butcher your reputation on top of it. He lured you in, made you believe he was some sort of white knight fairy tale, and then hurled you into the streets like a ten-dollar prostitute. It's what that family does. They deserve to have all their sins brought into the spotlight once and for all. Why aren't you doing that?"

As soon as he finished speaking, Angus flattened his bony hand over his stomach and leaned back. His face was flushed red. His chest was pumping faster and higher than could possibly be safe for a man of his health. As if out of respect rather than complete bewilderment, Belle waited for him to catch his breath before responding.

But rather than confirm or deny his suspicion about her baby, she decided to give the interrogation desk a little push. Knowing he'd come to the wrong conclusion gave her an advantage. Plus, there was something suspicious about the degree to which he seemed to loathe the Wickenhams. She suddenly wondered whether his goal was to eradicate all of the monarchies or just the one in Braddax.

"Wow. I don't think I've seen such intense hatred since my

mother found out my father was bankrupt," she said, raising her eyebrows. "What did the Wickenhams do to you? Steal your parking spot at the mall? Criticize your term extension? Kill your favorite cat without leaving a — "

"Not my cat," he interrupted, taking a sharp inhale through his nose. "My mother."

He held Belle's gaze for another few seconds, but then broke away, focusing instead on a section of rug between their feet. Belle's lips pressed inward as she contemplated how to proceed. What did he mean? They killed his mother? Was he speaking metaphorically?

"You remind me of her," he continued, his voice even softer than before. "She was kind and optimistic and had this inexplicable need to see good in everybody."

"She came from nothing but took everything life gave her with a smile and this undying sense of forgiveness that I'll never understand."

"She sounds like a wonderful — "

"And just like you, she fell for a deceitful Braddax King who promised to love her but turned tail the second something more glittery strutted along."

Belle's ears buzzed as she thought back to the day Penny picked her up from the hospital. She'd said something about Angus's mother working at Braddax Castle, a detail that seemed inconsequential at the time. But now, the pieces were finally bumping against each other and shakily starting to fuse. His mother had worked for Donner's father. Donner's father had been an infamous philanderer. He wouldn't have overlooked a pretty maid fluffing his pillows at the castle.

"So, your mother had an affair with Varek Wickenham?" she said, not sure why this was such a sore point twenty-plus years after the man's death. He'd had hundreds of affairs during his marriage to Hazel, possibly thousands. How could that possibly have impacted —

"Yes," Angus confirmed, knuckles white on the tops of his fists. "But it wasn't an affair at the time. And she rarely called him Varek when she spoke about him." He shook his head.

"Let me guess," Belle said, rolling her eyes. "She used secret pet names? Cuddlebug? Hercules?"

"No," he replied with just as much disdain. "*Your father.*"

Belle's tongue pulled into the back of her throat. She choked on it for a second, then swallowed. "Your father?" Her head did a full circle. She sank deep into the sofa. "How is that even— When did this—"

"It started long before Donner was born. Before he even met Hazel." The white knuckles flattened out for a split second, then curved back into a claw. "My mother wasn't the type of person to start a romance with someone else's husband. Like I said, she was good. She was in love and thought he was too. Even after he turned his back on us, she still believed that."

"So … he knew about you?" she asked, feeling drawn in. She'd never seen Angus Kane struggling to hold back so much emotion.

"Oh, he knew." His breath deepened. "They both knew."

"Both?"

His jaw clamped shut for a few seconds. "Hazel. That pureblood jezebel came along and made sure he tossed my mother aside. She convinced the arrogant prick that it was ludicrous for a man of his stature to make his life with a paycheck-to-paycheck servant. So out she went. And when she came back ten months later with a sickly baby in her arms— blessed at birth with brittle bones, apnea, and a weak heart— they stuffed ten thousand dollars in her pocket and told her to never contact them again."

Belle shook her head. She didn't even know what to say. That sounded awful.

"It covered fourteen months' rent in a rat-infested apartment in southern Riverfell. My mother worked three jobs for the next twenty years to make sure I had the medicine, food, and shelter I needed. I helped out as soon as I could fling a newspaper or pour a cup of lemonade, but she worked herself to the bone. And just when things were finally about to change — when I was preparing to take my graduation walk and make some real money to ease her burden — she collapsed. Her body was destroying itself from the inside. The doctors wanted to do some experimental treatment that would have eased her suffering and could have possibly cured her, but her insurance wouldn't cover it. She got put on a waiting list but there wasn't enough time as it was, and she didn't have the influence to bypass it like so many others." His lips crumpled as he said this. Belle scooted to the edge of her cushion. Angus shook his head. "So, I tried to get in contact with my father. I was desperate. She was everything to me. But Hazel wouldn't even deliver a letter, let alone allow me to see him. I was nobody then." He paused. Belle saw the unmistakable film of tears rise up and then drop, silently, over his lids. "My mother died three months later. It wasn't painless."

Belle started to speak, letting her emotions drive without proper instructions, but she couldn't find the words. "I'm so sorry, Angus," she finally whispered, shaking her head. "That should never have happened." She couldn't help but picture a little boy in squalor while his mother toiled away just to give him a decent chance at a halfway decent life. She could only imagine how painful that must have been. "I always knew Hazel was vain and selfish, but I never imagined her being that cruel. Maybe she's changed."

"She hasn't changed," Angus said with a snort. 'The money we needed would have meant nothing to them. They turned their backs on us and let my mother die in the most degrading way possible because they saw her as nothing more than a threat. Hazel Wickenham will protect her family at all costs — by letting an innocent woman wither away thirty years ago or by betraying the people relying on her today. How do you think the Marestam

Guard responded so quickly to the Hall of Curiosities today? Who do you think tipped me off?"

Belle flinched but contained her reaction. He had to be bluffing. Why would Hazel hijack them when they were trying to cure her son?

"My mother was brainwashed into believing there was good in the Wickenhams," Angus continued, "just like you. And now they're finally getting their due. I just don't want to see you tumbling down with them. It's too late to save my mother, but it's not too late for you."

Belle panned from one corner of the room to the other. The wallpaper was peeling in several places, and the painting over the fireplace made her think about the charm Angus had given her for the inn. The Trojan horse. The mole wrapped up in a pretty bow. It was just what she needed to yank her back to reality.

"I can't blame you for hating Hazel," she said, hardly believing that she was actually about to defend Donner. "And being a spineless oaf is no excuse for Donner's father's behavior either. But that's not my story. And Donner is not another version of his father. Neither of us were in a good place when he had his affair. And he only had one." She stopped, cringing at her own words but standing by them nonetheless. "Not hundreds. Plus, he wasn't even in control of himself. It wasn't even fair. And you know it."

Angus Kane's right eyebrow rose, then his left. His focus hardened. "What do you mean by that?"

She was too incensed to think straight, too overwhelmed to decide whether revealing what she knew was a good idea. But nothing could stop her now.

"How can you sit there and tell me how dishonest the Wickenhams are, while you're waging a war against the very magic you're using to attack them?" she said, jumping up and storming around the room. "Doing right by your mother is one thing, but launching a witch hunt on innocent people and trying to bring down a system that's been in place for generations is something else entirely."

She halted by the window and stared down at the square. Orderly lines of people were filing down the streets toward the docks. The castle was being evacuated. So much for Letitia's grand wedding.

"Excuse me," she heard, "but certainly you're not accusing me of using magic, are you? Forgive me but what sort of hypocrite do you think I am?"

Belle seethed and spun around. "The kind who would plant a charm in my house in order to spy on me and send blackmailing pictures to the newspaper," she snapped. "That kind."

Angus's brow furrowed as his lips curled up in amusement. "You think the painting I gave you is enchanted?"

"I *know* it is." Belle's fists were so tight, she thought she felt nails breaking her skin. "Just like I know you took Jacara's magic when Dawn's curse broke. I know you stole Ruby's powers and used them to curse Donner. And I know you did something to make the most beloved monarchs in Marestam vanish off the face of the earth. You're just using magic left and right, Angus. Don't even try to tell me it isn't true."

"It isn't," he replied, as easily as if she'd asked whether his turkey club sandwich was supposed to come toasted. Belle could practically see the wheels turning behind his eyes — his cold, dust-colored eyes — as he refocused on the purple orb topping his cane. He paused. Then he laughed.

Belle halted beside an ornate desk holding a stone bust of a regal looking old man. He had wide, googly eyes, fat cheeks, and hair that spiked off at the ends. She ran her hand along the spikes and wondered … if she threw hard enough in Angus's direction, would it kill him?

"You both under and overestimate me at the same time," he

said, bidding her back to the couch. Belle just narrowed her eyes and crossed her arms. "I'm not going to pretend I didn't contribute to that miscreant's rampage in one way or another. What kind of entitled egomaniac just starts getting monthly shipments of alcohol and doesn't ask any questions?" A wicked little smile popped up on his face but he forced it back down. "You'd be amazed what the right mix of hormones can do to a person's brain."

Belle felt her entire insides spasm. "Are you saying you —"

"I certainly didn't *curse* him. Nor did I harm the Charmés. They're probably happier than ever right now. Cinderella's mother was one of the only people who treated my mother with dignity during her final years. I would never hurt her daughter."

"But do you know where they —"

"And the painting? Yes, the painting is more than it appeared to be. I won't deny that. But its being a *charm* is news to me." He shook his head and flattened his hand over his heart. "That's just insulting. You should know by now how much I distrust magic. It's done far more harm than good and those who have it did nothing whatsoever to earn it — not unlike the monarchies. Had it not been for magic, that tyrannical mother-in-law of yours wouldn't have been able to ruin my mother's life to the extent that she did. And your father wouldn't have been taken prisoner by a monster. You would have been free to have a normal life with a normal husband and family. You wouldn't have lost the child you waited so long for because *he* went on a murderous, magical rampage." He uncrossed his legs, pushed himself up, and meandered a few feet toward the door. "No, I trust science. Chemistry. Technology. But if you'd rather throw your hat in with Ruby Welles and all of her magical supremacy ideas, so be it. I just wanted to give you a chance."

Angus was inches from the door when a little voice inside her called out for him to stop. "Wait," she ordered, her fist closing around her bracelet. "Why are you telling me all this? What do you want from me?"

By the time Angus faced her again, his lips were curved on both sides and his hands rested comfortably atop the cane smack in between his legs. "The monarchies are going to fall soon. It's not even a question anymore. Their midnight is approaching, and it's coming on fast. The people are finally seeing the whole system for the archaic, elitist institution it's always been, and they're not going to back down. The King of Braddax is a criminal. The Whites have been ostracized by everyone outside Tantalise. My niece's thirst for the throne is seconds from starting either a civil war or a revolution in Riverfell. The Charmés have forsaken us. And Regian ... well, I can crush them at any moment thanks to Dawn's lust for her husband's new business partner."

"You're a monster," Belle muttered under her breath.

"No, my dear. You married the monster. Your friends dug their own graves with their decisions. I'm just shining a light on them."

"What do you want from me?" Belle said again, stomping on each word like it was a mushroom in Beast's favorite part of the lawn.

Angus shrugged. "Like I said, you remind me of my mother. I just wanted to give you a chance to abandon the ship you've been bound to for the last five years before I send it to the bottom of the ocean. Tell the people of Braddax what really happened to their heir. Let them know Donner is the end of the line, and stop dragging out the inevitable by giving them false hope. It's a win-win for all of us. You get the sympathy and the support that you deserve, and I get to fulfill a promise I made a long, long time ago."

"What promise is that?"

"To bring the monarchies to an end. To stop this constitutional nepotism that puts the lives of thousands in the hands of a fetal lottery winner without any sort of merit or vetting. It's the right thing to do."

Belle didn't know what to say. She thought she'd been speechless before, but this was a whole new level of bewilderment. Angus appeared to know nothing about Jacara's powers, but Ruby couldn't have been more right about his intention to destroy the monarchies. Not that Belle didn't agree with a few of his points. Blood by no means guaranteed a qualified leader, for example. And taking the crown off the table was the best thing she could do for her baby boy. But this wasn't the right way to let that happen.

She was just about to tell him as much — minus the part about Rye — when a loud pop ripped through the air. She twisted up and around, expecting to see Hazel or Elmina or Grethel coming to her rescue. Instead, she spun right into Donner's waiting arms.

"Are you okay? I was two miles from Avalon when I heard what happened." He did a visual welfare check and then shoved Belle behind him. "Is this what you're resorting to now?" he barked, turning to confront his secret half-brother. "Kidnapping pregnant women and holding them against their will? What is wrong with you?"

Angus didn't move a muscle, save for the ones controlling the loaded smirk spreading across his cheeks. He looked directly at Belle but didn't say a word. He didn't need to. She'd heard all he had to say, and now had a decision to make.

"Why didn't you use the bracelet?" Donner asked, cupping both her wrists in his massive hands.

"I wasn't ready yet," she said. "I wanted to hear what he—"

"Never mind," he cut her off, just as both doors swung open and four guards stormed toward them. "Let's get out of here now."

"Donner Wickenham," one of the men shouted, stun gun at the ready. "Sir, you're under arrest."

Belle attempted to block him as the guard rushed forward

and the distance between them increased.

"Donner, you can't—"

"Go!" he ordered.

Belle lurched after him, suddenly aware that Angus had been right about one thing—she *did* want to protect Donner. The real Donner. The Donner who gave up his freedom when he handed her that bracelet, and was risking it again now in order to save her. He had his flaws, that was for sure, but more than anything else, he was a victim. He was the product of an infantile father, a narcissistic mother, a vengeful fairy, and now a hateful half-brother who'd used "science" to sabotage his own body and turn him into a raging beast.

"Just clear your head and go!" Donner commanded again, suddenly lost behind a crowd of struggling uniforms. "I can't get out of here until you do, Belle. Now!"

Chapter Twenty-Six

RAPUNZEL

Rapunzel couldn't understand why Ethan was being so manic. In the few hours since he'd returned from Stularia, he'd been moody, combative, grouchy, impatient, and even outright aggressive—but not in that sexy, tie-me-to-the-bedpost sort of way. Sure, she'd left him alone on a deserted island, but not by choice. Donner was pretty much calling the shots at that point. She expected him to be fatigued from all the jet setting, but also thought he'd be generally happy to see her. She thought twenty hours of isolation would have given him time to cool off.

But when she stepped into his father's viewing box just before the coronation, Ethan looked at her with eyes the color of blood. His hands were so shaky he could hardly hold the program, and he reeked of whiskey. The only thing he seemed to care about was finding Donner so he could refill the flask he'd given him just before they disappeared. He was talking like a junkie, getting more and more agitated until the ballroom launched into chaos and his mood took a sharp U-turn.

Now, as he sobbed into Snow White's loveseat on Tantalise, she was beginning to suspect foul play.

"What the hell is wrong with him?" Grethel asked as he bear-hugged her legs and used her beaded skirt as a tissue.

Rapunzel shook her head. She'd encountered highs and lows like this a few times before, but only with professional athletes who took too many steroids. That wasn't Ethan though. Ethan was always so cool under pressure. It was one of the reasons she'd fallen for him in the first place. *Her* Ethan always smirked through conflict and cut through tension to reveal the logical solution everyone else was too incensed to see. She needed that Ethan now. They all did.

"I have no idea," Rapunzel replied, wracking her brain for ideas. "I've never seen him this ... volatile."

Grethel made a painfully slow grimace, her eyes never leaving the emotional train wreck unfolding before them. "Do you know if he's taking any new medications? It's criminal the damage those can do to some people."

Rapunzel frowned at this reminder about Grethel's health, then frowned even deeper upon realizing she didn't know whether Ethan took any medications at all. Or any vitamins, for that matter. A little extra D? A multi? Fish oil? Maybe Donner had been right. Good, earnest girlfriends were supposed to make note of such things. Ethan probably had her entire maintenance routine down pat, right down to her go-to brand of hair elastics. But that didn't mean he was more serious about their relationship than she was. Did it?

"How about drugs?" Grethel tried again.

Rapunzel shook her head immediately. "No. I mean..." She faltered, unsure how to answer the question that usually preceded a story about her parents trading her to a witch to feed their rampion addiction.

"It's okay, I've heard the spiel." Grethel shifted her focus to the kitchen, where Snow was warming a bottle on the stove. She then panned to Ruby, who was perched in front of the news like Beast watching Gray prepare a steak dinner. "What do you think should be our next move?"

Rapunzel yanked her mangled dress from Ethan's fist and replaced it with a hemp throw pillow. "I don't know. But I was never a fan of this triad nonsense to begin with. I said from Day One that all we needed was a shred of proof and a good headline vilifying Angus. Though at this point, I might just pay him a visit at gunpoint and —"

A deafening roar swept through the house, followed by the sound of a dozen dishes shattering on the kitchen floor. Rapunzel jumped to her feet, sending Ethan face-first onto the cork flooring, and raced towards the noise. "Is Belle back?" she called, careening around the butcher block island. "What in the world was —"

But before she could finish, she caught sight of Elmina and came to a screeching halt.

"Oh," she said, not bothering to mask her disappointment. "You still haven't found Belle? Did you try every place I said? The Phoenix? My apartment? Braddax Castle and the old abbey on the far side of the property?"

Elmina gave her an exasperated look, then pulled off her sandal and tipped it over Snow's sink. A stream of dirt poured out.

"What about the zoo?" Rapunzel tried again. Elmina whacked her footwear against the sink five times, then reached down for her other foot. "She goes there sometimes when she needs to thi —"

"I checked the inn, the castle, the abbey, the gardens, the Hall of Curiosities, your apartment, as much of midtown Carpale as I could access, and every square inch of Selladóre — coast to coast. But like I told you before, I can't evaporate everywhere. If she's in a private building that I don't have permission to enter, I won't be able to…" She stopped, looked pointedly at Rapunzel, and let out an exhausted sigh. "I mean, do you *really* think she'd go to the zoo at a time like this? Chances are if she was wearing that bracelet you told me about, she would have come here. And if she wasn't, she couldn't have gotten that far from Selladóre without anyone noticing. The Braddax Zoo is what, a ferry ride and five miles away?"

Rapunzel stared at her but didn't answer. Even pregnant, Belle was known to take Beast for ten-mile hikes and still be back in time to fix breakfast for everyone at the inn. If she wanted to travel five miles without anyone noticing, she could. "You're the only one who can transport another person with your little magical teleportation act," she said. "Please."

Elmina shoved her sandal back on and leered at her. "Fine. Fifteen minutes. If I don't find her by then, I'm coming back and we need to talk about our other problems."

But no sooner did she disappear again than a second blast rang out. More pots clamored to the ground.

"Belle!" Rapunzel shrieked as she materialized directly behind Snow, knocking the teakettle into a tower of cookware. The lid of a saucepan rolled into the living room and wobbled frantically before finally stopping at the base of a potted aloe plant. "What happened? Where did you go? We've been worried s—"

"Where is he?" she hollered, racing into the living room, then down the hallway, then toward the window to look outside.

"Huh. Where's who?"

"Donner! He should have been right behind me."

"Donner?" Rapunzel repeated, unsure she'd heard her correctly. "Why would *Donner* be here? We don't even know where Hazel is. Apparently, she disappeared as soon as the Marestam Guard showed up, which *I* think means she might have sold us out."

"She did," Belle said, not at all the reaction Rapunzel was expecting.

"What?" Ruby asked, turning away from the news. "Are you sure?"

Belle nodded but still seemed intensely preoccupied. "Yes. I mean no. I mean that's what Angus seemed to in—"

"Hold on," Ruby interrupted. "You were just with Angus?"

"And Donner?" Rapunzel chimed in.

Belle stopped, then nodded, then launched into a wild rant about Angus being Donner's half brother and plotting vengeance against the monarchies for decades. "He didn't seem to know about Jacara's magic though. He swears he would never *use* magic because he hates it so much, but I'm pretty sure he had something to do with Donner's rampage anyway. He said something about science and hormones and how they can affect the brain. I think he spiked Donner's—"

"Spiked Donner's whiskey with enough steroids to enrage a rhinoceros?" Rapunzel interrupted, giving Ethan a nauseated—though moderately relieved—glance. "Yeah, that actually makes sense." Belle followed her friend's gaze, then gave her a look of both pity and solidarity. "But unless you were downing poisoned whiskey while you were pregnant, that doesn't explain Rye."

Belle paused. From the look on her face, this hadn't occurred to her.

"It was just horrible timing!" Ruby said, her tone almost one of relief. "That makes sense. *That's* why the curse seemed so much stronger—so much angrier—than the original." Rapunzel turned her eyes into slits and focused extra carefully on Ruby's tone of voice, on her mannerisms, on how long she maintained eye contact as she spoke. She hadn't forgotten the discussion with her friends a few hours earlier.

"He should be here by now," Belle murmured just as the skies opened up and the outside became a soaking blur. "Why isn't he here yet? He was almost safe in Avalon but came back to help me." Her huge brown eyes widened. "He could have been free. There's no way he's getting a fair trial if Angus is calling the shots. He'll probably resurrect the death penalty just for that day, and then I'd be responsible for Rye never knowing his father."

No one spoke — more out of fear than a lack of opinion — until a tiny voice from upstairs broke the silence. "Da!" it called, clear as a glass breaking during a funeral. "Dadada!"

Snow was at the foot of the stairs in seconds, warm bottle in hand. "I'll get him," she said as two more cracks rang out and a dark, hulking figure appeared in the rapidly shrinking room.

"Donner!" Belle called, rushing forward and throwing her arms around him. Donner stood there like a flagpole, then gave a humble smile, slid his arms under hers, and gently nudged her back.

"I'm fine," he said as Rapunzel ground her teeth. But before she could say anything, an even scarier sight appeared beside the schizophrenic who'd ruined her best friend's life: his mother.

Rapunzel immediately pulled Grethel aside and told her to go upstairs and keep Rye hidden. The last thing anyone needed was for Hazel Wickenham to realize Belle was no longer carrying her grandson — and was therefore fully expendable.

"*There* you are," Hazel proclaimed, staring down the room but barely glancing at Donner. Her ordinarily perfect hair was sopping wet and stretched out in all directions — across her forehead, around her neck, swirled over the mascara that had puddled atop her cheeks. She looked more like a half-drowned mouse than the former queen of a kingdom. "I've been looking everywhere for you people. I must have missed the emergency rendezvous memo. Someone neglected to inform me that we were all supposed to turn tail at the first sign of trouble and hide in the woods. You do realize this wasn't a dress rehearsal, right? My son is cursed and Marestam is in danger and you — "

"Oh, stop it," Belle commanded.

Hazel's head jerked back while her neck arched forward. "Excuse me?"

Belle pressed her hands into her hips and made herself as tall as possible. "Stop the act, Hazel. "We know you tipped off

Angus." Her eyes darted to Donner's, as if asking for verification—or forgiveness. His look was one of disappointment, but not shock. "You're the reason the triad failed and Donner's still cursed."

Hazel blinked a dozen times in five seconds but said nothing—which, for all intents and purposes, said everything.

Belle opened her mouth to ask why, but Donner beat her to it.

"How could you?" he snapped, lunging between his wife and his mother. "That was the only way for Rye to—" He glanced toward the stairs but stopped himself. So, he hadn't told her. "You have no idea what you've done."

"They were supposed to wait until after we broke the spell," Hazel said, sounding simultaneously guilty, weak, and furious. "I didn't want your curse to break just so these people could toss you in a jail cell for the rest of your life. But the only way you were going to keep any semblance of your old life was if I gave that snake something in exchange."

"Something like the destruction of Marestam and the death of a thousand innocent people?" Belle growled, the ferocity in her voice taking even Rapunzel by surprise.

"The death of a thousand innocent people?" Hazel repeated, her focus narrowing on her daughter-in-law. "Now that's more than a tad melodramatic, don't you think? All I did was give him the opportunity to arrest three purebloods breaking into a historic landmark."

"No, it's actually not," Belle countered, getting her mother-in-law up to speed on Jacara's abilities and how Angus could use them to undo the magic keeping every Selladórean alive. "Plus," she said as Hazel denied knowing anything about this, "you ruined your son's only chance to live a normal, curse-free life. Even if he had to do it outside of Marestam, at least—"

"Oh, that wasn't his only chance," Hazel corrected, quickly forgetting the whole Selladórean genocide thing. "There's one other way to break Donner's curse — a way that guarantees it will never, ever come back."

Silence descended as everyone waited for Hazel to continue on her own. But for minutes, she just stood there, arms crossed, weight on one leg, chewing on her tongue and staring at Ruby.

"No one here is in the mood for games," Rapunzel finally said, taking the wheel. "Unless you found the cure for all curses at the bottom of a hurricane glass, I highly doubt you know anything we haven't already thought of, tried, and discounted. So, spit it out already. I'm dying to know what it is you think you know that flew under everyone else's radar."

The whole room waited as a tiny little smile opened up along the far corner of Hazel Wickenham's lips and slowly rose up her left cheek. "What do I know?" she asked, uncrossing her arms and stepping forward. "I know that no one here actually cares about Donner. I know you think Ruby just used that as bait so I would join her stupid triad and find your missing friends — even though all *she* really wanted to do was get her powers back. And I know you believe Angus is the one responsible for what happened to my son even though — "

"He is," Belle said, just as Grethel slunk silently back down the stairs, shooting Rapunzel a discreet *all is well.* "I was just with Angus and he admitted — "

"He admitted what?" Hazel barked, shutting her down instantly. "The man is as worthless as they come. A conniving, jealous, whiny, spiteful skunk of a man. Evil, yes. But magical? Not one iota. No, Angus Kane didn't curse my son." She paused and leered at Ruby, who'd silently backed all the way up into the living room and was eyeing the door. "*She* did."

"That's a lie!" Ruby shouted even as she broke for the door. But the old, wheezing fairy was a sickly zebra compared to Hazel, who shot across the kitchen like a lioness, ricocheted off the couch on which Ethan was now comatose, and stopped Ruby before her toes even hit the welcome mat.

"I really have to hand it to you, Ruby," Hazel spat as everyone else stood frozen, doggie paddling through the shock. "This whole righteous, incontestable persona you invented? It's genius. Really. So genius that even though you lost your powers at the *exact* same time my son's curse came back, this group of fools couldn't even *imagine* you might be to blame."

Rapunzel gritted her teeth. That wasn't true. She'd made that exact assertion the morning Belle awoke at the hospital, and Penny had been all over it that afternoon. But now wasn't the time to play told-you-so.

"Instead, they preferred to swallow that ridiculous tale about Angus pilfering some ancient fairy's residual magic and using it like some sort of magical boomerang."

"More like a siphon," Ruby grumbled. "And that wasn't entirely wrong. What happened was a combination of—"

"Oh, just stop it," Hazel commanded. Ruby's jaw clapped shut. "You cursed my son for acting out when someone murdered the love of his life," Hazel said as Belle looked more confused than ever. "He was a brokenhearted wreck. He was beyond consolation. So yes, he took it out with booze and bad behavior, but he wasn't hurting anyone. I had it under control. But then you waltzed in, still high on your Cinderella glory, not knowing even a fraction of the story, and decided his behavior warranted a life-altering punishment—a punishment judged, levied, and executed by *you*."

"Believe what you want," Ruby mumbled, crossing her arms but visibly frightened. "It was an accident. I—"

"You're full of it," Hazel proclaimed, lunging forward and smacking Ruby right across the cheek. She fell into the wall and clutched her face. "You knew *exactly* what you were doing."

"I meant the second time," Ruby backtracked, pleading, red-eyed, with her assailant. "The second time was an accident."

"So you were justified six years ago?"

Ruby stared at the floor and shook her head like a guilty child.

"That was unfortunate. But I had my reasons at the time."

Hazel started to grunt something about jealousy not being a reason, when Belle joined the attack.

"How could you?" she demanded, her voice firm, angry, and pitiless. "Rye? The Phoenix? All the hounding and threatening and blame you threw on me? How could you stand right beside me this whole time and pretend like you were completely innocent? All because you couldn't handle the world turning in opposition to what you wanted. You may have cast that spell to turn Donner into a monster, but *you're* the monster, Ruby. *You're* the one who should be thrown in jail, not him."

Rapunzel could see Hazel's satisfaction as clear as glass—but not as well as she could see Ruby's terror. It was a sight she'd imagined so many times—the moment someone finally put the self-aggrandizing blowhard in her place. But now that it had come, she actually felt sorry for her. The dogmatic old fairy was boxed in. Her reputation would be tarnished forever. The closest thing she had to real friends were doing nothing to help her. And Hazel wasn't going to stop until every last shred of dignity had been scratched from her frail, magically-depleted bones.

"I'm sorry," Ruby said again, looking at Belle as she pushed herself away from the wall. With her mouth tight, her shoulders hunched, and her chest moving faster than a triathlete at the finish line, she looked so … done. "But it wasn't jealousy, and I never intended to hurt anyone. I just wanted to protect Marestam, like my parents wanted. The monarchies are supposed to be beacons of light, not debauchery and excess. Braddax deserved a queen like Belle, and no one can say she didn't make Donner a better man—even if it didn't last forever. But you're right. I shouldn't have taken it upon myself to arrange that."

Belle crossed her arms and glared at her. "Then why did you do it twice?"

Ruby laced her fingers together and shook her head. "I swear

I never meant to bring it back," she repeated. "I mean, I thought about it; but I knew I'd regret it. I kept hoping I could talk some sense into you instead. I kept trying to make you see that erasing your fairy tale would be detrimental to the very fabric of Marestam. But then I went to the inn and saw you kissing that … that derelict." Belle and Rapunzel shot each other panicked looks. Hazel's arms were crossed, and it was possible there was smoke rising from her ears. "I couldn't believe my eyes. After everything I'd told you." She sucked her cheeks in and shook her head, trying not to get pulled back into that moment. "My emotions took full control at that point, and I must have said something by mistake. You have to believe me, I never meant to. I muttered something — to myself. But almost immediately, you started screaming and Gray started hollering for an ambulance. I thought it was just a coincidence until Donner's blood came back from the hospital — though now I know that was skewed by whatever Angus Kane put in his body. And as soon as I found out about the baby, I — "

"Baby? What about the baby?" Hazel waited a split second, then amped up her volume and intensity tenfold. She stomped forward. "Ruby Welles, if I find out you cursed my grandson too, there is no way in the universe you're leaving this cottage alive."

Ruby's eyes widened and she leaned into the wall again, sliding further down the closer Hazel got. "I tried to take it back immediately but you know I can't," she said, her voice almost a whimper. "You know how magic works. Just because I cast it doesn't mean I can stop it. His curse is a curse to me too."

"Wait," Belle said, tears starting to force their way through. "I don't understand. If you cast it because you wanted me to go back to Donner, why didn't it break when I decided to?"

Ruby's eyes panned the ceiling. "Like I've said a hundred times, magic doesn't abide by any — "

"It didn't break because you don't love me anymore," Donner interrupted, his voice deep and grave. All heads turned to see him, arms crossed by the stove, a mess of dark hair obscuring his eyes while Snow's orange pot bubbled over behind him. "The cure is an act of true love, right?" He glanced at Ruby but didn't bother waiting for her answer. "Well, Belle doesn't love me anymore, so that's not the answer." He gave a weak, defeated smirk, then looked up. "Though on the bright side that means she did at one point."

Belle stepped towards him. "Donner, that's not—"

He waved her off. "No, it's okay. What you said a few months ago was right. We were ... how did you phrase it ... what each other needed under the circumstances. We weren't made for the long haul. That doesn't mean we should never have been, but you being metaphysically blackmailed into staying with a man who no longer has your heart isn't the same as returning out of true love. Is it?"

Ruby and Hazel said nothing as his words sank in. They were both guilty of trying to fabricate love, to force Belle and Donner together. For the sake of the realm. For the sake of appearances. For the sake of fulfilling what society deemed was best for a child—having both birth parents under one roof even if they were miserable ninety percent of the time.

"No," Ruby finally said, standing up tall and smoothing out her clothes. "It's not the same thing." She swiped beneath her eyes and flipped her hair as if preparing for a photo session—or an execution. "So, with that off the table, the triad was the next best option. And now there's only one more." She stared vacantly at Hazel. "Please don't drag it out."

"I'm sorry," Hazel replied, dropping her shoulders and drawing a short, sparkly wand from the top of her shirt. That's when Rapunzel recalled what Grethel had told her about Ethan's eyesight. When she dies, all of her magic dies with her. Killing Ruby would be the one sure-fire way to break Donner's and Rye's curse. She watched in horror as Hazel stretched the wand out to triple its original size, raised her eyes to the sky, and lifted her weapon—slowly, as if each hand contained twenty-pound weights and she was walking through quicksand. Donner yanked Belle out of the way just before his mother's hair began flying and Grethel conjured some sort of protective bubble around half the kitchen.

Suddenly, Hazel stopped, dropped her arms, and thrust her hips forward. A blinding light erupted from the wand, darted straight for Ruby, then hit the outside of Grethel's bubble and turned back. Rapunzel ducked as it ricocheted over her head and blew a hole through an exterior wall. A second shot grazed her left shoulder and knocked the pot of water off the stove. A third rammed into the ceiling directly above Grethel's head, sending a fog of sheetrock raining down and severing a two-hundred-pound oak chandelier from its anchor. The crash was deafening. The bubble shielding Ruby instantly fell.

Rapunzel didn't see what happened next, but she heard it—a sizzling sound, like steak being tossed into an inch of bubbling oil. Suddenly, a tower of orange flames flew across the stovetop and zoomed up the curtains on the west-facing wall.

She waited just long enough to see Belle leaping up the stairs two by two. Then she raced into the dust and tumbled into Grethel.

"Are you okay?" she hollered, the noise inside Snow's cottage now deafening. There was no response. She pressed her hands against both sides of Grethel's face and moved it side-to-side. Then she stopped, remembering some rule about not moving a person after a serious injury. But the cottage was going up in flames. Was there a rule for that?

She looked up for help and tried not to panic. Snow and Belle were still upstairs. Ruby and Hazel were exchanging—she blinked a few times and shook her head. Yes. They were *exchanging* magical fire while Donner hurled flying objects between them and hollered for them both to stop. In a matter of seconds, the reclusive little haven had become a claustrophobic war zone. And all the while, Ethan lay spread eagle on the wicker loveseat, staring out in a vacant trance.

She stomped to his side, concern for Grethel overshadowing all of her anger at his current condition—anger no longer directed at Ethan for drinking too much, but at Angus Kane for poisoning him.

"Ethan," she hollered, grabbing his leg and clawing into it through his pants. "Grethel's not moving. Ethan. Look at me." His head pivoted on a perfect plane, as if his body contained metal and wires rather than flesh and bone. He gazed blankly back at her. "Ethan!"

The left side of his mouth rose half an inch, but quickly fell.

"Dammit!" she shrieked, twisting his collar in both of her fists. "Snap out of it, Ethan."

His eyes flickered a bit as his body flinched, but his mind was still elsewhere. She held on harder, forcing him to focus, begging him to come back to her without saying a word. There was a reason her wild romantic life had two bookends that both belonged to him. There was a reason she gave a fuck when she thought he'd abandoned her the first time—and the second. There was a reason she hadn't sent him packing when she found out about Grethel. No one else in her history could have pulled even one of those things and still been in her life the next day. Ethan was different. The thought of losing him did something bleak to the way she envisioned her future—something that made her feel more alone than she'd ever felt in her life. And her life had some pretty lonely moments.

"Listen to me," she heard herself saying, pleading, giving in. Her cheek brushed against his chest, then hovered by his chin. She felt her entire body jolt. "I need you. I'm sorry that I'm still learning how to show it, but you have to know that you're *it* for me." She stopped, realizing what she'd just said. Donner had been right. She'd taken it for granted that Ethan knew those things, even though she'd never made a conscious effort to tell him.

"I'm sorry," she continued. "I was too busy punishing you to let you know how I really felt, to let you know I was so raving mad at you because I love you so freaking much. And I'm sorry I was distant with your family. It's not because I didn't care to make a good impression. It was because I was sick over making a bad one. Literally sick," she added, recalling the soul-churning nausea on the plane, the disgusting ginger tea she couldn't keep down, and the ten minutes she'd spent looming over the toilet before settling into bed. "I wasn't guarded because I thought it was pointless for me to meet them. Or because I don't want to have—" She paused, not wanting to get carried away. "Or because I'm opposed to the idea of discussing starting a family with you someday." Much better. His eyes seemed to stop on hers now, seemed to be trying to focus. "I just don't know how to be part of a family like yours. And I'm terrified that if I *do* get close enough to become a part of one, I'll lose them. Just like I'm terrified of losing the love of my life and my mother right now. So please. Fight your way out of this poison fog you're in, lift your ass off of this couch, and help me get Grethel out of here."

As soon as her last word left her lips, Ethan drew in a sharp breath, locked his eyes on hers, and wrapped both hands behind her head. Suddenly, it was as if they were locked inside one of Grethel's magical bubbles, away from the growing fire, away from the screams of panic, away from the world going to shit all around them.

"You're not going to lose anyone," he said, pulling forward and planting his mouth firmly against hers. A thousand bolts of electricity surged down her spine, through her arms and out her toes. Then came an intense heat—the sort of heat that came from cinematic love, or bananas flambé, or the walls of a two-bedroom cottage burning to the ground.

Her eyes opened just in time to see Belle and Snow sprint down the stairs and race out the front door with a baby-sized bundle of sheets. She looked at Grethel.

"We have to carry her o — "

"Already on it, love," Ethan chirped, hopping to his feet and struggling to push the chandelier away. She was bending down to help when a third figure pushed them both out of the way, tossed the wood aside as if it weighed nothing, and lifted the injured fairy into his arms.

"Belle's orders not to let you die," Donner said as a flaming beam plummeted off the kitchen ceiling and crashed into the sink. "Now, are you two finished making up, or do you need to consecrate it in a burning building?"

Rapunzel looked at Ethan, then at Donner, then at the trees swinging through the air outside like balloons in a tornado. "I think we're good," she said, feeling her cheeks flush. "Let's get out of here."

߭錹

The first thing Rapunzel felt as she crossed the threshold was a raging, soaking wind and ice-cold air. The next was Belle, hugging her and crying and bouncing all at the same time. She was babbling a million broken words a minute — something about help being on the way, a question about Grethel, an angry remark about Ruby, and more praise for Donner coming to the rescue.

"Okay, let's get something straight," Rapunzel interrupted, sick of this tune already. "Donner didn't *rescue* you. Angus wasn't going to kill you, and you were perfectly capable of zapping yourself out of there at any time with that bracelet. I'm not saying what he did wasn't noble, but let's call it what it is and say — "

"That risking everything to come back for me broke his curse?"

Rapunzel paused, then gave her a flabbergasted look. It

wasn't like Belle to crack jokes during times like these—or at all, really. She scoured her for head injuries and asked if she was feeling okay. "Are you alright? I mean besides the fact that Snow's house is going the way of the Phoenix and that you just found out I was right about Ruby being a villain all along, are you okay?"

Belle grabbed her friend's shoulders with both hands and squeezed. "Pun, I'm fantastic. Did you hear what I said?" Her eyes were dancing back and forth and her face could have lit up a nightclub—or was that just the reflection of the flames? "Donner's act of true love broke the curse! Didn't you notice? Ruby's powers are back. We were so obsessed with kisses and romantic love that we forgot about all the other kinds—like a parent for his child. Donner gave up his chance at escape to make sure Rye didn't lose me, too. About Rye though..." She drifted off for a second, her eyes panning to the right, then down, then back to Rapunzel. "Well, the important thing is he's going to be okay."

Rapunzel stood there, stunned, as Belle pulled her into another huge hug and ushered her towards the tree line. Everyone but Ruby was huddled beneath a swath of ancient evergreen boughs, which provided a makeshift shelter from the rain. Ruby was front and center in the yard, dousing the inferno with some magical ice concoction shooting from her wand.

"How is she?" she called to Ethan, who was folding his jacket gently beneath Grethel's head. But before she could reach him, the sound of a tiny cry stopped her in her tracks. She spun around to see a serene Hazel Wickenham standing beside Donner and cradling a red, wriggling newborn with black eyes, curly chestnut hair, and a body barely longer than her shoe.

"Umm, who is that?" Rapunzel asked, making a move to come closer but holding back. Hazel was gazing down at the baby with stars in her eyes and the sort of calm that had seemed impossible a few minutes earlier. "That's not ... I mean ... Where is Rye?"

Belle pressed her lips, gave a powerless shrug, and told her that magic could do a lot of things, evidently, but it couldn't do everything. It could summon icy winds to fight an inferno, but it couldn't reverse the damage. It could help lost lovers find each other, but it couldn't bring one back from the dead. It could protect a child from a traumatic assault by launching it forward in time, but it couldn't stuff him back into his mother's womb once he was out.

"Ruby thinks he's in some sort of suspended growth pattern now until his age catches up," Belle said. "So, it looks like I get to deal with those newborn cries after all — for an additional few months."

Rapunzel gave a hesitant smile. She didn't know exactly how to feel about this. Of course, she was thrilled that Rye would grow at a normal rate now. But would this pinched, ruddy creature remember her silly faces and the laughs they'd shared together? Or would she be a stranger to him now — a stranger with memories of a past that belonged to another incarnation of Rye? Then again, was there ever any way this story could have had an entirely happy ending? Perhaps if they had found a way to go back in time and ... no. Everything was too connected. If Ruby hadn't cursed Donner the first time, Belle would probably be working at a library somewhere, completely unknown to Rapunzel. If Donner had never cheated on Belle, Rapunzel would never have started the Phoenix or met Gray. Just thinking about it made her head spin.

Perhaps that's why Snow always found it so important to leave the past in the past; why Ethan thought one heartfelt apology was all their relationship needed to move on from his lies about Grethel; why Belle was able to forgive Donner for the things he did rather than cut him out of Rye's life eternally. Life was a series of imperfect but irreplaceable events, where a misstep could lead to something wonderful, and the best laid plan could result in catastrophe. Perhaps those people who flocked to church on Sundays were on to something. Perhaps there was some grand, master architect and everything did happen for a reason not meant to be understood in the present moment. Or perhaps it was all just dumb luck ... a world in which evil churned alongside the good, and each day was as unpredictably senseless as the next.

She looked up just as Ethan was helping a newly-conscious Grethel to her feet. "Oh, thank God," she said, hustling over and slipping her hand around the fairy's other side. "Don't ever do that again. You still owe me at least twelve years of nagging and power struggling, remember?"

Grethel flashed a weak grin and asserted that she was perfectly fine. But Rapunzel saw right through this. She saw that Grethel's lips were the same color as her skin, that her eyes were cast down and glassy, that her knees weren't holding weight as well as they should have. Grethel wasn't healthy enough for this sort of stress. She thought briefly about what Belle had just said about magic's limitations. She'd left one out. It couldn't eradicate cancer either, at least no magic she'd ever heard of.

Slowly, they all made their way back to the baby, who was now silent and still in Snow's arms. She had a blank look on her face, but there was far more happiness than sorrow behind it.

"I'm so sorry about your house," Belle said, tucking a corner of the blanket under Rye's neck. His huge black eyes focused intently on Snow, then panned a few inches to Belle.

"It's not your fault," she replied. "The only thing that really matters is right here. I'm just sorry he has to find a new home again."

Silence fell as the remaining drizzle disappeared and a bit of sun broke through the clouds.

"So, what do we do now?" asked Snow. "The curse may be broken but Angus has put a price on all of us and Cinderella's still missing."

"Actually," Ethan chimed in, pulling his phone out of his pocket, "I just got a lead on that. A colleague of mine in Ellada says he got a hold of the man who picked them up at the airport. The good news is he has no reason to think they're in danger."

"Great!" Belle, Rapunzel, and Snow shouted in unison.

"Where are they?"

"Let's not waste time."

"When Elmina gets back, she can just zip on over there and —"

"No, she can't," Ethan said. "There's a problem."

"What sort of problem? So long as she knows where to go, Elmina's powers allow her to take someone with her when she does that teleportation thing."

"It's called evaporating," Hazel corrected.

Rapunzel gave her a dirty look. "Whatever."

"It doesn't matter what it's called," Ethan said, rubbing the back of his neck. "It won't work either way. The Charmés are stuck in a town they can't leave, and they have no reason to want to."

Rapunzel nearly pounced on him. "What do you mean they have no reason to want to? They have four children who need them. They have an entire kingdom to run. They have friends who've been worried sick."

"Yes, but they don't know that," he said, giving a frustrated sigh. "They don't remember you or their kids or Marestam. According to this guy, there's some town on the southeastern fringe of Ellada that was cursed decades ago and still is. Anyone who crosses its borders instantly forgets everything about their life up to that point, and loses any desire to leave. Cinderella and Aaron think that's their home now. And if anyone goes in to get them … well, they'll forget too."

All eyes stared either through him or into the ground. How had this become normal?

"Okay. Looks like we have another curse to break," Belle said just as Elmina appeared between them with Dawn in tow. The latter looked like she was in a functioning state of shock.

"I don't even want to know right now," Elmina said, panning vacantly over the smoke drifting off the charred cottage. She looked more frazzled than a mother of two-year-old quintuplets. "Belle, what exactly did you tell Angus about Jacara's powers?"

Belle unhinged her jaw but took a few seconds to answer. "I … I mentioned them, but I don't think he knows a thing about the – "

"That's not what I asked. What did you *tell* him?"

Belle shrugged and furrowed her brow. "I said I knew he took her powers when Dawn's curse broke."

Elmina pulled her right cheek between her teeth. "And you mentioned Jacara by name?" Belle nodded. Elmina's left cheek joined in. "Anything else?"

The lines deepened across Belle's forehead. "I said I knew he used them to steal Ruby's powers – which I guess was wrong but – "

"That's enough." Elmina shook her head and panned the circle. "I think Belle was right that Angus knew nothing about Jacara's powers a few hours ago. But he certainly knows about them now." She pulled a newspaper bulletin out of her front pocket. "In addition to this witch hunt disguised as a state of emergency, Parliament is holding a zero-hour referendum on two things tomorrow: the future of the monarchies, and the fate of magic."

No one made a sound, not even Rye.

"Angus says that in light of the inability of either the Carpale or Braddax monarchs to uphold their duties, as well as the Tantalise monarchs' refusal to obey federal law, the confusion over the Riverfell throne, and the likelihood that Belle was involved in the attack on the Hall of Curiosities – which he is labeling magical terrorism – the people have a constitutional right to reform their government should they so choose. And as for magic … well, he says he has in his possession a weapon that will erase it from the face of the earth in a matter of seconds."

"It's the orb atop his walking stick," Ruby interrupted, her nose buried in the bulletin. "But because he doesn't want to be seen as a hypocrite harboring the magic he so despises, he's giving the public the choice to pull the trigger or let magic remain. It says he's going to display the stone in the undamaged wing of the Hall of Curiosities until midnight tomorrow. That's when the polls will close and the votes will be tallied."

"He might be making it up," Elmina said, plucking the paper right out of Ruby's hand. "And there's a decent chance that it's a trap. But I don't think we can afford to gamble on this one. We have to try and grab it."

A flurry of ideas came forward. Most were horrible. A few were impossible. One was moderately less horrendous than all of its peers.

"Disagree if you want," Belle said, kissing Rye on the forehead and pulling out her phone, "but I still believe there are more rational, intelligent people in Marestam than there are fear-mongering sheep." She flashed Rapunzel an energetic smirk and then glanced at the four fairies, who'd split off into a smaller circle and were brainstorming how to break into the Hall of Curiosities—again. "Let them handle the magic," she told the remaining mortals as Matilda Holt's number popped up on her screen. "We'll take the media. After all, who can ignore the exclusive of the century?"

The Marestam Mirror

Diamond Ropes and Velvet Cake
By Perrin Hildebrand, King of Gossip

S PEECHLESS.

That is the only word that can possibly describe how I felt after reading Matilda Holt's exposé this morning. I am sure the book rights are already in the works, and feature film ideas are being tossed around behind closed doors everywhere. To summarize would be an insult to both my colleague (of whom I am now obscenely jealous) and to my readers (who I'm sure have already gobbled it up from headline to contact line half a dozen times), but far be it for insults to stop the King of Gossip from doing his job.

So … boiled down to one earth-shattering run-on sentence, here's what you REALLY need to know about the people who have been running our kingdoms for years: Belle's baby was born over a week ago; Hunter and Dawn Tirion have even more marital woes than we thought; Ruby Welles cursed the King of Braddax twice in the last six years; Cinderella and Aaron Charmé aren't giving us the cold shoulder—they've been trapped in a magical town that sucks up people's memories; Angus Kane is actually the bastard son of the late Varek Wickenham, and whether or not he succeeds in toppling the monarchies with tonight's vote, he'll be either impeached, assassinated, or arrested before the next sunrise.

For details, check out Matilda's award-worthy feature in the early edition. For public reaction, here's what I overheard this morning at Grand Capitol Station:

Regarding Belle's big pregnancy cover-up:
• "The poor thing! First her husband kicks her out, then her home burns to the ground, and then she has to hide her firstborn child like a canker sore? That woman should be given sainthood immediately—and probably Donner's crown!"
• "Never thought she had it in her, to be frank. Before Donner's scandal, that Belle was a bit of an insult to females everywhere. Not that I wish such misfortune on anybody, but I'm glad she's finally grown some muscle. Pin me for Team Belle."
• "I just hope this doesn't mean we're going to have a child king in Braddax—no, scratch that, an *infant* king. Look, I feel for Belle and all, but this isn't changing my vote. The monarchies have had their time."

Regarding the allegations that Angus Kane poisoned Donner Wickenham, covered up the Charmés' disappearance (or quite possibly organized it), and misused government property (a.k.a. Selladóre) for his own personal gain:
• "First, let me say that I'm skeptical of anything I read in the papers these days, so only a court of law can convince me. But if all that is true, I think Angus Kane should be held responsible for everything Donner Wickenham is on the hook for—jail time, hospital bills, emotional trauma, arson, all of it. Ruby Welles too. They should split it."
• "No big surprise here. That rat bastard's been angling for unrestricted power from the get-go. I never voted for him to begin with. What's the phrase his first opponent used way back when I was in high school? Oh yeah, 'doesn't play well with

others.' But he certainly plays others well, ha. I'm sure there are many more iniquities where these came from."

• "I am appalled that the *Mirror* would publicize such partisan nonsense on the morning of a historic, long-overdue exercise in civil liberties. Where are the opposing views? Where is the journalistic integrity? Do a couple 'declined to comments' really check the boxes nowadays? I swear, if today's vote upholds the current political system, I hope this rag gets sued into the history books."

• "Long live the crowns!"

In response to Dawn Tirion's affair with her husband's business partner and international distillery magnate Liam Devereaux, who is actually a 332 year old native of Selladore:

• "This is a real-life soap opera! Holy crap. I never thought I'd say this, but poor Hunter!"

• "Good for her. That walking manila envelope snatched her up before she even had a chance to see what a real modern man was like. That's like picking house keys out of a hat and being forced to sign a sixty-year lease. Of course she wasn't going to be satisfied. I just wish she'd given me a call. I've always had a weakness for redheads."

• "There is no excuse for infidelity. She took a vow — however unfair it might have been. Upon my word, where would society be if everyone broke the rules just because they felt miserable? It would be chaos. Misery is part of life."

• "I knew she couldn't really be as stale and conservative as she let on. I mean, just look at her hair — there had to be a little fire on the inside too! Well, at least Regian's queen is no longer a giant bore — not that I expect her to remain queen for much longer."

On a few additional points:
• "If Donner had a thing with that Karen Epson person before

she died — horrible story — and she left behind a young son … Well, what do you think the chances are that this kid is half Wickenham? Is it possible? What would that mean for the Braddax throne?"

• "I'm cancelling my subscription to *Ruby Magazine* this instant!"

• "So, if Donner was both under a curse and 'roid raging while he was being such a jerk, do you think that means he and Belle will get back together if he's better now? OMG I'd give anything to see a Donelle reunion!"

• "Crap. I think my neighbor is on the magical registry. I'm not trying to stereotype or anything, but … maybe I should sleep at my mother's house tonight. I can't see this ending well for anyone."

• "I'd find it much easier to believe Donner's story if he hadn't skipped bail like that. Or if he turned himself in now to await a fair trial."

AND now for a rare reprieve from the King of Gossip whimsy:

Marestam voters have a lot to think about today. We've been given a bloodstained sword and the option to slit the throat of our internationally admired royal heritage. We've been given the power to demote five members of our beloved femme fatale sextet, making them nothing more than former figureheads with fizzling celebrity status. Yours Truly would be forced to tack on that horrid qualifying adjective each time I referred to "former" Queen Cinderella, "former" Princess Penelopea, or even "former" King Donner. And not even two years into your King of Gossip's reign, at that! It's a cruel, cruel twist of fate, dear universe. A cruel twist of fate, indeed.

But if that's not enough to knock your head off and send it toppling down the East Bank Expressway, the people of Marestam are also being given the ability to do something that (rightfully) has the international community up in arms: end magic for good. Now in full disclosure, I'm doubtful that the baseball-sized orb now sitting in the Hall of Curiosities actually has the power to turn magic into a myth. I find it hard to believe that our shrewd, if not calculating, prime minister had this power attached to his walking stick for the last ten years but thought it nothing more than a pretty rock.

Still, it's my duty to relay a "VERY IMPORTANT" (she insisted on all caps) warning about calling Angus Kane's bluff. According to the now wanted, most powerful known fairy in the world, the power contained in that stone belonged to the very same fairy who cursed Dawn Tirion more than three centuries ago.

"People today can't even comprehend how much power Jacara had," says Elmina Goodman, "but there's one way I can put it into perspective. If the government uses that stone to try and erase magic from existence, there's a distinct possibility that every Selladórean who woke up in this realm and anyone who has since descended from them will die. Anyone whose life was saved by magic will die. Any evil that was toppled by magic—assuming the evil was not magical as well—will return. Jacara practiced black magic to an extent no one born in this century can possibly comprehend, and there's no way of knowing whether such a curse will simply remove magic going forward or undo everything that it's ever touched. It's a butterfly effect we can't even begin to understand. The people of Marestam might be holding the code to a nuclear bomb carrying enough ammunition to destroy the world."

Excuse me a moment while I polish off this gin—all three bottles of it. Happy voting.

Chapter Twenty-Seven

BELLE

"New count just in!" Gray called as Belle crawled around the kitchen floor on her hands and knees, wiping Beast's dribble off the floor with a brown dishtowel. "So far it's only eighteen percent in favor of using the stone. I knew that wouldn't pass. I mean, I know there are far too many irrational people out there who let fear run their lives but—"

"What about the monarchies??" Belle hollered, using a kitchen chair to pull herself upright and grab a box of flaxseed crackers. Any minute now, her tiny groundskeeper cabin was going to host Griffin, Snow, Rapunzel, Ethan, and—though she hadn't yet shared the news with her significant other—Donner.

"Not to worry," she heard him reply. "The polls don't even close until midnight. Only a few districts are reporting so far, but right now the thrones are all—"

His sudden silence caused Belle to dump the entire box of crackers into the porcelain bowl. Tiny seeded hexagons bubbled up like over-boiled rice and spilled onto the floor. Beast handled cleanup while she cursed, dropped the box on the table, and raced into the living room.

"Fifty-seven percent in favor of dissolving the monarchies," she read, her hands suddenly limp. She resisted as Gray wrapped his arm around her and pulled her close.

"Don't worry," he said, picking a crumb from her hair. "They only just started counting." She melted into him. "Believe me, it's going to be okay. That article was phenomenal and exactly the sort of honesty people have been waiting years to see from their leaders. There's no way Angus is going to win."

Belle opened her mouth to reply, but couldn't decide on the words. Matilda's article *had* been phenomenal. It cast off Angus Kane's fleece to expose a calculating, salivating wolf. It handed the entire realm access to their rulers' deepest, darkest secrets. It created a political climate so tense, she could have slashed it with a corkscrew. It gave Belle and her friends a certain level of protection as the world scrutinized Angus Kane's every move. But without the Charmés' confirmation that he was responsible for their imprisonment ... without his confession or a receipt in his name for anabolic steroids in bulk ... was it enough?

"I'll get it," she said as the doorbell rang and their first four guests toppled in hauling glass bottles, bakery boxes, and tight, jittery faces. As if the vote wasn't nerve-racking enough, they were also waiting to hear from Ruby and the other purebloods, who were gearing up to swipe the stone at any moment—just in case.

"Thanks for having us," Snow said, making a beeline for the bassinet in the corner. She'd finally ditched the excessive makeup and was looking like herself again—with a few, subtle upgrades. "I know we should be on Tantalise tonight of all nights, but with our cottage uninhabitable and the castle still being used as a spiritual learning center, we figured the people would understand."

"That and she's going through baby withdrawal," Griffin said, his voice forcing amusement though his eyes held a mixture of sadness and concern. "Please, any time you need a babysitter, call us." He paused to accept a beer from Gray, then tipped it back and turned toward the news. "Really. Any time at all."

∽◌∾

At nine o'clock, the vote to dissolve the monarchies was still unnervingly close but support for ending magic had dropped all the way into single digits—leading Gray to once again question why Angus even floated the idea in the first place.

"Was he just trying to scare us? Was it a distraction?" he asked, shaking his head from the couch. He was sitting on the middle cushion, feet on the coffee table, between Belle and Snow. "I just don't get it."

A slumbering Rye smacked his lips together in Gray's lap, as if agreeing in his own infant way. A smile crept up the far side of Belle's mouth. She liked the way they looked together, and was beginning to regret inviting Donner even though he had nowhere else to go. For someone who'd come careening into her life with no fear of death and absolutely nothing holding him down, Gray certainly had changed. And while she couldn't deny missing his cavalier spirit sometimes (especially when he became overprotective instead), she knew that was better for her and Rye. Better for being part of a family. Better for raising a child.

She reached out to hold Gray's hand as Rapunzel flashed her a proud, knowing smile. Then she rested her head between his shoulder and the side of his neck. It fit her like a winter hat, the fun kind with pom poms on top and flaps covering both ears. Gently, her thumb ran up and down the scars on his forearm— the scars she'd decided never to ask him about because she didn't need to know all the details. Everyone had secrets. Everyone had done things they were ashamed of. Whatever these meant to him, to her they were simply part of the road that had brought him here.

ல்கூ

By ten thirty, the proposition to destroy magic was formally declared dead, but the vote to end the monarchies was too close to call. Kingdom by kingdom, Tantalise was overwhelmingly in favor of keeping their monarchs in charge. Carpale lingered at a surprisingly low seventy percent, possibly because no one knew exactly how, when, or in what condition the Charmés would be found. Regian was hopping back and forth across the halfway mark. Riverfell was bringing up the rear. And Braddax was sinking like a bowling ball catapulted from a lighthouse.

"Don't take it personally," Gray said, pretending to give Rye a pep talk. "They're just used to someone a little … taller."

Belle smirked and gave his arm a playful jab. She would never admit it out loud, but she wasn't entirely against Marestam becoming a full democracy—or at least Braddax. That's presuming Angus was removed from office immediately and her friends still got to live in their castles. She just didn't want that life for her son. But either way, they'd survive. They'd make the best of it.

"Has anyone heard from Ruby?" Snow asked. "Or the others? Should we tell them they voted to keep magic?"

A short discussion began, during which they decided the vote shouldn't deter them from taking Jacara's powers out of play. That rock, or charm, or whatever it was, had to be destroyed. They just couldn't risk it falling into the wrong hands—or Angus deciding to use it regardless of the people's wishes.

ல்கூ

Forty-five minutes before midnight, Ruby sent Belle a message saying they were closing in on the stone, and frazzled newscasters announced that Donner Wickenham had just turned himself in at Marestam Central Prison.

Belle leapt from her seat to call him, but after catching Gray's eye decided to plop down and cuddle with Beast instead. She would probably have to walk a fine line between these two men forever, but was proud of Donner for prioritizing the greater good. If only the people of Marestam would feel the same way.

bn

Ten minutes before the polls officially closed, the pro-monarchy numbers in Braddax rocketed past those in Regian. Riverfell received a noticeable boost as well. Dawn called Belle within seconds of this change.

"Did you tell him to do that?" she asked, her voice piercing. "I never thought I'd say this, but thank you, Donner!"

"Yeah," Belle answered, relieved that she'd taken the call in the kitchen—and hadn't put her on speaker. "Me too. But no, it wasn't my idea."

"Well you can't deny that those numbered leapt up as soon as he turned himself in. I don't think it's a coincidence. I don't see how there's any way we can lose the vote now. Now all we need is to get the all clear from Ruby and we're—"

The line went dead as the entire cabin quaked and everything went black. Belle heard something fall from the counter and shatter against the floor. She stretched her hands out and felt her way back to the living room, grabbing a flashlight on the way.

"What the heck was that?" she asked, following the beam to Rye's room and finding nothing amiss. She jumped as something brushed against her leg, then saw the dim reflection of Beast's eyes. She shined the flashlight on the floor and led them both back into the living room.

"Snow," she said, skirting a poorly placed ottoman, "you'll be happy to know that Rye's still fast aslee—"

She stopped, centering the flashlight on Snow's end of the

couch. She was slumped over the armrest beside Griffin, who was trying frantically to shake her awake. "Babe!" he called, not acknowledging anyone else. Snow's neck flopped limply to the side as he tapped her cheek. He then tried to pull her up, but her arms did the same thing. "Sweetheart, open your eyes!" Desperate, he cupped her face and slammed their lips together. Then he pulled back and flashed the room a look of pure horror. "Why won't she wake up?"

A few seconds later, the lights flickered back on. Everyone sprang up to help Snow. Everyone, that is, but Ethan.

"What's going on?" he asked, reaching for Rapunzel but missing by a mile. His eyes cast downward but at nothing in particular, and there was a rising panic spreading across his face. "Rapunzel, where are you?" His hands rose again.

Belle gaped from Snow to Rapunzel to Ethan and back again, then heard three concentrated explosions in the front yard. She reached the door in two seconds flat and flung it open.

"What's going on?" she shouted as Hazel, Ruby, and Elmina stared back at her. They were doubled over and ragged. Ruby appeared to be crying. Elmina had a limp. All three of them seemed to be covered in soot. "Are you okay?" she pressed, her arms and legs suddenly jelly. "Did you get the stone? Are we —"

"Where's Grethel?" Rapunzel suddenly shrieked, racing over the threshold and into the yard. The three fairies looked at her, then each other, then down. The devastation on their faces was undeniable. Rapunzel repeated the question, her voice beginning to shred.

Then Elmina hobbled forward, looked Rapunzel in the eye, and gave her the news. Their powers had overloaded the stone. Angus must have planned it. They barely escaped with their lives, but Grethel … Grethel didn't make it.

The next thing Belle felt was a strain around her heart, her friend's full weight on her elbow, and the cold, hard ground.

Chapter Twenty-Eight

RAPUNZEL

In most cases, the Pulse only lasted a few minutes. For others, it was hours. For an unlucky few, days. Everyone who had magical abilities found themselves temporarily ordinary, and everyone who'd been affected by magic found out what life would have been like had they not. For some, this meant encountering a different spouse. For others, it meant grieving the loss of a loved one who, in reality, magic had saved. For the people of Selladóre, it meant either a black void or a white light or a second life as a lobster — depending on whom you asked.

The experts said Jacara's powers had self-combusted. They explained that between the Hall of Curiosities' charms and the powers of four purebloods, things just got out of hand. The stone went on overload and sent out a supernatural shockwave, short-circuiting magic all over the world. Thankfully, this was only temporary. It was all just a glimpse.

Everything seemed back to normal the following Thursday. Snow was walking and talking just as she did after Griffin's kiss so many years ago. Dawn, Morning, and Day, were healthy and happy to be alive. Almost everyone experienced a new lease on life, a determination to "live for today," and a resolution to not let things like regret or anger bog them down — except, of course, when it came to Angus Kane, who many believed planned the Pulse and expected it to be permanent.

In the southeastern corner of Ellada, a brave group of hikers who'd heard about the Charmés plight ventured into the cursed town while the magic was down and guided twenty-seven people to safety. They'd taken a tremendous risk, not knowing when or whether the magic would return, and were being hailed as heroes worldwide. The people of Carpale were overjoyed to see Cinderella and Aaron returned safely, as were their children and everyone else who'd held out hope that a lost loved one would someday turn up.

But no one was more surprised than Belle. For when Cinderella stepped off the plane at Marestam International Airport, she had by her side a frail-looking woman with dark cherry curls and a nervous, unworthy smile. Belle's heart stopped the moment she saw her.

"Belle," the woman said, looking her youngest daughter up and down in amazement and asking — ever so humbly — for forgiveness.

Belle hardly said a word as she processed what was happening. "You ... you left us," she finally managed to whisper. "Why did you —"

"Oh, my dear, sweet Belle," her mother interrupted. "I left your father. I left because he was no longer the man I fell in love with. Because the choices he made ruined our reputation and robbed my children of the lives they deserved. And yes, because I fell for someone else who wasn't a heck of a lot better, as it turned out. But there's a difference between needing a few days away and disappearing for twenty years. I was a mother. I *always* intended to come back for you. I left your father," she said again, taking Belle's hand. "But I never in a million years would have left you."

It was the sort of reunion that spread a blanket of hope from

the western shores of Regian to the eastern reef of Stularia.
Nothing was ever lost forever, it said. No story was ever fully
known. No one was doomed to repeat the mistakes of their
forebears, live and die under the shadow of the past, or give up
their dreams because the deck seemed stacked against them.

For Belle, that meant showing Rye what strength looks like in
a woman, and going to bed each night without regret. For Snow,
it meant finding a way to be the mother she'd always wanted to
be, regardless of what her body allowed. For Dawn, it meant
diving headfirst into her family and giving them everything she
had. For Penny, it meant staying true to her ambitions whether
or not she wore a crown. And for Rapunzel, it meant exposing
her heart to the messy, unpredictable world that had sprung up
around her while she wasn't paying attention.

Weeks later, she still lived for the occasional, thinly
researched story saying the Pulse wasn't completely over. That
some effects were still waiting to be lifted. That Ethan's
continued blindness might mean Jacara's powers were still
circulating somewhere—not that Grethel was truly gone. After
all, no one ever found her body. Perhaps she just wanted to be
alone for a while.

After a month, however, the reality began to set in—as did
the food aversions, the fatigue, and the daily after-breakfast hurl
she could no longer blame on motion sickness. In all of the
commotion with Belle, she'd lost track of her monthly check-in.

"There's just so much I wish I'd told you," she whispered one
day at the foot of a marble obelisk a few blocks from Marestam
General Hospital. The Realm had erected it in honor of Grethel,
whose funeral had closed down half of Carpale. "I assumed
there would be time after we saved the world. I wanted you to
know that I believe everything you did, you did because you
loved me. To me, you were always my mother, and I wouldn't
have had it any other way. I should have told you this while I
had the chance. But I'm not going to make the same mistake

twice."

She paused, jostled a blue velvet box between her fingers, and smiled. She'd have to leave in a few minutes to get ready for the dedication of Tantalise Castle, which Snow and Griffin were turning into an orphanage, but she wanted Grethel to be the first to hear this.

"I know Ethan worries about being a burden. Perhaps you guys could have bonded over that." She forced a sad smile and looked around to make sure she was alone. "But to me he's just my Ethan. He still looks the same, talks the same, laughs the same, jokes the same. He still makes me smile, dream, think, and hope like no one else. And his kisses—" She stopped to laugh. "Believe it or not, his kisses are even better. Must be a heightened senses sort of thing. Sure, some things are different. He won't be making any late-night pickle runs to the supermarket for me, but so what? At the risk of sounding like pre-independence Belle, he fills up parts of me that I never even knew were empty. I have no problem being his eyes. It's a fair trade for the rest of him. I hope you approve."

৵৹৵

"I can't really describe it other than to say we spent every morning cuddling, every day dancing, and every evening—pardon my candor—every evening making love. We had no worries, no cares, no fears, no regrets." Cinderella laughed and took a long sip from her wine glass. "Honestly, if it wasn't for the whole memory-draining imprisonment thing, I'd advise all of you to take a romantic getaway to, ah, what was it called again?"

"Circadia," Aaron said, shaking his head but smiling at his wife's ability to find the silver lining even in being kidnapped. "And yes, there is some bliss in ignorance. No responsibilities, no stress, no regrets, no worries. But if you ladies hadn't organized that magical blackout, our poor kids would be spending the rest of their lives trying to figure out whether their parents abandoned them or were murdered. Let's not forget that."

"I know," Cindy cooed, giving her husband's shoulder a playful push. "I'm not justifying what that reptile did. Angus Kane deserves every second of his sentence. The judge was absolutely right to throw the book at him. But Ruby … I mean Ruby at least *meant* well. And if you think about it, the Pulse kind of vindicated what she said about broken curses returning and all that."

Aaron rolled his eyes but beamed. "My wife is the only one who thinks one year in jail and five more of supervised probation is harsh for turning a sitting monarch into an animal."

"Oh. No, I'm fine with that," she clarified. "It's not the *legal* sentence I think is harsh; it's the social one." She shook her head but then pulled her fading smile back up. "But this is a celebration so … Sorry. Happy thoughts. See what I mean about ignorance being bliss?"

Now it was Aaron's turn to shake his head. "Well, as much as I'm enjoying this, I think I'll take a look at the bar. Dare I ask what the Whites are considering libations these days?"

"Non-alcoholic beer," Penny grumbled.

"Virgin margaritas," said Rapunzel, raising a glass filled with a neon green liquid and tipping it in a mock toast.

"Bona fide thirty-proof merlot," Cindy chirped, then leaned forward and shielded her raspy, top-secret whisper. "Use the bar by the fireplace and ask for the cranberry cooler." A wink. "I planned ahead."

Aaron laughed, asked if he could get anything for anyone, and turned around to navigate Tantalise Castle's former throne room—now the auditorium for Second Chances Orphanage and Grammar School.

As soon as he was gone, Belle launched forward, threw her

arms around Cinderella, and repeated what seemed to be the theme of the month — how happy they were to have her back.

Cinderella blushed and thumbed the sash wrapped around her burgundy dress. "It's good to be back," she replied. "Hey, Belle. How's your mother doing?"

Belle's eyes lit up. "She's great. I still can't believe she was lost in that town for all those years. I never understood how she could just abandon us like that but..." She sniffled and gave Cinderella a huge smile. "Anyway, she's babysitting Rye tonight. And last weekend we actually got together with all of my siblings and — "

"Wait. *All* of your siblings? You mean including — "

"Yup." Belle nodded. "Including Julianne. I actually think having our mother back might change things between all of us." She shrugged. "I think the idea that she tossed us aside impacted everyone differently. Not that Julianne and I would have been best friends otherwise, but ... who knows how things would have turned out if she'd stuck around."

Everyone nodded, not sure what to say. It was one of those impossible "what if" questions for which there would never be an answer.

After a minute, Cindy cleared her throat and mercifully changed the subject. "And how's the inn coming along. Think you'll reopen by spring?"

Belle glanced at her partner and swirled her cider.

"It's coming," Rapunzel said before explaining that they'd finally finalized the plans last week and would officially break ground on Tuesday. The new layout consisted of a two-story building with ten guest rooms, three separate cottages with private suites, and a single-family house that would be categorically off-limits to all Phoenix guests.

"That's great," said Penny, now Riverfell's first co-queen and the founder of a private law firm in her southern Riverfell dream house. "So, you're going to live there with Rye? How many bedrooms, if you don't mind my asking? Logan doesn't think we need to add on just yet, but I say it doesn't hurt to plan ahead." Her eyes wandered toward the make-your-own s'mores station, where Dawn's only daughter and Cindy's oldest son were pouring hot fudge and rainbow sprinkles over melted marshmallows. "After all, if we want to do three in five years—" she smiled and tapped her watch "—the clock's ticking."

"Three what in five years? Children?" Dawn looked overwhelmed just thinking about it. "Penny, take my advice and have one kid before you start making plans for another two. It isn't a walk in the park, you know. And babies have a way of putting brand new businesses on the back burner."

"I know," Penny said, the light from the fireplace reflecting off the gemstones in her hair. "But I'll have a five second commute and an overbearing mother-in-law just dying to help out."

"You're kidding," Dawn said as everyone else's jaws dropped. "After all the time you spent trying to get Logan away from her … you're really going to ask Letitia to help bring up your kids?"

"Not bring up," Penny corrected. "Just babysit once in a while. Take them to the park. Give me time to shower. But she's never getting her own key to the house." She shook her head like a toddler refusing to eat broccoli. "Logan and I had a looooong conversation about this. But Belle, you never answered my question. How many bedrooms? I mean, I have to assume Gray won't be sleeping in that cabin when you move out. And if the two of you want to give Rye a sibling—"

Penny stopped as Belle choked on her drink and launched into a coughing fit. Rapunzel held her glass while they all waited for it to pass.

"What makes you think Gray and I are having kids?" she finally blurted, her hand splayed out below her neck. Her eyes were bright red and watery.

Penny looked around for backup. Her mouth hung open for an embarrassingly long time as she struggled to gather her thoughts. "I ... well ... you guys are great together and I just assumed ... I mean, isn't that what usually happens when the villain goes down and the skies finally clear?" She glanced out the window. It was starting to snow.

"*What* usually happens?" Dawn asked, tugging at her lace bolero. "People have babies?"

"No!" Penny said, shaking her head vigorously. "People get married. That's how all the fairy tales end."

"Yeah," Belle said, dragging the word out into five syllables. She flicked at her wrist. "That formula didn't work too well for me last time. Besides, Rye already has a brother." She paused to wave at Donner, who was here with his new love interest, Kim Epson; his newly discovered son, Jasper; and the ankle bracelet Judge Ford insisted he wear in lieu of serving jail time.

Penny furrowed her brow and cocked her head. "So, Gray won't be living with you, then?"

"What, are you kidding?" Belle balked. "Heck yes, he will! I need all the midnight feeding help I can get. That child may be almost normal now, but he eats like a fiend!"

Everyone laughed as Rapunzel panned the room and excused herself for a little fresh air. She found Ethan leaning against the patio doors, talking with Elmina Goodman. She'd just been named temporary prime minister following Angus Kane's incarceration, and her approval ratings were through the roof so far. Everyone expected her to make the post official in the special election after the holidays. At the top of her campaign platform: a promise to recognize Selladóre as a legitimate sixth kingdom, monarch to be determined.

Rapunzel gave the fairy a warm smile and apologized for interrupting—even as she grabbed Ethan by the elbow and guided him outside.

"Hey," he said as they stepped onto the patio, snowflakes

immediately resting atop his springy salt and pepper hair. "Elmina and I were just in the middle of rating people's outfits. It was really quite riveting." Rapunzel gave a sarcastic laugh and nudged him into a bench. "Is Kiarra Kane really wearing a see-through dress?" he continued, flashing that sideways smirk that still made her knees weak. "Oh, if I could only get my sight back for one day."

"Stop talking," she half teased, half ordered. Then she pulled the box from her pocket and slid down beside him. "I have something I need to show you."

His smirk flatlined for a second, then forced its way back up. "I assume you mean *tell* me," he corrected. "What is it? I'm all ears. Those still work."

"No, I mean show you," Rapunzel insisted, her hand shaking so much that she dropped the box. She cursed as it bounced off her boot and tumbled behind them. "Just one second."

Her insides quivered as she hopped to her feet, rounded the bench, and bent down to scoop it up. Her fingers were two inches away when a pair of patent leather shoes seemed to appear out of nowhere.

"Hi," squeaked a tiny voice.

Rapunzel's heart skipped three beats. "Holy crap!" she yelled, pulling upright and grabbing her chest. Ethan whipped around immediately to make sure she was okay. The helpless look in his eyes was undeniable.

"Yes, I'm fine," she said, continuing to stare at the little girl. She looked familiar somehow. Perhaps she was one of Snow's orphans and she'd seen her in a brochure. "Can I help you?" Rapunzel asked, leaning her hands on both knees.

"Are you Renpuzzle?" the girl asked. She had strawberry blond pigtails and was holding an envelope, one hand on each side.

"Rapunzel," she corrected, having the distinct feeling that she'd had this exchange before. She looked exactly like the little girl who'd delivered Ethan's letter during the inn's grand opening party—but that was months ago. "Yes? What can I do for you?"

"For you," the girl said, straightening her elbows and presenting the envelope as if it was a serving tray. She scurried off the instant it touched Rapunzel's hands.

"Wait," Rapunzel called after her. "What—"

"Who was that?" Ethan interrupted, his voice still showing concern—and frustration.

Rapunzel straightened up and looked at the envelope. There was something hard in it, and by the light of the moon she could make out her name scrawled across the front. "No one," she replied, tearing at the paper. "Just someone's little gir—"

A folded note and a chunky silver heart slipped into her palm. A locket. A locket dangling from a black leather cord. She gasped as it flew open on its own and revealed two tiny photographs. On the right was a shot of her and Ethan during Letitia's fortieth anniversary gala way back in the spring. On the left was a picture of her and Grethel decades earlier. Rapunzel was in Grethel's lap wearing pigtails secured with bright green ribbons, and Grethel was smiling as if it was the happiest day of her life.

Rapunzel bit her lip and unfolded the note.

My dearest Rapunzel, she read, her breath suddenly paper thin against the chill, November air. *No one is ever lost who has love, and nothing is impossible when it's true. Please think of me whenever you wear this locket, and know that you are always in my heart—forever, truly, and undeniably loved. I could never have asked for a better daughter. You deserve even better than a fairy tale. Yours always, Grethel.*

P.S. Congratulations

P.P.S. Told you I was there for everything

Rapunzel whipped her head up as a tear dropped onto the letter, smearing the ink. Her mind raced back to their reunion on Blood Island. "I never actually left you," Grethel had told her. "I was there for everything. You just didn't recognize me. You weren't supposed to."

"Hey!" she suddenly called out, hustling to the edge of the patio and peering into the darkness. "Little girl?" she called again, pulling the locket into a tight fist. Then, in a much smaller voice, "Grethel?"

She felt a tiny shock in her palm, then heard a confused voice answer. Only it wasn't Grethel. It was Ethan, still on the bench, staring at everything and nothing all at once.

"I'm right here," she answered, pulling the locket over her head and reaching the bench in six quick steps. She stood behind Ethan for one more minute, struggling to process what had just happened. Then she took a few salty breaths and tried to plug the flow of tears trickling down her cheeks and dropping onto Ethan's forehead as he leaned back against her hand.

"This snow melts fast," he said, wiping her fallen tears from his eyes. "Too bad. I was looking forward to beating you in a good snowball fight."

Rapunzel laughed and slid back onto the bench. She placed the jewelry box in her lap. To anyone else, it contained a strange-looking blob of wood carved to show one large oval supporting a smaller, jagged circle. To her, it was a three-dimensional rendering of her and Ethan's nine-week-old baby.

She'd taken the test a few weeks after her return from Blood Island, when her motion sickness refused to go away. By then, he'd already lost his sight and she had no idea how to tell him. A month earlier, he would have been elated. He would have flown his entire family in from Stularia to celebrate, while she tried to hide a full-blown panic attack every other hour.

But now, Rapunzel feared she would have to carry the hope and joy for both of them. She worried he'd hear the news and mourn the father he'd intended to be but no longer could — the kind who played catch with his son or raced alongside his daughter while she learned to ride a bike.

"Ethan," she whispered as his fists began to rub his eyes harder. Too hard. "Ethan, are you okay?" He removed his hands and blinked a few dozen times, staring first into the sky and then down at Rapunzel. "I'm sorry, I think you might have gotten tears in your eyes, not snow. Maybe the salt's bothering you. It'll probably pass in just a few —"

"Indigo, huh?" he asked, reaching awkwardly towards her face and running her chest-length waves through his fingers. "And ..." he bent forward, getting a closer look and almost nuzzling into her shoulder. "And turquoise on the ends? I like it."

Rapunzel's jaw dropped as her hand jerked up and pressed off his chest. Someone at the party must have told him what her hair looked like tonight, and he thought pretending he could see it might be a fun joke. "Not funny," she said, turning away. "Don't tease me about that. It's not —"

Suddenly, he cupped three fingers beneath her chin and rotated her face back towards his. With perfect aim, his lips fell against hers and pressed, pulling what felt like all of her insides up to her chest and out into the atmosphere somewhere far above them.

"Rapunzel," he said a few moments later as their lips fell apart. "I don't need eyes to see how beautiful you are." He caressed her cheek with the back of his thumb. "But damn, have I missed them."

"What?" Her words tumbled together. "Are you saying you — Can you really see?"

The floodgates opened again as Ethan nodded and pulled her into his arms. They sat this way for what seemed like an eternity, nuzzled into each other, breathing, struggling to process the enormity of what had just happened. Then Ethan's gaze fell to the locket around her neck. It was glowing, a thousand times brighter than she'd seen it glow in Grethel's tower, a deep, vibrant purple. Perhaps some of Jacara's magic had survived the

Pulse after all. Perhaps they'd saved Grethel or cured her cancer or given her enough power to enchant that charm with something that would protect Ethan's sight. Or perhaps she'd never know for sure. Perhaps she'd just have to take each day as it came, reveling in the good times while she had them because there was no telling when they might end.

"You know," Ethan said, as his eyes migrated a little further and settled on the box in her lap. "Blind or not, *I'm* the one who's supposed to pop the question. Not you."

Rapunzel responded with a snide, sideward glance and a quick censure about perpetuating outdated gender roles. "But this isn't an engagement ring," she clarified. "It's better. Close your eyes."

"Really? I was kind of planning on never closing my eyes again, but—"

"Just do it," she ordered, bending back the velvet top and pulling out his hand. "I took you out here to show you something." She dropped the tiny figure into his palm, closed his fingers around it one by one, and then leaned back to watch. He bobbled it in his fist for a few seconds, tilted his head, and rubbed it with his other hand. Then he froze.

"No!" he shouted, his eyes flying wider than she'd ever seen them open before. "Are you trying to tell me that you're ... that we're..."

He stopped and cupped her face so that their eyes were inches apart, connected by the magnitude of everything that ever was and the promise of everything that could yet be.

She nodded wildly as a smile blew up across her face.

"Yes," she exclaimed, tears starting to flow again. "Yes. We're going to have a baby. There's an ultrasound picture in my purse, too. And plane tickets so we can go tell your sister in person. But Ethan?"

He opened his mouth a few times before nodding at her, as if even a three-letter word was impossible to find in a moment as wonderful as this.

Rapunzel took a moment to make sure she was certain about what she was about to do—what she was about to ask. It was completely unplanned, but nothing had ever felt so right.

She didn't even remember hearing the words as they tumbled out of her mouth. She wasn't even sure they were comprehensible. But maybe Penny was right. Maybe this story *was* supposed to end with a wedding. Maybe, after everything Rapunzel had spent her entire adult life railing against, she did deserve the kind of happy ending they recorded in the history books. Or, even better, the kind of happy beginning.

The End

"So he wandered for a whole year in misery, till at last he came upon the desert place where Rapunzel had been banished and lived in her sorrow. As he drew near, he heard a voice which he seemed to recognize, and advancing towards the sound came within sight of Rapunzel, who recognized him at once with tears. Two of her tears fell on his eyes, and so healed and cleared them of the injury done by the thorns that he could soon see as well as ever. Then he travelled with her to his kingdom, and she became his wife, and the remainder of their days were spent in happiness and content."

— The Complete Brothers Grimm Fairy Tales, *edited by Lily Owens*

Note to Readers

Wait! Does this mean the series is over?

Keep in touch with your favorite Desperately Ever After characters at laurakenyon.com. Here, you'll find playlists, dream casts, character interviews, links to the centuries-old tales that inspired this series, and news about future endeavors — including Desperately Ever After novellas and short stories!

If you enjoyed these books, please consider posting a short review to help spread the word. They are invaluable to new authors and very much appreciated.

Finally, to read the tales that inspired this series, please see:

• *Cinderella* by Charles Perrault

• *Beauty and the Beast (La Belle et la Bête)* by Gabrielle-Suzanne Barbot de Villeneuve, as well as its adaptation by Jeanne-Marie Le Prince de Beaumont

• *Rapunzel* by Jacob and Wilhelm Grimm

• *The Sleeping Beauty in the Wood* by Charles Perrault, as well as its earlier inspiration, *Sun, Moon, and Talia* by Giambattista Basile

• *The Princess and the Pea* by Hans Christian Andersen

• *Snow White* by Jacob and Wilhelm Grimm (1812)

• *The Story of a Boy Who Went Forth to Learn Fear* by Jacob and Wilhelm Grimm

Additional tales mentioned in passing: Charles Perrault's *Bluebeard;* Hans Christian Andersen's *The Little Mermaid;* and the Grimm brothers' *The Robber Bridegroom, Hansel and Gretel*, and *The Golden Goose*

About the Author

LAURA KENYON is an award-winning journalist, freelance writer, and the Amazon bestselling author of three novels, *Desperately Ever After, Damsels in Distress,* and *Skipping Midnight.* She lives in the kingdom of Connecticut with her heroic prince charming, two beautiful princesses, and a noble steed.

www.LauraKenyon.com
Facebook: LauraKenyonWrites
Twitter: @Laura_Kenyon
Instagram: LauraKenyonWrites

Acknowledgments

Above all else, I want to thank everyone who read the first two Desperately Ever After books and waited so patiently for the third. The two years in between were fraught with unexpected obstacles and blessings, but neither you nor the women of Marestam were ever far from my mind. Thank you for keeping me going and for giving meaning to what some might call complete madness.

In addition to the many friends, family members, and colleagues who have lifted me up over the years (I hope you all know who you are), there are a few individuals I would like to thank specifically:

Andrew Brown, for once again taking the jumble of ideas in my head and showing me what I really want. (In other words, creating a kick-ass cover! Twice!)

Annie Hwang, for handling my email freak-outs with grace.

Marlene Engel, for her last-stop proofreading expertise.

Chris, for believing in me and for sacrificing so many evenings together so that I could hunker down in front of a computer.

Mom, for giving me the gift of time and peace of mind. Without you, this would have taken an additional two years.

Dad, for reading about princesses on the train, and for once using my books and "Game of Thrones" in the same sentence. Your enthusiasm for my writing means so much to me.

Allie, Shadow, and baby Caroline, for keeping me grounded and for inspiring more than you'll ever know.

Some people say this is a cutthroat line of work, but in so many ways I've experienced the exact opposite. Thank you to all of the wonderful writers, bloggers, and editors who took the time to show me the ropes, offer a shoulder, pen a blurb, or just make me laugh. In particular: Hazel Gaynor, Stephanie Evanovich, Elizabeth Blackwell, Tracie Banister, Eric Wilder, Becky Monson, Danielle Poiesz, Amanda Prowse, Marisa Iallonardo, and everyone at ChickLitChatHQ.

And finally, to Jacob and Wilhelm Grimm, Charles Perrault, Gabrielle-Suzanne Barbot de Villeneuve, Jeanne-Marie Le Prince de Beaumont, Giambattista Basile, and Hans Christian Andersen, for writing the tales that inspired this series.

Made in the USA
Middletown, DE
11 February 2023